SHOCK W.

By

Fred Crampton

Copyright © 2011 Frederick A Crampton

First Published 2013

ISBN 978-1-909424-27-2

Printed and bound in Great Britain By;

www.direct-pod.com

SHOCK WAVES

Contents	Page

ARCTIC CIRCLE

EUROPE

UK

ATLANTIC OCEAN

PORTUGAL

GREAT
METEOR
BANK

BERMUDA

SARGASSO SEA

CAPE VERDE

NORTH AMERICA

TROPIC OF CANCER

AFRICA

EQUATOR

TROPIC OF CAPRICORN

ATLANTIC OCEAN

TRISTAN DA CUNHA

SOUTH AMERICA

MIGRATIONAL ROUTE
OF ALBERT'S ARK

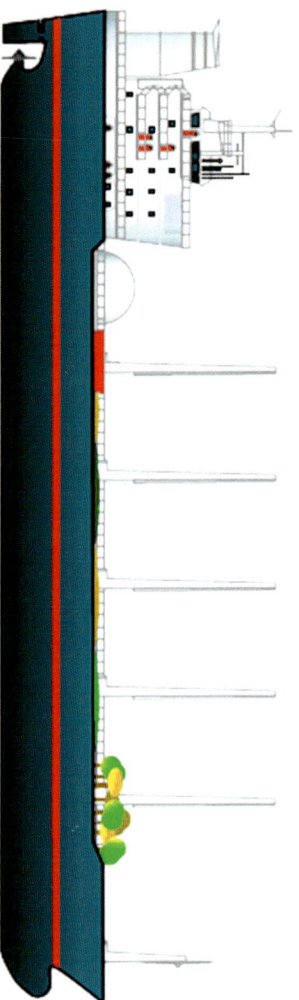

LIVING
QUARTERS

BIODOME

DESALINATION
PLANT

FIELDS AND CROPS

MECHANICAL
SAILS

ORCHARD

HERB AND
VEGETABLE
GARDENS

WIND TURBINE

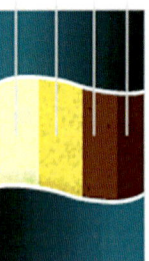

SOIL STRATA ONBOARD

TOPSOIL
SUBSOIL
SAND MIX
SANDSTONE

ALBERT'S ARK

1. A SURPRISE PACKAGE

Miles Overstrand was the Ark's multi millionaire benefactor whose life had been cut short when it came to an untimely tragic end, in an unusual way. He was later believed to have been an associate of villains, leaving an unexplained stash of millions of US dollars and Euros in cash, discovered on the Ark, two years after Miles' death. Albert's dream project to set up the Ark was financed by Miles who they assumed suffered a fatal heart attack just as they were about to set sail to the southern hemisphere after the first five month trial of the Ark's journey off the coast of Wales. They buried Miles in the orchard rather than have the authorities probe the situation causing them delay in moving to their winter home.

The Ark's community, formed by Albert and Amy Crowther has been on the high seas in their converted Oil tanker for almost three years. Many things have challenged them during this time, from the constant threat of the Russian Mafia to nature itself. But Albert was a man with a tremendous history of active service for the British Government and then came the appetite for action as a mercenary, surviving all that had been thrown at him through that period, plus during the past three years protecting the Ark's community, so to sustain their ideal way of life, Albert and his community of now experienced farmers and sailors, continue to try and defend their home, sail on.

Designed as a floating ecological island, the Ark's holds were filled with sandstone, sand, subsoil and topsoil, with a drainage system, to represent the earth's structure. A smallholding with almost seven acres of well kept fertile land, was managed by Millie almost single handed from her haven at the bow of the ship. This was complete with ever increasing livestock, kept at a manageable food productive level, plus crops, produce, orchard-cum-graveyard and a huge biome greenhouse for delicate salads etc., situated at the foredeck, making them totally self-sufficient for the years ahead. The bonus was the prolific fishing grounds they had around them when at anchorage. The ship was driven by huge mechanical sails powered by hydraulics, with

1

the backup of gas turbines for propulsion, fuelled by methane gas processed from farmyard waste and other organic matter. Albert's idea of season hopping from the North Atlantic for the northern hemisphere summer and then moving to the South Atlantic for the summer there was so far considered a success. Their dream was to survive on the Ark away from the mainland societies of the world with their political turmoil, ongoing workers' disputes, terrorist activities, big brother issues and heavy tax burdens and on top of that, the disproportional cost of living related to earnings for the average worker.

The last encounter with the Mafia involved a hi-tech luxury yacht 'Revelation II' that had stalked the Ark, with the intention, they believed of boarding and taking control of the ship. Who knows what would have happened to the community had they succeeded? But Albert had other ideas and thwarted the Russian Mafia's plan. He took young Italian Antonio on a spying mission in the black yacht which ended up being attacked by the stalker. Albert launched a grenade from their yacht in defence, surprisingly removing all onboard the Revelation as they panicked at the impact, jumping into the sea to be met by hungry sharks. Albert's 'luck' had reigned again. This left the Revelation behind with its contents of a computerised control room, various pieces of equipment and an arsenal that a squad of military men would be proud of. After stripping and storing useful items, the luxury yacht was sent to the bottom of the Atlantic. Originally, Albert wanted no truck with hi-tech modern technology but he reluctantly changed his mind, realising he had to embrace it to stay ahead of the criminals, hopefully to use the equipment for defence against enemies known and unknown, but also to bring Albert back into the twenty first century. So he organised setting up the salvaged computers etc., in a suitable area on the Ark.

During the Ark's life there had been additions and subtractions to the community, with Miles being the first to depart. The birth of Venus followed: the firstborn baby girl on the Ark to proud parents Gunter and Greta. Antonio and Marcello were rescued from their stricken yacht after losing their grandfather overboard in a storm that damaged its mainsail. The two lads were found dehydrated, malnourished and unconscious. Antonio stayed with the community marrying the lovely Jane, who was Miles' previous partner. Marcello was later taken back home to Italy initially via a helicopter thanks to the Salvation Army's repatriation service that came looking for survivors of the lost yacht.

Zimbo, a lucky young man from the Cape Verde Islands, was saved from the sea after another failed attempt by the Russians to attack the Ark during a hurricane. The first attack came by helicopter that Albert and company put to the bottom of the sea by water cannon. Zimbo had been hired to pilot the speedboat that carried the armed assailants. The boat was smashed to pieces in the storm with Zimbo the only survivor. At first a prisoner and then accepted into the community having nowhere else to go, he made the Ark his home and went on to marry Scottish teenager Melanie. Then there was the strange loss of Monty, the aged hippie whose disappearance was put down to eating magic mushrooms he had found in the orchard. Everyone assumed he fell overboard. He left a lonely widow Marigold and child Lucy behind. Another arrival was a baby girl named Rose. Farm manager Millie assured husband Ched that the child was his, but the general consensus was that the father was Antonio. Jane gave birth to the first boy and named him Alberto. There was no doubt Antonio was the father this time. The new baby delighted Albert and Amy personally, but not every member of the community.

Albert performed two weddings onboard, Antonio to Jane and Zimbo to Melanie. Melanie was now awaiting the birth of her first child. But the big shock to all was Albert's wife Amy falling pregnant after so many years of trying.

ALBERT'S PRIVATE LOG - September 2018
We're finally back in the southern hemisphere. What a year we've had since being here last!

3

My shock and joy about Amy's pregnancy! She is the proudest expectant mother I have ever seen. Of course it does help knowing I played a big part in putting it there. She shows her bump to everyone each day saying how big it's growing. I think it's tiny but I dare not say a thing. Now on the other hand, I think Melanie is huge. Her transformation in almost three years, which in my eyes is a short time, from a spotty-faced, negative schoolgirl to a radiant, proud and happy young mother to be, is wonderful.

The older children, Gunter and Greta's Stella, Ched and Millie's Vicky, seem to be more and more inquisitive as to what's going on and why they are living like they are and not like others they read about in books. Amy and Jane are helping Greta with schooling now that the two older girls require a broader scale of education. It is amazing how much work and attention it takes to look after and educate a few children. Jane has been excellent in all that she gets involved with. Both she and Antonio are very proud of Alberto who is growing rapidly.

We have a lot of work to do trying to recreate an operations room and control centre with the computers salvaged from the Revelation. I am surprised the grenade I launched didn't do more damage than it did. The roof of the room housing it all must have had armour plating which protected the equipment but did not help the yacht's panicking occupants. Magnus, Ched and Gunter have already been busy setting up the simulated computer room in an area below the Ark's bridge. There is ample space for it all there.

Community numbers are more or less static in adults. If I class Melanie as an adult in the beginning, we are still thirteen. There are five children with two on the way, so that part of things is working. But we have a lot more females than males, which has been the case from the start and really hasn't caused the problem that I thought it would, yet!

DOWN ON THE FARM

Marina has a family of four, one of which is a bull that Millie will keep until another bull arrives then it will be beefsteak on the menu for a change instead of Tuna. Pigs are at a good balance. Pork's always on the menu and there's lots of bacon for breakfast. Chickens are plentiful laying good quality eggs, really dark, tasty yolks. The sheep and goats are kept at a manageable number. Millie has more help now to run the farm with Antonio and Zimbo's strong arms. Melanie kicks Zimbo out of bed to go to work earlier since she became pregnant. Ched has been known to help his wife on occasions, when asked, and usually does so without resentment: dealing with the animals, sowing crops, spreading manure and harvesting etc.

Marigold seems reasonably content, but is still without a man in her life. I'm sure, as I have proved in the past for others that someone will turn up for her too.

My next task is a new defence training programme for the able male and females who now realise their responsibilities for the ultimate protection of their families and home. We must be fully trained and prepared to use the cache of weapons we now have. I had better find out how to use some of them myself first! There are a few I have never seen the like of before and this will be quite a challenge as will be the development of unarmed combat exercises that are already in progress.

It was only a few days after anchorage at their favourite place to stay in the southern hemisphere, near Tristan da Cunha, and the Ark's community had settled to their various routines. Vicky often wanted to be with her mother on

5

the farm and took a real interest in growing produce. She would be there on Saturdays, Sundays or after school and even had her own little vegetable patch and was tending it one day when she heard a faint thumping noise. Standing up straight, she looked around, then ran quickly to her mother.

'Mummy I can hear a thumping noise.' Without even looking to where the noise was coming from,
Millie called Albert on the shortwave.
'Albert I can hear a helicopter but I can't see it.'
'Ok Millie, you know the drill. Are the boys on their way up here yet?'
'Yes, they must have heard it too.'
'Please keep out of sight and under cover.'
'Yes Albert.' The three boys, as Albert called them, were running as fast as they could through the fields to the upper decks to take their defence positions; the two younger men racing against each other, leaving Ched behind, flagging and well out of breath. Antonio looked back at him and started laughing, Zimbo followed suit.

Normally, the only visitors when they were in this area were from Tristan da Cunha's coastguard, who would call near to Christmas to have free booze, food and ogle at the women onboard. Albert had already armed himself with his new toy: a Heckler & Koch mp5 sub machine gun. By the time he got to a viewing point in front of the swimming pool, the helicopter was in sight. The drill was for the armed force to be out of sight and positioned for defence. This consisted of Albert, Gunter, Ched, Antonio and Zimbo. As planned, Albert then took a position where he was in full view of the unwanted visitors, with the others able to see the situation, but hidden. Anyone else would be well out of harm's way. Brandishing his weapon so the pilot could see he was armed, the chopper suddenly veered away. Unbeknown to Albert, his old friend and fellow Marine veteran 'Package Pete' was a passenger inside the craft with his new bride. Their aim was to join the Ark to be part of its community.
'What the fuck are you doing? I want to land on that ship,' Pete ranted. The pilot moved up his visor and turned to face him.

6

'Did you see what that guy had in his hand? He looked ready to use it.'
'That's only Albert; he's just bluffing.'
'Well I'm not calling it; this chopper is going back to Tristan.'
'Shit!' Pete replied, sinking back into his seat.

As the helicopter headed away Albert's squad assembled by the swimming pool to discuss the event.
'What that was all about?' Ched asked.
'They didn't like the look of my weapon,' Albert replied.
'It was probably a private helicopter, hunting for a news story like before, I doubt if they will be back.'

Pete calmed down and thought of another approach.
'Captain, er… what is the maximum ceiling height of this fine machine of yours?' he asked the pilot politely.
'12,000 feet on a good day; so it would be about 10,000 feet today.'
'Would you have a parachute I could buy off you?'
'I have and it's expensive, but what about the lady?'
'I only need 5000ft you can go higher if you want, just stay within sight of me landing on that ship; he won't shoot at a parachutist.'
'You must be bloody mad!' said the pilot as he raised the power of his engine and turned back towards the Ark.

The defence team members were just about to disperse and go back to their routines when they heard the helicopter again. They were soon back at their posts ready and waiting for Albert's commands. Albert focused on it through the binoculars and wondered why it was flying so high. The pilot took the chopper to its safe ceiling. With the outside wind speed and direction in mind, he positioned it so that Pete could take advantage of it to manoeuvre his chute to the Ark. The door opened and Pete was out leaving his new bride holding her head, terrified and fearing the worst. No such thoughts had he, but only, I'll show the bastard! Free falling, guiding down to the Ark, he pulled the ripcord and the first part of the chute opened, followed rapidly by the main, bringing him to what he thought was a near standstill compared to the free fall. He manipulated the control lines, putting him in circles to accurately position himself over the ship. He could see a figure standing in front of the swimming pool.

Albert was unsure what the visitor was up to and gave a burst of automatic fire to the side of the parachute, thinking that would show him who is boss. He squeezed the trigger quickly three times. Immediately he heard a faint voice shouting at him.
'Stop shooting you daft bastard! It's me, Pete.' Albert heard the word Pete and laughed as Pete repeated his apoplectic ranting. Lifting the shortwave radio he spoke to the others.
'Don't shoot! It's Package Pete!'

The squad made their way to the foredeck where Pete had finally guided himself down. Once he released his harness he ran to Albert shouting at the top of his voice.
'What the fuck did you shoot at me for?' Standing in front of Albert waving his arms about, the fit, lean, muscular man in his late forties, with dark hair slightly thinning on top and sharp, carved out of wood features, was expecting an apology from Albert.
'How the hell was I supposed to know it was you? And besides you've been shot at before; you should be used to it. If I had shot *at you*, you would be dead by now and if you're mad enough to jump out of a helicopter, a few bullets whizzing by won't make any difference.' They both looked at each other and burst into laughter.

'Anyway, it's good to see you and that you're still about old buddy. I told you I would find you,' Pete reminded Albert. They greeted each other clasping their arms around one another.
'It's good to see you too. Come on, let's get you a drink, you deserve one.'
'No, not just yet, I want the helicopter to land with my wife and luggage.'
'Your wife! And who in their right mind would marry you?'

'Don't be like that Albert. I know I've had my problems and have caused a few too, but I need to settle down. She's a lovely lady. I've finally found someone who puts up with me; well so far anyway.'

Albert told Antonio to assist Millie as soon as they could, to get the animals as far to the bow of the ship as possible to allow the chopper to land without frightening them. The helicopter gradually drew nearer, finally landing in view of the rest of the community, who had formed a large circle to show the pilot the landing spot, also eager to see the unexpected guests. Pete gathered up the parachute rolling it into a bundle, thinking he neither needed nor wanted to pay for it. He walked slowly to the helicopter allowing the pilot time to shut down the engine and for the rotors to stop before opening the door. The pilot led Pete's wife down the steps where Pete took her hand. She stood there staring at the onlookers with all their eyes on her. She turned to Pete.
'I'm frightened.'
'You have no need to be, it is just as much a shock to them as it is for you my darling.' The pilot handed Pete their luggage and he passed the chute back.
'Here I don't need this, so please don't charge me for it. How much do I owe you?' A wad of cash changed hands as Amy went to Pete's bride to welcome her and lead her to the other women.

As the last piece of luggage was taken from the pilot Pete intervened and presented it to Albert.
'Here's a gift for you; I thought these were missing from your Ark. I wouldn't be surprised if they've been at it on the way here.' Albert peered into the box with a metal grill at one end to see two rabbits in good shape.
'They survived the altitude you were at to jump, what was it?'
'About 6000 feet.' Albert was delighted but wondered what Millie would think about these new additions to her livestock. But on the other hand, he thought, perhaps I could persuade her if I promised to keep them under control; then again she doesn't like guns. Oh shit! The dilemmas we have to sort out!

9

'Aren't you going to let them out then Albert?'

'No, not just yet Pete, I need to check with Millie, our farm manager, if you don't mind; but thank you very much. They seem to be fine specimens.'

Gunter and Ched helped carry the luggage away from the helicopter to allow it to take off then joined the others for introductions. Amy had already made Pete's wife welcome and now Pete introduced her to the whole group.

'This is my wife Mi no hou Dunhill. She just prefers to be called Mi.'

'Mr Albert, I've heard so much about you. You are a great man.' She bowed to him, embarrassing Albert. There was a slight pause as they all looked at the pretty, petite young Thai girl.

'We are all very glad to have you both here with us on the Ark and you deserve a round of applause followed by some celebratory drinks,' Albert announced. The applause was drowned out by the noise of the helicopter lifting up from the deck then circling to put it in the direction of Tristan da Cunha. The sound of the chopper soon faded into the distance leaving the Ark to its normal tranquillity.

'Did you hear her name?' Ched asked Gunter on their way to the canteen.

'No.'

'Mi no Hou. I bet she does!'

'I don't understand Ched, know what?'

'Oh forget it, let's go and have a drink.'

The welcoming party was in full swing in the canteen. Everything else stopped while they drank and chatted, because making the new arrivals feel at home was a priority. Amy soon made Mi feel more at ease, as she sensed her nervousness at first meeting everyone. She asked her where she was from and what she did, congratulating her on how well she spoke English. Meanwhile Albert and Pete sat at a table where Melanie soon put two pints of bitter in front of them.

'Amy's put some weight on since the last time I was here; must be the contentment of the good life you have created Albert.'

10

'She's pregnant.'

'What! I never thought you had it in you?'

'You cheeky bastard, but I must admit we have been a lot more active since living on the Ark together; something has altered.'

'How old is Amy now?'

'She was fifty one last December and we'd almost given up hope of having a child.'

'Well she certainly doesn't look it. Cheers Albert. Here's to the good life.'

'Cheers! It's great to have you onboard.'

They supped a couple of mouthfuls and looked around to see if Mi was alright. She was surrounded by the women. They all seemed very jolly and Mi was smiling,

'How did you meet your wife and convince her to come here to this way of life?' Albert asked.

'I had my mind set on joining you. Knowing what you told me on my last visit and your need for some armaments, I thought you could do with some help. I knew I would struggle to settle to civilian life and I'm sure that's one of the main reasons you're here too. The only obstacle I had was I didn't have a partner. So I went about trying to find a woman that could bear children and wasn't much hassle. I ruled out Euroland and that left me with the tried and tested method for many years by ex-servicemen, old age pensioners, misfits and other sad bastards that can't find a partner in the good old fashioned way. I just happen to fall in one or two of those categories as you know. So I went to Bangkok to try and buy me a wife.'

'You mean you just took a flight to Bangkok, went to a shop and selected a woman you fancied, tried her out, if you were satisfied you took out your wallet and paid for her; a bit like buying a car?'

'No, not quite like that, I did go there for that purpose though and that service is available and still legal, but I did not meet Mi in that way.'

'Does Mi know that you were there looking for a bride?'

'Yes, she does now.'

'So how did you meet?'

11

'Strangely enough it was a typical 'boy meets girl' situation. I was in a bar in Bangkok, I can't remember the name. I was trying to catch the eye of a waitress to order a drink. I was getting somewhat frustrated in being ignored, you know how we British are. Then this lovely lady walked by me. Thinking she was a waitress I shouted, oy! *Bar tart* can you get me a beer please?'

'That's a bit uncouth to say to a lady.'

'Albert. Where have you been all your life? Anyway it was obvious she understood because she gave me a concentrated glare of resentment then she turned on me, and asked. "What type of beer would I like sir, Tiger, Singa, or Leo?"

'Any bottle that's cold will do, thank you.' Off she went to the bar for my beer, only to return with two.

"Here you are sir. That will be five hundred Bats," she said.

'But I only wanted one drink and five hundred Bats is way over the top for two beers,' I replied.

"The other beer is for me and the high price is for the insult, I'm not a bar tart or even a waitress."

'I had to apologise immediately and asked if she would join me?'

"I don't see why I should,' she said, "considering the way you spoke to me, but you have apologised so yes, I will join you for this drink."

'What is your name?' I asked.

"It's Mi, just Mi, Mi No Hou Chei." And then she asked me my name.

'Just Pete,' I said.

"Are you on holiday looking for cheap sex or looking for a wife? That's what most Europeans come here for."

'This direct question flustered me for a short while, so I answered as a politician would do, and avoided to answer the direct question. I said, I was retired and I had promised myself a holiday to give me time to think of where to live in the world and what to do next. She said I looked too young to retire and then asked me about my job, if I was married and if I was really looking for a wife. I told her I was a Royal Marine to begin with and still am at heart, but I ended up as a coastguard Captain in the Euro-Navy, just before I retired.

I wasn't married because I hadn't found the right woman yet or she hadn't found me.'

"So you are here looking for a wife then?" she asked. I didn't want to sound desperate.

'No not in particular,' I explained. It is usually the case with me that I try to chat up a certain lady, I succeed and then find out she is married. But I don't normally find out until the next morning when the husband is banging on the hotel room door!' Then it was my turn to buy the drinks again but at the correct price from then on. I was amazed at how well she spoke English. When she came back with the drinks, she asked me how I would go about chatting her up.

I already have done 'I replied. 'She looked me straight in the eyes and gave me a beautiful smile that melted me and that was it. We told each other our life stories and got on like a house on fire. We started dating and before long I thought, she will do for me. I explained to her about you and the Ark and asked her if she would join me to live on the Ark. She said yes so I proposed to her. Of course she accepted and now here we are.'

'What about her family Pete, did she not mind leaving them behind?'

'No that wasn't a problem she is the daughter of government officials, her mother and father. The regime changed and became out of favour and they disappeared, leaving her and her brother alone. Her brother was forced to join the military and Mi was educated as a doctor and made to work in the poor areas of Bangkok. I did have to pay officials quite a lot of money to get the papers to marry and for her to leave the country with me, so really the end result was I bought a wife.'

'That's some good news to hear, Mi is a Doctor.'

'The main problems bothering me at the moment Pete are: number one, the ongoing attacks by the Russians, and we could face possibly others in the future. Number two is the maintenance of the ship. She needs her bottom looking at.'

'Do you have you diving equipment onboard?'

13

'Yes and top notch too, several sets complete with compressor. I don't have the full experience in that field, but will soon get to grips with it, how about you Pete?'

'Well being a member of the Special Boat Squadron, or should I say ex-member, it was one of the skills that was forced upon us.'

'But you couldn't possibly think of going down there to maintain the whole of this ship's bottom?'

'No, but if a few of us trained, we could look for any problem areas and deal with them, albeit on a temporary basis. Then perhaps a programme could be put in place for the future.'

'Yes you're right, how about another beer?'

'Why not? It's not too bad, probably the best I'll get around here eh Albert?'

They both smiled as Albert refilled the glasses at the bar.

'Cheers!'

'Cheers, Albert. I see you have a couple of male additions to the crew: the young black kid and the Mediterranean looking chap.'

'Yes, a few strange things have happened since we last met. We rescued Antonio and his brother Marcello just after the first assault by the Russians. We found them barely alive in their storm stricken yacht when we were returning to the north for the first time. They had lost their grandfather overboard in the storm, leaving them without sailing knowledge, water or food and they ran out of fuel going round in circles. Lucky we spotted them. Another couple of days and they would have died from dehydration. Antonio's brother was repatriated by the Salvation Army who came looking for survivors. Antonio had fallen for Jane and wanted to stay and would you believe it, they have since produced a son named after me: Alberto?'

'Wow, Albert you certainly have a lot of respect here.'

'Hmm, yes, well as for the other lad, Zimbo, we were heading south to our favourite spot here in the southern Atlantic, when passing the Verde's, we were approached by a very fast speedboat. It was armed and fired at us. At the time we were heading into a storm, hurricane status. The dickheads went down. Zimbo was the only survivor. He had stolen the boat for the contractors

14

and was the getaway pilot. He is a lucky lad and not a bad lad. He's married to young Melanie now and she is expecting too.'

'Married, you've performed a marriage onboard?'

'Yes, not one but two, Antonio and Jane in the same hit, It was a very joyful occasion.'

'You do surprise me. Your talents are never ending.'

'There's a lot more to tell and show you, but I think we should sort out your living accommodation. Not being pre-warned it will be makeshift for tonight and maybe a couple of days at the most. We'll sort out a permanent residence for you tomorrow. There's plenty of room.' They finished their drinks then Albert asked Amy to organise a place for Pete and Mi to sleep.

The bell rang for the evening meal. Head cook Patricia was hot and slightly flustered, but ready. She had been busy making sure of a good welcoming spread for the new additions. Her cooking and seeing peoples' faces when they tucked into her food made her delighted and proud. Serving the community had increased her self esteem and she had become a very happy-natured person. The main course was roast lamb, marinated with garlic, rosemary and red wine. Pete could not get enough of it. He was so ecstatic he went over to Patricia, kissed her on the cheek and thanked her for such a wonderful meal. She turned bright red and shuffled quickly into the kitchen.

'You old charmer,' Albert said as Pete returned to the table.

'You must look after your stomach first, before you can attempt any task. You of all people know that. I was just ensuring the excellent food she delivers will continue.'

'It has never been a problem before. I must admit that was exceptional though, don't you think so Amy?'

'Yes, her skills as a chef, considering mainly self-taught, have been fantastic.' Mi sat back in her chair rubbing her tiny stomach.

'I am so full; it was a lovely meal, thank you very much. When Pete explained to me about the Ark I did not know what to expect, but now I'm beginning to understand why you want to live this way of life.'

15

'Albert, did Pete tell you that Mi is a qualified Doctor?' Amy asked.

'Yes, he has, but not in detail.'

'She hasn't worked since we've been together, it is a bonus though,' commented Pete.

'What area did you practice or specialise in Mi?'

'I'm just a General Practitioner for mainly minor ailments. I would refer anything out of my field to the specialists.'

'You are certainly going to be useful. We've never had a proper doctor onboard before and with a growing community, it couldn't be better timing.'

'I'm going to help Patricia clean up the kitchen. She's been on her feet all day and Melanie has gone to lie down. Please excuse me.'

'Can I help you Amy?' Mi asked.

'You are most welcome. It will give Patricia a break.'

'Pete, would you like another glass of wine?'

'Yes please Albert. What was it?'

'Red grape, with the addition of raspberries and blackcurrants to give dryness and fruitiness; it's only twelve months old, not bad eh?'

'I think it's very good and on top of that I haven't a bill to pay. I don't think my plastic will work here will it?'

'No it won't, but I've got something in mind that will contribute to your upkeep and I think Mi will pay her way quite easily.'

'What are you thinking? I know you need help with defence and I'm expecting that. Is there something else?'

'Let's sleep on it and I'll show you a few things tomorrow and run through some of my ideas then.'

Amy and Mi had finished cleaning up in the kitchen and returned to Albert and Pete.

'I'm very tired,' Mi said to Amy….. 'Pete, Amy is going to show us where we sleep tonight.'

'OK, I'm coming.' They were taken to the cabin that Melanie and Zimbo first moved into. It was originally Monty's room before his departure presumed

16

dead, lost overboard the previous season there. Melanie and Zimbo had moved to a larger cabin to accommodate their new baby and possibly further additions.

'It's on the small side,' Amy apologised, 'but it will only be for one or two nights at the most.'

'It's very good,' said Mi.

'Thank you. It's just great,' Pete added.

'Pete this is bigger than my place in Bangkok.'

'As Amy said, it will do for a couple of nights. We'll need a bit more room if we're going to start a family though. Talking of which, there's no time like the present?'

'On that note I had better go.' Amy quickly headed for the door.

'Sorry Amy, we are so pleased to be in our new home.'

'Goodnight to you both.'

'Goodnight Amy.'

'Oh Pete, our baby, that's a nice idea.' With arms around each other they swirled in a clockwise direction, and he led her to the bed. Collapsing backwards onto the pillows they caressed each other, removing their clothes in between. She lay on top of him kissing and nipping his neck, which has an instant effect on stiffening him. Feeling him pushing his way between her legs, she held it and guided it gently into her.

'Oh, oh that's lovely,' Mi said, sitting up on top of him. Steadily she moved her little body up and down, knowing that if she got him too excited he would finish too quickly. While she tried to control him with slow movements, he held her tiny breasts, fondling them gently. Then he arched his back to thrust into her and quickened the pace.

'Pete no, please, please take your time, do it slowly!'

'Ah, ah, aaah.' He sank down along with his deflated penis. Moving off him, Mi was disappointed. 'You always do this to me. I haven't even started yet.'

'Sorry Mi, you just drive me wild. I can't help it.'

'Well maybe you should think a little bit for me next time. I want to feel something too!' Mi had a big appetite for sex and would not let Pete get away

17

with just a *wham bang thank you mam*. She decided to let him have a rest and then it was arousal time until she was happy; then she would sleep.

'Night, Pete.' No reply came, except his snoring.

'Morning Pete,' said Ched. 'Did you sleep alright; you're looking a bit bleary eyed? Was the bed uncomfortable?'

'No, it was fine and I did sleep very well *eventually*,' he chuckled and then looked Ched in the eye with a beaming smile.

'Oh, that's fine then.' Ched disappeared quickly thinking to himself, the lucky bugger's been shagging all night. I could do with some of that myself. I'll go and find Marigold. She's always pleased to see me and it's been a couple of days since. Ched grew excited at the thought of some extra marital Marigold.

2. WHAT'S ALL THIS WIZARDRY?

Pete's first port of call after leaving Mi in bed was the bridge. There was no one there, which he was pleased about. He just wanted to look about and have a good study of the layout and see what was going on. When he visited the ship a couple of times in his coastguard days, he didn't have a real feeling for the Ark, only the concept. He liked what he saw with only limited information to go on. But now he was bemused at the enormity of the project that Albert and co. had achieved.

'Wow, this is great, our own mobile country!' he said out aloud to himself.

Taking a pair of binoculars he focussed on the bow to see if anyone was there. He spied a girl watering plants. Moving from her he spotted a young man guiding pigs into the orchard. Sheep and goats frolicked in the fields. He scanned again and picked out Millie just inside the sheds leading a cow out. This is something else he thought: the crops, the trees, the animals and most important of all, everyone seemed content. Ignoring the door opening behind him he continued with his study.

'Like what you see?' Albert asked.

'Can anyone not like it? It's amazing what you've created. I congratulate you Albert.' Lowering the binoculars, he turned to face him and shook his hand.

'That was the original idea, but sadly there are people in this world who are not what they seem and use other people at any cost for their own means.'

'Well that's nothing new; did you think you would escape from that?'

'Yes, that was the intention, but me being the optimist, I tend to trust my own kind and then when I smell a rat, I am vigilant and go on the attack.'

'Knowing you as I do from being together in past action, I can understand you thinking that being here on the Ark you would be in control of yours and the others fate. By all accounts, and from what I've seen, the others trust you without question. This must make you feel you have to be more vigilant and very strong to look after the people that love you.'

'Now you're getting soppy and sentimental. Come on, I've got something to show you.'

19

Albert led Pete to the floor just beneath the bridge and they entered a door marked 'Communications Room'. Pete followed Albert only to get another shock. Before him were several tables with computer screens. They were not the type you would buy from your local PC store, they were military standard. He stood there taking the layout in. Magnus, Jane and Gunter were busy positioning various cables marked to go to designated points.

'Where on earth did you find this lot?'
'That's only a bit of it, come with me.' Pete followed Albert to a hold below the foredeck to reveal his new arsenal.
'Fucking hell Albert! What have you been up to?'
'Let's go to the canteen and get some breakfast and have another chat then we can come back down for you to identify some of the tools I've not seen before. You must be more up to date with all that wizardry.'
'Sounds like a good idea, just looking at all this makes me hungry.'

'Good morning Pete,' Patricia called out as soon as he entered the canteen. 'Did you have a good night's sleep? And where is your young lady wife? I've cooked a nice full English breakfast for you all. Would you like some fresh orange juice and herbal tea? We're a bit restricted on coffee and ordinary tea at the moment.'
'That's fantastic. I'm sure Mi will be along shortly Patricia.'
'Just come and help yourself when you're ready.' Picking up trays at the self-serve counter Pete and Albert filled their trays with a plateful of goodies.
'Good morning,' a little voice said from behind them.
'Good morning,' they both replied to Mi.
'This is so great. I feel very happy, and look at all this food. You are very well organised Mr Albert.' Albert thought he must put this straight.
'Mi, please, I'm not *Mr* Albert, I'm just Albert. There are no titles on the Ark, we call each other by first names.'

'Sorry, I am not used to calling Western people by their first name. It is normally Sir or ma'am. I've only just got to really know Pete and our relationship is still growing.'

'Well that's sorted it out before carrying on and not saying anything and letting titles get in the way of who we really are.'

'It will sort itself out in time,' commented Pete.

'Well I'm worried about you already.'

'Why? That's what she's used to. What difference is it going to make?'

'I'll tell you when we are sat down, because my bacon and eggs are getting cold.' The three of them laughed at the silly situation. They sat down and started their meals.

Albert quickly filled his face with the things he liked to eat hot.

'There is no hierarchy on this ship. We are all equal. Nobody gets any more than anybody else. If they want more, it will be only food or rest. But if it comes to notice that someone is not pulling their weight, it will be dealt with. It's not a written rule. No one has been keel-hauled yet!'

'What do you think Mi? Do you want to stay under these *draconian* rules?'

She paused before answering.

'Pete, you are making fun when you say 'draconian' I know that, but let me tell you, when we first arrived here less than twenty four hours ago I was very nervous and almost frightened, but very shortly I felt at home, my biggest thought is this really possible and how long can it last?' Albert deliberated while stabbing his fork into his last piece of fried bread and mopping up the remainder of his grilled tomatoes.

'Nothing lasts for ever! But what we can do is make our quality of life the best we can, and fortunately, we have been provided with a good education and training background to sustain this way of life, not like other parts of the world where it's just being born to suffer a miserable existence.'

'Albert, you are getting soft in your old age.'

'Pete, listen to him, he makes sense.'

'There is part of my military life not even Amy knows about, we can always be wise in hindsight when we reflect on the past. When our baby is born and

Amy has recovered and both fit and are well, I will tell her of my misdemeanours as a mercenary.'

'You mean you were a man of the cloth in the jungle?'

'No Mi, that's a missionary.'

'Sorry Pete, it sounded similar.'

'You are not far off though, they can both cause death.'

'That's a very profound statement Pete, yes when you think about it and it is still happening now.'

'You are definitely mellowing Albert, you are thinking of your past, and I was right when I mentioned about looking after the people you love.'

'Perhaps.'

Albert got up and took his tray back to the counter, then returned to the table where Pete and Mi were still sitting.

'It has been on my conscience for a long time now. I needed to say something to someone who I knew would understand. Knowing you have had front line experience I thought you would know where I'm coming from. The past can be such a burden and you want to escape it, but it just follows you. What I said about being a mercenary, please don't let it leave this table?'

'Albert, that goes without question.'

'Thank you.' Albert left the canteen feeling he said too much and was annoyed with himself. He wanted to take his mind off things and headed for the communications room to see how the team were progressing.

'Hi again,' said Jane. 'We are just off for a break. There's still a lot to figure out but Magnus is very methodical and besides, there's no rush to have it all up and running tomorrow, is there Albert?'

'No there's not. It may even be a waste of time,' he replied.

'I don't think so, not on my part anyway,' she replied, 'I would like to see what is really going on! And see if there is any indication to Miles' involvement. Oh, by the way,' Jane pulled Albert to one side out of earshot of Magnus and Gunter, 'there is a question the adults are asking each other: why did Package Pete take such a risk to get on the Ark? He could have hitched a lift with the coastguard when they make their visit at Christmas. I know that's a couple of months off. But could it be to show you how much you need him, him being the younger ex-marine with up to date military knowledge? Oh, and there's something else that Ched is putting around, that Package Pete is named that because he has a big dick, sorry for being so crude, but even Marigold was getting the 'hots' when she heard about it.'

'Oh shit! Ched and his loose mouth, thanks for telling me Jane. Perhaps we should monitor the situation and brief each other if something awkward happens. I know what you mean about Pete though, but I can say this in his defence, he was always waiting there for us when we had finished an "op" and got the squad and any baggage out of the front line very quickly.'

'I'll see you later Albert.' Magnus and Gunter broke off from what they were doing to take a break.

'Oh, one thing while the three of you are here. Please do not mention anything about the money to our new arrivals and pass the word to the others. I don't think its necessary or a good idea at this stage.'

'Sure Albert,' Jane replied and the other two agreed.

Albert stayed in the room to take a view on the computer layout so far and to review the situation now that other elements were at work, after his brief conversation with Jane. Yes he thought to himself, I better go and see Ched and Marigold right now. No sooner had he turned to exit the room Pete arrived.

'Hi, I thought I could make a start and familiarise myself with this control layout, but before that, you haven't explained how you came by this equipment.'

'Can I explain later over lunch, I've just remembered something I must do straight away.'

'Yes no problem, a few hours won't make much difference.'

'I'll see you later Pete.' Albert left, wondering where to find Ched and Marigold. The canteen might be a start for Marigold and I can try Ched on the short wave he thought.

'Ched, do you read me?' He paused, 'Ched come in please. Do you read me?'

'Yes Albert, go ahead, I hear you.'

'I want a word with you and Marigold. Do you know where she is?' He cleared his throat. 'Shit,' Ched groaned to himself, 'He's found out about us.'

'Err, no I don't. What's it about?'

'I'll tell you when I see you.'

'I'll go and find her now Albert. Shall we meet on the bridge in say twenty minutes?'

'That's fine, ok I'll see you both then.' Strange, that didn't sound like his normal self Albert mused. He seemed agitated, a little thrown off guard. Hmm, for him to volunteer to find her, he doesn't usually volunteer for anything, Albert pondered as he slowly made his way to the bridge.

Ched was panicking, thinking the worst, how the hell did he find out? I must see her first she might know something. What time is it? Just after ten, canteen, she's bound to be there. He rushed into the canteen where she sat, drinking her regular cup of herbal tea, then slowed down immediately as the others stared at him as he entered the room.

'It's not like you to be in a hurry Ched,' someone said.

'Oh, I've got a terrible thirst, a very dry throat.' He faked his voice disappearing by coughing and went straight to the counter to self serve a drink, wondering how he was going to speak to Marigold without the others hearing and suspecting something going on. I know I'll politely ask her if she would like another drink, he decided.

'(Cough.) Marigold, would you like a top up?'

'Yes please Ched.'

'We'll have one too,' said Jane. 'About time you did something for someone else.' Shit, he said to himself, calmly now Ched.

'I won't be a moment Jane and what flavour would you like, jasmine or *stinging nettle?*'

'Very funny, ha, ha!'

He took his and Marigold's drinks over to her table and whispered with his back to the others.

24

'Drink up quickly and get out of here I need to talk to you, urgent.'

'Here you are three teas as requested, would there be anything else for you Lady Jane?' Jane glared and kept quiet knowing if she started on him it would not be in anyone's best interest, they had to try and get on with each other. Ched returned to his drink.

'You go first,' he whispered again. 'Wait for me on the stairs before the bridge.' Ched remained there for a few minutes taking sips of his tea that he didn't even like. The others finished then returned to the communications room.

'Marigold, Albert wants to see us both. He called me on the short wave and wouldn't say what about. Do you think he's found out about us and if so how? I haven't said a thing. Have you heard anything?'

'No, and why all the panic? The only interesting gossip I've heard came from you about Package Pete and his *lucky* wife.'

'No need to be like that, I do my best, I can't help it if I'm not stud of the year. Come on Albert's waiting for us.'

'Just keep your mouth shut Ched! Deny anything he accuses us of.'

'What's this all about then and why just us two?' Ched spoke out first.

'Two things at the moment, number one I hear you have mentioned to others, your impression of why Pete has the nickname Package.'

'You told me to use my imagination.'

'Using your imagination and telling everyone of its conclusion are two different things.' Albert replied. Marigold giggled. 'Number two and that's why you are here as well Marigold,' they both went very still, quiet and bright red. 'I want you to promise me that you say absolutely nothing to Pete and Mi about the money.' A feeling of extreme relief came over the lovers.

'Is that it? What about the others, have they been told?' Ched asked.

'Most have, I'm just doing the rounds without making it obvious.'

'Why not tell them about the cash? Don't you trust them?'

'It is not a question of that. At the moment Ched, we have enough to contend with the Ark's security.'

'You have my word. How about you Marigold?' a very relieved Ched asked.

25

'Of course, goes without question, can we go now?'

'Yes that's all. Thank you.' Odd behaviour, Albert thought. I'm sure there is something going on between those two I think I'll keep an eye on them.

'Mummy, Mummy, come quickly,' Vicky shouted for Millie.

'I'm coming, I'm coming. What is it darling?'

'Look over there, there's two birds, what are they?'

'Oh yes, they look like sparrows, I wonder where we picked them up from. That's wonderful. Let's hope they stay.'

'Can we give them names?'

'Yes why not? How about Gus, a sparrow named Gus, a-sparrow-Gus, (asparagus) that's something we attempt to grow and the other must be Mrs Gus.' Albert was approaching and he heard them both giggling.

'That's wonderful to see, mother and daughter laughing together.'

'Yes Albert, for the first time we have what I think is a pair of sparrows onboard. Vicky spotted them, and wanted to name them. A sparrow named Gus and Mrs Gus.'

'Very good, talking about multiplying, have you seen the present Pete bought for me, I mean us?'

'Yes Albert, I have,' she frowned.

'Oh, you don't approve then?'

'It's not that, it's how you are going to control them safely. I know that all you and Antonio would do is to go out and cull them with guns. He's all for them being let out to breed and I know it's another source of good protein food. But I'll only agree if you have a cull at certain times of the year and no one other than you and Antonio are in control of the shooting, everyone else stays in the canteen together.'

'I agree Millie. Thank you. I came down for something else I wanted to ask you. I would like the question of the money to be kept silent for now, for reasons I'm sure you understand.'

'Yes, I totally agree.'

'Shall I bring the rabbits down?'

'Antonio has already done it and let them out.' She grinned at Albert and he looked flabbergasted, then smiled as well and walked away shrugging his shoulders. He checked the time, thinking to himself, its lunchtime already and I haven't done a thing yet, other than running around having words with all and sundry. I said I would meet Pete to explain how we came across the cache of equipment, now he is going to ask why the attackers went to such lengths to try and take the Ark. I'll just say that they probably think Miles is still alive and he must be very important to them.

Pete was already tucking into his food when Albert arrived. He dished up a few things onto his tray and joined him.

'Where's Mi?'

'She's with Amy, sorting out our cabin. It's very spacious. I'll need some help to get the furniture they picked from the store hold.'

'I'll organise that for you after lunch. The sooner you get settled in the better.'

'I can't imagine how you got hold of that very up to date, hi-tech arsenal.'

'Well, it was surprisingly easy. It was our last encounter with the Russians. They were stalking us with a luxury yacht, and stayed with us for a few days and disappeared, then appeared again. It was obvious they were stalking us because we were just doing a steady eight to nine knots. They were probably capable of thirty, but just kept their distance all the time. So during the course of this I had the yacht we salvaged from the rescue of Antonio and his brother, painted black including the sails. We went out using the Ark as cover, away from their sight line to get the hang of sailing it. Then I picked the right night to go and have a closer look to see what they had onboard. But we were spotted and fired on, so I used your present you managed to deliver to me when you were still working as coastguard down here. I used it to launch a grenade to the stern deck. The crew must have panicked and jumped overboard to some hungry local sharks. I went back, boarded the boat to find it more or less intact complete with control room and arsenal. We stripped it later, marking every connection and detailing the layout. When we had what we wanted, I used my expertise and their semtex to sink it.'

'You do make it sound very easy. Are you sure it was the Russian Mafia?'

27

'Most of the equipment we took is labelled in Russian. The other attacks were just hired hit men I think, could be any nationality. When we picked up Zimbo, he said the men who hired him only spoke English to each other. The man shouting at us through the loudhailer from the helicopter at the first attack used English.'

'I just want to be clear in my own mind Albert. What are we up against and do you think they have had enough now, just putting it all down as a bad experience?'

'I don't look at it like that.' Albert replied. 'They will have studied the situation. Even without Miles, what better cover for their international operations than being set up on the Ark as a bunch of alternative lifestyle hippies? The only thing I have a problem with is the idea that communications can be tracked. They probably have access to rogue satellites that I believe are in operation for those who can pay.'

'That certainly makes sense, I've heard of these satellites and that the CIA are trying to knock them out. They are so small and extremely fast, Chinese made and launched in Iran,' commented Pete.

'There you have everything up to date Pete. Now you can see why I have had to go back to the drawing board and get involved with modern technology, to defend the Ark and its community. And to think all I ever wanted to do, as did the others, was to get off the planet and have some peace!'

'You have no chance of that! Come on show me the goodies and I'll see if I can identify them.'

Amy and Mi were picking out the furniture and soft furnishings which Mi wanted in her new home. The store had a vast array of goods to supply, what was hoped by Albert, an increasing community. Spacious cabins were available for up to twenty couples and their offspring. With the new arrivals they were at eight suites, although Marigold had not a partner as yet, she was classed accommodation-wise as a couple. Unless something drastic happened like picking up a number of strays, it should stay status quo until the children reach adulthood and wanted to find partners. At present, if the population stayed as it was, Alberto was going to be very busy in years to come, being the only male child, but then as Albert has always said, "You never know what's over the horizon."

'I think that should be all we need for now Amy. Could you arrange for the furniture to be moved to our cabin? I'm sure Pete will help.'
'Yes Mi. I'll radio Albert now to organise it.'

Albert and Pete had just got to the arsenal so that Pete could identify what he could, when Albert had a contact from Amy on the shortwave asking for muscle in moving the furniture.
'That's fine. I'll call Ched to give us a hand. He won't be doing much.'
'Ched can you read me, we need your help?'
'Now what the heck does he need me for Marigold? I'd better answer him and see what the old bastard wants. Yes I read you, *and how may I help you?*'
'Are you being sarcastic, because if you are and you are laid on your back somewhere, the next time I see you you'll be on your back holding a bloody nose!'
'Oh shit I've upset him now. I'd better go. I need to talk to you Marigold. We can't carry on like this. If he finds out, he will have me walking the plank, especially now his big buddy Psycho-Pants is with him.' Albert was annoyed with Ched's attitude and was even more by the amount of time waiting for his response.
'I'm on my way Albert where do you need me?'
'In the furniture store please, to help us move Mi's things to their cabin.'
'I'll be there in ten minutes.'

Ched arrived and Albert was still not happy with Ched's general unhelpful approach to the community.
'So what have you been up to then Ched that made you answer in such a sarcastic manner?'
'Nothing! Well the truth is I've not been feeling myself just lately.'
'Oh, and who have you been feeling?' Pete tried to contain himself and turned away.

29

'No, no, nothing like that, I'm just under the weather that's all.'
'Well then you can be Mi's first customer. She's a Doctor you know. In the meantime let's shift this lot. A bit of physical exercise will do you good.'
'You are a hard man chief; I'll go and see her tomorrow.'
'Make sure you do.' The rest of the day was spent fitting out the new cabin. Mi was very excited with her new life. To her it was luxury to have the choice of high quality furniture and soft furnishings, a roof over her head and the best of good food, just for helping the community with her medical skills in return. And then there was the bonus of the chance of having a family. She could hardly wait to get her man under the duvet!

'Pete we best leave looking at the gear until tomorrow. You would be better giving Mi a hand to get yourselves settled into your new home.'
'Yes you're right. I'll see you at meal time.' Albert started to think about Ched and his attitude. Should he have a word with Millie to see if anything was wrong with her husband? Or if he did that, would it cause a problem? I know I'll talk to Amy about it she's a bit more diplomatic than me and will advise me what's best. It must be time for a beer, checking his watch. Oh it's a little early. What the hell, he thought, I'm way off track today anyway, and I'll make a fresh start tomorrow. Ched was at the bar with his head propped in his hands, arms resting on the bar and looking into space when Albert arrived.
'Penny for your thoughts,' Albert remarked. Ched stood up straight and faced Albert.
'You threatened me with violence today. Was there any need for that?' Albert paused before answering, using the time to think as he poured his pint.
'No, perhaps it was a bit too strong for someone who, (raising his voice) just needs a kick up the arse.'
'What have I done wrong?'
'You had better ask yourself that. When you compare yourself with the rest of us, you're the only one, oh sorry, I'll rephrase that, *and you* are one of two who do not pull their weight fully for the community.'
'And who's the other one?'

30

'Oh, so you admit you are one.' Albert managed to get some of his pint down him while Ched was thinking about an answer.

'Stop trying to be clever Albert, it doesn't suit you. I told you earlier, I'm not feeling too good.'

'Is it illness or other problems?'

'I'm going. I'll sleep on it,' replied Ched. He left quickly without looking at Albert or saying goodbye. He said he'll sleep on it, Albert immediately thought, so it's not illness! Pondering again, as his pint went down, he started to mellow. Perhaps I'm being too hard on him. He may need someone to talk to, to open up about his problems I'm no good at that. It needs the Amy's of this world. As if stressed, he pushed his head down between his hands with arms resting on the bar. He heard a voice behind him.

'What's wrong Albert? You look worried.'

'Melanie, how are you? Is *he* still kicking you hard inside there?'

'Yes it is and it's not a he or she until we know and that will be on its arrival. I asked you what's wrong and you have changed the subject, so, in my way of thinking, there must be something wrong.'

'Yes, you're right. I do have a problem with something. But it seems, from my perspective, I'm not the right person to sort this one out, so I'm going to pass it on to Amy and that's where it stops and I would very much appreciate if nothing was said to anyone. So don't you go worrying about it, you concentrate on having that baby.'

'Ok Albert, if you don't want to talk to me about it, I'll just go away.' Albert returned to his head held position as she left.

'Shit,' he said, and thought the day was getting worse.

He finished his first pint and poured another just as Amy walked into the room.

'I hope that's your first,' Amy spurted out.

'No it's my second and the way things are going I'll sink another ten!' he fired back.

'Albert!' She raised her voice, looking around to make sure no one was within earshot.

'What's wrong? Melanie has just come to me to ask me to talk to you. She says you have a problem.'

'I was going to talk to you later in private because here and now is not the right time. It's coming up to mealtime and the others will be calling in for a teatime drink and then the food will start with all the rest here.'

'But if you drink too much you won't be able to explain the problem to me later.'

'I promise you Amy I will not have any more than I normally have, besides, I'm looking for an early night. Things haven't gone too well today in some departments.'

'Alright darling, no more talk about *things* until we are in our cabin,' she smiled. He pecked her on the cheek as she put her arms around him.

'Albert, it can't be all that bad. Cheer up and let's see what Patricia's cooked for us tonight.'

'So what's the problem?'

'I had a run in with Ched today. His attitude was way out of order when I asked him to lend a hand to move furniture for Pete and Mi.'

'What did you say to him?'

'I threatened to put him on his back.'

'Albert! Have you apologised?'

'No, not really, only that it was a bit strong and he just needed a kick up the arse.'

'You're going to have to restrain yourself. You could do more damage than you may think at the time. You know what Ched is like for opening his big mouth. The threat of violence between members of such a small community could have awkward repercussions.'

'Yes Amy, I know, I know you're right. I've just got to find it in me to apologise to him properly.'

There's something else, I have a strong suspicion that Ched and Marigold are having a liaison, an affair, same thing I suppose. If you think about it, Marigold's a young fit woman but doesn't seem bothered about the Ark bumping into somebody new for her, and Ched, I can never find him when he's needed.'

'I hadn't thought of it before, but yes, I can see it. I have an idea. Don't apologise just yet. Let's see if we can find out more about them and use the information to our advantage, if possible. Plus if it is just the four of us that know, it won't go any further to do untold damage and there would be the bonus of an indirect kick up Ched's arse!'

'Amy, that's a very good idea. It's usually me that comes up with that sort of thinking.'

'I've got to know you very well these past few years. It must have rubbed off on me.'

'Talking about rubbing off darling,'

'Albert! Don't be so crude.'

'Oh, alright then I'll go to sleep.'

'Albert,' she whispered and reached over to him, put her hand on his disgruntled cock. 'is this what you mean?'

'Hmm, that's nice, that's very nice.'

'This is all I will be doing for you until well after our child is born and if you are a very good boy, I might give you a treat now and then.'

'Oh, oh, hmm!'

'Now you can go to sleep.'

'Pete, look this is very nice and so spacious. The furniture is good quality and look, a king size bed. Come on, let's not waste any time and tonight you can do something for me, before you think about putting your little package in me.'

'Little! I'm supposed to be big.'

'Well that's what they all believe and if it comes up in conversation, I will tell the women that it is small.' By this time she'd finished the sentence laying completely naked with her legs apart, gesticulating with her hands and pointing to her bushy hair. She held his head into her and as he worked his tongue gently, soon finding the spot she wanted him to touch.

'Now, oh, oh, uh that's more like it, don't stop, don't stop, uh, uh, ah……, Pete, you do that so well, it makes me want to fall asleep now. Night Pete.'

'Eh?' He grunted as he pulled himself up. 'Mi, can't I have a quick burst on my banjo?'

'Oh go on then. But be quick!'

'I don't think that will be a problem!'

After breakfast the next day Albert and Pete went to view and identify the arsenal. Albert had also asked Magnus to be there to make notes about the weapons and to do a proper inventory.

'I know about most of the small arms Pete but I still want a record of make, model, rounds, clips, magazines and numbers.' They went through the small arms first making a detailed file, then they moved onto the various grenades and launchers, rockets and guided missiles etc.

'Got your clipboard ready Magnus?'

'Yes, fire away, well not literally.'

Hand guns: Taurus 1911 series pistol, 20 of plus 500 clips of ammunition.

Heckler & Koch 9 mm USP pistol, 20 of plus 500 clips of ammunition.

Heckler & Koch MP5 sub machine gun, 9 of plus 1000 magazines of ammunition.

'That's an odd number Albert nine.'

'Make it ten Magnus I've got the other one.'

Heckler & Koch G3 assault rifle, 10 of plus 1000 magazines of ammunition.

105 mm surface mounted light machine gun, 2 of plus 1000 magazines of ammunition.

Missiles: Advanced Short Range Surface to Air Missile, 4 of with software. (A.S.R.S.A.M)

Sting Ray Lightweight anti-submarine torpedo Ship launch model with software, 4 of.

VLS Quad Pack Missiles with software, 12 of.

Short Range Attack Projectile 95 mm, 10 of with software. (S.R.A.P.)

Evolve Sea Sparrow Missile with software, 10 of. (E.S.S.M.)

Exocet Block 4 Anti-Ship Missile with software, 12 of.
Objective Individual Combat Weapon Grenade Launcher, 2 of plus 100 grenades. (O.I.C.W.)
A quantity of Semtex with10 detonators and numerous timing devices.
A box of 20 limpet mines with timers.
A box of 100 light hand grenades.

It was lunchtime by the time they had completed putting together a full list of equipment.

'You were right to replicate the control room Albert because a couple of those guided missiles will not operate without data supplied by the computers,' Pete said.

'If that lot was set up with a control centre, there's enough hardware here to make the Ark a pain to anyone wanting to take her on from sea or air. But I think most of it is out of our depth. The military training programme on this type of weaponry is very extensive. You and I can only train our defence team with the knowledge we have of the arms we are well acquainted with. We would be foolish to start messing around with high-tech equipment we know nothing about.'

'Perhaps you're right Albert. After all, we only want to stop anyone boarding the Ark. An enemy would have a hard job blowing us out of the water, especially with the type of missiles you recovered.'

'I'm not so sure Pete. They could probably sink us if they really tried. The main danger area is the methane gas storage tanks but they aren't visible. The rest of the ship is more or less inert, nothing of any quantity to burn, I still think they wanted to take the Ark and set that lot up on her,' Albert replied.

The three of them sat down for their lunch break and continued discussing the weapons. Magnus listened, taking it all in.

'Albert, we will have the computers ready to log on tomorrow. Why not wait and see what we can find out about everything we have because it will all be stored on them. I'm worried about switching on to any communication

35

satellite, though as soon as we do that people will know where we are. That's if they don't know already by conventional means.'

'Will you be able to understand the Russian Magnus?' Albert asked.

'I've never known a computer yet that is not a multi-linguist.'

'Oh really?'

'You are out of date Albert,' said Pete.

'In that case I'll leave you all to it. Just call me when you need me for the rough stuff, I'm well on home ground with that, as you well know Pete!' Pete gave him a knowing nod.

As Albert walked away, he wondered where Ched was. I'll have a quiet wander around he thought, but first to save me the trouble of trekking up to Millie, I'll radio to see how she is and if she needs any more help.

'Millie/Antonio come in please, do you read me?'

'Yes Albert, I hear you. Millie is mucking out the pigs with Zimbo, they're welcome to it!'

'I just wondered if you needed any more help up there.'

'No it is OK thank you Albert the three of us are managing very good!'

'That's great Antonio, see you all later.'

That was worth doing and I know he's not in the communications room, he is not out fishing that's for certain, so I'll go to the canteen and see who's there. He entered the canteen, no one about. He tried the kitchen and found Patricia with Amy assisting her, and Patricia looked up.

'Albert this is unusual to see you in here.'

'Yes, err I just fancied a cup of tea with my wife.'

'It will have to be "mint" because that's all we have at the moment. I do miss a good cup of Tetley's tea, don't you?'

'I know what you mean Patricia, but mint will be fine. We'll get it ourselves won't we dear.' Amy quickly got the message and followed him out of the kitchen.

'Now what's up?'

'We are going calling.'

36

'Oh, have you checked everywhere then?'
'Yes.'

They left the canteen to call at Marigold's living quarters.
'You knock. Just say it's Amy and you could do with a hand in the kitchen because you are tired and need to lie down.' She knocked at the door.
'It's Amy Marigold. Can I come in?' Trying the door as she spoke, it opened, she walked in.
'Marigold! Ched!' She quickly closed the door. The deed had been done. Not saying a thing she grabbed Albert, looked at him with her finger over her lips to be silent, and they disappeared rapidly.
'Yes Albert. You were right. They are having an affair.'
'What were they doing? I should have opened the door.'
'I'm glad you didn't. You would have stayed and watched. They were very careless to leave the door unlocked.'
'Yes but what were they doing?'
'They were at it doggy fashion.'
'Were they completely naked?'
'Yes they were. It was quiet erotic.'
'Shit, I missed it!'
'Albert stop it! You don't need that to turn you on. I'm in charge of that department.'
'Now how should we deal with this?'
'We leave it because I'm sure they'll approach me first. They won't know you were there.'
'OK, I'll leave it to you, the outcome should be interesting Amy.'

It was not long before Marigold knocked on Amy's door.
'You'd better come in and sit down. So how long has it been going on?'
'A long time,' she sighed weakly, 'it's been over a year. Monty didn't care for me. He had his own type of pleasure. But Ched cared for me and made me feel loved and wanted without any hassle. He was always worried that Millie might find out. You won't tell her will you? Please don't tell her.' She burst

into tears. 'I'm sorry it's my fault, it was me who led him on.' Amy gave her a handkerchief she took from a drawer.

'Telling Millie is not going to do anyone any good,' she said, 'in fact, it could do untold damage to the whole community, but this must stop immediately. It will not go further than this room, I promise you. Albert and I have discussed it already. You have our word.'

'So Albert knows then?'

'Yes and will want to see Ched as soon as he has the courage to come to us with an explanation.'

Marigold was shaking.

'Now what will I do? There's no one for me now. I don't think I can cope with that. What will I do?'

Then the tears came again.

'Try not to let it get to you. It's strange, Melanie always used to go to Albert with the same worry thinking she'd never find someone for herself and look at her now, married to a nice young man with a baby on the way. So don't throw in the towel. You are a young, pretty and a healthy woman. We also have room for expansion on the Ark.'

'Albert can I have a word with you please?' Ched asked.

'Certainly, I wondered when you would. I'll see you at our cabin in twenty minutes. I want Amy to be present if you don't mind.'

'OK, I'll be there.'

'Come in Ched. Let's close the door and get this sorted out.'

'Hello Amy.' He looked embarrassed knowing what she'd seen.

'Hello Ched.' She tried to look him in the eyes, but his eyes were on his shoes.

'Right Ched, it's a simple as this: from now on you will cease the affair with Marigold.'

'Yes Albert.'

'Do you realise that if Millie found out it would do so much damage. We have all come a long way together to get to this level of contentment and we don't want you throwing it all away. Do you understand?'

38

'I'm very sorry and want to apologise and put this all behind us. I'm more worried about Marigold and her happiness. Our relationship has grown and she has been able to cope better with me as a special friend.'

'I understand that,' Amy said softly.

'Now there is one other thing Ched,' Albert continued.

'Oh! What?'

'Before I asked this we will promise that not one word will be said to Millie or anyone else about the matter.'

'You have our word,' Amy added.

'I've accused you of being slack compared with the others to the extent that I got so frustrated I made a threat to you. I can only apologise for that. But now I want your word that you will go about your duties and be of assistance wherever required, without waiting to be asked by someone who has spent ages looking for you. Can I have your promise on that?'

'Yes and you won't say a word to Millie because if she finds out she'll kill me.'

'That is an alternative, but we are short of men at the moment.'

'Albert!' Amy snapped.

'Thank you both for being so understanding. But I'm still worried for Marigold. I best go now to collect Vicky and Rose from the crèche. A relieved yet sad Ched left their cabin growing more concerned about Marigold by the minute. He realised now how strong his feelings were for her.

'Everything went to plan Amy. That's that sorted then.'

'No Albert it's not. You can't plan people's emotions and there is more between those two than I think we all realised.'

'Oh shit!'

3. RAIN, SODDING RAIN

The southern hemisphere was entering autumn; the end of summer and the season changing had not been that kind to them with less daily sun hours than the Ark had become accustomed to. During February and the beginning of March they were pounded by persistent rain, not even a thunderstorm that would give them hope that it would clear afterwards, just continuous drizzle and heavy spells of downpour. This was a shock to their system comparable to the short stay last year in the Sargasso Sea, but with the exact opposite weather conditions. Millie had just returned from the Bow farm to go to the canteen for a break, she was completely soaked when she bumped into Albert.

'Albert, I think we need to move north earlier this year. Some of the crops will fail if we don't get a stable period of sunshine.'

'Yes, Millie I completely understand. The only problem I can think of is where do we go? I feel a lot more confident about the Ark's security. In fact I'm more worried now about the media than the Mafia.'

'Well don't you think we should all sit down around a table and let others give their points of view about the whole situation, let alone where to go? It's a long time since we've all sat down for a good discussion.'

'Yes, again, you're right. I'll call a meeting tonight after dinner. Where would you like to go?'

'I like the climate near the Azores. It suits all aspects of growing and Ched likes fishing there; he hasn't been out for a while because of poor visibility.'

'That's true. Let's see what the others have to say.'

Word got around and the canteen was buzzing at mealtime, the last desserts were finished as Albert got to his feet.

'I've called this meeting so that each of you can have a say on where we move to next. It will be a little earlier than normal because Millie is worried about too much rain and not enough sun on the crops. Please have a chat amongst yourselves for a while and then I'll go around the table for your opinions. Amy will take a few notes.' A lot of muttering went on with heads going from side to side.

40

'What are our realistic options Albert?'Gunter asked.

'We could go to the Azores or even somewhere in the Mediterranean. There's a lot of shallow water there. It could be a little busy with tourists etc; though at the end the season, there's the Suez Canal and out into the Indian Ocean and try south of Madagascar.'

'Didn't they make a film once about Madagascar?' asked Patricia.

'Yes, it was a cartoon.' Pete said.

'That's right, they had funny little chipmunk type animals talking, I remember now,' continued Patricia.

'They were supposed to be lemurs with an Indian accent, I think,' Pete replied.

'Ah hmm, excuse me. We are digressing, so could we get to your decisions on where to go please?' 'How about going to the Azores for half of the season and stock the freezers with good Atlantic fish etc; and then go into the Med for the remainder before going through the Suez to the south again? I'm sure we can muster up a few bob to pay the toll through Suez, if there is one,' Ched piped up. Conferring with each other again they ended with an air of agreement. Ched sat back and his face beamed, as if he had come up with the solution entirely on his own.

 'Can I take it that Ched's suggestion is the favourite for all of us?' Albert asked. They looked around at one another and nodded their heads followed by a unanimous 'yes.'

'OK. It will be subject to any outside interference, of course. Thank you all. Meeting ended.'

Albert went to the bar and pulled himself a beer. Millie joined him.

'I'll try one of those Albert; you know I've never tasted your brew yet, other than the wine.'

'It's certainly more consistent than it used to be and it's always best when we have been stationary for a while, which makes sense. Real ales don't travel too well.'

'Hmm, that's not bad at all, I think I'll be changing to your bitter rather than the wine. Oh, and thank you for calling the meeting. It went well. I've never been to the Mediterranean or any further East. It should be interesting going through the Suez Canal.' She returned to her table with Ched, Marigold and their children.

'Where's mine?' asked Ched.

'Sorry Ched, you have this one, can I get you anything while I'm up at the bar Marigold,' she asked, heading for the bar.

'Yes please, a red wine, thank you.'

Pete left Mi at the table to get them some drinks.

'What do you think about the plans?' Albert asked as he poured.

'I just hope I don't get too bored. It's hard when you have always been active, facing difficult decisions, controlling men and being in the thick of it. You know what I mean? I've found out something on the computers database that might be of interest to you.' Pete went on.

'What are you getting at Pete?' Just then Millie was standing behind Pete and had overheard the last part of his sentence to Albert.

'Yes Millie what can I get you?' Albert asked quickly, to stop any further conversation.

'Another pint and a red wine please Albert. What database Pete?'

'Oh, just talking shop, nothing of any interest as yet.' Millie returned to her table with the drinks, none the wiser but still with database on her mind.

'You know that for years now,' Pete continued. 'Somalia has been the home to every modern day pirate, a sanctuary for all sorts of terrorist drop-outs. Strange that it's been suggested to go through the Suez and out into the Pacific just happening to pass by a certain Russian Mafia base, it's a little bit inland but it's there.'

'That's very interesting. Please keep it to yourself. I've got a few months to think about it and study the situation and I know what you're thinking. It's not out of the question. We could do a lot of damage!'

Millie and Antonio were on their way to the animals as usual early next morning.

42

'When will this sodding rain give up? I've never known such a time like it before.'

'It is very miserable all the time. I like plenty of sun on my back,' Antonio replied.

'Antonio, you've been involved with the new computers. Do you know anything about the database Pete has been studying?'

'Only that Magnus has broken some passwords to access stored information. There is a database that has a lot of detail on the Russians operations.'

'So it's nothing to worry about at the moment then?'

'No, no Millie, nothing at all.'

'What a mess that grazing field is. We can't let the animals on that. They'll just trash it to a mud bath. The drainage system and pumps must be working overtime. We'll feed them hay in the pens today.'

Heavy rain continued throughout that day. Millie was exhausted and sat down on a straw bale. She started to shiver and sweat at the same time and knew something was wrong.

'Antonio, Antonio, please come here quickly?'

'What is it? Do you want me to make love to you?'

'No, we agreed that was over after Rose was born. I'm not well. Feel my forehead. I'm sweating yet I'm so cold.'

'Yes. I must get you back to your cabin and bring Mi to you. Put on your cape. Let us go.' They reached the upper decks and Albert spotted the pair. Antonio was holding and helping Millie along. He saw that there was a problem and rushed to over.

'What's wrong?'

'Millie's not well. It looks like she has a fever. We must get her to her cabin and call Mi.'

'Right, I'll call Mi and Ched to help.' Albert did so immediately. Millie was in her cabin when they arrived, with Antonio and Albert still there.

'OK, you two can go now and thank you.' In came Ched.

'What's wrong with her Mi? Is she going to be alright?'

'I haven't had a chance to examine her yet Ched, but I'm sure she will be fine. Why don't you collect Lucy and Rose, take them to the surgery room so that I

43

can examine them too. How are you feeling Ched, any symptoms hot and cold sweats?'

'Not just lately, are you sure she's going to be alright?'

'Ched, please go?'

'Yes, I've gone.'

'Now lie down Millie I want to take your temperature and pulse.' She placed the thermometer under her tongue, and then took her pulse reading. When Mi checked the thermometer it was 39°C degrees, worryingly high and her pulse racing. Mi was dreading that it was something like malaria, which she had seen before. She ran through the symptoms and asked Millie a few basic questions.

'Millie have you pain in your joints?'

'Yes, I ache all over and there's pain in my chest.'

'Have you noticed any unusual insects like the mosquito on the ship?'

'No.' Mi called Albert on the short wave.

'Albert I'm not sure at the moment until I have taken some more tests, but as a precautionary measure I want to make this cabin isolated. No one comes in and I will stay here with her and call you for anything that I need, probably some more linen. Oh and antibiotics, but I'll get them myself when I go to the surgery. I need to check Antonio over too, to find out if he has any symptoms.'

'Yes Mi, I'll see to that and tell the others.'

'Ched,'

'Yes Albert.'

'When Mi has examined your girls can you stay with them in Melanie and Zimbo's old place, it's just a temporary thing until Millie is diagnosed.'

'Yes Albert, I understand. I hope it's not serious.'

'She will be fine. She's a very strong Yorkshire lady.' Greta burst into the room.

'Albert where's Mi? Melanie has gone into labour,' she said.

'Oh shit! That's all we need.'

'Mi's with Millie who's gone down with a fever, and she can't leave her yet. Can you get Jane? I'll get Amy. I just hope she hasn't gone into labour herself, because she's due.'
'OK Albert, I'll stand by as well.'

'Thank you.' Amy was taking a nap in their cabin, Albert felt awkward when he had to disturb her.
'Amy we have problems. Millie's gone down with a fever. Mi has isolated her and will stay with her until she can identify the illness. Now Melanie's gone into labour. I've asked Greta to get Jane and I was wondering if you were up to assisting?'
'Of course, help me up will you?'
'How are you doing, any signs yet?'
'No I'm fine. Let's go to Melanie.'

Jane was already at Melanie's side going through the motions of preparing for another newborn to the Ark. Melanie was very big and everyone guessed it would be between seven and eight pounds. Now they were about to find out.
'Amy, are you alright with this?' asked Jane, 'it must be nearly your time to deliver?'
'Yes I'll be fine, but I won't be able to stand up for long. My back aches like mad, Greta will you stay with us?'
'Yes, just tell me what to do.'
'Albert, you can leave us now.'
'Yes, I'm just going.'
'Albert,' Melanie cries, 'Look at this!' as she put both hands on her huge stomach, 'I didn't think I'd see over a horizon like this.' He looked at her and smiled, quickly leaving the room.
'I bet nobody's told Patricia,' he mumbled to himself and then headed for the canteen. Rushing through the door he saw a line up at the bar: Zimbo, Magnus, Gunter and Ched all with drinks.
'Ched, I thought you were with Vicky and Rose?'

45

'Marigold's got them. I know it will be alright with Millie, she's babysat before.'

'Where's Antonio?'

'He had to get cleaned up; he was covered in shit.'

'Oh, I assume you are waiting to wet the baby's head and already started by the look of things. Did you remember to invite Pete? He's one of us as well.'

'Sorry,' said Ched, 'we forgot about him.'

'And where's Patricia?'

'She left ten minutes ago. She must have gone to her cabin first before going to Melanie,' Zimbo explained.

'Shouldn't you be at Melanie's side?'

'Oh no, that's woman's work. I would only get in the way and probably pass out at the sight of it all.'

Albert raised his eyebrows and tried to keep a grip on the situation.

'Who's looking after Stella and Venus Gunter?'

'Marigold.'

'Marigold, are you sure that's wise for her to look after all the children? That's not been a good idea in the past. Has she got Alberto as well?'

'No, Antonio is going to bring him here to wet the baby's head as well.'

'What at nine months old? Right lets get this straight, I know it's a special occasion, but I think you are forgetting another problem, Millie is with Mi, who is trying to look after her and identify and treat the fever she has, so can we all make sure we take it easy and think of others that are caring for the ones we care for?'

'Ched let's go and see if Marigold is alright with the children,' Gunter suggested.

'Yes you're right.'

'Zimbo, go to Melanie and don't pass out. Just come back here when you know that mother and baby are well and you know if it's boy or girl.'

'Yes Sir!'

'I'll accept the 'Sir' on this occasion.'

'Well Magnus pour us a pint while I call Pete and get him here. I don't suppose Antonio will be long. I haven't heard from Mi to ask for anything. I hope Millie's alright. She always stretches herself, over-doing it, and then the body is low in its resistance to ailments.'

'Pint coming up Sir.'

'Magnus don't you start.'

'I just thought it was fitting for you.'

'Pete, come in please. Do you read me?'

'I hear you.'

'What are you up to?'

'I'm just scanning files. I heard there's a couple of problems do you need me?'

'Not particularly, it's just that there will be a gathering to wet the baby's head when it arrives. Melanie has gone into labour and hopefully not too long to wait. It's mainly Millie I'm worried about. Mi is still with her. She said she would call me if she needed anything. I haven't heard.'

'I'll call to see how they are on my way up.'

'Just knock on the door. Don't go in. She wants it isolated until she has an idea of what's causing the fever.'

'Roger.'

Albert took his pint to sup a welcoming mouthful, as Antonio arrived with Alberto in his arms.

'Ah, I needed that, Antonio. Oh Alberto, just think, one day we'll stand here and have a pint together, hasn't he grown?'

'Yes and he can stand up for a short while and tries to walk. It won't be long now. He is very strong,' the proud father boasted.

'What would you like to drink Antonio?'

'I will just have a soft drink please until Jane gets here. I hope it won't take too long, Alberto's hungry. Patricia normally makes him something special.'

Just then Mi walked in with Pete.

'Millie's ok then?'

'No, not exactly, she has pneumonia and is fast asleep. I gave her antibiotics and something to make her sleep. She needs rest. She has overworked. The

constant rain making her wet through all the time has completely drained her. I do not want her to work for at least three weeks.'
'Antonio, you'll have to take the management of the farm on. You have Zimbo, but Ched will need to be with Millie. Will you manage?'
'Yes we will.'
'I'll give a hand if you need it,' came out of the blue from Pete.

Later Zimbo rushed in, in a burst of excited shouting.
'It's a boy! It's a boy! I'm a father! I'm a father!'
'What's his weight and have you named him?'
'I don't know but he's black!'
'Congratulations!' came from everybody there. Soon all but Millie, Patricia, Melanie and son were in the canteen relieved and celebrating the birth of the new arrival.

Early next day everyone called in to see the new baby, wondering what they would call him and his weight. Melanie gave them all the same answer.
'We haven't thought of a name yet. His weight was seven pounds twelve ounces, whatever that is in kilograms and he is gorgeous, so cuddly.' Zimbo got a look in when they were finally left alone.
'What do you think Zimbo, have you any thoughts for a name for him?'
'I would like to call him after my father, Zaptu.'
'No definitely not! I'd rather call him Magnus II.'
'No it is too long, how about Chuva?'
'Chuva, what does that mean?'
'That is what we call rain at home, it is from Portuguese.'
'Yes Zimbo, I like it Chuva! It will remind me of the weather when he was born and he turned it into brightness.' The name was soon on everyone's lips. All saying, 'that's a strange name,' but Albert knew exactly what it meant.
'It means rain and I think it is a good and very apt choice,' he explained to the others.

The next few days was a critical time for Millie. Slowly her condition improved. If it had not been for the antibiotics and other medicines they had in stock and also those retrieved from the yacht they sunk, together with Mi's skills, the situation would not be as it was, Millie on the mend. Albert realised this and was worried about the future, a serious injury, or, as they had just experienced with Millie another serious illness. He thought of Amy and a heavy burden fell on him. What if something goes wrong when she gives birth? We have been lucky in the past, even when Monty was shot! It wasn't an internal wound which needed surgery. His mind was riddled with bad thoughts of disaster. I'm going to look at this area more closely and somehow create a proper emergency service with better medical care instead of taking chances all the time and that means sitting down with everyone again. I'll wait until Millie is fully fit and hope our baby's birth goes well. I had better go and see Amy now.

'How are you doing my dear? You're five days overdue now.'
'Yes I know. I just want it over with. I hope it goes as easily as Melanie did with hers.'
'I'm sure it will,' Albert comforted her.
'I thought we were going to head north earlier this season. We should have been moving by now according to the plans at the meeting.'
'We will be moving within the next few days my dear. Things are being prepared as we speak, ok?'
'Yes of course. I just hope it's not thunder and lightening when our baby arrives because it won't be called that.' They both laughed at her joke.
'Yes that would be a mouthful, have you any ideas for names?'
'No Albert. Let's wait until it's born.'
'I must pop and see Millie and Ched to find out how things are. I won't be long and I'll be back soon.'

He not only went to see Millie, he called around to all the adults to find out how preparations were progressing for the move north. Just as he thought, they were ready, so very keen to leave the rain behind. It was suggested to go at first light the next day. Gunter had already plotted a course.

The turbines were running and were soon pushing them away from the area of Tristan da Cunha in the South Atlantic. They had always enjoyed it there and most of this season the weather was good, but the past four weeks had been dreadful for them. They all agreed that it would not deter them from returning again sometime. Now they were looking at part of the next season around the Azores, south of an island called Vila Do Porto, the most southern of the archipelago and then onto somewhere in the Mediterranean. Later they would return to the south via the Suez Canal, through the Red Sea, the Gulf of Aden and out into the Indian Ocean to head south down the East coast of Africa.

Two days into the journey and Amy went into labour. Mi, Jane and Albert were with her, with Amy clinging onto him as if fighting for her life. Her pain was excruciating during the whole birth allowing a tiny little girl into the Ark's world weighing only three pounds two ounces. The baby was very weak and frail with its mother in the same condition. Albert stayed with them for two days, just having meals brought in. Amy was struggling to feed the baby let alone herself, so Mi took what milk Amy could give and topped up by giving the baby to Melanie to feed, gradually strengthening it to relieve Amy of the task of producing milk. Jane and Mi nurtured that baby constantly, which allowed Albert to give Amy total attention, building her strength back up. It took eight days before Amy could stand on her own two feet and the Ark almost at their destination before she could walk about carrying the baby.

The sailing north went very well. They stayed right out into the Atlantic to avoid any visitors. This meant it took longer, but then they were not in any hurry anyway. The only downside was that they used up most of the methane gas supply they had stored. Because they relied on the turbines instead of the mechanical sails made the longer trip less work, not like on other passages. Gunter, Ched and Pete took full control in shifts with others helping on lookouts. Albert would have made these decisions but with him distracted and concentrating on other pulls of his heart strings, something that he had not been affected by so much before, it was left to the rest of the crew. The usual rituals for some of the occupants took place' as the centuries old sailor tradition has it of doing something outrageous when crossing the equator; but this time some had other concerns. It was late March and the early evening sun was edging its way over towards the western horizon before dropping down rapidly like a huge fried egg falling off the edge of the earth. The sky was completely clear apart from the odd evening star eager to show itself first, the short reddish pink vapour trails of the busy jet flight paths criss-crossing the sky faded into the deep blue night. A suitable area to anchor was found and now all the community wanted to do was wet the baby's head.

Amy and baby made a brief visit to the canteen to show those who had not seen her because of the fragile state the pair were in. They were all waiting for a view of the tiny little mite.
'Come on you two you haven't told us her name,' Millie now very much better shouted out. Albert and Amy looked at each other and then at the gathering.
'It's been very difficult because of the struggle both of them had. We first thought of 'Shrimp' but she has to live with that the rest of her life. We were inspired by Zimbo's Portuguese name for rain,
'Chuva' set us thinking. We have hope for our late-in-life-baby. The Portuguese name for Hope is Esperanca.'
'How unusual and a lovely sound to it, Esperanca,' said Jane. They all applauded and soon a toast was given to the new arrivals wishing them a full, healthy and complete life.
'To Chuva and Esperanca!' glasses chinked around the room and the names repeated.

Gradually Amy and Esperanca built up their strength to be able to have a normal daily routine although Amy was unable to feed the baby with her own milk. Albert would always get up through the nights to bottle feed the baby, to give Amy maximum sleep. The other new parents, Melanie and Zimbo, took it quite easily in their stride, having the strength of youth on their side, with Melanie able to quickly satisfy feeding Chuva at anytime and still be able to kick Zimbo out of bed in the mornings to do his duties on the farm.

ALBERT'S PRIVATE LOG – March 2019

I've gone through some shit in my life but the last few weeks has beaten all the lot so far, but Amy and Esperanca survived that makes me carry on with strength. I just don't know what I would have done if I had lost them, it was that close. Perhaps it's a getting old thing, when you value more the things you have got, compared as to in the past when you possibly had a cavalier attitude towards never ever losing it, having youth on your side, thinking it will always be there for you. Disregarding the thought that most soldiers have, that you won't be back, you have to think that you will be back with your loved ones to make the risk worthwhile.

I'm very glad the passage here went well to give me the time to spend with Amy through a horrendous challenge she had to go through for the thing she always wished for: to bear me a child, such a different case with Melanie and Zimbo producing such a fine specimen of a child. The combined genes of the two of them should make him a gentle giant.

Pete and Mi have really made a difference, Mi especially. At the moment, her doctor's profession has been a saviour to us. It's strange how sometimes certain things can fall into place where other things are often at a loss. As to the business of the Russian Mafia, it's been about ten months since our last encounter with them, albeit a total loss on their part. We have a lot of information on them now, as they must have on us. We have sufficient arms to protect ourselves but do we leave well alone or use what we have got to hit them hard at one or two of the places we know they are and let the world know about it? That's my dilemma and I have a couple of months to *make a decision. The training must not slip just because we have had a relaxed period of aggression. I must install that on the trainees.*

Food stores were being replenished by Ched and Zimbo going out fishing regularly and Pete took a fancy to go out with Ched to try his hand at something he'd surprisingly never tried in all the times he's been out on water or at sea. Ched agreed to take him fishing and they came back with a fine catch of netted fish, lobster and crab in the pots. On one particular trip back to the Ark it was silence between them, but Ched's mind was working overtime. He thought to himself, fuck it! I'll ask him.

'Err, Pete you know that nickname you have of Package, I'm only guessing of course, but is it related to having a big cock?' Pete laughed at him, stood up and dropped his trousers to reveal all.

'Fucking hell, that is *not* fair!' Ched looked away holding his hand over his eyes, shaking his head.

Pete was still laughing while he zipped up, then he sat back down, with Ched quiet for the rest of the journey.

Ched was frustrated with his discovery and could not keep the display he had seen to himself, so after dinner that evening with Millie, after a few drinks and just for the lack of conversation, he mentioned what he had seen. Millie was relaxing with a pint of beer.

'You are surely joking?'

'No, honest, I couldn't believe my eyes, I had to look away I was so embarrassed.'

'Wow! Lucky Mi.'

'What do you mean?'

'Oh, sorry,' said Ched, 'Mi as in his wife's name.'

'Ched, you didn't think anything else did you.'

'No it's just the name Mi, it sounds the same as 'me' it's confusing.' They both laughed the situation off, Ched thinking no more other than envying Pete.

Ched was doing his best to make things *okay* between Millie and him, even more so now that for some strange reason Millie had accepted Marigold, almost feeling sorry for her. The more the two were together the more Ched was with them. Marigold would talk of her past and the relationships she had when living back in the West Yorkshire town of Todmorden. Her disclosures were not happy ones. Millie felt for her and they became very close with Marigold respecting someone who had been quite hard and intolerant towards her in the past. Ched saw this and more felt at ease, although not being where he would like to be: *inside Marigolds knickers,* but he was close.

Millie, now back to full health and approved by the resident doctor, returned to her duties in charge of the animals and crops having been absent for many weeks. She was not happy with the state of things down on the farm. She went around inspecting everything, criticising anything she could find that was not to her standard. She found the farm machinery not at its place of stay, bales of hay that had fallen over and not restacked, the pig pens had not been cleaned out and she was annoyed that some gates had been left open on her way down. Where's Antonio? She thought to herself, I'm going to give him a right rollicking. Not knowing that Pete had offered to help while she was extremely ill, she was shocked to see him in the cow shed tending to the animals and she mellowed instantly.

'Pete, what on earth are you doing here?'

'Sorry Millie, I hope I haven't startled you, it was weeks ago, I think! Time doesn't mean much here. It was when you were first ill I offered to help when needed. Antonio asked me, so here I am.'

'You surprise me. You are obviously a man of many talents. Shouldn't you be defending the ship or something?' Millie could not stop glancing at the bulge in his trousers. 'Pete, that's great! Err, I mean to see you helping out right here where it matters for our community.' She turned away to skedaddle, coolly but walked as swiftly as she could. She knew she had become excited at the thought of his obvious package. 'Bloody hell, Ched was right,' she said to herself. Then, after about one hundred metres she was going nowhere. Shit, you silly cow she thought. You've got that urge for it, just like when those young Welsh lads were planting the trees. Then there was Antonio's irresistible smooth lean commanding body and now Donkey Dick! I must control myself. I know, I'll have a word with Albert to let him know Pete isn't needed down here now I'm back at work. Shit! If I do that he won't come down here, he's a nice chap, hmm, but then I'll see how it goes. Millie's head went haywire with her wild thoughts. She soon put her mind back to her first love, the farm.

She wandered through the fields checking the condition of crops, the weeds, insects, anything new that she had not seen growing before. She saw a lot more activity everywhere, even butterflies and wondered how did they make it here? The wind, I suppose, when we are close enough to land. It's a good job rats can't fly. That's one creature I do not miss. Some field mice would not do much harm but then you need the rest of the food chain to check them. A barn owl or falcon, no! Too complicated, I like the way things are. I'm still concerned about shooting the rabbits. When it's time for a cull, I know, as another thought came to her stimulated mind, I'll say to Albert that I've changed my mind on shooting them with guns. They will have to use bow and arrow or a crossbow. That will be a challenge to them and it will save them ammunition for other more serious matters, hmm. She smiled to herself and felt quite perky, and thought, oh it's great to be away from that sodding rain and have some sun on my back. With the thought fresh in her mind, she went to Albert to ask him about the bow and arrow idea.

'Albert,'
'Yes Millie.' I don't like the sound of this he thought.
'You know I said that I would agree to you shooting the rabbits, well I've changed my mind about the type of weapon to be used. I would prefer bow and arrow or a crossbow. It would be quieter and save on high-powered ammunition.'

'That sounds like a challenge for Magnus, but an excellent idea. The crossbow would be the favourite it's a lot more accurate and powerful than the longbow. I'll have a word with him. We have plenty of time to make and practice using them. Thank you Millie, so be it.' She walked away thinking how easy that was. Albert pondered over Millie's request and came to the conclusion that it would definitely be a good idea to have the crossbow in their arsenal.

4. THIS LOT

The summer had begun and the two sparrows, Mr and Mrs Gus, had stayed on the Ark during its travels. Vicky would watch them while they were busy feeding their chicks with grubs and small worms. There were more than two rabbits as well, although very small ones. The cries of the unwanted seagulls were constant as they stood about on any perch they could fit, waiting for the slightest morsel of food to scavenge at. The battered ruined crops from the wet southern stay were ploughed into soil and fresh crops sown, rotating the type. All the fields, orchard and gardens were showing their worth with greens, pinks, red and white shades, a vibrant countryside floating on the sea. All they would see of the outside world was the regular once a week fly by from the coastguard in a twin engine plane. Albert named it a 'Fokker Friendship' others a 'noisy Fokker', scaring all as it flew so low across midships port to starboard and sometimes the other way. They probably had a different navigator when that happened. It was almost harassment. There was the odd cruise ship, local fishing boats and the inevitable life on the ocean waves "the weekend yacht's person." Some came close to have a look but no further and that is just how Albert wanted their life onboard to be, left alone to get on with the important things in life, living as a happy family.

As they all discussed at the meeting the decision was made to spend half the northern stay around the Azores and then go and anchor in the Med somewhere before exiting through the Suez Canal, into the Red Sea and out into the Indian Ocean to go south for the winter. It was now time to make the move, some were happy staying where they were because of no interruption and excellent weather conditions and some wanted to see the Mediterranean and have the sightseeing tour of going through the Suez. Albert, encouraged by Pete, also wanted the Suez option. It was no big deal for those that wanted to stay. They knew that the weather would be much the same as where they were at present. Options were mulled over during conversations at the evening meal. Ched was one of those who was quite happy staying around the Azores because the fishing was good in the Atlantic besides, he had never been keen on the Med, not even for a holiday. Millie wanted to see that part of the world, so he was won over.

'That's you happy then. What about you Marigold? Have you been to the Med before?' Ched asked.

'No, what chance would I have had to go holidaying there? I would be lucky to have a night out in Halifax. I still would have been stuck in Tomordon, back in Yorkshire if it hadn't been for Monty. On thinking about it, that's the only really good thing he did for me, which gave Lucy and me the chance to live a pleasant life here on the Ark. As long as the sun shines does it matter where we are? I could do with a man though.'

'I know what you mean,' replied Millie, and they both laughed.

'Alright Millie there's no need to be like that, embarrassing me in front of Marigold, just because we have a 'Supercock' onboard.' The two women started chuckling as Ched got up to leave.

'I'm having a beer, do you two want anything while I'm up?' They both looked at him and laughed again.

'Bloody hell, what are you two like?' and he laughed back. 'I meant what would you like a drink, *girls?*'

'Yes please Ched, same again, two red wines.'

Albert came into the canteen and was surprised to see Millie there. Normally she wouldn't have finished down on the farm until seven or eight, when everyone else was already having or had their food.

'It's good to see you here at dinner time Millie. Is everything ok?'

'Yes it is. I've realised that all work and no play makes Jack a dull boy, that's the old saying. What it should say now is that, all work with no rest and play makes you old, knackered and ill, so I've completely changed my attitude since my life-threatening illness, but I've been influenced by others.'

'Well that's good that you've come to that conclusion yourself. There is nothing worse than somebody else trying to advise you when you know it already but need time to process and put it into practice. You make sure you get some enjoyment in life. It's too short, make full use of it.'

'You are a very wise man Albert and I promise you I will,' she replied, as her thought of a certain male organ sprang to her mind.

'I had better get some food Millie. I'm late tonight. Baby is playing up, problem trying to feed her. I'll have to get back so that Amy can get her meal while I look after Esperanca.' Off he went quickly.

'Now there is a true man Marigold. He is totally devoted to his wife and child, yet spent many years on and off being on active service front line do or die situations, and now, here he is doing the same thing for us, protecting at all cost.'

'I know what you mean Millie, but I couldn't do with all that. I just want a simple, loving, uncomplicated man. Where will I find one of those?'

'You should have married Ched,' she replied as Ched arrived back with the drinks. Marigold immediately thought, I'll have him if you don't want him.

'Am I still the butt of the joke between you two? Do you want me to go and sit at another table so you can continue?'

'No, come and sit down,' they both replied together.

'You stay here with us,' Millie insisted. 'Don't be such a wuss.' The three of them sat happily together, lifted their glasses, chinked them and then said.

'Cheers.'

Preparations to move did not take long, two days and all was ready. They always left at first light when a move was properly planned. First light it was. A boost from the turbines to get some motion and then the sails were raised to catch any breeze that was about. It came nicely from the south-west, a regular pattern there that time of the year. From their position south of Vila do Porto on the island of Santa Maria they would head for the Straits of Gibraltar. Gunter set a course for the next 1100 nautical miles. This would take them to the mouth of the Mediterranean where they intended to change course to pass the most southern tip of Spain at Tarifa, then through the straits. It would be four to five days sailing by the time they entered the Mediterranean. They planned to head towards Sardinia and then south-east to the south of Sicily at the foot of Italy, coincidentally, not that far from Antonio's home town of Salerno, south-west Italy. But he had no thoughts of old home, only of his new life. It would only be a short distance then to where they could anchor somewhere north of Malta not far from the North African coast.

Three and a half days into the journey, about 150 nautical miles south of Cape Saint Vincent, Portugal and Europe's closest point to America, a boat was spotted drifting eastwards. Ched, who was on lookout, did not report the sighting until he had a clear view. It had no sails and was not under power. First he thought it was just an open fishing boat, but then realised it was too far from land. Focussing as they were getting closer he saw it was full of motionless people.

'Shit!' More bloody problems,' he mumbled under his breath. 'Albert, Gunter can you read me?' he called on the short wave.

'Yes Ched,' Gunter replied.

'Open boat spotted south-east with people onboard, not under power and a long way from home wherever that is.'

'I will call Albert and alert the others then I will be with you to take a bearing.' Gunter was already there when Albert arrived with Pete not far behind.

'What do you make of it, any sign of life there?'

'Yes,' Gunter said, 'there are some children moving about. I count seven adults and three children.'

'It's been quite common in these waters for the past twenty years or more for people from North Africa to try and get to mainland Europe and I don't know why they keep trying because they always send them back,' reported Pete.

'What do you think then, this being more in your recent field of work?' enquired Albert.

'They are almost certainly economic migrants and usually well organised, European dressed, designer jeans etc., with the inevitable mobile phones. They try to look as if they've been in the country for some time and get accepted, providing they can beach undetected. They will have contacts whom will shelter them and then find them black market work. It's a modern form of slavery and an impossible task to stop it. It's not much different now than it's been in the past. The thing is now you have a humanitarian problem on your hands Albert. I know what I would do and I can guess what you would like to do, but it would not go down well with the rest now would it?'

'If it means leaving them,' Ched spoke out, 'I've no qualms with that. They made their choice. There will be some other ship in the area soon. It's a very busy shipping lane and we've passed no end of container ships.'

'I would like to agree with you Ched, but as Pete said, it's the others you know the *females* 'or have you forgotten what they can be like?'

'Yes alright, I give in.'

They all grimaced at the situation, knowing the problems they would have in picking them up, feeding and housing them. Then what would they do with them? They had no intention to take them to a port if they could help it. Albert came up with an idea.

'Right listen.' The four faced each other to hear him.

'Gunter what is our distance from Gibraltar?'

'I think maybe two days maximum, without checking the charts.'

'Then we slow down to one or two knots, making it four, five or six days to get to Gib. In the meantime we pick them up and do the female/humanitarian bit; lift their craft onboard, get Magnus to fix it then drop them all off as close as we can get to Gib.'

'Yes that's alright,' Pete replied, 'as long as Magnus can fix the motor, if that's the problem. But what if it's just run out of diesel? We haven't got any diesel.'

'Good point Pete, because it's bound to be an old diesel engine, any other suggestions?'

'Yes I have.' Pete put his plan forward. 'How about picking them up, along with their boat, it's probably an old traditional African fishing boat and could come in handy when fishing off the coast of Africa.' All of a sudden Pete's thinking hit Albert.

'When we get near Gibraltar drop them and the black yacht with provisions to go the few miles to safety then they will not be our problem anymore. We don't have to slow down and just think of the brownie points you'll have with

61

our better halves.' They looked at one another and thirty seconds later Albert came up with a more detailed plan of action.

'Let's slow the Ark down to enable us to pick them up, we'll get the inflatable and fishing boat from the hold ready to lower over the side. I suggest Pete and Gunter take the inflatable and Ched and Antonio the fishing boat to take them in tow. Don't forget the arms.'

By the time they had slowed down, the drifting boat was well behind them. As soon as it was safe to do so the fishing boat and inflatable were lowered from the Ark, complete with occupants. Amy and Jane were watching what was going on from the bridge and could see the predicament the drifters were in. Amy called Albert on the short wave.

'Albert, why haven't you asked for emergency medical help from us?'

'From the look of things they were moving about ok. They don't seem to be in danger at present.'

'Oh, I'll get things ready anyway.'

'As you wish, my dear,' Amy sensed Albert's resentment in having to pick up these people.

The inflatable and the fishing boat powered their way to the stricken boat. All four had packed side arms from their new arsenal, feeling in a strong position if there was a problem. Approaching the boat with extreme caution, Pete circled it several times. He waited for some response from the adults. They were well aware of their presence, conferring with one another as though discussing what to do. There was no evidence of anyone suffering. Then a spokesman got up and shouted to them in very good English.

'Can you help us please? Our engine has broken and we need to get back to Algeciras our home.' Pete knew straight away the guy was lying. He radioed Ched.

'That's bullshit Ched. Did you hear it? Algeciras is in Spain I'll guarantee they've travelled from Morocco.'

'Yeah, they must have been on *some* day trip. I suppose we'd better go in and put them in tow. It would be best if I did that and you keep up close, then we'll get a better view of them on the way back to the Ark.'

'Good thinking Ched, we might make a military man of you yet.'

'Cut the crap Pete. I'm just doing what we have to do.'

'Sorry Chum. Let's do it then.' Ched moved his fishing boat just ahead of the potential migrants. Antonio displayed a hand on his firearm, while Ched did the seaman bit of throwing a line to tow them. Pete and Gunter moved in very close with the intention of looking menacing. Pete was used to this practice, Gunter was very apprehensive.

'Don't worry we are just showing them who's boss. You have to be very careful in these situations. They could be armed and waiting to catch you off guard.'

Two hours later, the trio of boats were by the side of the Ark waiting to board. Pete went onboard first to brief Albert on what had happened so far and what had been said.

'Pete let's put in standard interrogation tactics and don't start with anyone who speaks English. If they are from Morocco they will speak some French. So a combination of our knowledge and the first bit will be Passports please!' The group were taken onboard to the canteen. It consisted of three children, three females, thought to be their mothers and four adult males. The female adults were brought to the bridge one by one to be questioned. Amy and Jane wanted to be present. Mi wanted to check them over for any ailments that could affect the community. She was concerned that the more this community was isolated from the rest of the world, their resistance to outside viruses would change and they could be affected by the slightest bug. The adult males were closely guarded by armed Ched and Antonio. The children were fed and looked unaffected by the situation, as if it was just another day.

The three boats were lifted from the water by Magnus, Gunter and Zimbo as quickly as they could to enable the Ark to get underway again. Albert, Amy

63

and Jane were waiting on the bridge for the first female to be questioned, escorted by Pete.

'Can I see your passport please?' asked Albert. This young woman bowed her head took a cloth from around her neck and covered her head Muslim style.

'It gone,' she replied.

'There's no point wasting our time with the rest. It's obvious where they are from and we don't want the problem.'

'What do you mean Albert?' Amy was confused.

'They are economic migrants, Arab Muslim probably from Morocco who want to get to Spain or Portugal and then disappear into mainland Europe working on the labour black market. Just look at the way they are dressed. They are not fishermen! If you saw any of them walking in the streets of any European town or city they would not seem out of place in these times. They look respectable. But that's not the point. They are potential illegal immigrants and just having them here onboard is a big problem for us. If the authorities from Spain found out they'd probably confiscate our home.'

'Oh,' Amy feebly replied. It struck hard. She realised the real problem; the Ark's protection which was paramount.

'Let's go back to the canteen and sort this out,' Albert said. All the boat people and most of the community were there when Albert addressed their guests.

'Right Mr English speaking spokesman, stand up and listen.' The man obeyed immediately, 'you want to get to your *'home'* Algeciras in Spain? We know that is not your home but will help you providing we don't have any problems with you. You will stay here in the canteen under guard until we drop you off for the short trip to your destination. You will be fed and the toilets are there. Please use them. It will only be for two days at the most.'

'Thank you Sir. You are very kind. We will do as you say.' Albert went to see Patricia and Amy followed.

'Patricia, I'm sorry about this but it's not as easy as you might think, so don't go and feed them piles of food. What have you got the most of in meat?'

'Pork, bacon, ham and fish,' Albert shook his head.

'Patricia my dear, pork, bacon and ham are from the same animal.'

'Yes but each is so different.'

'I don't want to go through all the connotations of the pork ingredient, please do not offer pork or serve it to these people, it would be an insult to them, give them mainly cod and potatoes.'

Albert then went to see Pete.

'I'm a little reluctant to let the black yacht go. You never know when it might come in handy as it has proven to be in the past. I know that, that style of fishing boat would not look out of place meandering off the coast of Somalia. Do you know anyone at the naval base in Gibraltar?'

'I used to do, but we don't need to know anyone. What if we slow down the Ark a few miles before, drop me and one other off in the inflatable, go to the coastguard say we've picked some people in an open boat drifting and get them to collect them. Just be straight with it. They can repatriate the people. Why should we have the problem? It would also give us a chance to get a few medical items that Mi wants. Some diesel would be handy for that old fishing boat too if Magnus can fix it.'

'Yes you're right Pete. That's what we'll do. I'll let the others know but we won't mention to the drifters where they'll be going. It may cause unrest.'

Magnus came to the bridge to see Albert and Pete who were still there.

'The fishing boat is in a bit of a state. Are you going to put them back into it? Because, if you are, it will take me four or five days to fix it, we haven't any diesel but I could get it to run on our own grown cooking oil. There's something else, we've found about twenty kilo of hashish in the bow of the boat. What shall we do with it Albert?' asked Magnus.

'Dope smugglers as well! The best thing to do with that is to weight it down heavily and put it over the side. We don't want it found onboard and I think it will be best if we transport these people to meet the coastguard on the water rather than them coming onboard. It's too risky. They might want to look around. So don't bother fixing the boat for the moment Magnus, just get rid of the dope.'

'So do I go to the coastguard or do we radio them to rendezvous?' asked Pete.

'We'll put them in one of the lifeboats because they won't all fit in the fishing boat and escort it with Gunter and you Pete in the inflatable. There would be a security problem in guarding them anyway. Ched and Antonio, as armed guard, can go with the migrants. We'll radio the coastguard to meet you then you can transfer them to the coastguard vessel with Ched and Antonio bringing back the lifeboat. That way, we don't have too much risk with them on the lifeboat.'

'When will this be likely to happen?' asked Magnus.

'The day after tomorrow, when we are very close to Gibraltar. Why, have you any problems Magnus?'

'No, the lifeboats are always ready.'

'Pete, you mentioned about some medical things that Mi needs. Let's get rid of this lot first then a couple of you could go into Gibraltar for a list of items. I trust you'll be able to use your plastic to pay?'

'Yes, that's not a problem.'

It was very uncomfortable for the community at mealtimes because of all 'this lot' as Albert named them. They were confined to the canteen and guarded twenty four hours a day. They had to be segregated to one area where they ate and slept on mattresses from the stores laid on the floor. Anyone that questioned Albert on the strictness of security would be answered with, 'you cannot trust anybody that peddles dope.'

Drop off day came and there was an intense relief to the Ark. The inflatable was lowered first and then the lifeboat complete with Ched and Antonio brandishing his firearm complete with the migrants inside. Pete and Gunter escorted the boat to the coastguard who Albert had radioed earlier as planned. They were only three miles from the harbour at Gibraltar and it did not take long to meet up and transfer them over. Pete described where they were picked up and explained what had happened. Ched with Antonio then took the lifeboat back to the Ark followed by Pete and Gunter. After lifting the boats back onboard there was a gathering in the canteen, mostly to help clear up the mess created by the unwanted guests. There were questions asked why this

66

sort of thing was still happening in this so called modern world. Albert had asked if there was anything anybody wanted from the mainland shops. The biggest surprise was that no one could think of anything they were short of. 'A descent barrel of beer,' Ched jokingly shouted out, which raised a few laughs. Happily they were back on their own and keen to get moving again. Albert told Pete not to buy any diesel because Magnus had a large volume of spent vegetable oil, collected over the years that could be filtered and used. Pete and Ched made the trip to get the supplies mainly for Mi's new doctor's surgery and pharmacy. By the end of the day the Ark was on its way towards Malta where they planned to anchor for the rest of that season. The place they had chosen to anchor was ten miles north of Gozo, the island just north of Malta. It would take them another four to five days sailing. There was a slight air of excitement throughout. A new place to go and even though they would still be at sea, to them it was different. The atmosphere, the smell in the breeze, the type of fish, the sun and light, they could sense the changes. On their way they would pass the North African coastal towns and their countries of Tangier in Morocco, Algiers in Algeria, Tunis Tunisia and to where Malta is situated north of Tripoli in Libya.

ALBERT'S LOG - July 2019

What a strange few weeks it has been. The time that we are most likely to bump into a problem is when we are on the move. It might have been better to stay off Vila Do Porto. You just don't know what's best. It looks good here. The sea is still like a millpond, and clear. Our fishing boat that Ched uses is tied up to a buoy that was laid down just metres from the Ark and a few of the younger adults use it to dive and swim from. Pete has started snorkelling and scuba diving lessons. Even Millie has taken to scuba diving. It's an ideal place to check the bottom of the ship. I will definitely start scuba diving myself while we are here and now Amy and Esperanca are at a thriving normality, I'll have the chance.

The Ched and Marigold affair seems to be settled at the moment and oddly, she is very friendly with Millie. They enjoy a bottle of wine and chat together, always making fun at Ched's expense. He just shrugs it off and seems to be glad they are happy.

Mi has set up a proper clinic with assistance, when required, from Jane and Amy. Amy's knowledge of herbs, which she extracted from Monty during the short time he was about, has not been rejected by Mi. She believes, as I do, that there is a formula to cure sickness in nature. Finding it is the problem. But unless you try from known remedies it is difficult to expand the data you have collected.

Ched goes fishing on a regular every other day basis, and comes back with mainly crab and lobster. As he predicted, the fish is better in the Atlantic, so we're not short of any type of food. This is as good as paradise even though I haven't been there yet.

5. MEDITERRANEAN STYLE

Albert got his wish to scuba dive with a crash course of training from Pete. As soon as Millie heard about scuba diving she wanted the opportunity to be involved. It became a regular daily exercise for the three of them and the novices' confidence grew. Albert wanted to put into practice a full survey of the Ark's hull, the ships bottom that is the part always below the water line. The hull was mapped on a chart so that each day a team of divers that consisted of Pete, Albert and Millie, who had temporarily signed over the running of the farm to Antonio. Starting at the stern of the ship they dived each day covering the huge hull of the Ark, marking the areas they had completed. While the weather was good to them, which was most of the time, this would happen day in and day out. The survey was almost complete and with very little problem to report so far, meaning the hull would not need attention for many years to come. The last section to check was the bow, the front of the ship and its massive bulbous nose which breaks the waves, parting them aside for the ship to float smoothly on its way. The routine for the final inspection went ahead. The three checked their equipment. All was ok until Albert was concerned about the air pressure in his tanks. It was down and not enough to do the diving safely.

'My tanks have lost pressure. Can you finish without me?' Pete looked at Millie they both looked back at Albert. 'Not a problem,' they agreed, 'there's not much left to do, is there Pete?'

They both got down into the inflatable and powered to the Ark's bow, tying up the craft to the bow anchor chain. Pete knew he would have to mount the nose of the ship to check the top side of the nose which takes normally a heavy pounding from breaking into the waves; he came prepared with rope and a soft tip grappling hook. He explained to Millie that it would be best if they tackle climbing that first, leaving the gear in the boat and then go back to do the underneath.

'That's fine by me. I'm not much of a mountain climber, but I'll give it a go.' Pete finally got a grip with the hook and quickly pulled himself to the top making sure the rope was well fast. He shouted to Millie to climb. She made it without difficulty because of the slope being gradual. She sat down to take breath and Pete joined her on this totally isolated spot where they were unable to be seen by anyone on the Ark. She rested her arms on her knees and her head on them then looked out at the sea and sighed.

'I hope that's a happy sigh?' said Pete.

'Yes, it most certainly is, it's just wonderful here. How on earth could farming have led me here to be doing this? Just look at it it's beautiful.' The morning sun was heating the air nicely and making the sea glitter in its brightness. She lay back to soak up the sun and was quiet for a few minutes with her eyes closed.

'Pete I want to see your dick, I'm told it's some size. Is it true?' Pete laughed. 'No, Mi tells me it's small,' Millie pulled herself up.

'Well let's have a look then.'

'He stood up to drop his trunks revealing all. Her eyes lit up with delight. It was just as Ched described it. Millie could not resist holding it in her hand. She looked up at him with a smile. It began to swell. Holding it and then with her automatic movement back and forth she made it bigger. She let it go, stood up and removed her bikini top and bottom. Pete removed his trunks completely and they pulled each other together kissing passionately as the bond of their naked bodies excited them. Bending her backward, he laid her gently on the warming steel. She opened her legs to let him enter her already willing and eager. Slowly, inch by inch, she accepted the thing that she had fantasised about for the past few months just wondering what it would be like. He moved in and out more controlled than he did with Mi. Strangely he wanted this to last and neither of them expected it, Millie came to a climax of such strength which Ched had never brought her to.

'Oh Pete, Pete, Pete, oh please don't stop, finish yourself inside me as fast as you like.'

Pete moved in and out as she commanded, just several more movements and he ejaculated and collapsed on top of her to continue passionately entwining each other's tongues. She rolled him over to be on top of with him still inside

70

her. She held it tight, controlling her muscles to make him stiff again. She fondled her own breasts, moving erotically, then lowered one hand to hold the base of his cock to keep it prisoner inside her. Gradually it gained its strength and she could feel the volume of it expanding, she climaxed again, moaning with pleasure collapsing on him. Both of them were drained and they lay in silence for a few minutes. Then Millie rolled off him and put her swimwear back on as Pete slipped on his trunks.

'Well Pete, I don't know about you but I would like some of that on a regular basis. What do you think?'

'I would too. But how will we do it without the others finding out? We can't go scuba diving to inspect the ship's bottom every time we want each other.'

'I don't know yet but there will be a way. I only want to know if you want me enough to take the risk. I'll sort Ched out. Can you sort Mi out?'

'Between the pair of you, you will have me knackered!'

'Now there's a thought I've never tried that, a threesome. Have you?'

'What, you mean you, Mi and me?'

'Don't get me wrong I have no lesbian tendencies, but I would do it for you. She's very pretty and I like her complexion. What's she like with you in bed?'

'She is the opposite of you. I can never make her climax and I'm finished far too quickly for her. She has a good appetite for sex and I'm worried she'll find it elsewhere.'

'Well there is little choice for her here, so perhaps we can work on it then it won't matter her finding out. I'll give it a go just to have that lovely beast inside me regularly.'

'I must admit it was wonderful and I'll have a job to resist you.' They resumed their work and Millie felt on top of the world, full of excitement about herself, not a care in the world, thinking how she didn't feel like this before her illness, and determined she was not going to miss out on enjoying life to the full anymore.

They completed mapping out the bulbous nose and prepared to climb back down to the inflatable to complete the final section of the hull's inspection. Looking around to see if there were any local boats close by that may have been in sight of their performance, to their amazement, their eyes were fixed on a huge five masted fully rigged tall ship heading towards them and getting close. Pete was worried about the wake it would leave behind. Being in a small inflatable it could throw them all over the place.

'Quick Millie, get down to the inflatable, we must move to the other side of the Ark.' She obeyed and Pete quickly followed. He started the outboard and manoeuvred to the other side of the ship. They waited until the ship passed and felt a few minor ripples but nothing like the trail of the wake pounding the starboard side of the Ark where they had previously been shortly before.

'That was close. It would have thrown us and the equipment into the water.'

'Did you see all those people taking photos of us and the ship? It's a good job it wasn't twenty minutes earlier Pete.'

'Yes that would have been something for their family holiday photo albums!'

Both were excited about their little escapade, daredevils, a surge of adrenalin energised them. When the sea returned to its millpond state, they finished the final inspection.

It became a regular pattern when evening fell, instead of dining in the canteen they would gather around the swimming pool. Ched had fabricated a Bar-b-que. The menu was nearly always lobster, prawns, fish and various kebabs, along with boiled new potatoes and fresh salads drenched in olive oil with white or red wine vinegar. Albert provided this by some of the less successful wine making. Everyone enjoyed the facility to the full in Mediterranean style. Stella and Vicky, the two older girls, were becoming excellent swimmers, constantly chasing each other in and out of the pool, having races across it. Lucy at only three and a half years old, making her first strokes without aid. It just seemed natural to her, as it was with Stella and Vicky. During the days each adult did their various tasks without hesitation and were pleased to be up early and out in the sun as soon as they could. Even Patricia liked to sit out for short stints of sunbathing. Albert, and occasionally Jane, would leave the brewing to make use of the swimming pool etc., until it was too hot to be out and better off in the comparative coolness of the brewery cum distillery. Amy would go for a regular daily swim, doing thirty lengths of the pool along with other exercises, bringing her self back in trim and fit after the traumatic birth, while Albert looked after Esperanca. Melanie was conscious of being overweight but excused herself by saying it was because of giving birth to Chuva, thinking she would lose it soon. Gunter and Greta were still very content in their life with then daughters Stella now aged seven and Venus nearly three years old, both so much like her father.

Ched and Millie were still on very good terms, having *almost* a normal married life when together, but they both yearned for their other desires. Ched took more of a roll in parenting Vicky and Rose. Millie resumed work on the farm hoping there would be an opportunity to have Pete when he came to help but Antonio or Zimbo would always be about, so her passion eluded her. Marigold still wanted Ched and vice versa, both were behaving themselves. Pete and Mi got on with their jobs and fitted in well to the community. Millie made a point of befriending Mi, concentrating on her plan to achieve her goal of sex with Pete whatever the situation she might fall into. This would leave Ched and Marigold in each others company quite often and became very much the norm with their children close by. Being patient, the pair of them talked and enjoyed moments together, said goodnight in a formal way took the children and retired to their respective quarters. Marigold would take Lucy and Ched would take Vicky and Rose, Ched would wait for Millie who normally came later after having some drinks in the bar, mainly with Mi and Pete, but sometimes with Albert as well. When he could make it now that he had parental duties, he would look forward to a pint with other company. One night Millie came in and Ched was waiting as usual. He asked her if she would mind if he went out for a late evening stroll, as he felt restless and would find it hard to sleep. Millie was quite happy to go to bed having had a full working day.

'Yes, go on but please don't wake us all up when you come back in.'
'No I won't, I promise.'

He went up to the pool area and sat down looking at the glittering night sky and tried to pick out stars and constellations in between the wispy clouds. He looked to the north and an electric storm was beginning to show its incredible theatrical performance. He was amazed and wondered how that could possibly happen without any interruption to the weather nearby. He heard footsteps and turned his head reluctantly, not wanting to miss the spectacle. Then in his eyes stood in front of him, was more amazement, Marigold.

'Hi, I didn't know you'd be here,' she said as she sat beside him.

'Just look at that up there, it's fantastic,'

'Not as fantastic as you Ched,' she murmured looking each other in the eye. He put an arm around her and said the ultimate words.

'Marigold, I love you,'

'I love you too, Ched.' They kissed each other tenderly, but soon stopped knowing it would probably end up with an interruption and more problems. They behaved themselves and continued looking at the night sky until the electric storm faded away.

'What can we do Ched? I can't carry on like this. I want to be with you.'

'Things between Millie and me haven't been the same since Rose was born. I haven't said this to anyone or even accused Millie, so please keep it a secret, but I have a gut feeling that I'm not Rose's father.'

'But then who?'

'Antonio,'

'Of course,'

'I like the life here on the Ark. We've had some risky times with attacks and all that, but Albert has seen us through. I would find it very difficult to live back on the mainland and I don't want to even try it. It wouldn't be fair to the children. They love being on the Ark. Since we were caught '*at it*' I've realised how much I miss you and not just the sex thing but the friendship, you know? The looking out for each other and the silly banter, so my dear Marigold, we have got to find a way to make it work that's acceptable to all the community, including Millie. I'm sure there'll be a way.'

'Ched, I really understand you and since our forced separation you've become more sensitive. I don't know if I've picked the right word. Hmm, how can I say this? You have definitely changed. You're not as happy-go-lucky as you were and it makes me feel more for you, I don't want you to be sad. There's something I want you to know that I'm not taking any more precautions when

74

we get together. I want your child.' Ched looked about to see if anyone else was interested in the night sky and then kissed her with the passion of true love.

'Good night Ched.'

'Good night Marigold.' He stayed there thinking things over, trying to see a way to be with her.

The beginning of September was with them it would only be a few weeks before they would lift anchor and head for their next destination. Albert and Pete got their thoughts together, going through firstly, should they forget the Mafia and give them a wide berth and secondly, if they did anything what would be the risk and the gain? Albert was thinking things out in his own mind.

'What was the name of that chap who died that you suspect is the cause of this problem, Russian background or something?' Pete asked him.

'Yes, Miles Overstrand or his former Russian name of Elo Mikovich.'

'That's interesting, because there's a list of people in the structure of their organisation and I'm positive he is, or was, chief accountant. Let's go and check that now, it may make a big difference.'

The pair went to the communications room and Pete did his search, this time by putting in the name of Elo Mikovich and, bingo, his details came up.

'Well well, the plot has just thickened. It's more than Mile's they wanted they wanted the Ark all along.'

'That seems to be the case Albert. Oh and by the way, this database is worth a fortune.'

'Yes I can imagine.'

They studied the information. The place that always came up on the database on the computers that were taken from the destroyed yacht Revelation II, was in Somalia, just off the coast, a small town on the peninsula of the Xaafuun Cape. The peninsula is about fifty kilometres across. There is a small town named Caluula on the Gulf of Aden side just before the point of Gees Gwardafuy. Albert and Pete discussed an outline plan, it was to lower the refurbished Moroccan fishing boat with their equipment when they were west of Caluula, drift close into the shore as safely as they could to the town, beach the boat and steal a vehicle of some description. Then head for the target, destroy it and drive to the other side of the peninsula to be picked up by the inflatable piloted by someone from the Ark which should be just off the coast as it entered the Arabian Sea. The fault in the plan lay there. Who would be capable and willing to do that task? Their joint initial idea was to keep it to themselves, a major task just for two of them, but they knew that a speedy well-armed couple of well-trained veterans could do a lot of damage. They chewed it over and over and kept coming up with the same answer: Antonio, because Gunter and Ched would be the only ones who could sail the Ark pointing it where it would need to go. There was always a question over Zimbo. Given the chance he might do a runner so they carefully worked on Antonio. Albert trusted him and after being out on the last night op he knew he had the nerve. But it wasn't as easy as that. It was how should they tackle telling the females? And should they bother? They came to the conclusion that they could prepare and be over the side without the ladies knowing, then Antonio would not be pressurised in any way not to join in because the women would want him to pick them up. So that was decided as the plan of action and they would give it a go. Antonio was pulled aside and sworn to secrecy. They taught him how to use a compass and chart and went over and over the plan. Pete took Antonio out in the inflatable for instruction under the pretence he wanted to do some scuba diving on the reefs.

Pete and Mi were sitting by the pool one evening, Millie left Ched and Marigold to join them in a drink, as had become the norm.
'Mind if I join you both?'
'No not at all, please do.'
'Mi, I've been meaning to ask you for some time now, how do you keep your hair so shiny and vibrant? It's beautiful and your skin, just look at mine. I need your help with it.'
'It's just using natural oils from the olive and lavender. I know I have an idea which could help all, even the men if they wished. Why not set up a health

and beauty salon for one day a week, in the clinic, to pamper each other with massages using the natural ingredients we have here on the Ark?'
'What a fantastic idea. I'll put my name down for that Mi. When can we start?'
'Well I need to do some preparations and collect herbs and make some compounds etc. I will make some josh sticks to burn, they help you relax. There's a lot to do so it may take a week.' Millie was so excited.
'Oh Mi, that's fantastic I can't wait.'

The next couple of weeks took Pete, Antonio and Albert away from the normal routine, which meant Millie was busy on the farm with just Zimbo, and occasionally Ched, when available, to help. A little exhausted and feeling low, she told Zimbo to finish up for her as she was going to have an early bath.
She called in to see Mi.
'How's the health and beauty club doing? I could really do with some pampering tonight.'
'It's ready. Why not call round at about five o'clock. I could spend an hour on you before dinner. Is that alright?'
'That will be brilliant Mi. I've just time for a shower.' She could not be more pleased. Oh an hour of being pampered, she thought to herself, I must control myself and just see what happens. Five came and Millie was on her way to the new beauty clinic very excited but also wondering what to expect. She arrived and knocked. Mi opened the door.
'Please come in, I will lock the door Millie because you will need to take some clothes off for the massage.'
'Yes of course.' Millie was slightly nervous but the intake of the herbal aroma of burning josh sticks soon made her relax.
'Please get undressed and lay on the couch. You can leave your pants on if you wish. It does not make any difference.' She decided to leave them on.
'If you lay face down first I will massage the back of your body.'

She poured an olive oil mixture onto her hands and then applied it to Millie's back and rubbed it gently into her skin and found the knotted joints in her spine. Gradually working down her back, then lower to her buttocks, she rubbed underneath her pants and then down the back of her legs, Millie was in a state of delight at the sheer pleasure of it.

'You can turn over now Millie and I will do your front.' Over she turned and adjusted herself to be comfortable and a repeat performance began. Without hesitation Mi massaged her breasts, and Millie's nipples became erect.

'Is that good?'

'Yes, wonderful!' Gradually she moved down over her stomach and pulled her pants down as far as her pubic hair. She worked on her abdomen just slightly into the triangle.

'Oh sorry, I slipped.'

'No that's alright, it's wonderful Mi. Just carry on.' Mi put more oil on her hands, rubbed it into the hair, gently working the oil in. She pulled the pants further down for better access.

'Take them off Mi, please.'

'Yes it would be easier.' Mi removed them completely for her and Millie relaxed even more and slightly spread her legs. Mi resumed with her fingers in and around her inner thighs and up to the apex, Millie felt unselfconscious with a small gyration of her hips. Mi could see the expanded and moistened lips.

'You are feeling good.' Mi said. 'Do you want to climax?' Millie was panting and could hardly speak. 'Yes,' she moaned. Mi touched her and rubbed her and sent her to orgasm.

'Oh, Oh, Oh, Ah, Ah, Hmm,' A silence followed for a few seconds.

'Oh I'm sorry Mi. You must be embarrassed. I am so embarrassed, I was so tensed up I just couldn't help it.'

'Don't worry about it it's natural and I'm not embarrassed. I wish I could do it as quickly as you. Come on there's not much time left before dinner for you to massage me.' Millie slipped her pants back up and they changed places with Mi stripped completely and laid face down on the couch.

'I've not done this before Mi. Shall I just try and repeat what you did to me?'

'Oh yes *please,*'

Millie wondered if that meant what she thought it did. She rubbed her gently all over her back and down her legs. She looked and admired the beauty of her shape and softness of her skin, her small perfectly formed buttocks which she gave plenty of attention. She couldn't believe how much she enjoyed giving her friend pleasure. Mi began responding with sighs and groans of obvious gratification then it was time to turn over. Millie did as she requested by starting the massage on her breasts, rubbing them gently and thought I'll pay a little attention to her nipples and see what response there is. She gently caressed them and they increased in size. Mi liked it.

'Hmm, that's nice don't stop yet,' she commanded. Moving from her very small tits now with hard firm nipples, Mi replaced Millie's hands with her own tweaking and pulling herself vigorously. This made Millie stir inside as she continued down Mi's perfect tight, narrow stomach massaging all the way to her hips caressing her inner thighs and back up to the base of her opening. Mi slowly spread her legs to show Millie access to her moistened pussy. Millie put her thumbs to the top of it touching gently, giving Mi more pleasure.

'Millie a little harder at the top, the hard bit, oh that's it, just there, oh that's so nice.' Mi increased the intensity of the sighs and groans to panting, but it seemed like ages to Millie and she remembered what Pete had said. She wondered what she could do to speed things up and her answer was, if done properly, what most women like done by a man. She crouched over her and put her tongue on the right place, pushed at it moving over the hard point. Mi went wild holding Millie's head into her and opened her legs wider thrusting her buttocks up and down. In seconds her climax was there and then settled down. Letting go of Millie's head, Mi slid off the couch, put her arms around Millie and kissed her passionately, Millie was in shock. She hadn't expected such a response.

'Oh Millie thank you, that was wonderful. Let's get showered together and go and have dinner with Pete.'

They showered, washing each other. Mi was tiny compared with Millie. They fooled around in the water with Mi holding and biting at Millie's nipples. Millie held her to one to suck, which she did with delight. Millie pulled her away and held her at arm's length.

'Please don't tell anyone about us Mi, I like this. I would never consider myself gay or lesbian. I still want a man inside me as much as I can. Do you understand me Mi?'

'Yes, I do. I am the same. But what about Ched, he makes love to you doesn't he?'

'No, I can't remember the last time, it must be ages ago, but when he did, he always finished before me. It's so frustrating.'

'I like Pete inside me but he must be the same as Ched and finishes too quickly. We could help one another. This doesn't have to be a one off. I will do this for you when you feel you need me. Will you do that again for me? You are far better than Pete at that.'

'Yes I will, but what if Pete finds out about us?' She looked at Millie and shrugged her shoulders.

'That's his problem. He will have to work around it.' They both resumed washing each other and laughed.

'You two look happy. What have you been up to?' asked Pete.

'We have just had a massage each. It was very good, wasn't it Millie?'

'Very good, so relaxing and soothing, I'd recommended it. Mi certainly knows how to massage,'

They both giggled and sat down to dinner.

Albert and Pete were now committed to carry out the action they'd planned. Magnus just thought that the fishing boat he had restored was for Ched to do some fishing off the coast of Africa to blend in with other local boats. At this stage only Antonio knew. Albert did wonder to himself about the risk and the outcome. His big question was would it make any difference? He was spurred on by the thought that it would delay any further action against the Ark for a while, as it has done for the past ten months making the Mafia think twice about attacking them. As far as Gunter and Ched were concerned, they did not need to know a thing until it was time to lower the boat and Albert would work the shifts on the bridge to coincide with the timing. Having been able to use mostly sail power from the Azores to Malta, gave the adequate savings on methane gas for the Ark to power its turbines and be able to negotiate the Suez and for changing courses when going around the peninsular and into the Arabian Sea. With only a matter of weeks left the pair needed to start on their fitness regime alongside weapon choice and practice. They knew it would be a problem, if they suddenly started to use rounds of ammunition onboard, so they picked hand held automatics that they were very familiar with, and then they would practice with the crossbows that Magnus was to make. It was then up early in the mornings running around the ship with backpacks on amongst other exercises. This did raise questions from the others but they both fobbed the questions off, saying they were putting on too much weight with all this Mediterranean style living!

6. MAGNUS' CHALLENGES

Magnus was a very busy man. He had completed the final part of setting up the communications room with the help of others, and it was fully ready for use. Albert and Pete agreed that it was not a good idea to switch on to satellite yet until they were near the danger zone. Magnus had almost finished work on the fishing boat they had retrieved. Ched's input with this project was invaluable. They re-corked some of the timbers, painted it in traditional colours and rebuilt the engine so it ran quietly and with very little smoke. When it did run, it smelt like a fish and chip shop because of the processed cooking oil that fuelled it. Now Albert wanted Magnus to make two powerful and accurate crossbows and a large quantity of bolts (arrows).
'Of course they will be top notch Albert. I've got all the materials and the machinery to finish them. I bet I can make it reach three hundred metres.'
'In that case can you fit them with telescopic sights on and night vision?'
'I thought they were for the rabbits or did you want to shoot at them from the bridge window?'
'I like your sense of humour Magnus. Let's leave it at that thank you.' Albert left quickly to prevent conversation getting any deeper.

Magnus got to work on his next piece of engineering. First he did some research by visiting their library and found information on its history. He discovered that the crossbow was also known as an arbalest, used as a weapon for war and sport in the middle ages throughout Europe, with common use in England in the thirteenth century. He could not find construction details of the modern crossbow, but found enough to make a version of his own. The stock was fabricated from a combination of hard wood and steel and the bow from tempered strip steel. Ched helped with the tempering, using skills from his metal fabrication days.
'Whatever will the old man think of next Magnus?'
'It wasn't Albert, it was Millie's idea.'
'Millie? Well I'm not surprised, she doesn't like guns.' They used high tensile piano type wire for the bowstring, which wound back on a ratchet wheel

mechanism to a spring loaded trigger. This would gain maximum tension when the trigger was released propelling the bolt or quarrel. He made the two bows together making them identical. The bolts originated from short straight lengths of cane that Millie had grown a plentiful supply in her garden for climbing beans. They were tipped with steel bullet shaped points and had feathers from the seagulls as flights, and looked very professional.

Ched was with Magnus for the first trial in the workshop. The geared ratchet was wound back pulling the bowstring along the stock to the catch on the trigger in the centre of the handle. A bolt was placed on a guide fixed to the stock. Ched aimed it at the far end of the room about forty feet away. He pulled the trigger. The bolt hit the side of an upright steel strut, ricocheted of it, hit the steel wall at an angle, hit the steel wall to the side of them again at an angle, then headed back to them passing within feet behind were they were stood.
'Shit!' Ched said, 'that was close.' Magnus was speechless and sat down shaking.
'Err I think we best try it outside next time Magnus, don't you?' He replied by just nodding his head.
'It certainly is very powerful. I bet it would go through you and out the other side.' The comment did not help Magnus one little bit. He just looked up at Ched still in shock. Ched thought it best to leave.
'I'll see you later Magnus.' Magnus nodded his head again. Finally he pulled himself together and thought about the telescopic sights that Albert had asked for. He converted a pair of binoculars, separating the sights and mounting one on each bow parallel to the bolt chamber.

Later he asked Albert to test the bows out when he was satisfied with the set up. They put a sheet of nineteen millimetres thick board on the port side of the ship, with circles on it. Pete was interested and joined them. Aiming and firing from the starboard side some hundred metres away Albert hit the target with his first shot.

'That's not bad Magnus let's go and see the damage.' To their amazement, although not a bull's eye the bolt had penetrated clean through the plywood. 'How's that then?'

'It's excellent Magnus. Well done, we just need to practice. If we use straw bales instead of the plywood I think we would be able to salvage the bolts. We could try at different distances. What do you reckon Pete?'

'I'm very impressed Magnus and you have made two so both Albert and I can go rabbit hunting together. That will be exciting.' He looked at Albert and winked.

'Well don't kill all the rabbits. Leave at least one buck and a couple of doe to keep him happy,' said Magnus.

'Yes rabbits have all the fun like that. It's a pity humans aren't the same. But then governments might introduce a type of myxomatosis to control the numbers.'

'You mean like VD or HIV aids?' Albert quickly added and continued. 'The humans have already done that to themselves don't you think? Perhaps we should check all that come onboard for Aids. Have you had a check, being facetious?'

'You cheeky sod, do I look as though I have it,' Pete bit. Albert just laughed at him. Millie arrived on the scene and was inquisitive having heard the last part of the conversation.

'Who's a cheeky sod?'

'Hi Millie,' said Magnus. 'They are like two schoolboys with their new toys and banter.'

'Millie we were just testing out your idea of using crossbows to cull the rabbits,' Albert explained.

'You're a bit premature. It will be ages before they become a problem. Pete only brought two. They will have four to eight litters a year. A litter will consist of between three to eight young, and they won't become sexually mature until six months. Apart from that we could keep a reasonable amount of rabbits grazing and they would manure the land. It can help maintain the ecosystem that we depend on.' The three men just stood there dumfounded by her *sermon,* trying to work out the mathematics and give an answer.

'Thank you for that information.' Albert replied. 'Now there's no need for us to panic about an invasion of rabbits. So we will put the bows away and practice when we need to cull and I'm sure Millie will advise us when that will be.'

'I know you Albert, you and action man here are up to something.'

'I don't know what you mean Millie. We are just keeping ourselves occupied and being prepared, aren't we Pete?'

'Yes Albert, definitely, just a little enthusiastic you might say.'

'You were right Magnus, just like two schoolboys.' She turned and walked away. Albert and Pete looked at each other not saying a word.

The next day Albert made another visit to the workshop as Magnus was checking over the cross bows before moth balling them.

'Good morning action man or is that the other one?'

'You've been listening to Ched too long. That's the sort of shit he puts out and not like you,'

'Sorry, I thought Millie was very good in her 'putting you two right' don't you?'

'Well if that's what you think, yes. But I've come here to test your knowledge and ability,' Albert teasingly commented, knowing that Magnus would not turn down any mechanical challenge.

'Fire away. What is it?'

'I want to put up a high voltage electric, but low in amperes fence on the sides of the ship, as you would do in a field to keep animals in, but in our case, it's to keep certain *animals* out.'

'What do you mean animals out?' Two seconds later, 'Oh you mean from attack?'

'Yes, a little defence from unwanted visitors because we will be passing a region off the coast of Somalia that has been, and still is, notorious for pirates and, as always, protection of the Ark is paramount.'

'Of course, now let me see. Probably a couple of kilometres of thin trip wire, plastic tube to insulate at fixing points, and a number of DC batteries or transformers, some coils. Yes I can do it but not on my own, I'll need a lot of help to do it properly and in the time. It's only a couple of weeks until we move to that area.'

'That's not a problem. I'll explain why we are doing this and you will have all the help you want. Oh and there is one other thing for you to put in place, I'm sure we have plenty of light bulbs.'

'We stored enough to last us for decades.'

'I want to cover the inside landscape, the inner walls of the ship, with lighting that will come on and point to the sides to dazzle anyone who manages to get over the electric fence, using the same method to activate as the security beams.'

'That's easy. I'll map it all out today.'

'Brilliant Magnus, just ask for any help you need. I'll get Ched to come down for a start.'

Albert went to the bridge to talk to Ched and Gunter to explain his plans for defending the Ark from intruders while on passage into the Indian Ocean. They were well aware of the problems shipping had for years in that area, but he did not disclose the other plans he and Pete had for "Operation Shock waves." That would be left until the last minute. After that he went to find Pete and called into the communications room as first guess. Pete was there alone going through, sifting all that he could find on the databases.

'I've set the ring fence and lights installation in motion, but we will have to give Magnus our full support to achieve the task. He has been fantastic and never ceases to amaze me. Now we need to work out our window of opportunity to make sure that when we leave the ship, it will arrive around the other side of the peninsula at the lower part of the Arabian Sea to meet us when we have finished. So Gunter and Ched have to calculate the exact speed and course to take so we will not be waiting about and neither will they, I plan on leaving here in two weeks. That brings us to the last week of September.

86

We should be south of Madagascar by mid October for the winter. Are you ok with that?'

'Yes,' acknowledged Pete. 'It sound's alright and putting an electric fence around is a good way to protect the ship while we are away, which should only be about five to six hours max. I don't understand why the practice has not been put in place on ships before, perhaps there are some health and safety regulations, like they have to put up warning signs and floodlight areas showing intruders the way across safely.'

'Yes, you are probably right,' Albert laughed then continued with his plan. 'The thing we'll do nearer the time is to get an aerial view printed off so we can identify the buildings when we approach it. There will be a generator of some size to destroy plus communication dishes and a mast. It's unlikely to be very well fortified and not have many armed guards. They will probably feel comfortable in an outlaw place. It will be very rare that anyone could be mad enough to venture to such an area, so it will be hit and run. It sounds simple enough Pete, lets hope it works and it keeps them at bay for some time, because after that I will only defend the Ark from aboard the Ark, they will need a submarine and some torpedoes to get us.'

The electric fence was stretched all around the top of the sides three centimetres above the flat surface of the gunwales so that anyone trying to climb over would put their hands or grappling hook on to it and have a twenty thousand volt surprise, and an even bigger one if they were hanging onto their rope while dangling in the water. If they managed to get over the sides, the flood lights set in the ground would dazzle them so much they will not be able to see where they were going. The final work was completed and a test was required. The floodlights came on as soon as someone accessed the deck but Albert didn't have any volunteers to touch the fence.

'Come on, it won't kill you, there's no amperes and it's only a few volts. Zimbo you're a strong daring lad, it might even straighten your hair for you.'

'No thank you Albert I like my hair curly just the way it is and so does Melanie.'

87

'Right then, there's only one answer to it,' he said to all the men there. 'It's short straw time.' Millie and Jane were present and they looked at each other expecting some fun.' They both giggled, one of the rare occasions they found something in common. Albert crossed to a field and gathered seven lengths of straw and cut them the same size. He showed them to the men.

'There are seven of us. These seven straws are the same now. I'm going to cut this one shorter than the rest. I will place them into Millie's hand for her to conceal the short one leaving all the seven exposed at the same length. Then she will offer each of us a straw and whoever gets the short straw tests the wire. Is that clear?' Spreading the straws out for them they each took one, first Pete, Ched, Gunter, Magnus, Antonio, Zimbo and Albert.

'Shit it's me!' Albert gasped. They all laughed and were relieved it wasn't any of them.

'Magnus are you sure about your calculations?'

'Yes I've tested the volts and its twenty thousand, well thereabout.'

'I don't like the sound of the thereabout bit, but here goes.' He reached up and put his hand on the wire. With immediate effect it threw him away from the side.

'Ah, it works Magnus and quite a belt too, that should do the trick.' They all clapped their hands for his bravery. Millie and Jane put their arms around him and planted kisses on each cheek.

'Crikey it was worth it just for that!'

'I'm jealous now, Albert,' Pete said.

'Oh,' said Millie, 'do you want a kiss as well Pete?' They repeated the performance with arms around him and kissing Pete's cheeks. Millie dug him in his waist with her nails, just enough to make him aware.

She whispered in his ear. 'I have something to tell you,' while the three were still hugging

'Wow!' he said, 'if this is what you get for being brave I'll volunteer next time as well.'

The atmosphere was jolly. Everyone was pleased with their achievement and without hesitation they headed for the canteen for drinks. It was still early and the children were all together with their parents just socialising and having a laugh at Albert's expense about his predicament in being the guinea pig. Mi, Pete and Millie sat together, as was now commonplace. Millie and Pete purposely let their glasses stay empty, hoping that Mi would get up for more drinks. When she did, it gave Millie the opportunity to speak to Pete. Quickly Millie told him about the massage session.

'Bloody hell! Really? I'm getting a hard-on just thinking about it!'

'I told you I would do something. Well I did and she loved it. She wants to do it again and doesn't mind if you find out and I must admit. I didn't mind doing it myself. It seemed a bonus on the way to having you.' Mi returned with the drinks, and Millie sparked off a conversation.

'This is great, everyone's here and enjoying themselves. Albert and Amy have done a wonderful job of creating our community. We all get on very well together, don't you think?'

'I couldn't agree more,' replied Pete, 'Picking this spot to spend the summer has been fantastic. What do you think Millie?'

'I feel the same. It's been fantastic. There are three things I'm very grateful for, first the time you pulled me through my illness when we were in the south, then the massage you gave me, we must do it again soon.'

'Yes, yes,' Mi agreed with a smile.

'The third thing was the scuba diving! It was wonderful. I loved every moment,' Millie stopped there, she was getting excited herself.

Ched sat with Marigold and their respective children. Melanie had Chuva with her and asked to join them. Ched would have preferred Marigold to himself, but decided to be polite.

'Yes of course, join us. We were only discussing the weather, weren't we Marigold.' They were not. They had eyes on Millie and Pete especially when Mi got up for drinks. Albert with Amy, holding Esperanca sat with Magnus. Jane sat nearby with Alberto on her lap looking into Antonio's eyes. Patricia was talking to Zimbo. Gunter, Greta and family were all together, happy as ever.

The time had come to lift anchor and move on to their winter destination. This trip was going to be very different from their previous migration routes. There would be a lot of expert navigation required. Gunter was well aware of the task he had to do, with all the turns and the narrow Suez Canal. Prior to the journey he spent a lot of time going over the planning with Ched, marking it out on the charts for a route that had plenty of depth for the Ark's draft, waterline distance to the lowest point on the keel of the ship. He still preferred to set the navigation calculations manually and then would check it through on the GPS. They estimated the trip to take them about three weeks, leaving the place they all loved with very fond memories at the north tip off Gozo, north of Malta. They would sail east to Egypt to the mouth of the Suez Canal at Port Said through one hundred and ninety five kilometres of canal into the Gulf of Suez, passing Egypt on their right and South Sinai on their left. Then out into the Red Sea across the Tropic of Cancer, with Saudi Arabia to the Arabian Peninsula and Yemen on the left, leading them out into the Gulf of Aden. Then they would turn east along the north coast of Somalia to its Peninsula where the Gulf of Aden meets the Arabian Sea around the Peninsula, and turning south into the Indian Ocean to Madagascar, travelling between Madagascar and Mozambique on the east coast of Africa, and finally over the Tropic of Capricorn to find a suitable place south of Madagascar.

As usual they aimed to leave at first light. The Ark powered its turbines to get the momentum going for this huge vessel. Once they were moving they put up all the sails, enabling them to cut the turbines and conserve methane gas. Four days later they were ready to enter the Suez Canal. This historic canal dates back to the thirteenth century BC. It was neglected for a thousand years, and abandoned after several Egyptian rulers tried to excavate and maintain it but giving up in the eighth century AD. The main canal opened to navigation in 1869 and in 1888 gave access to all vessels of all nations, without discrimination. There were many problems on the way, such as the post World War II formation of the nation of Israel. The narrow canal has been extensively widened in recent years for the larger oil and container ships on their way between east and west and their return, although more container traffic than tankers now use the passageway. The Ark's passengers spent much of the time during the fifteen hour or so journey through the canal looking out at the historic and war torn areas. This was the closest most had been to land for over three years and were amazed that people still lived in mud built adobe homes and in such poverty. An even bigger spectacle was for the people on the canal banks looking at this giant oil tanker with its trees and bleating animals. The passage went very smoothly mainly because of the lack of traffic coming the opposite way. Gunter gave a sigh of relief when they entered the Gulf of Aden, open water. Albert, Ched and Pete were there to congratulate him on his handling of a very nervy task.

Albert and Pete resumed the planning of "Operation Shockwaves" the moment they entered the Red Sea. They knew that as soon as they were in the Gulf of Aden the mission would be very close. There was a vast choice of weapons and explosives and they wanted to cover all eventualities, but not to carry much weight which would make it difficult to run any distance. After a few meetings they put together a list. It was then a matter of getting that equipment together to inspect it and make sure all was in tip-top condition for the operation. They picked two Heckler & Koch mp5 sub machine guns, two Heckler & Koch 9 mm USP pistols and the two crossbows with a quantity of bolts each, plus the standard commando knives. These were their hand weapons. They chose a rucksack each to spread the load of explosive devices which consisted of limpet mines, Semtex 10, detonators and timers, hand grenades and night vision glasses.

Now they were through the Red Sea and entered the Gulf of Aden and passed south of Aden itself, it was time to brief Gunter, Ched, Magnus and Antonio on what they must do to give Albert and Pete the best chance of returning safely. A meeting on the bridge was organised and then Albert announced the planned operation. It came as a shock to most of them.

'It's ridiculous!' Ched said immediately, 'and what happens if you don't make it back?'

'Will it make any difference to the ongoing threat and could it make it worse for us?' Gunter questioned. Magnus was concerned for the protection of the women and children if they did not return. Antonio was quiet.

'Because we took out the Russians boat dismantling all of their communications,' Albert explained, 'they probably think it's all at the bottom of the ocean. We haven't had an attack for almost a year now and that doesn't mean that we have won and that's the end of it. We have located where one of their communicating transmission sites is. Quite conveniently it's on the Somalia Peninsular that we just happen to be passing.'

'Oh very convenient,' Ched cut in, 'or was it on the cards since leaving the Southern Atlantic and planned all along?'

'It had been discussed, but not seriously until recently when we found the structure of the Russian Mafia's organisation in the database. And guess who was chief accountant, assumed missing?'

'Miles!' they all said together.

'Now isn't that strange? I still don't know whether he wanted to escape the clutches of the Mafia or the idea was to take over the ship and use it as a floating communication and operation centre. I'm beginning to think the latter. So on that basis it's not over yet and if they believe that Miles is dead, or alive and has changed his mind, it will not make the slightest difference to the organisation. They will still want the ship for the original use that they bought and paid for it.'

'Oh, I see where you're coming from with that scenario,' Ched said. 'So you are going to do them more damage by knocking out one of their communication transmitting stations?'

'Yes Ched, you've got it.'

'But why all the secrecy keeping it away from us like you did?'

'The less time you have to worry about it and upsetting the girls the better. It meant we could concentrate on our plan without unnecessary stress to them and us by worrying.'

Having realised that there was not much choice but to go ahead with the plan the pair went over the operation again with the others, and it would be repeated twice more to them, so that it was indelible in their brains. Albert also instructed them all to carry side arms from the moment the pair leave the ship until their return. Gunter, Ched, Magnus and Zimbo were to be on the bridge and lookout for that period as well. Antonio needed to be rested and ready to be at sea for a number of hours in case of any delays. The final thing they wanted to do was to go online and check if where they were going to attack was still operational. It was something they were very reluctant to do, but if they didn't, and found the site abandoned, it would all be a waste of time with a big risk taken. The dilemma was if they did make a communication, then it could alert the Russians that something was amiss prompting them to reinforce the transmitting site.

7. ALBERT'S REVENGE

Gunter altered course to south-east heading towards the coastal town of Bendar, northern Somalia, passing quite close by. They made a course due east to the drop off point just before Caluula, near to where they were to leave the Ark, for in Albert's case, terra firma, the first time in well over three years. They took the chance and went online to check if the site was transmitting, leaving it to the very last minute to do so. That would give the Russians only a few hours to call up extra defence if a problem was suspected. The drill was repeated for the last time and Albert gave the men his final orders before his and Pete's departure over the side.

'I'm going to ask you all a very straightforward question. What is the most important thing to you all?'

'Our women and children,'

'Right, then how will you defend them?' There was a pause as they looked at each other.

'With our lives,'

'Then this is my final word to you, if anyone manages by whatever means to board the Ark without a formal request and permission to do so, you shoot to kill, or you will lose your women and children.'

Reality had sunk in and they were going to be on their own whilst Albert and Pete would try to defend them all by attack. The Ark had slowed down late that afternoon, Albert and Pete did their well-practiced preparations; no distinctive smells, nothing shiny on them, gear all at hand and no ID; they were ready. Magnus switched off the electric fence for a short period while they lowered the fishing boat over the side as a precaution, then it was action stations.

'Albert what do I tell the women?' Magnus asked.

'Nothing until they ask where we are.'

'OK.'

The old fishing boat was going back to Africa, albeit several thousand miles away from where it was found. It was lowered over the side with the men and equipment inside, at 20.00 hours. The sun had long gone down but it was a clear night, much to their disadvantage by heightening the possibility of being detected, but they had to seize their only window of opportunity. Hopefully by posing as a local fishing boat they hoped no one would take any notice as they approached the shore. They estimated that if all went well, they should be in the inflatable by 02.00 hours so they had six hours to do their stuff. A splash as they hit the water, the shackle released and then they were on their own drifting away from the Ark. The engine started up and off they went to the coast as the diesel engine powered by cooking oil, phut, phut, phut, was the sound it made as it headed into the distance.

'Have you seen Pete anywhere?' Mi asked Amy.

'No Mi. I've been looking for Albert. I tried the shortwave but there's no answer. They're probably in the communications room. Let's go and see.' The pair were quite concerned because Amy could usually always get hold of Albert quickly. When they got there the lights were out, nothing was switched on, and no one was there.

'We'd better go to the bridge and ask some questions.' Amy's heartbeat started to race and she quickened her pace to the bridge pushing the door open hard.

'Oh shit!' said Ched, 'here comes trouble!'

'Come on tell me where they are and why have you got side arms on?'

'Where's who Amy?' Ched asked.

'Don't you fuck with me, Ched!'

'Oh in that case they have gone overboard for a little while, haven't they Gunter?' Gunter was trying to stay out of it.

'Yes they won't be long.'

'Ched tell me what the fuck they are up to or you and Arnie here will be thrown overboard by all the women?'

'You're very persuasive Amy,' Ched stalled.

'Ched tell me now!' Amy shouted extremely mad and loud.

'Well they've found a place on the mainland not far from here that is the communication centre for the Russian Mafia. Gunter and I were only informed about all this a short time ago. Their plan is to destroy it and give us all more time without threat, as Albert did when he destroyed their yacht. There is another thing that we discovered in the data stored on the computers. I know you were involved as well as Albert in picking Miles, but he was their chief accountant.'

'Now I understand why Albert's doing this, it's his revenge.' Mi, started to get hysterical.

'Oh no Pete why do this to me? He will get killed.'

'No Mi. They have planned this operation meticulously to every detail, and Antonio will pick them up in the early hours of the morning. Don't worry it will be fine,' Ched assured her.

'Come on Mi, let's go and tell the others what's happening!'

They left the bridge and called the women to meet in the canteen. They soon arrived and Mi went straight to Millie clutching her and crying.

'Pete's gone, Pete's gone.'

'What do you mean? Amy what's going on?'

'Can we please calm down? Millie please comfort Mi and tell her they will soon be back. I know my husband.' Millie soothed Mi as Amy explained what was happening.

'In the past few minutes we have discovered that Albert and Pete have gone on a little mission to destroy a transmitter place or something that the Russians use. They left the Ark about two hours ago and it is planned that Antonio will pick them up in the early hours of the morning.'

'Antonio is involved? I'll kill him!' Jane burst out. Jane rushed to Amy as she became hysterical and threw her arms around her and burst into tears. Amy tried to calm her.

'You can't stop him. We need Antonio to bring them back.'

'Oh Amy what are we going to do? What if they don't make it?'

'It means they have sacrificed themselves for us.' That had a very sobering effect. 'Jane can I stay with you tonight I don't want to be on my own, not this time,'

'Yes of course Amy we best let the men get on with it.'

'What part has Gunter played in this deceiving?' Greta asked Amy.

'As far as I can see he just kept his mouth shut, which I would expect from a comrade of Albert's.'

'Oh, yes of course.'

'Melanie where is Zimbo?'

'He's on lookout duties,'

'That makes sense,' Amy said.

Millie was still comforting Mi and led her off to Mi's cabin, thinking she knew then they were up to something.

'Don't worry Mi the two of them are used to doing that sort of thing and remember they have done it for us. We have to make sure when they get back we look after them no matter what. I'll stay with you tonight and by the time you wake up tomorrow he'll be back in your arms.'

'Millie you are so kind to me, thank you.'

'I must tell Ched that I'm staying with you tonight and I'll ask Marigold to look after the children. Let's get you to bed first then I'll join you, OK?'

'Yes Millie.'

'I won't be long.'

Millie scooted off to the bridge to see Ched, thinking on the way. Why do men do these things? He had better come back in one piece.

'Ched, you won't mind if I stay with Mi tonight? She's in a hell of a state as you can imagine.'

'Yes I saw her. No problem, just ask Marigold to have the children because I've got a long night here with Arnie.'

'What is this Arnie thing?' Gunter asked.

'Thanks Ched.' Millie rushed off to see Marigold.

97

'Arnold Schwarzenegger, famous film actor, Arnie is his nickname. Amy thinks you are like him.'

'But he is not German.'

'Fucking hell!' said Ched in exasperation.

Millie let herself into Mi's cabin where she found her sitting on the sofa. She sat next to her and put her arm around her shoulders.

'Oh Millie he never said a word to me, not a goodbye. How could he do this to me?'

'That's because he didn't want us to worry and they were hoping to be back before we realised they'd gone. Now let's have a drink, go to bed and snuggle up. Before you know it they'll be back and you can give Pete a lovely welcome home. Now what have you got to drink?'

'There is some clear stuff that Albert makes. He calls it "Flash." It's alright with water.'

'Well let's have a glass each, neat down the hatch and get to bed to sleep it off.' Mi got up and did exactly that, poured two large drinks. They took them straight down and the distilled liquid had the usual effect on its victims.

'Wow!' They both looked at each other as the burning sensation took hold to convert to a very mellow feeling. Millie started giggling. Mi followed with a snigger as they entered the bedroom leaving a trail of clothes behind them.

'Thank you Millie,' a slurring voice said a little later.

'Any time my little star.' They fell on the bed together, entwined and completely naked only to soon pass out and fall fast asleep.

The engine was cut about a thousand metres from the shore letting the tide take them in and onto what they hoped was a sandy beach. It was a mixture of rock and sand. They hit a rock close to the shore. Pete jumped out of the boat where the water was almost a metre deep and guided it through channels between the rocks to the shore. Now they had the task of gearing themselves up with backpacks and weapons ready to head to the town, and hopefully pick up a vehicle. The crossbow was the choice for their defence and first attack if necessary, being quiet to use and effective. They could see lights as soon as they climbed from the beach. Then swiftly on towards the town of Caluula where on the outskirts they stopped to assess the situation, on the lookout for vehicles. As they crouched down Albert tapped Pete and put his nose up in the air. Pete did the same and smelt the distinctive smell of cigarette smoke, someone was close by. They took note of the direction of the breeze. The tobacco smoke grew stronger and then they saw puffs of it rising against the night light. They moved forwards and heard soft voices, a conversation of some description. They crept towards the sounds, and spotted a young couple up against a pickup truck fooling around with each other. The man was feeling the young woman's breasts, picked out and shone in the moonlight. She was giving him a hand job and being very successful by the size of its glistening tip. They were sharing a smoke of some description, which reminded Albert of the odour the cannabis spiffs that Monty produced before his disappearance.

Albert and Pete looked at each other and decided to wait until she has brought him to his goal before they acted. It didn't take long. In they moved and stuffed cloth into the mouths of the startled couple, throwing them face down to the ground and binding their hands behind their backs. Albert handled the female with delicacy knowing she would be scared out of her wits. Pete needed to use more force as the innocent chap fought back. They hauled them to the side of the road, the man face down with his trousers dragged to his ankles.
'I bet he's got a sore cock now after it being through the dirt,' Albert said on return to the truck.

They put their packs in the back, started up the engine and they were on their way, no speed and screaming engine with wheel spin, just calmly. The road ahead was just a dirt track, hard and well used. They estimated it would be about thirty kilometres to the hit spot and, considering the state of the road, probably take an hour. Hands on weapons keeping their eyes peeled ready for anything, Albert realised he needed a pee.

'Pete pull over, shut the lights, I need a leak. You should have one too, there's no rush. Pete pulled off the road near some rocks. They pulled out their penises and begin to relieve themselves. Albert sighed with relief. Then they heard a vehicle coming and it wasn't far away. The exercise was hurried, shaking was rapid. Albert could not cut off as quickly as Pete, and dribbled. 'Shit!' cursing himself for getting old. They cocked their other weapons ready for action and ducked out of sight, watching as a truck with four white men with bottles of drink in their hands, obviously drunk, careered along the road and passed them, not even seeing them or their truck at the roadside.

'Let's hope they're coming from where we're going and there's minimum security left.' Pete got back into the truck, and wondered where Albert was.

'Albert come on, let's go,'

'Sorry Pete I didn't finish.'

'Yes Albert old age is creeping in. Just stave it off for as long as you can and I think you are well above average, keep it up buddy, we need you.'

Moving on with a few kilometres to go they slowed down to look at the map and the outline of the area. It was barren. Nothing was showing up on the night skyline. They were looking for a mast about a hundred feet tall. Pete scanned around with night vision binoculars and picked out some trees and shrubs but no mast. Going around again, he noticed a tall tree, a bit like a monkey puzzle tree but very symmetrical.

'Got it Albert!' and passed the glasses to him, pointing out the tree.

'Yes that's it, it's manufactured to look like a tree, just like the Madeira pine, and with all the branches it doesn't need to be so tall, but I can't see any satellite dishes,' Albert whispered. They moved closer to get a better view. Pete stopped again and signalled to look.

'There, Porta-cabins. There must be about eight of them. They'll have the dishes inside one of them with the roof cut out. There will be living quarters and one with a generator in. It must be well insulated because I can't hear it.'

'It's got to be the target, so let's go and get it over with,' Albert said.

'Ok it looks as if it's about three hundred metres from the road.'

'Then we'll coast quietly past the site, even if we have to push the truck and leave it on the exit route. Then we'll return to check out where everything is, see what personnel are there, deal with them, plant the charges and then get back to the truck.'

Crossbows at the ready, they moved towards the fixtures, walking slowly at about ten metres apart and within view to signal each other. The dim lights strewn around the place showed the outline of a guard moving slowly and sloppily around the perimeter of the cabins and not being aware. They stopped to watch and timed him on his complete circle. It was three minutes and the same guard. On the start of his next circuit, he lit the inevitable cigarette. Pete fired his bolt right into his back. They both rushed forward. Pete's knife was ready to cut the guards throat, he lifted his head there was no need. Albert scanned around waiting for any other movement or sound. They crept around the structures listening and looking in windows, trying to locate the generator, the operations room and where the dishes were housed. They soon found the generator. It had sandbags stacked up against it. Albert went in quickly through the access door, timed and laid the charges while Pete watched the outside. Three minutes and it was done. He was out. The strange antenna was next. A charge was fixed to blow upwards to mangle the metal mast. They came to a cabin that had grilles over the window and no light. Albert put a flashlight through the glass. Moving it around there he spotted a man tied up either asleep or unconscious and not in good shape. He handed the light to Pete to take a look.
'Shit! We have to get him out of there,' he whispered to Albert. Albert shook his head whispering a reply.
'Let's do the operations room first.' Pete put his thumbs up to agree.

That cabin was brightly lit and not far from where they took out the guard. Peeking through the window they could see that all was well in sleepy town, just one man with his head on the desk and he looked sound asleep. Pete walked straight in and slit his throat. Albert watched outside, then changed over positions for Albert to place the explosive charges. They took a chance on which were the containers that had the satellite dishes in and laid charges on those that had plain structures, then they headed back to release whoever was captive and predictably it was the only door that was locked.

'We are going to make a lot of noise shortly anyway,' Albert said. He fixed a small quantity of plastic explosive and then inserted a detonator. They both stood aside and bang, the door was open. Pete ran straight in, automatic at the ready while Albert guarded outside. Pete dragged the guy out, still bound, before cutting him free. He was shocked and dazed and had not a clue what was going on. The pair took one of his arms each and headed for the truck, dragging his feet behind. Suddenly, floodlights lit up the perimeter. A man ran out from a cabin brandishing a gun and pulling his trousers up at the same time. The trio hit the ground, Albert turned and bellied, aimed and fired a short burst, a painful yell then quiet, the man was dead. The one hundred and fifty metres or so to the truck seemed a long way with their added burden. There still was no communication with him and they both wondered who the hell he was. On reaching the truck they loaded him in the back and were soon on their way to the rendezvous place hoping Antonio would be just offshore. They had gone about five kilometres and a bright light with several flashes lit up the night sky behind them. They looked at each other and shrugged their shoulders.

'Job done!' they said and high fived.

'Now let's see if we can get home in one piece,' Albert said, as he drove on.

Pete did the navigation and concentrated hard, he knew that a turning should be coming up shortly. Just then they were startled by a thumping on the rear cab window, the passenger was awake and shouting in a broad American accent.

'Hey do you two guys speak English?'

'No shut up, we're busy.' Pete shouted back.

'Oh.' Their passenger nodded his head then pulled himself up to a sitting position against the back of the cab.

'Left here Albert, quick,' He swerved to take the turning throwing the poor sod in the back against the side of the truck. Pete looked back at him.

'He'll be alright. He looks as if he's had a bigger pounding than that. Another five kilometres and we should be there. They slowed down as they approached the coast. They could see the shimmering sea in the moonlight and the outline of the Ark. Albert drove as close as he could to the shore and stopped. They got out of the truck and both helped the guy off the back after lowering the tailgate, moved him quickly away from the vehicle to the water, with their weapons still ready.

'I can hear him but I can't see him. Give out the signal Albert.' Albert flashed his light to the planned sequence. The water was quite choppy with breakers from over a metre to much smaller in size. Albert noticed the pattern of the larger waves which counted three and then calmer ones for a longer period of time.

'We knew it was going to be a problem for him to reach the shore,' said Pete.

'We're going to have to swim to him,' said Albert.

'What about our man here?' Then Albert spotted Antonio's signal and returned it.

'Come on after the third big wave we go. Now there's no time to wait. We'll take him between us and grab the side ropes of the inflatable, we'll cling to the side while Antonio heads back to the Ark. Fifty metres, that's all we have to go.'

In they went dragging their guest in between them. They were swimming for their lives and carrying their weapons, the burden of the man and Albert flashing his light. Antonio was soon there and they grabbed the side rope.

'Go Antonio, Go!' He turned the inflatable and headed back to the Ark away from the shoreline. When they were well away from the shore line Albert signalled for him to slow down.

'Help pull us onboard. Take this one first.' Antonio pulled as the other two helped the American out of the water, then Albert, then Pete.

'Before we carry on Antonio, has anything happened, any visitors?' asked Albert.

'No, just some very upset women and a very angry Amy.'

'Yes, I can imagine. I noticed a few boats about quite close to the Ark. Did you see them?'

'Yes and they saw me leave. They looked like fishing boats but that's all I could see.'

'Pete you must have a full clip in and I've hardly used any, are you ready?'

'Yep, I can't wait.'

'Right get as low into the boat as you can and we'll approach very slowly circling the Ark before you signal to Magnus to pick us up. Ok?'

They could see the silhouette of a sizeable motorboat that was too close for comfort. Albert signalled to Antonio to head for the boat, which was now alongside the Ark. A rocket was launched from that boat to land just over the Ark's side.

'I can see a grappling iron following on behind that rocket to get a rope onto the ship,' Pete said.

'Full speed to the boat Antonio,' Albert instructed. One of the occupants of the boat was now feeling Albert's electric shock experience, the others were busy picking up their weapons to fire on Albert and co., but they were too late, Pete and Albert let go a full clip each into the pirate boat and were ready with another. Antonio slowed down and his comrades stood up to look at the mess. Antonio was shocked and dismayed. Their passenger was still laid down semi-conscious in a daze wondering what was happening.

'Pull away Antonio and go around the Ark again. When there's no threat we'll board. Twenty metres away Albert lobbed a grenade into the motorboat and seconds later it was blown apart as they fled away.

'Why Albert they were dead?' Antonio was puzzled by his action.

'I don't like leaving evidence around. It causes questions,'

'Oh.'

All was clear after their trip around the Ark. Antonio got Magnus on the shortwave to organise the lift. The hoist was lowered rapidly. Albert connected the shackle and they were soon up out of the water and onto the deck. Zimbo was there with Magnus. Albert and Pete helped the young American out of the inflatable. There were many pairs of eyes looking down from the bridge on to the foredeck to see them return. Amy and Jane grasped each other, Amy clutching Jane tightly.

'They're back. I'm angry but I'm so happy they're back.' She wiped away the tears to look again as the men helped the American up to the canteen.

'Jane there's someone with them. They must have taken a prisoner.' Albert picked up the shortwave and took a deep breath.

'Amy come in please do you read me?'

'Of course I read you, you bastard!' Albert moved the radio away from his ear. Pete could hear her voice cursing him.

'See you in the canteen in ten minutes we want a glass of "flash." He quickly turned the radio off. Amy heard and told Jane that they were going to the canteen as the night was not over yet.

'Antonio, did you see Mi tonight before you left?' Pete asked.

'Yes Pete, as I said earlier, the women were very upset, Mi could not stop crying for you so Millie took her to your cabin and I think she is with her.'

'Oh!' said Pete.

The American staggered along supported by Antonio, asked.

'Where the fuck am I?'

'You are on Albert's Ark and very lucky to be here.'

'And who the fuck is Albert?' He immediately dropped him to the deck and walked away. Pete was following on and shouted.

'Antonio what's wrong?'

'He was disrespectful to Albert after you both saved him.'

'Antonio he hasn't got a clue where he is or who we are. He's been through some heavy shit. Now help me with him to the canteen to get some food and drink into our bellies.' They picked him up and caught up with Albert.

'Albert, are you on another mission?'

'Yes I need a drink and it's the hard stuff. Antonio give me the shortwave please, Ched or Gunter, come in please?'

'Gunter here,'

'Is Ched with you?'

'Yes, he has been here all the time.'

'Good, it's going to be a long night for you two so burn some gas. Let's get out of here.'

'Sure,' he replied.

'What did he want?' Ched asked.

'He just said burn some gas.'

'Oh that's alright then.' Ched increased the engine power.

Amy, Jane and Patricia were waiting for them in the canteen. The rest were asleep or looking after their own or someone else's children. As soon as she saw Albert, Amy weakened and couldn't shout at him face to face. She just rushed over, hugged and kissed him.

'That's it Albert. No more or I'm going back to England with Esperanca.'

'Amy, that's it. I'm done. Any defending in the future will be from the Ark.'

'Who's that you have with you?'

'Don't know yet. The only clue we have is that he's got an American accent and he was a prisoner at the compound. Apart from that at the moment I couldn't give a shit!' Albert left Amy's clutches and got to the bar. Patricia was ready and willing to serve.

'Patricia darling, is there any chance of a pile of bacon sandwiches as soon as you can please?'

'Oh, I don't know. Are you sure that chap is not Muslim. I don't want to offend him with bacon.'

'No Patricia he's Jewish,'

'Oh, will he want ketchup with them?' Albert laughed, Patricia moved as swiftly as she could and thought Albert had flipped. He went behind the bar took a tray, a bottle of flash, several glasses and a jug of water to the table where everyone had congregated. Amy was concerned about the American.

'Albert shouldn't we get this guy to sickbay and Mi to tend to him?'

'Why, Amy? He's American and they're all tough!' Pete smiled and knew the way Albert was thinking.

'Would you like a drink young man?' Albert asked the chap propped in his chair.

'Yea, I'll have Bourbon with ice.'

106

'Certainly,' Albert poured drinks for everyone, passing the jug of water to the ladies who are bemused by Albert's attitude to the newcomer.

'Here's a toast to being back with the ones we so dearly love and to a successful operation cheers,' Albert said.

'Cheers.' Albert and Pete stood up to shake hands congratulating themselves on the teamwork and thanking the expert training of the Royal Marines for their success. The Yank heard.

'Royal Marines?' he stood up and spoke out. 'My Commander never told me the Royal Marines would be involved in this operation.' Albert and Pete turned and looked at him. He immediately saluted them in true American Military style, standing to attention.

'Lieutenant Buster Manta, 101 Airborne division, Sir, at your service Sir, and who might I be addressing Sir?'

'This here is Wing Commander Gung-Ho-Happy Hogan and I'm Albert. Relax cowboy. Sit down and enjoy your drink, there will be some food very shortly,' said Albert as he and Pete burst out laughing. Amy and Jane saw the funny side and joined in, leaving the American having to laugh as if he was watching one of their sit-com's on television.

'Sir, please could I have another glass of Bourbon?' Albert topped up all the glasses.

'That's my last. After I've eaten I'm going to bed, we'll find you somewhere to sleep Buster so don't worry you are in very good hands, we will talk tomorrow,' Albert told him.

'Pete, Millie is with Mi they must still be fast asleep, Mi was very upset.'

'Yes I know Amy, Antonio told me so it will be on the couch for me for what is left of the night.'

'Albert, where are we going to put Buster for tonight? The only bed that's available at the moment is Ched and Millie's but you best ask Ched first because he will want it as soon as he can be relieved.'

'OK,' he replied as a big tray of bacon sandwiches arrived. Within minutes the men had demolished them.

'Patricia you are the woman of my dreams,' said Pete. She quickly disappeared back into the kitchen blushing and all of a flutter.
'I'll go and see Ched. I need to anyway, I'll be with you shortly darling,' said Albert.

Jane and Antonio left for their cabin with arms around each other. She was so pleased to have him and the others back. They put Alberto in his bed. He had been asleep all through the toing and froing and never murmured.
'I want a shower with you before we go to bed,' Jane said.
'That will be nice,' he replied. Within a minute they were naked and entered the shower. She couldn't wait to be with him. She clutched at him, kissed him and felt his very masculine torso then dropped down to his semi erection and did the same to him as she did when she first had desires for him, gently she pulled his foreskin back and entered his now rapidly expanding rod into her mouth, giving him a delightful sensation in seconds,'
'Jane, Jane, Oh, Oh, hmm,' Not letting go of him until he was weak at the knees, she gradually pulled herself back up his body kissing and pecking at him, stopping at his nipples to tantalize them bringing them to hard knots. She knew he loved these little bits of attention and she was in control as she moved to his lips to almost swallow his tongue. Then she pulled away from him touching her own body bringing her hands to her breasts pushing them up and down swallowing water from the shower and releasing it provocatively at him. This aroused him and he wanted her so much. He lifted her up and to her delight, he parted her legs and forced his increasingly hard tube of flesh into her. She gasped at the speed and force, but that is exactly what she wanted. His strong arms moved her up and down, in and out holding her neat buttocks with his hands.
'Antonio, Antonio I love you,' she cried, climaxing and holding him tightly with her arms around his neck. On his final stroke he still held her tight and they did not part for several minutes then he lowered her, and she told him she loved him again.

'Ched we have a one night temporary problem to find somewhere for our American fugitive to sleep. Would it be alright if he uses your bed? I know Millie is with Mi and Marigold has the children so your place is all that's available at the moment, because you will be on the bridge for the rest of the night.'

'Why can't he bed down in the canteen like the others did?'

'Ched, this guy has had a rough time and as much as I dislike the Yanks, he needs some rest. So-called friendly fire killed a lot of our lads when I was on active duty in the Gulf war. I have to be diplomatic because he is an American soldier on a mission for his country and it affects our own security.'

'OK, no problem Albert, but who is going to relieve us and at what time?'

'Now that is a difficult one. Err, call me and Antonio at 08.00 hours and we'll be here to change shifts at 09.00 hours. Ok?'

'Yes, alright I'll do that.'

He started to think. If the Yank is in my bed and the state he is supposedly in he won't want to be running around until mid-day at least so where? Ah yes, what an opportunity for us, Marigold's. As long as I tell her to be away from the cabin and be seen with the children at all times, that will do me. What's that old song I remember from a child? He started to sing as the memory hit him.

'Inch worm, inch worm, measuring the Marigold,'

'What are you singing about Marigold for Ched?'

'Gunter, I'm not singing about Marigold. Well yes I am. No I'm not. Shit. What's our position navigator?'

'We are both on the bridge chief engineer.'

'Now that's more like it,' and they both laughed.

Albert showed Buster, Ched and Millie's cabin and in no time at all he was on the bed and fast asleep, still in the salt-encrusted semi-dried clothes he had worn for probably not even knowing how long nor cared at that moment.

Albert entered his own cabin. Amy was sitting on the bed waiting for him, naked.

'Shower Albert and make it quick, I want you,' she said. About five minutes later he was drying himself off eager to be with her and was striding to her, still wet in places.

'Albert you haven't dried yourself properly. You'll make the sheets all wet.' She stood up full frontal to him and smiled, thinking what does it matter? She took hold of his dick and guided him to the bed.

'Are you sure you're alright now Amy? I don't want to hurt you. This will be the first time since before Esperanca was born.'

'Yes I'm sure and I think there will be a bonus. You'll be able to have me every day of every week because I won't be having any more periods.' Caressing each other, it didn't take long for Albert to be strong inside the one he loved but he worried that he might hurt her recovering insides. He was very gentle and she was very appreciative to have her man fully connected to her again and did not want to let him go. They held each other tightly through the remaining hours of that night.

As quietly as Pete could possibly be he opened the door to his quarters, crept in and locked up behind him. The door to the bedroom was open and the bedside table lamp gave a dull light over a scene that made him stop, stare and smile. The two were fast asleep huddled together totally naked. He thought to himself you said you would do anything to get me regularly and you have kept your word, that's good enough for me. I had better shower before joining them. I hope I don't wake them up I need to rest first. Very quietly he moved to the bathroom and when thoroughly clean and dried, he approached the bed. Just looking at them turned him on, slowly and carefully he climbed in behind Mi, straightened out, snuggled up behind her and put his arm over the two of them then closed his eyes. Millie felt a hand on her, raised her head slightly and saw it was Pete. She smiled to herself took his hand and held it on her breast and fell back to sleep.

8.   THE TRUTH AND OTHER DECEPTIONS

Albert's alarm went off. He had only been asleep for a few hours, but being seasoned in this sort of thing moved to sit on the side of the bed because he knew if he put the alarm to snooze he would have to shift his arse rapidly to achieve his commitments. Shower, canteen and the bridge was his plan. He stood up, turned to look at his lady and thought, you are something else my dear, it's you that brings me back.

'I didn't expect you here so early Patricia after such a late night and thanks again for those bacon sandwiches, they were fantastic.'
'Thank you Albert we were all happy to see you back safe and sound and that poor young Jewish lad you saved.'
'What?' His memory lapsed for a second. Oh dear he thought. 'Patricia I have an apology to make. I had a tough time and when we returned. I was not quite myself, I'm sorry, I was jesting.'
'Oh I wondered why, you were a bit odd.'
'I'll have a quick bacon sandwich and then I must go and relieve Ched and Gunter. They've done a straight two shifts. They must be knackered and when Antonio arrives, feed him as quickly as you can and tell him I need him on the bridge. Thank you again.' As soon as he finished his breakfast he was off to the bridge.
'Morning Albert, I don't know about you Gunter, but I'm knackered, I'll probably sleep all day. I'm off, oh, please don't disturb me.
'You have a guest in your room Ched? Where are you going to sleep?' asked Albert.
'In Marigold's quarters, she'll be with the children in the crèche. Check if you want.'

Antonio arrived as Gunter was about to go to his cabin.
'Just a minute Gunter before you leave,' asked Albert, 'I need to check our course with you.' They went over the chart from their present position, to the direction they needed to maintain for the day.

'Thank you Gunter. See you later.'

'Antonio could you please go and relieve Zimbo on lookout, he must be exhausted.'

'The animals, but what about them? They should be out and the cows milked by now. We need Millie.' Antonio was unhappy with the situation and left to relieve Zimbo only to find him fast asleep! He gave him a slight kick to wake him.

'Zimbo you are a waste of space. I'm here to relieve you. I bet you have been asleep all night.'

'No I've only just dozed off.'

'So you must have heard the grenade attack only ten minutes ago?'

'Yes, but I knew Albert would have the situation under control.'

'You lie Zimbo. The grenade went off several hours ago. I know because I was there when Albert threw it. Now that you are the only one that has had a full night's sleep, you can get to the animals, milk the cows and let them all out.'

'Yes, I will after I have some breakfast.'

'No Zimbo, the animals come first, understand?' Zimbo departed without another word.

Mi opened her eyes and glimpsed at Millie but felt the familiar closeness of Pete stuck to her back and fast asleep. Before she moved and disturbed him, the weight of his arm across her was heavy with his hand on Millie's breast and she held it tight to her. Mi turned to Pete and woke them both.

'Sorry Millie I tried not to wake you but Pete's back and I wanted to welcome him, do you mind?'

'No go ahead, can I welcome him back as well?'

'You best ask him yourself.' Pete stirred himself, rubbed his eyes to see the two lovely naked ladies next to him. First he paid attention to his wife, clutched her and moved on top of her. Her hands were all over him, 'Don't ever leave me like that again,' she commanded. By this time he had already entered into Mi. Millie watched him going in and out of her. She put her hand on his shoulders as he thrust into Mi, who was so grateful for his safe return.

112

She got closer to Mi and lay alongside her. She looked at Pete and put her left hand on Mi's right nipple, gave it a tweak as she liked, the other on Pete's left nipple touching it.

'Pete will you do that to me too please?'

'Yes.'

'Pete, you can stop if you like before you come and do as Millie asked.'

He withdrew his long thin penis, Millie watched it, hard and shiny with anticipation of what she was going to feel made her start small gyrations of her hips. Pete moved across to Millie as she lay on her back, opening her legs for him to get between. He guided it in gently as he did on the nose of the ship that day. Mi fondled Millie's breasts as Pete moved in and out sending her wild. Mi, turned on by the climax Millie was having, kissed Pete and then Millie as Pete let fly his ejaculation well into Millie.

'Oh Mi that was fantastic, thank you for letting Pete have me. I hope you didn't mind Pete and it was nice for you.'

'It was wonderful.' He turned to Mi.

'What is your pleasure my lady?' She looked at Millie and fondled her breasts.

'Millie show Pete what you can do for me, then he can have me.' Millie gulped a bit but knew she must do it and admitted to herself it was nice to see Mi pleased and well worth the reward she knew she would get hopefully on a regular basis. Millie started by kissing her. They played with each others' tongues then Millie moved down to Mi's breasts and sucked and flicked with her tongue which made her nipples hard and made Mi pant with the sensation. She felt so excited and moved her hips erotically. Millie realised how much Mi loved this and worked on her, when Mi wanted her to move down she put her hands on Millie's head to guide her. Pete stayed calm and interested, holding and moving his cock about and deciding on his preference. Millie finally reached the place Mi wanted her to be. Millie knelt to bring her neat little arse into the air, crouched between Mi's legs, placed her tongue on the spot to Mi's delight. Millie showed all of her juicy pussy which gave Pete an irresistible invitation and he entered Millie from behind a complete surprise for her, and at that stage, very welcome as it pushed her hard on to Mi's tender spot bringing her to a climax. Pete had never seen Mi on such a high before. Millie kept her position knowing he would finish inside her again and wanted him to. It did not take long and was over by the time Mi had come round. The three lay together, Pete in the middle, with the arms of these two beautiful women around him, all three exhausted. Millie got up.

'Shit! The animals, there won't be anyone to milk and let them out. I must go.' She moved as fast as she could. There was no time for showering and no point. She quickly dressed then returned to Mi and Pete kissed them both. 'Thank you,' she said, 'it was fantastic. I hope you will include me again sometime, it's the best I've felt for a very long time. See you later. Bye.'

'Well my darling what did you think about that? She enjoyed having you inside her. How did you feel?'

'It was very nice I must admit. But how often will you want a session like that and how do you feel about me making love or having sex with her regularly? I thought this was a one off to welcome me home safely. It's obvious that you two have been pleasing each other before, so you tell me?'

'Yes but it was only the once when we gave each other a massage and we adventured a bit further and liked it. For myself, she can do that to me anytime she wanted to or when I can get her to, but I think she would like you to have her as well.'

'Well the choice is yours. I'm just the stud.' He rolled over on top of her and kissed her passionately. Mi responded and aroused him again.

'Oh, that's nice, having Millie seems to have improved you,' she said to him.

'It's you mentioning it makes me harder and last longer.'

'Oh, Pete don't stop, I'll say anything you want. Don't stop, Oh, Oh, have her when you want as you want, oh, oh, ah, ah.' He finally stopped and pulled out of her.

'Oh Pete you haven't made me feel as good as that before. It was wonderful.'

'I didn't come. It must be right what you said. Looks like I'm going to be busy with you two then.'

'Yes,' she grinned. 'You are, so don't let me down will you?'

'No I won't. That's what you wanted all along isn't it?'

'Yes Pete.'

'You little minx,' he chuckled as he kissed her. 'Come on let's get some breakfast.'

Ched explained to Marigold about the temporary sleeping arrangements and that he told Albert that she wouldn't mind if he got his head down in her bed, while she looked after the children in the crèche.

'Albert said he understood considering the circumstances, as long as we behaved.'

'Oh,' she said and thought about it.

'What time will you want to wake?'

'About four o'clock,'

'Well I'll tell Greta I have to get something from the cabin. She won't mind because she has Melanie there as well to help with the children and I'll come and give you a special wake up call.'

'That would be nice.'

After breakfast Pete went to Albert on the bridge to discuss what to do with their guest and the fact that he was still a soldier.

'Our American must be out for the count. There's no sign of him yet. Should we check on him?'

'Leave him until just before we have lunch. If he is not up by then wake him, and ask him to get showered and join us for lunch then we can find out why the US had a soldier in civilian clothes held prisoner by whom we believe to be the Russian Mafia.'

'I must admit it is a strange one. I could understand it if he was CIA. Still, no good thinking about it until we have the information from him, but the fact still remains that we will have to return him to the mainland somewhere. He has no passport, no money and no clothes.'

'Clothes won't be a problem, but, like you said, let's hear what he has to say first.'

There was no appearance from the American so Pete went to wake him. He knocked on the cabin door of Ched and Millie's room where he had slept. No answer, he tried the door and it opened.

'Hello, anyone home?' He moved into the bedroom and could hear the shower going.

'Hi Buster, are you there?'

'Yea, I'll be out shortly. I could do with some clean clothes.'

'Ok, I'll see what I can find.' He looked in the wardrobes and drawers, then he grabbed a few of Ched's things and put them outside the shower.

'There are some clothes there for you, I'll wait in the other room then we'll go and have lunch.'

'Gee that's great.' He appeared with over sized trousers and shirt.

'Wing Commander Sir,' he said and saluted. 'Sorry Sir I didn't realise it was you Sir.' Shit Pete said to himself, Albert in the canteen last night, I didn't think that this poor sod would believe that, no wonder he was a prisoner, I had better put the chap straight.

'Buster, forget what you heard last night? Or I should say early hours of this morning. I'm Pete and the other guy is Albert and that is all you need to know at the moment. Is that clear?'

'Yes Sir and thank you for saving me.'

'OK, let's have some lunch.'

'You best give me your soiled clothes I'll get someone to wash and iron them as soon as they can.'

'Gee, that would be great. Thank you.'

The pair arrived at the canteen and Pete introduced him to those who were there.

'This is a very important lady on the Ark. Patricia this is Buster. He was not in very good shape when you fed him early this morning.'

'Nice to meet you hope you enjoy your stay.'

'I'm sure Patricia.' Amy walked in with Esperanca in her arms.

'I do remember seeing this lady, but don't know her name. I apologise Mam.' Pete turned to introduce her to him.

116

'Amy, this is Buster, Buster this is Amy and Esperanca, Albert's wife and daughter.'

'Pleased to meet you both Amy, Albert must be the boss of this outfit Mam?'

'You could say that but he doesn't like you to think so. Would you agree Pete?' Pete just smiled.

'There was another very attractive lady with a young guy and then it went blank,' Buster recalled.

'That was Jane and Antonio. Jane will be here soon with her son Alberto,' Amy added.

'Yes Mam,' Pete replied.

'Pete don't you start that, it's bad enough with Albert.'

'Sorry Amy, his humour has rubbed off on me.'

Buster was bemused by the banter and what the ship was all about but extremely happy to be on it and relaxed by the attention he was given. Pete guided him to the serving area.

'Let's get something to eat Buster. Some of the others will be along soon, but tonight we should all be together for a short period so just relax and enjoy it. This ship is the best place on earth, believe me.'

They soon sat down with trays of food and dug in. Buster wanted to know more about the Ark. Only seeing the ship in the dark, he had not been fit to remember much, and started asking questions.

'I don't understand. This oil tanker has military men onboard that do hit and run operations making the CIA look amateurs. I tell ya, you Brits are darn clever and got balls. How come we didn't know about it?'

'Sorry I'm not at privilege to say.'

'I get it, Secret Service and all that. When will I meet the boss again?'

'You mean Albert? We will go and see him after lunch.' Mi entered and came over to Pete, shocked to see a new face.

'Pete you never told me we had a guest.'

'Sorry Mi, we have been a little busy don't you think?'

'Oh, yes of course.' Buster stood up. 'And who,' he asked, 'might this pretty young lady be Sir?'

117

'Mi is my wife.'

'It's a pleasure to meet the wife of the man who saved my life Mam.' He took her hand and kissed it, embarrassing her.

'I didn't catch your name.'

'Buster, Mam.'

'Nice to meet you Buster, I'm sure I will be seeing a lot of you. I'm the Ark's Doctor and you will be required to have a health check to make sure you are not carrying any viruses or diseases that could harm the rest of us.'

'But I'm already here amongst you.'

'All the more reason to give you a full medical with some tests as soon as possible.'

'Pete could you bring him to the surgery immediately after lunch?'

'Certainly we'll go and see Albert after that, OK?'

'Sure Pete.'

Mi went to the counter for a tray of food while Pete and Buster continued eating theirs. Then Greta, Marigold and Melanie came in with the rest of the children running about screaming and laughing as they do. Being inquisitive, Stella and Vicky spotted the new face and made a beeline for him. They stood at the table, and just stared.

'Who are you?' Vicky asked.

'Are you a bad man? Because if you are? Albert will sort you out.' Buster was speechless, thinking these Brits are weird. They use kids to intimidate you.

'I'm a good guy, honest I am.'

'What's your name?'

'Buster Miss.'

'Bustermiss? That's a funny name.' The pair ran away giggling.

'Pete can you pinch me, I want to know if I'm dreaming, dead or alive. I'm totally confused?'

'No need to. You are alive and in good hands.'

Buster has now been introduced to most of the community. Just a few were left because of either not being able to leave their duties or asleep, due to the

circumstances. Mi reminded Pete to bring Buster to her surgery for a check. She left to make some preparations for it. Pete took him and left him with Mi.
'How long do you want him for Mi?'
'Twenty minutes. It is only the basics. He looks fit enough.'
'Ok, I'll see you both shortly,' and left for a wander.

'Can you sit on the couch please and remove your shirt?' He did so while she put on her stethoscope. She then went through the usual routine of breathe in breathe out and listened for any abnormalities at the front and back of his lungs, then asked him to stand up to attention while she asked him some questions.
'Have you had any problems with passing water or burning sensations while doing so, or any problems with your solids like bleeding for instance?'
'No Mam. I'm ok in that area.'
'Fine, could you drop your trousers and underpants for a final check?'
'Yes Mam.' He did so while she put on protective gloves.
'Can you lie back down on the couch please I'm just going to look at your penis, ok?'
'Yes Mam.' She took it in her hand and closely examined it for spots or blisters. She moved it about to check it all around and looked at the whole picture of this fine fit young man. He became erect. Oh dear she thought and flicked the swelling end with her finger.
'Ouch.' And it returned to a deflated droop.
'That's all good. Please dress and resume whatever it is you were doing.'
'Yes Mam, I'm sorry about my pecker getting excited. That's because you are so pretty, I just couldn't help it.'
'That's alright Buster and thank you for the compliment.' Pete was waiting for him outside as he closed the door behind him.
'Everything alright then?' he asked.
'Yep sure is. That sure is a fine lady you have there Pete.'

It was early afternoon and the Ark moved steadily south along the east coast of Africa towards Madagascar. Pete showed Buster to the bridge to meet

119

Albert who was at control. Buster walked in and immediately went to the forward window to look out and saw a farm, crops, animals, green trees and all different colours of flowers, then turned to look at Albert in his big leather chair.

'Sorry Sir, I should have acknowledged you first but I could not wait to see the ship. It's fantastic! Unbelievable! You can't see this from the canteen window.'

'Do you like it Buster? We like it and don't want it changed. So we have a problem and have to find a way to solve it.'

'What might that be Sir?'

'Well, at the moment, it is you and what to do with you. You have no passport and no money to get yourself back to your home wherever that might be. So why don't you start by telling us who you are and what were you doing held prisoner in that place?'

'I can only give you my name rank and number Sir.'

'But you were in civilian clothes. No passport or ID and no dog tags, so what are we to believe?'

Albert paused and then said. 'Put it this way, number one we saved your arse. Number two if we hadn't checked all the containers you would have been splattered about inside one. Number three, how can we repatriate you if you don't tell us anything and the icing on the cake: we are both, and I stand to be corrected, are fighting the same enemy, does that help you?'

'Yes Sir, it sure does, and I'm sorry for my stance. It's training Sir. We are drilled and drilled over and over again.'

'Right, can I take it you will answer a few questions?'

'Yes Sir.'

'Why were you, a military person in civilian clothes, captive in a transmitter station in Somalia?'

'The CIA was short of Russian speaking frontline experienced staff and asked the Pentagon to help out with Military personnel. I was seconded to pose as an out of work Russian mercenary in Mogadishu, I was dropped off by the US navy Sub Tina Turner in a small inflatable that I hid.'

'The what?' Albert and Pete asked.

120

'Yes Sir, the Tina Turner. It's a brand new Sub launched by the president. My job was to steal the codes for the access to their satellites and blow up the station. But you did that bit for us, Sir.'

'So what went wrong Buster?'

'My Russian wasn't good enough, Sir.'

'And how did you plan to get back?'

'The inflatable boat that I had hidden had a transmitter in it. I would activate it when I got back to it and put to sea, then the Sub would pick me up.'

'So how do you propose to be picked up now?'

'Well Sir, if I can use a transmitter of some description I can send a coded message to be picked up from you.'

'I don't see any alternative, do you Pete?'

'No, not really but the Yanks will want to ask us questions and will be interested in other things, won't they?'(He did not want to say anything about the communication set up etc in front of Buster)

'What other things Sir?' Albert quickly stemmed the situation.

'We just had a bone to pick with our common friends. They upset us and we upset them, that's simple enough don't you think?'

'That's fully understood Sir.'

'Well on that point, you can use the ships radio to tell *Tina Turner* to get her arse over here and pick you up.'

'Yes Sir.'

Marigold kept looking at the clock. It came around to three thirty pm, half an hour before it was time to wake up the love of her life, Ched.

'Greta I just need to pop to my cabin for something, I won't be long.'

'That's fine. They are all playing nicely, see you soon.' Brilliant, she thought. He will be woken a little earlier with a nice surprise. She let herself in and was careful to lock the door behind her this time. She could not wait to strip and snuggle up to him in bed. He was still fast asleep. She pulled back the thin white sheet that covered him and was very happy to see him totally naked in her bed where she hoped he would be every time, as soon as they could work it all out, but now is now she thought, and they say tomorrow never comes.

She kept looking at him while she removed her clothes and dropped them all to the floor, climbed in beside him and kissed him all over the top of his neck. He woke.

'Marigold you're wonderful.' He moved from his side, to lay on his back. She followed to be astride him, and felt for and held his stiffened cock to guide it into her.

'Don't move just be still and leave it to me.' Looking up at her, he moved his hands to the back of his head in a resting position and admired her beauty as she moved up and down on him. The more he saw the more he became determined to sort things out. She sensed him about to ejaculate, pulled off him quickly and held him in her hand to finish, letting it pump into the air several inches to let it land perfectly onto his stomach. She then lay on top of him, and they held each other passionately and whispered to him in between kisses.

'Ched I've missed you so much. My heart beats faster every time I see you.' She became emotional and tears came to her eyes.

'It's not right for us to be apart anymore. You and Millie have been cold for a long time. What can we do?'

'I've been thinking about it and Amy came to mind to help us. You know when we were caught together and we spoke to her and Albert, we both got the impression that there was a little bit of sympathy, for you more than me.' Marigold sat up on Ched, still astride him, wondering what he was getting to.

'Yes I did get that feeling.'

'Well you don't spend much time with Amy, so if you did do, and spoke to her about how much you miss me, but no further than that, don't mention to her about the problems you know between me and Millie, otherwise she'll think you are trying split us up for your own gain and that you had been privy to knowledge from me. Then in the meantime I am going to talk to Millie about our marriage. But please remember, I know things are not right between us but I still respect and will never hate her. So there will be no nastiness about it all and I know you would not think that way, I just wanted to let you know where I stand. Ok?' She fell back down onto him, her breasts firmly on his chest holding him, tightly pecking at his neck,

'Ched I do love you.'

'Marigold that's lovely, but please don't mark me at the moment. Let's try and sort this out without anyone being hurt, I love you too and I'm determined to sort it out.' She laid on him for a few minutes before he spoke again.

'I've got to go. Albert will need me on the bridge. I need a shower and something to eat.'

'Sorry Ched I don't want to let you go.'

'Hmm, it's strange my love but, who would have thought that a pair of red knickers would have led us together? Remember they were beside Antonio's bed and that I found them when I had to wake him up for work that day. It was when he and Jane first got together. Then I was trying to find the knickers rightful owner and thought they might be yours.'

'I remember that, but I couldn't get my head around the pair of red knickers.'

'You wouldn't have wanted to, knowing where they'd been.' They both laughed as they held each other and rolled on the bed.

'Ched you are so funny.'

'Come on I must go.'

Ched managed to get to the bridge for 17.00 hours to relieve Albert. Gunter was already there checking their position.

'Hi Ched, I bet you slept well.'

'I bloody well did, like a log, right through until the alarm went off at four. That's a very comfortable bed Albert, far better than mine.'

'Stop it Ched.' Ched smiled to himself and changed the subject.

'What's the score then, have we hit Madagascar yet?'

'No, and I hope we don't. We are slowing right down and taking it easy now. We're out of the danger area. Tomorrow we are to rendezvous with an American sub to offload our guest. Hopefully that will be the end of that little episode and we can get back to normal. Antonio is on first watch tonight. You may have to drag Zimbo away from Melanie for the second.'

'Where's Buster Crabbe sleeping tonight? Now Pete's back they will want to be on their own, so Millie will be back in our cabin with the children.'

'Buster Crabbe! Crikey that goes back some years. What was that series and films he was in? You know we should have a weekly canteen quiz on this sort of thing, could be quite entertaining.'

'You wouldn't be a match for me on that type of question. That's my forte, old films and their stars. Buster Crabbe, Clarence Linden "Buster" Crabbe, American athlete and actor. He was the only actor to play Tarzan, Flash Gordon and Buck Rodgers, the top three comic strip heroes of the 1930s. He achieved Olympic Bronze and Gold medals for men's freestyle swimming 1928 and 1932. I was a big fan of Tarzan.'

'You always amaze me Ched, when you just come out with knowledge like that straight out of the blue. Anyway we have a temporary bed because it should only be for tonight. He is sleeping in one of the sick bay beds. In fact I don't know why we didn't put him there last night.'

'I didn't mind him sleeping in my bed Albert.'

'The way we keep bumping into people we need a permanent guest room,' said Ched. 'Right I'll leave you to it I'm going to have a beer.'

'Have one for me while you are there.'

9. BIG BROTHER

Pete relieved Ched at 02.00 hours and Ched was surprised to see him because Albert forgot to mention it. He was expecting to go through until 06.00 hours when Albert would be back, Gunter was not needed and went to his cabin at midnight.

'Pete, I wasn't expecting you here. Shouldn't you be snuggled up to your lovely young wife after the risk you've been through? I'm alright here until Albert relieves me at six.'

'No, I'm fine Ched. You get back to Millie, you and Gunter did a very long stint yesterday and last night. It was much appreciated by all, and for the Ark to be in the right place at the right time to get us back, that's teamwork.'

'Thanks Pete, that's good of you. Gunter's set the course, there's no change, so see you tomorrow.'

'Night Ched,'

Ched went off to his cabin, quite happy. He let himself in very quietly so he wouldn't disturb Millie and the children then changed into his pyjamas. Since it became a mutual understanding by default, he carefully got in bed beside, yet apart from Millie. Because he had had a very restful day he just laid on his back thinking things over while Millie was asleep but restless. Ched thought she must be dreaming, I'll try and dream as well and get some sleep, but he could not because Millie started saying things in her sleep, mumbled at first but then increasing in clarity.

'Pete,' pause, 'Pete.' This continued for a while making Ched think, why is she calling his name? Her dream had stopped and she was quiet and it wasn't long before Ched was asleep too. Millie was long gone to the farm by the time Ched woke and when he finally came round, he remembered Millie and her dream and wondered about it. Is something going on like I thought there was with Antonio? Hmm, I should do a bit of investigation see what, if anything is going on.

10.00 hours and a submarine had appeared and moved parallel with the Ark. Albert called Ched, Gunter and Pete to the bridge, where they were all assembled very quickly.

'I haven't called for Buster to be here yet because I wanted to discuss a few things with you first. Now during the past couple of days things have moved rapidly. All of a sudden we are in the middle of an operation that the Yanks were trying to deal with. They cocked up and unbeknown to us we did part of their job for them, in our own little way. What they do not know is that we have access to the rogue satellites, which by all accounts is the real thing they are after. They can't identify them, and the Yanks would not be very popular if they knocked out a Chinese satellite or anyone else's by mistake. They need positive ID of the rogue satellites. Now they will not understand why we took the risk to blow up that communication post. The thing that is really going to bug them is how the fuck we did it, how we knew where to hit and what did we do it with. They won't believe us when we tell them we just had two home-made crossbows. Now what I want to happen is to repatriate Buster and let them submerge into their own world and leave us alone to get on with ours, here where we want to be. If that happens fantastic but I doubt it. So, hopefully we just say goodbye to Buster and nothing else. Are we alright with that?'

'It sounds good sense to me, what about you two?' asked Ched.

'Albert's right, we don't want a ship full of Yanks sniffing around do we? Let's send the young chap on his way and then we can fuck off P.D.Q.,' said Pete.

Gunter frowned. 'What's P.D.Q.?

'Pretty Damned Quick! Pete smiled.

'In that case then we'd better get Buster up here to communicate with Tina Turner so she can take him onboard A.S.A.P.' Albert continued.

'Albert, what on earth has Tina Turner got to do with it am I missing something?'

'Sorry Ched, that's the name of the American sub.'

'You are joking?'

'Ched can you go and find Buster Crabbe and get him up here?'

'Yes Ming.' Ched replied. Albert and Ched laughed, Gunter and Pete did not understand why.

'Albert what's that all about?' asked Pete.

'It goes back to Flash Gordon and comic book heroes. Ched is very knowledgeable on the subject.' 'Oh.' Pete felt like yawning.

'Good morning Albert Sir.'

'There's your sub. We'll lower you in the inflatable with Pete and he'll ferry you over. Is that Ok?' 'Yes Sir. I just want to thank you all for saving my life and the hospitality you have given me and when I was told I was in good hands, I was in the best hands in the world. Thank you all. I wish I could be part of your crew, good luck to you all.' Pete escorted him to where Magnus was waiting to lower him over the side. All the community were there at various positions to view the departure of this brave and fortunate young man. Millie, Antonio and Zimbo watched from the Bow farm, Amy, Mi, Marigold, Patricia, Melanie, Greta and children with those on the bridge. In the short time that he was on the Ark, those that had the opportunity to meet him and speak to him had respected and liked Buster. Magnus lifted the inflatable with its occupants over the side and into the water, and it was soon on its way. Pete and Buster bobbed across the waves to the submarine where the Commander of the sub and Buster's superior were waiting to receive them. A line was thrown to the inflatable to secure it allowing Buster onto an access ladder to climb onto the vessel. Pete shook his hand.

'Good luck Buster.'

'And to you Pete, thank you again. See you around.' He jumped to the ladder. Pete released the line and piloted back to the Ark. He turned to look back and watched the men disappear inside the sub, by the time Pete was being lifted back out of the water and onto the Ark the submarine's propulsion had moved it quickly away.

Back onboard Albert was in sail mode.

'Let's get the sails up to catch this nice warm breeze that's coming from the coast of Africa while we can. And get ourselves tucked away somewhere south of Madagascar.' The men did not hesitate at the request for sail power. The sails were raised from their housings and positioned to get maximum effect from the light wind available pushing the Ark to speeds of twelve knots in record time. Gradually they moved along the east Africa coast, passed by the capital of Somalia, Mogadishu, over the equator then moving further away from the coast southwards to pass Kenya and its capital Mombasa to Tanzania and Pemba Island. Then they sped onwards to Zanzibar and Mafia Island between them and the east coast of mid Africa. Next the Comoros Islands, an archipelago at the northern entrance to the Mozambique Channel, the area of sea between Mozambique East Africa and Madagascar, a large island in the Indian Ocean with the Tropic of Capricorn passing through its southern tip. They sailed out of the channel and changed course eastwards, to a place on the chart about twenty miles south of the town of Taolagnaro at the foot of Madagascar where they could anchor for their winter in the southern hemisphere's summer.

Onboard the submarine USS Tina Turner Buster was taken to a room to be debriefed by his senior from the CIA who congratulated him and shook his hand.

'Well done for a very successful operation. Our reports are that you completely destroyed the site. It will be some time before they will be able to set up again. Now tell me how you managed it Buster?'

'Sir, I didn't. It was two guys from the Royal Marines. They saved my arse, Sir.'

'The Royal Marines! I thought it was all Euro Marines or some shit like that now. No one told me that they would be involved, are you sure?'

'Yes Sir, they operate undercover from that old oil tanker posing as some sort of hippie type community with their women and children. It's some set up they've got. They are completely self-sufficient including fuelling the turbines, to using the decks as farmland to produce all their food. Those Brits are sure clever and cunning. It seems they can stay at sea for years doing operations wherever they are required.'

128

'That's amazing Buster I need to get on to the Pentagon to find out from MI5 in London about their outfit. It must be very secret. In the meantime give me a detailed report on everything, from the day you landed in Somalia, to the boarding of that ship and then an even more detailed report on all you saw, the people you spoke to and what they have told you. Is that clear?'
'Yes Sir, right away Sir.'

Buster was left to make out his report while the CIA man went to the sub's Commander to make some communications with the Pentagon.
'Commander I need to send a coded message to the Pentagon urgently.'
'Go right ahead Chief you know where to go.' Some hours later he had a reply.

> Checked with London and Brussels.
> Nothing is known of an outfit of Euro
> Marines operating as you described.
> Investigate. You have the sub and crew at
> your disposal. Permission granted from the
> White House.
> Signed.
> The President

'Commander can you find that oil tanker we rendezvoused with earlier, we need to board it and find out what the hell they are up to?'
'Why sure. They were heading south. We'll catch them in no time.' The sub was soon behind the Ark and followed it keeping well out of sight, just tracking to see where it was heading. The CIA Chief got frustrated with this.
'Where the fuck are they going? At this rate they'll be in the Antarctic.'
'We can fire a torpedo into them to stop them if you want,' said the Commander facetiously. The Chief took it seriously.
'No, I need to talk to live people not dead ones. Just keep tailing them. They must stop and anchor soon.' The tailing went on for the full remainder of the trip to the Ark's anchorage place just south of Madagascar. The CIA chief

was curious why they would stop there and immediately communicated with the Pentagon to ask what operations where going on in Madagascar. The reply was:

No known operations in Madagascar.

The Ark had settled to organising themselves for their winter stay, doing the things they enjoy; just wanting to be left alone to get on with their lives as any normal people would. The sub stayed at a distance, making sure the Ark's crew were unaware of them for the time being while they decided on how to tackle the situation. Buster was hoping for a period of leave, but the Chief called on his help. He wanted him to communicate with the Captain of the oil tanker and gain access to them without any hostilities. Buster agreed to give it a go and the sub surfaced very close to the Ark then sent a radio message to Albert. Buster and the CIA Chief set out a plan to board the Ark to meet the Royal Marines to try and find out diplomatically what they were all about, but the Chief did not tell Buster that while they talked to Albert and co., a team of US Navy Seals would secretly board the Ark and take a closer look at everything.

'Albert of the Ark come in please this is a message from Buster on the submarine USS Tina Turner. Please acknowledge.' Albert was in the distillery with Jane when Pete called him on the shortwave.

'Albert, Pete here, come in please.'

'Yes Pete, what is it?'

'Tina Turner has turned up and Buster wants to talk with you.' Just then Antonio called Albert on the short wave.

'Albert, that sub is right alongside us with armed personnel on the tower.'

'OK, tell Magnus to switch the electric fence on immediately and take it as a defence drill, action stations!'

'Yes Albert, right away.'

'Albert,' Jane jumped in. 'You're not seriously thinking of taking on the US Navy? You must be mad?'

'Jane, calm down. I'm not taking them on, I just don't want them running about this ship and defence is our first option, lets see what they want.'

'Sorry Albert, I hate these situations, I just want to be at peace and not bothered by anyone.'

'That was all Amy and I ever wanted Jane but unfortunately life hasn't treated any of us like that has it? Could you go and prepare the women, just as a precautionary measure, so that I can concentrate on the present issue. I need to talk it over with Pete on how we tackle it.'

'Yes Albert, give us half an hour and I'll have it explained to them.'

'Pete I'm on my way to the bridge, I'll see you there in five minutes.'

'Albert here Buster. Why has the US Navy parked their sub next the Ark? We don't need anything. We are quite happy just being left alone. Now tell your Commander to please go away and leave us in peace. Is that understood?'

'Yes Sir.'

'Pete I have a strong feeling that big brother won't take no for an answer and that they'll want to board the ship. What do you think?'

'I agree but how can we do it diplomatically and trust them.'

'Number one, I agree in diplomacy, number two, I don't trust them. So where does that leave us?' The ships radio received another message,

'Albert Buster Manta here, please come in? My Chief would like to meet you to thank you personally for saving my life and for doing my job. It won't take up much of your time.'

'Albert, that sub has not tracked and followed us here several thousand miles just to tell us we are jolly good fellows.'

'No Pete, I couldn't agree more.'

'Buster, does that mean he will give us the Congressional Medal of Honour and he just happened to have them on his person to give us, travelling thousands of miles for that purpose?'

'Did you hear that Chief?'

'Of course I heard the Limey Bastards! Commander I order you to get the Navy Seals to board that fucking thing.' The radio was still on and both Albert and Pete heard the order.

'Magnus is that fence switched on?'

131

'Yes Albert.'

'Jane is everyone back to the upper decks and do they know what's going on?'

'Yes Albert.'

'Thank you.'

'Right Pete let's see what happens next.'

The commander was hesitant to send armed US Navy Seals to board the Ark and spoke out.

'Chief I know you have orders to investigate what's going on with that outfit, but there are women and children onboard, and apart from that, they have posed no threat to us in any way or form. In fact they've done the opposite by doing your job for you, with the bonus of saving your man.'

'I don't give a fuck about my *man* or doing my job for *me.* I want to know how they operate, how they pinpointed that target, put it out of action and what's in it for them.'

'Well I'll be making a full report and show my objection to your actions and if anyone is injured or killed from either side I will hold you personally responsible. Is that fully understood Chief?'

'Yes, now get those fucking men on that ship and take it.'

Buster heard it all and was mortified at the comments and action that the CIA Chief was about to take against the Ark and had to speak out.

'Sir, I protest at this line of action. They are good people on that ship and just want to be left alone.'

'You shut the fuck up! Commander, have those men left yet?'

'Navy Seals, Commander here. This is my order: Board the ship and take control. Do not hurt, injure, maim or kill anyone. Is that fully understood?'

'Fucking hell Sir, how do we do that? That wasn't in the training. We only know how to blow things up and kill.' The Commander was exasperated by the response from the squad leader and poured out his contempt to the CIA Chief.

'You are a fucking moron. I am disgusted with your mentality and did you hear that from the squad leader? They only know how cause explosions and kill. What is it with you? Do you want brownie points at the Pentagon by taking an easy target, you're a dumb shit!'

'Navy seals' this is the Commander have you left yet?' he screamed in anger. 'Yes Sir, we're on our way.' In broad daylight four US Navy Seals' fired grappling hooks over the side of the Ark. Antonio watching the action from his view point immediately informed Albert on the short wave. Albert gave Magnus the order to cut the power on the electric fence but be ready to put it back on. Pete smiled.

'You have a sadistic side to you Albert,' he said.

'Magnus,' Albert called again, 'Which control is for the starboard side thrusters. We haven't used them yet have we?'

'No we haven't. They are the buttons on the right next to the main control. But don't forget we have the bow anchor down.'

The four Navy Seals pulled on their ropes and climbed up the side. Albert timed them. He knew how long it would take a young Royal Marine to scale the shear height. Five seconds before they should be at the top he called Magnus.

'Switch power on Magnus,' The shock to the four men was so unexpected they fell into the sea between the sub and the Ark which dwarfed the sub. Swimming like hell to get back on the sub to safety they realised the Ark was getting closer to the sub which made them frantic. The four entered the hatch just as the Ark hit the side of Tina Turner. It moved steadily against her and made her tilt and unstable. It threw her crew and company into disarray, panic was suddenly rife.

'What the fuck's going on?' shouted the CIA Chief.

'This is your fucking fault *Dick Head.* 'You just don't understand diplomacy do you? Those men on that ship, aren't stupid, they're the sort I want with me, not power crazy twats like you.'

Albert cut the side thrusters. He knew if he went too far he would put the sub on its side and do more damage than he could justify. He switched on the port side thrusters and pulled away from the sub and allowed it to recover to an upright position, to the relief of its occupants. The sub Commander called for two duty guards and instructed them to arrest the CIA Chief on charge of putting US military personnel and others at unnecessary risk of injury and possible death, also putting in danger of damage to the United States Governments Property.

'You have made a big mistake here Commander. The orders come to me from the Pentagon. They will court marshal you for this.'

'Please take him away?'

'Yes Sir.'

'Lieutenant Manta,' the Commander addressed him.

'Let's cut out all the formalities while we are together from now on. Sit down and let us have a chat and see if we can come up with a sensible solution that satisfies all.'

'It's a bit quiet on that sub at the moment Albert. Do you think they're changing their underpants?'

'It could be Pete. Just keep a watch out for the white flag waving about. I think they'll try proper diplomacy next. It is obvious they want something we've got and they can't go home empty-handed. So how far do we go?'

'We could come clean and say this is what we have and how we got it, take it away and leave us alone. But that doesn't guarantee any advance on our safety in the future. The thing that I think at present is that whoever is making the decisions on that sub is not making the right ones. So if they're going back to diplomacy, then I would ask to speak to someone superior, make them bring someone from the States as a first, *to parlez'* as they say. That would give us a little time to discuss our situation properly, because these pricks won't go away.'

'Yes Pete I think you're right and we need to talk to all the others to let them know what's going on.'

'Buster.'

'Yes Sir, Commander.'

'Now tell me about these men on the tanker they call the Ark. How old are they?'

'That's a difficult one Sir. They are very fit. I would say that Albert must be fifty or more. He's the Captain although no one calls him that, it's just Albert. The other main man is Pete; he is younger probably in his mid forties, both very experienced military men. Then there is a young guy called Antonio who was waiting to pick us up just off the coast. He's in his early twenties. That leaves other crew members and many women and children. They live in a well organised community and want for nothing it's pleasant to be there. They made me so welcome that I felt at home.'

'So where does the Royal Marines come into it?'

'Well Sir, from what I can remember, that night when we got back to the ship we went straight to the canteen and had some drinks while a lady made some food for us. I was exhausted from my ordeal and trying to take it all in. The two guys, Albert and Pete, were congratulating themselves on a successful mission thanking the Royal Marines for their training, so I took it that they were Royal Marines.'

'What weaponry did they have?'

'They had an array of automatics, hand grenades. Each had a crossbow strapped to their backs. They must have used plastics and timed detonators to blow the target. They seemed to handle the part I remember like clockwork.'

'Yes, that sounds like Royal Marines, but the thing that puzzles me is their age. They should be retired not still doing missions, so there must be more to this than meets the eye. How can we have a proper meeting with them without showing the big brother tactics that your CIA chief tried and fucked up? Because now we are not trusted.'

'I can only radio them and try to explain the problem we've had with the Chief, tell them he's locked up under your orders Commander. But they will still say they want to be left alone and I don't blame them.'

'Call them and talk to the Captain and then introduce me and I will see if I can get their respect.'

135

'Yes Sir….Albert of the Ark come in please. This is Buster onboard the USS Tina Turner.'

'I hear you Buster and before you say any more, I will say that I'm very disappointed in the mentality of your superior to order personnel to try and board the Ark without our permission. We know they managed to re-board the sub. They are lucky to be alive and I apologise if any suffered injury. Now what is it?'

'Albert Sir, the Chief that gave those orders has been locked up and the only navy seal injury was their pride. Can I pass you over to the Naval Commander of the sub who would like to talk to you.'

'Go ahead Buster, put him on.'

'Captain Albert, I'm Commander Grey of the United States Navy. Please accept my apologies for the way the situation was handled. I'm embarrassed at the disrespect for life and limb that the CIA Chief showed, especially against someone who had saved one of his men. How can we meet and talk about what is obviously a common enemy and see a way forward to benefit us both?'

'I'm pleased to hear that from you Commander. Apologies accepted but before we talk, I need to know what authority you have to make any decisions, when you have just locked up the person you were taking orders from. As I see it your duty is to your sub, those who sail in her and to the United States Government, and that is no disrespect to you. We would be honoured to have you and Buster, join us on the Ark for some hospitality food and drinks, but that's as far as it goes at present.'

'Thank you for the invitation. We would be delighted to attend. Just give me a time and the method of access and we'll be there.'

'At 1800hrs a side ladder will be lowered. You'll need the means to get to it. After you have boarded the Ark, it will then be raised, and the security circle we have will be in place throughout your visit.'

'Understood Captain Albert, we look forward to meeting up with you.'

Later Albert, Amy, Pete and Mi greeted the Commander and Buster. The rest of the males and some females were acting and posing as guards, each carrying a side arm, to show organised strength.

'Welcome onboard the Ark Commander. This is Amy, my wife, Pete and his wife Mi.'

'Hi Commander and Buster nice to see you again.' Mi blurted out with a big smile to everyone's amazement.

'Sorry,' she said, looking embarrassed. Pete thought that she looked really especially pleased to see Buster.

'Thank you for the invitation. This is an unusual experience for me. My wife would have loved to be here now unfortunately the US Navy does not cater for wives and family onboard in any situation other than home base. Your government look after you very well while you do your operations.'

'Commander please, as I said let's not talk shop. This is a social visit for us and as you can see, although a farming community, we are well protected. So please enjoy these moments with us. I'm sure you will be delighted with our hospitality,' Albert replied as they all strolled to the canteen.

A table had been prepared for the six of them and pre-dinner drinks were offered and taken followed by a formal dinner. Albert's theory was that if he kept the Commander impressed with the civility, good food and wine and talking rubbish, hopefully he would go away contented. The evening went well, past experiences were exchanged, but nothing was divulged about the present situation. There were two people in the group who couldn't help making quick glances at each other, well aware of their mutual attraction. Although not too obvious to the others, it was very clear to them a bond was growing, just through smiles. The evening came to an end and as the guests had boarded the Ark, they left in the same manner. Goodbyes were exchanged, hands shaken, and very nice to meet you Commander etc., Mi could not help herself from planting a rapid peck on Buster's cheek and then shaking his hand and saying, not goodbye but, 'See you.'

The next day at breakfast the Commander pondered on what he had seen the previous evening and began to weigh up the situation in his own mind. He came to the conclusion that these guys were ex Royal Marines who were on their own mission, but could be very useful to the US Government if they could be coerced and introduced to the right people. It could also be good for him under the circumstances, what with the ignorant CIA Chief and possible repercussions that may not work in the Commander's defence. He thought about what stood in his way and what he needed to do to bring this all together. He needed a strategy; what to tell the CIA about their man's whereabouts and a period of time to stay along side the Ark and get more friendly with them, even perhaps inviting them onboard the sub, showing them around and entertaining. Buster arrived for his breakfast and spoke to the Commander.

'Good morning Sir, (saluting.) May I join you for breakfast?'

'Yes Lieutenant, you may. Sit down and as I said before cut out the formalities please. At the moment it's boring me.'

'Yes Sir.'

'Now Buster you seem to get on very well with the people on the Ark. What's your real gut feeling about them?'

'They are very good people, as I've said before, and I feel comfortable in their company. Nothing fazes them. They tackle life in a way that I've not seen before. They survive very well on their Ark. It's well organised. But if they are not funded by a European government or a cavalier London MI5, then what are they up to and who has funded them?'

'Yes Buster there are a lot of unanswered questions and the only way to get those answers is to do it little by little with diplomacy and tact, not by the method your no-brains Chief took which was destructive and lost trust. We achieved more in one night and it was enjoyable too, than he would achieve in a decade.'

'Yes Sir, I can see that, but you have a few problems in being able to maintain such a situation because the CIA have full command over this sub and you.'

'This is where I need your help Buster. I know it seems strange for a Commander of a sub to ask a Lieutenant in the US Army for help in such a

138

matter, but at the end of the day I'm only on hire to the CIA. If we turn back home now without some answers about why the Chief was locked up, questions will be asked by men in positions with the same mentality as him. I'll lose my command and pension. Who knows where you and I will end up?'

'I don't understand how can I help? I was hoping for some leave time back home. I'm lucky to be alive, so please don't ask me to do anything to damage the wellbeing of those people on the Ark.'

'No Buster, nothing like that. I need to make time so that we can stay here and improve our relationship with the Ark. The first problem is the CIA chief in custody here. Would you back me up in telling the Chief's seniors that he has come down with a fever and is mentally unstable at present in the hands of medics? And that we are continuing in our diplomatic methods in talking to the professional people responsible for the successful raid on the Russian Mafia. Then we can say we are making ground and we just need more time to be granted, probably a couple of weeks I think should be enough. What do you think, could you relay that to them? We need to sing from the same hymn sheet, do you understand?'

'It sounds reasonable but when it comes to a hearing back in the States, it's going to be mighty difficult to explain things.'

'That depends on how successful we are with getting the information we need from the Ark for a mission accomplished. It could be good for your career.'

'I don't know Sir. I won't deceive those good people in any way. I would rather put our cards on the table and tell them straight Sir.'

'Yes I agree Buster. But how are you going to be in such a position of trust to be able to sit around a table to lay your cards down?'

'I see what you mean Sir. Let me give it some thought. Can I meet you at lunchtime Sir for my decision?'

'Certainly Buster, but if we have communications to attend to I will expect a rapid response.'

'Yes Sir, of course.'

Buster had a huge dilemma and spent the morning going through the options. His first thought was the lovely lady Mi, but she is married to one of the guys,

Pete, who saved him. Secondly he did not want them to be harmed or changed in any way, which if the Chief had succeeded in his assault, who knows what the consequences would have been. Thirdly, if they just went away and left them alone, which is what they wanted on the Ark, the CIA would not be satisfied with that, as long as they have something the CIA want. That would be big trouble.

'Shit,' he said to himself, 'why is life so difficult?' He lay on his bunk still turning all this in his mind when a message came through to him from the Commander.

'Please report to communications room immediately.'

'Shit! Shit! Shit!' Buster repeated to himself, knowing exactly what he must do, but didn't like it one bit.

Buster entered the communications room where the Commander was alongside an operator. The Commander explained that they had a request to communicate with the Chief.

'Sir have you answered them?'

'No, I was waiting your response to our discussion, and by the way, I didn't want to mention it but it was you who failed your mission, so don't you think you should put in an effort to gain some good points for yourself?'

'OK, I'll do it, Sir. If you would give your answer to them first I will confirm the situation.' The Commander dictated his message to the operator which was sent automatically coded. As expected, a further request for confirmation from their field operative, Buster Manta, was required. He complied, and they were committed.

'That's it Buster it's down to us now, either way. Let's go get some strong coffee and wait for approval. Let's think positive.'

The Commander was a shrewd man and knew that the CIA or the Pentagon would not want them to pull away from the situation when they said they were gaining ground. The CIA was satisfied that the Ark had information on it and the capability to do destructive operations and by all accounts, was ungoverned. The approval followed within twenty minutes while they were

140

still sipping their coffees. The Commander was delighted, Buster not so, still very apprehensive about the task ahead.

'Right Buster that's it. We have the go ahead for two weeks to find out how they operate and report back to the Pentagon. Now they, the top boys, are involved with the operation, it must have gone over budget. We need to plan how we can get a regular day-to-day communication going with the Ark. Can you think of anything they need we could offer them, like whisky, brandy, cigarettes, chocolate or ladies nylons/tights you know?'

'Commander how come a United States Seawolf Class Attack Submarine has ladies' tights in its stores?'

'Its policy these days, we have to cater for all male and female and others. Please don't ask me to explain further.'

'The only thing I can think of that they might want is good coffee and tea, but I don't think they will take a gift. They will see it as a bribe. You're not dealing with some tribe in downtown New York where things only get done by bribes. It's a whole new ball game now. I think you're better off just saying come on over and see what a fine sub we have here and see our technology. Anyone who wants to be on top of military technology would not be able to resist having a chance to see the world's best war machine.'

'Yes I can see where you are coming from. We mustn't take them for idiots, falling into the same category as your Chief. We will do as we said and invite Albert and whoever over for a visit and tour if they would like, against all regulations, but what the hell, I was already past that stage when I locked up your man and lied about his illness. I'll feel better with that scenario and I could still give them some coffee and tea anyway.'

'So please Sir, a requisition for as much ground coffee and other beverages as you can spare, with your permission Sir, then I'll contact Albert.'

'Granted Lieutenant. We now have a mission to accomplish. Let's get on with it.'

'Yes Sir,' he replied in military fashion, stood up, saluted and marched away from the meeting, full of the joys of spring! He was a man of at least two missions, one of them more personal than official.

10. THE BASIC THINGS

'Albert of the Ark, Buster here, do you read me? Come in please?'

'Gunter here Buster, Albert's busy at the moment. Can I help you?'

'Yes Gunter, could you ask Albert to contact me when he has the time. We would like to give him and anyone else who's interested, a tour of the most advanced submarine in the world. We have two weeks to kill before we leave to go home.'

'OK Buster I will pass on that message.' The nature of communications between the Ark and the sub was purposely made nonchalant in the hope that it would delay things and the sub would run out of time, leaving the Ark alone. That was the theory but Buster was persistent, and he kept calling. Albert gave in two days later.

'Buster, Albert here. Sorry for not responding sooner. I've been very busy making a new batch of "Ark's Best Bitter" and some of our "Flash Spirit." It's a delicate process to get it right. Gunter tells me we have an invite to tour your submarine. I've asked our people and some of them would be delighted, including myself. So organise it as you wish and we will ferry ourselves across to you. It may be a couple of separate trips to accommodate everybody, just let me know when.'

Buster was delighted with the reply.

'Yes!' he said as he punched air.

The first group to see the sub was Albert, Gunter, Ched and Mi, leaving enough skilled men on the ark capable of defending it with the added electric fence. The Commander had drilled his crew on how to accept the visitors to make sure it went without any hitches and their visit was relaxed and enjoyable. Albert and the Commander took the lead, with Gunter and Ched in between, followed by Buster who escorted Mi. She did not seem particularly interested in the submarine. The Commander explained the basic things about the sub to Albert. He told them that the Navy began construction of Seawolf class submarines in 1989. They were designed to be extremely quiet, fast and well armed. It is a multi-mission vessel capable of search and destroying enemy submarines and surface ships and to fire missiles in support of other forces. Other missions range from intelligence gathering and delivery of "special forces" to anywhere in the world. That is the roll of U.S. nuclear attack submarines.

The group left and thanks all around were exchanged, only to be replaced by the next tour which consisted of Pete, Magnus, Jane and Antonio. Magnus and Pete took a serious look at the technology asking questions that had guarded replies.

'We are not at liberty to answer that question Sir.'

'Oh, yes of course, we understand.' While the Commander stayed with Pete and Magnus, he repeated his speech that he gave Albert about the submarine's basic facts. Buster escorted Jane and Antonio, and asked them questions about relationships on the Ark, its history and why they operated in the way they did.

'That is the way we wanted it to be. It's our form of harmony for our life,' Jane replied. While Antonio and Jane smiled at each other, Buster could not resist asking them why they were involved in missions against the Russian Mafia.

'Buster,' Jane answered. 'We protect the Ark, our home, against anyone who is a threat. How we do that you will need to ask Albert, so please don't try to get information through the back door. If you are straight with him, he will be straight with you. That's the basic thing you must remember when dealing with the Ark. I will not say anymore than that. Is that understood?'

'Yes Mam, I'm sorry, it's a problem for the Commander and me at the moment. We are under pressure from the Pentagon to find out why and how you were able to pinpoint a target, blow it up as if it was your daytime job and walk away. We have been trying to do that for months and with all the weight and technology of the US Government behind us.'

'Well it seems to me that you have been wasting US tax payer money,' came Jane's quick-fire reply.

'You know Jane I really envy you all on the Ark. You are free to do as you wish, uncontrolled by any government, but it seems like I'm going to have to confront Albert himself. How I will get that opportunity I just don't know.'
'Best of luck Buster.'
The four returned to the Ark with Magnus boring Pete with high-tech details about the sub. On the way back Jane commented to Antonio about Buster's dilemma saying what a nice chap he was. He immediately got the wrong end of the stick.
'Jane do you like him, the American, you know, fancy him?'
'Antonio, don't be silly. No I don't fancy him. I'm saying he has a good character, he seems like a good person.'
'Oh, sorry, I understand now.'

The two weeks were almost up and the Commander was taking in the cost of his failure of not being able to get any information from the Ark to report back to the Pentagon and put them, the Commander and Buster in some good light to their superiors. Buster was frustrated in being cooped up in the submarine and forever thinking of Mi. He thought he must do something before leaving this all behind. An idea came to him; He wanted to walk around the Ark, through the fields and the farm to get some fresh country air full of fragrances from the various grasses combined with the aromas from the herb garden before he left, Albert surely wouldn't deny me that pleasure? He thought.
'Albert, Buster here. Come in please. Can we speak before we leave you?'
'Pete here Buster, give me ten minutes and I'll get Albert for you.'
'OK.'
'Yes Buster. What can I do for you?'
'Albert Sir, we will have to leave you tomorrow, and I would like to do one thing before we go. I want to spend a few hours walking and looking at that beautiful prime farmland you've created that will always be in the middle of nowhere, I wish I could be there with you. Would you grant me that pleasure, to walk your land?'

144

'Yes Buster of course. Just let me know the time you want to board and it will be arranged.'
'Thank you Sir.'

Shortly after breakfast the day the sub was due to leave the Ark, Buster boarded and went on his walkabout. His first stop was the huge Biome greenhouse to see what was growing in there. To his amazement there were cucumbers, several varieties of tomato, peppers and chillies, lettuce, herbs and melons. Then he went to the foredeck which led through the fields of crops, marked out by fences with mature hedgerows. He caught a glimpse of sparrows flitting about, bees working away doing their stuff like nothing else on earth. Albert saw him from the bridge and felt for him. He left the bridge to join him meeting at the Bow farm where Millie, Antonio and Zimbo were busy tending to the animals, like any farmers would be toiling, elsewhere in the world.
'Hi Buster, nice to see you, are you interested in farming?'
'Yes Millie, I think it's fantastic what you have all done. I love it. It's a shame I have to leave you all later today.'
'Ah Buster, that is a shame. You leave that silly job you've got and come and join us. I'm sure we'll find someone to look after you.'
'That would be good but I cannot see it happening. Thank you for your kind words, I will remember you all.' Albert appeared and caught some of the conversation.
'Are you from a farming background Buster?' Albert asked.
'Yes Sir, Montana, it's a very fertile and beautiful State, cold in the winter and warm in the summer.'
'Just think, you'll be there in a couple of weeks at the most. You will forget the trauma you've been through. You're a fit and tough lad. You'll survive.'
'Yes Albert.'
Albert noticed he dropped the Sir.
'That's better Buster now we are on the same level.'
'What I was going to say was that I don't think they will let me go home because of the situation we are in, the Commander overruled the CIA Chief

and locked him up telling the Pentagon he went down with a fever and we were conducting the case ourselves and making progress. This gave us some time to get some snippet of sound information about how you do better than the whole of the US defence force.'

'Oh I see, so what happens if you go home empty handed?'

'An investigation and with the CIA having so much power these days it all tends to go in their favour, no matter what, so it will be a reduction in rank for the Commander, losing his pension. They will send me on another even more dangerous mission and you know what that means.'

'I understand Buster and I appreciate you telling me of your predicament. You could resign from your post if that's possible, pull out some stress disorder. It happens all the time these days in active military service personnel, some genuine, some not. I'm sure the community would accept you here with us if you had no wish to return to the outside world.'

'Thank you Albert, that's very decent of you and I would take that offer if my circumstances allowed me the choice, but they do not and I have to be realistic and do the best I can in the situation I am in.'

'Buster, this snippet of information you need to justify the Commander's and your actions, how little would satisfy the hungry jaws of the CIA or Pentagon?'

'It's the rogue satellites. We can't pick them up. The only way they can be destroyed at the moment is to launch a missile from the space lab, which is a joint project between the US, Russia and others. So to get an agreement to chase them around the world is out of the question. Practically, orbiting at incredible speeds with a million to one chance of collecting or destroying one of these satellites is something else, and the budgets don't stretch that far. So it's back to the foot soldiers.'

'It's strange Buster, even with all the modern technology that billions in various currencies have been spent on, the basic things still rely on humans to provide the answers. We still grow and produce food by hard toil. We still fight our wars and skirmishes in the same basic ways throughout humanity, by elimination of the enemy. It's just the tools are different.'

146

Strolling back together exchanging their views on things Albert was busy thinking of a solution to Buster and the Commander's problem. Albert had already been told by Pete that he had located the full network of sites throughout the world and wondered if he should pass it on.

'Buster, I tell you what I'll do. It's obvious to you that we have a common enemy, but we have more information than you on him, so I will have a meeting with my defence committee to see if we can help you out. You may stay onboard and enjoy your time here. I'm sure you'll be welcomed by everyone. Shall I see you in the canteen at 1600 hrs?'

'You bet, Albert.'

Albert contacted the defence team, and they met in the canteen. He explained the Americans had a dilemma. He also explained that whatever information they passed to them about the Mafia, they would probably still be a target, but on the plus side in meant they had the Americans as an ally, still the most powerful nation on the planet. The consensus was to cooperate with them and to give a detailed grid reference of the places they knew the Mafia operated from. Pete went off to the communications room and printed the information, rather than sending anything electronically.

Mi asked Albert if Buster was still on the ship.

'Yes he is, wandering about the fields somewhere. If you go to the bridge you will probably spot him.'

'Thank you Albert, I would just like to say goodbye. I think once he has the information they will go away and leave us alone, but he is a good young man. Tell Pete I've gone to find him to say goodbye, he will understand.'

'That's saved me going to find him. Please bring him back to the canteen Mi, and we will give him a send off.'

'Hi Buster,'

'Mi, I didn't expect to see you. It must be a special trip because I know you're not the farming type, which means from the smiles I've had, you've come to see me. I'm pleased but I don't want to cause any conflict between you and

Pete. He is a man that you would not want to be on the wrong side of, along with Albert. I wouldn't do anything to upset them, even though I like you so much.'

'That's why I came here to see you, because I like you as well, but I also like Pete and I love being here on the Ark. It's as good as paradise gets. Don't worry about any problems you think you might cause. Pete is not a jealous man. What he and Albert have been through in their lives they don't have time to be jealous. They are glad to be alive and their women are proud of them. We all live in harmony. Albert has asked me to bring you to the canteen for a final meeting before you have to leave us.'

'Yes sure, let's go.' She grabbed his arm with both of hers snuggling to him with affection as though they had known each other for a long time, then she lead him towards the upper decks.

'You know this is like crazy Mi. How can this work? I'm going back home and I don't know what to or where I will be posted. I've met a community I want to be with, especially you. You're married to a top Royal Marine. I'm sorry I'm struggling to work this out.' She turned to face him reached and up put her arms around his neck and kissed him hard on the lips.

'You will just have to come back and work it out won't you?' she said pulling away.

'Mi, you're mixing up my head. I can't promise you anything. I don't even know where I'll be myself.'

'Don't worry Buster, you will find a way. The Ark would like a fine young man like you.'

'That's strange, I heard something similar from Albert, saying I would be welcome to join the Ark if I resigned from the service, but it's not that easy to resign these days.'

They reached the entrance to the upper decks. Nothing more was said as they went up to the canteen. Others were coming and going as the pair joined Albert and Pete who were having a drink at the bar.

'What can I get you to drink Mi and Buster?'

148

'I'll have some red wine please Albert.' Mi replied. She immediately greeted Pete with a kiss.

'I'll have one of those Flash things you brew Albert, thank you.' The group's glasses were full and Albert gave a toast.

'Here's to the future of the Ark and all who live within her.' The toast was acknowledged wholeheartedly.

'So Albert, Pete, what's the verdict, are you going to send me and the Commander away in disgrace or can you help us?'

'Well Pete, what do you think? Is he worth it? If we help him we might have to save his sorry arse again somewhere else in the world, if we don't, we may never see him again.'

'Stop teasing him you two,' Mi jumped in, 'and tell him you have something for him.' Albert and Pete said sorry for jesting and then Pete showed Buster some papers.

'See here, there are more sites like the one we destroyed. They are all around the coast of Africa in the places that are in turmoil, but then here you have two sites in your own backyard. How come your mighty intelligence service hasn't picked them up?'

'Shit!' Buster replied.

'How can they not know what's going on?' Pete asked as he showed him another page with names on which Buster recognised as government men.

'Oh, shit, the bastard traitors!' He paused for a while taking in the severity of the information he had in his hands.

'But how did you get this? How can I be sure it's correct?'

'Put it like this Buster, you would not be here now if our intelligence was incorrect.'

'Sorry Albert, of course. You were spot on and I am still indebted to you both.'

'There's one thing that must remain paramount in all this, we must be able to protect ourselves, so we will not be giving up the ability to do so and will not bow to pressure from the CIA. If you want help in being supplied with information we will help, but only through you Buster. So put a feather in your cap, blow your trumpet, you know what I mean?' said Albert. They all laughed at Albert, trying to advise Buster on how to use the information for his own benefit as well as the US government's.

'Thank you both for your trust and goodness towards me and thank you Mi for checking my health after my ordeal. I am very grateful to you all. Can I inform the Commander that I have something of great interest for our Government?'

'Yes Buster,' 'Pete would you please take Buster to the bridge to make a brief communication.'

'No problem Albert. Let's do it quickly Buster or we'll miss the party.' The pair were soon back in the canteen ready for a little celebration.

The rest of the community began to arrive and join in. Gunter, Greta and their children, Millie came straight over and joined the group giving pecks on cheeks to greet them, with smiles all around.

'How's your day been Millie?' asked Pete.

'Great so far, there are all sorts of things happening, *down on the farm.* We've had some new arrivals: different birds some like buntings with yellow feathers and others I've not seen before. We have another litter of pigs so there will be plenty of bacon.' Then a big distraction arrived putting the conversation to an early end. Marigold came in with Lucy and Millie's two. She was holding Rose and then passed her over to Millie. Millie thanked Marigold and asked where Ched was.

'I think he's on the bridge. Have you not spoken to him?'

'No, I've been busy, no doubt he'll be here soon,' Then she asked Marigold to take Rose back until Ched arrived.

'No problem Millie. That will be fine.' Millie returned to Albert and company receiving a large red wine from Pete.

'Cheers everybody!'

Jane, Antonio and Alberto came in next, and then Magnus followed by Melanie holding two babies, one in each arm, Chuva and Esperanca. Amy and Patricia were busy in the kitchen preparing a special meal for Buster's send off. Zimbo was on watch duty and Ched finally turned up to a relieved

Marigold who had the burden of three children although Vicky was very well behaved.

'Thank heaven you're here Ched. I've been saddled with all the children again. Millie seems to be taking me for granted. I don't really mind because though I do it for you.'

'Thank you my love,' he said quietly. 'I'll take Rose, Vicky will be fine she'll play with Stella. It won't be for long. After dinner, they'll be ready for bed. Oh bed, I wish it was like it was before being caught. The risk was well worth it,' he whispered again.

'Yes I miss you. It wasn't just the sex, it was the whole combination of loving, trusting and sharing thoughts and dealing with day to day things, I want that back again,' Ched stood up and asked Marigold to hold Rose while he got the drinks.

'Do you want the usual, Marigold?'

'Yes please Ched,' as they looked each other in the eye, knowing what they really wanted.

The meal was finally ready and there was a rush to the counter to take their trays and plates to help themselves to a selection of delicious vegetables, salads, meats, seafood and fruit-filled desserts.

The tables were set out in a long row with places already designated. Albert and Amy were to sit opposite each other at one end with Patricia at the head between them for easy access to the kitchen. Melanie was next to Albert, still with a baby in each arm and tits out, feeding them both. Magnus sat across from his daughter and next to Amy, Jane next to him. Antonio was opposite her with Alberto on his lap. Gunter sat by Antonio and Greta was opposite with two children sat to attention along side. Then came Millie next to Stella with Mi on her other side. Pete faced Millie with Buster next to him and then Marigold with Vicky on the end. Ched was next to Mi with Rose on his lap and Lucy next to him.

'This is fantastic! You Brits certainly know how to put on a spread. You don't have to go to a supermarket that has flown in the produce from all parts of the world. You have it at your finger tips. It's unbelievable. You put the rest of

151

the world to shame in what you are able to achieve, making the basic things in life into a luxury.' Everyone heard Buster's compliment and he was thanked for his kind words. The happy evening continued then the parents and carers gathered their flocks to put the children and some of themselves to bed. This left Albert, Pete, Millie, Mi and Buster in the canteen. Buster was supposed to go back to the sub, but Albert said because everyone had enjoyed the evening so much it would be a shame to send him off, especially having drunk Flash. It was Albert's turn to relieve Zimbo on watch, leaving the four in the canteen. They sat and chatted, drank and crashed out with heads on the table until Patricia arrived for her duties in the early morning hours to prepare breakfasts.

'Oh my goodness,' she said to no one in particular. 'I'd better use that coffee Buster gave us and make a pile of bacon sandwiches for them. Looks like they've been on a bender, they'll need it.' She moved to the kitchen and got to work. Very soon the smell of frying bacon and brewing coffee reached the intake breath of Buster and Pete's nostrils and they simultaneously rose to the aroma of that lovely combination. Patricia placed four cups of strong coffee and a pile of bacon butties on the table.
'You're an angel,' Pete told her.
'Most definitely,' Buster agreed.
'Shouldn't Millie be with her children and Ched? She's normally on her way to the farm by now. Just look at her, I've never seen her like that before.'
'Patricia, don't worry about it. She wanted a break and let her hair down. She's like you she works so hard for us all. Without her those fantastic bacon sandwiches wouldn't be in front of us now.' Pete was determined that nothing derogatory should be said about her.
'Patricia, I don't know if I will see you again, but can I please thank you for the most delightful evening and now the best breakfast I've ever had in my entire life. You are wonderful.'
'Oh' Buster, thank you.' Flustered by a compliment as usual, she turned and headed for the sanctuary of her kitchen.

152

'Hey girls do you want some coffee and bacon sandwiches before we demolish them?'
'Ugh what?' Millie and Mi groaned.

Buster left the Ark with farewells, hugs and kisses from a community that had only known him for a short time. Even Albert warmed to him despite his long memory of the problems he had experienced during the Gulf war in 1991, of the so called friendly fire, mainly by the US forces that wasn't friendly to the allied soldiers it killed. He became to like and respect Buster as a man just like himself that fought for and believed in his country and was prepared to make the ultimate sacrifice for them at home.

ALBERT'S LOG - October 2019

I surprise myself sometimes. You hold reservations about a certain nationality dismissing them as all the same useless bastards being biased towards them, then by a freak chance you pull someone from the depths of a criminal's jaws and he turns out to be the nicest guy you could ever meet. He was naturally polite, respected all. Far better than the shabbily dressed youth I used to see walking the streets in England, aggressive to anyone in their way, often obese, face pierced with scrap metal and an IQ less than an orang-utan, fed on tax payers' money and the actions of a do-gooder society that has destroyed the very thing they naïvely believed would make society better. The key to this degeneration is a lack of discipline and a proper diet, instead of junk food full of "E" numbers and harmful fats. Well that's my answer to the problems of the so-called modern world. Perhaps it's a good thing that we don't live a lot longer life, the changes in youth on mainland Europe that I saw were disturbing to say the least. I can't imagine what it would be like if I had to go and live back there today or in the future. I like it here with these people and generally I think they

153

are content with a good quality of life and that compensates for all the problems we've had.

Our raid turned out to be a bonus, because now we know the US are at work and also the Mafia know that they are on their trail, when they captured Buster. I should imagine that they were going to use him as a trade for something. But the thing is they don't know who blew up the site and rescued the American. If they think it was the Yanks then that might take the pressure off us. I hope that is so. Unfortunately only time will tell, so it's still a full alert situation.

Pete has made a big difference here and I certainly couldn't have done the raid and saved Buster without him. His wife is a strange one in that she was so familiar with Buster but Pete doesn't seem to be bothered about it. Perhaps it's because he knows he's going away. Millie and Mi are very close. She spends more time with her than Ched! I wonder if he's behaving himself. There doesn't seem to be any rows or confrontations between anyone at present. Perhaps it's the sea air that calms everyone, long may it continue. It will be interesting to see the outcome of the information supplied to the Yanks!

11. LET'S FIND SOMEWHERE PERMANENT

With Buster repatriated and who knows where he will be sent after his due term of leave? Nowhere, if the restrained CIA official gets his way at a hearing and they believe his version of events against the solid information that Buster has supplied to the Pentagon obtained with the help of the Commander of the submarine USS Tina Turner. Buster left the Ark with sadness and hoped one day in the near future he could return. The people of the Ark made him feel so welcome and ideally he would have liked to be a part of them but he had three years more service to do and could not imagine it being the same if he went to them in three years time.

The Ark had returned to normal daily routines very shortly after the hangovers had dispersed from Millie and Mi's heads. The only affect it had on Pete was a pain in his kidneys like a backache. He knew exactly what it was and went completely dry from alcohol, drinking only water and soft drinks for a couple of weeks to hopefully repair the binge drinking damage he had done. Albert and Amy heard from Patricia, the state that the four were in when she arrived for her duties that morning.
'Well at least they weren't all in bed together.' Albert remarked.
'Albert, how could you think of such a thing?' Amy responded.
'Sorry Amy!'

The weeks passed, each person became content with just living in one spot, not having the upheaval of having to keep moving and beat the seasons and they wondered if they could find somewhere that was shallow enough so they could just anchor and stay permanent for all the years to come. The seabed could possibly house them making the Ark a fortified island, even just for them to bottom if necessary and rest letting nature take its course. The idea was sparked off by Gunter after a discussion with Greta, their theory being that if the ship could not move and was left to nature, it would not be of value to anyone to take and if the world authorities knew where they were, eventually it could be accepted. But where could that place be? It intrigued

155

Gunter making him scour the charts for that perfect spot. First he made a list of the places with the most stable weather conditions, then, with the aid of Ched, for the best fishing areas and Millie for the best agricultural climate with a balance of sun and rain. Millie thought north of Malta but was thinking of her goal, rather than a permanent place in the right climate and the Mediterranean was out of the question. But none of the places they had anchored in the past would be suitable either because of being so deep or extreme weather conditions in winter for a permanent stay. Gunter's idea would mean some exploration in moving to the east or west along the areas a little north or south of the Tropic of Capricorn as opposed to the Tropic of Cancer, which had far more land mass on its circumference of the earth. Gunter gradually put his thoughts about to the adult community, suggesting his and Greta's ideas for a place somewhere in the South Pacific Ocean where there are an abundance of small uninhabited islands in the Polynesia area through to the American Samoa Islands. Albert was well aware of his ideas and did not dismiss them in any way. His own thinking was that the Ark could not keep roaming the globe indefinitely, besides major mechanical breakdowns can happen. They didn't want to push things until they break, and then find out that Magnus is unable to fix problems because of needing a dry dock situation for the repair.

Gunter had enough information and some feedback from the rest, to ask Albert if there could be a more serious discussion on the matter, favouring the eastern side of the South Pacific.

'Albert, as you know, I've been doing a lot of research on this. My studies take us to the islands of the Polynesia group that range from the Pitcairn Islands although just outside the group to the thousands of islands owned by many different countries, a large number by the United States. How do you feel about staying somewhere permanent?'

'Yes it is inevitable that we should stop in the next couple of years and forward planning is a must, so yes, let's start the ball rolling and have discussions amongst ourselves to get everyone's point of view. We are doing very well in the self-sufficiency department so we could spend a considerable amount of time searching without it affecting our stores of methane gas and foods etc. If you want to put it to the community we could move to the area you have suggested and take a look. It may take a long time to find our ideal location, and by the way don't forget the fresh water issue, we must have plenty of fresh water, we'll not always have the backup of desalinated water.'

'Yes Albert I will. It's about time I did something positive for a change. Greta and I feel very strongly for this plan and I don't want the worry of the navigation anymore, besides there is no one to continue if anything happens to me.'

'That goes for me too Gunter. I'm not getting any younger and if anything happened to me, I don't know who would fill my shoes either. The main problem we have is the age gap between us and our offspring. There are Antonio and Zimbo but they haven't the experience and life know-how to be able to cope with the sort of problems we have come through.'

'but what about Pete? He is a leader and has experience.'

'Gunter, Pete is great in the front line battlefield that is what we were trained for. I don't know how he would cope with being in one place. But when you are in a tight corner he is the man to have with you. So don't count on him to stay because if he gets too bored he may decide to leave.'

'So Greta and I are correct in thinking that we try and find a permanent place to anchor soon?'

'As I've said, we can't keep roaming the seas forever.'

Gunter left Albert to find Greta and tell her of Albert's approval and it was left to them to discuss the idea with the rest to get more in-depth feedback. They both went to each adult and asked them in a detailed survey fashion, clipboard in hand and a series of questions in a methodical manner. Strangely Millie was the only one opposed to the idea, the rest were quiet happy to go with it and hoped it might reduce the risk of attack from the Russian Mafia. The results were brought to Albert and then a meeting was called to get the full consensus. There was not an emergency on the issue so a meeting was planned for the next week. This gave Gunter more time to study the areas in detail using the newly installed computer system and a well known Earth

Look programme which focused in on every detail of the earth's surface. Gunter inadvertently gave away their position to the Russian Mafia as soon as he switched on the computer system. This happened on numerous occasions while doing his research. He had not been informed of the 'sat-silence' or, what it used to be called, 'radio silence' taking it for granted that when Albert and Pete knocked out the transmitter station, there wouldn't be a problem. Gunter spent hours searching for his and Greta's place of permanence but it would have to be looked at and a trial stay if they found the right spot, so it was a long way off for a permanent stay. The day of the meeting came and Gunter was about to deliver his speech on the places he would like to put forward. He set down full colour photocopies of satellite photographs on the table. Albert and Pete were furious. 'You dumm-kopf! Do you realise what you've done by using the system to connect to the satellite? You've given away our exact position to the Russians,' said Albert.

'Well in the light of that we best move on,' said Pete.

'That's it, we move to Tristan Da Cunha for the winter, we know we are relatively safe there,' Albert told them. 'Make preparations now. We leave at 1200 hours today, so let's jump to it. I would rather be moving than at anchor if we are attacked. Gunter when was the first and last time you logged on to the internet to get your information?'

'Just over a week ago and again yesterday afternoon,'

'Pete, would it be possible to monitor any of the Mafia's movements?'

'Yes, but it might take me a while to work it out.'

'Could you do that? I'll take charge of defence. Gunter, Ched. You make sure we get the Ark moving as soon as possible.'

Ched and Gunter went to their duties.

'What's it like being a dumm-kopf then?' Ched asked him.

'Not good Ched, especially the second time. It seems I only make big mistakes. I feel bad about myself. I thought I was doing something good for everyone, just like Albert does.'

'At least he didn't rip your head off.'

'No, but being called a dumm-kopf is worse than my head being ripped off.'

'I'll take your word for that. Let's get this ship moving.'

A couple of hours of propulsion from the turbines and then reliance on sail power took over. Gunter set a course of south-west as a first leg to the Cape of Good Hope and into the South Atlantic. Pete finally found out how to use the system to scan the activities of most known Mafia craft, both at sea and in the air. It did not matter now about sat-silence because of the huge exposure of the Ark's whereabouts. The case now was not if, but when would they be attacked.

Two days into their transit Pete had been monitoring the radar when he detected they were being followed by a submarine. A message came from Gunter at the lookout post said it was the USS Tina Turner the conning tower shape gave it away. He called Albert to the bridge to show him on screen and discuss the possibilities of why they would shadow them.
'Right Pete, what have we got?'
'The sub is only a nautical mile away and they must know that we know of their presence. Why don't we call them to say hello, it may work in our favour letting anyone listening know we have a bodyguard.'
'Yes Pete, that's a good idea.'
'This is the Albert's Ark calling the USS Tina Turner. Nice to have you with us again and we look forward to having dinner with you Commander and Buster if he is with you.' There was no immediate reply.
'Albert we have an emergency, Ched called Albert, there are two very fast low flying aircraft heading towards us showing on the radar.'
'OK Ched, usual drill. We'll see to it.'

'Come on Pete we need to use that new arsenal.' The pair rushed to the top deck to the defence system they had put into place since leaving the South Atlantic some eight months ago. By the time they got there the two small jets, which looked like old RAF Hawk Trainers with missiles attached under the wings, had flown over and were banking to turn and return on them. Albert did not want to take any chances and ordered Pete that they would fire as and

159

when possible, Albert aimed the 105 mm calibre stand mounted machine gun and Pete adjusted the VLS Quad Pack missile launcher. The jets were lined up in an attack approach and released a volley of machine gun fire just to show they meant business. It raked the foredeck each side of the sails which acted as a restriction to the attackers so they had to go each side of the sails. They peppered the Biome and continued to the upper decks hitting the bridge and through Albert and Pete's defence, not giving them a chance to take a clear shot at the predators. The jets did the same again, banked and did a u-turn to attack from the stern. This time Albert and Pete were ready. Albert lined up his sights and Pete had already locked on to them and launched another volley of missiles. Suddenly the attackers were two plumes of smoke and falling debris. The only explanation Albert and Pete could think of was that the USS Tina Turner had launched surface to air missiles and knocked the planes out. 'I don't believe it Pete. We've had accurate help from the Yanks and they didn't hit us. Things are looking up! Let's check our damage. Everybody should have been well covered, they know the drill.'

Damage to the Ark's upper deck was quite substantial. The Biome had two sides shattered and the port and starboard sides of the upper decks, including the bridge windows, had been damaged. There were no injuries just extremely shaken and frightened people. This attack was too close for them. Even Albert was very pleased with the US Cavalry. If the jets had had a third and fourth run on them, it could have been disastrous. Their main problem now was the shattered glass. They did not have enough to replace so much damage. Albert had only catered for the odd accident, so it meant a covering with polythene until they could think of how to replace the broken panes. The rest of the community were told the attack was over and that the American sub had destroyed the jets. There were clasps and hugs all around with Pete hugged by Mi and Millie, Ched by Marigold and the children around them and in full view of all, Patricia and Magnus, Jane and Antonio who was holding Alberto, Gunter holding Stella and Venus in his arms, Greta in between them and Melanie with Chuva and Zimbo. Amy cuddled Esperanca close and asked if anyone knew where Albert was?

160

'He's gone to the bridge I think to assess the damage.' Pete said.
'Thank you Pete.'

She rushed off to look for Albert clutching Esperanca and there he was sat in the Captain's chair rocking to and fro just staring, with his hands clasped together supporting his chin and elbows resting on the side of his stomach.
'Albert what's wrong? Everyone's together comforting each other with relief. The attack is over and you are sat here on your own pondering. Aren't you pleased that we are still here and unscathed?'
'Yes of course I am pleased. Come here and sit on my lap and give me her to hold, I want to tell you something.'
Amy made them comfortable on his lap and smiled up at the man she has always and would always love.
'I've wanted to tell you this for a very long time. You know the time I was a security expert after leaving the Forces and went to work in Africa?'
'Yes, I remember it well I was always worried about you. You never talked about your work.'
'Well I was basically a mercenary, and still thirsty for action. I was hired by the government of the day in the northern Congo, to seek out enemies, opposition, etc. But one day out on a patrol we were ambushed and I lost my dear friend Chopsy Finnon. It was betrayal from one of the people that employed us. I was supposed to die as well, but I survived and now I'm here in a similar situation, betrayed by someone we trusted although not with us now, leaving a legacy of persistent attacks for the money and the Ark.'
'Oh Albert you poor thing, the reality is you've survived it all.'
'You've asked me what's wrong, well I'm getting too old for the action. I was too slow out there just now and I have to call it a day. When we started out on this way of life we didn't expect this much attention and have to use my military skills to keep us alive. So I've been thinking again about how to get out of this constant threat. The answer lays less than a mile away and has just saved our arses and I hate to say it but, the Yanks saved the day and I'm willing to congratulate them on being in the right place at the right time.'

'Albert you are a wonderful man and I know you've taken a lot of risks in the past. You once being a mercenary does not surprise me. The decisions you've had to make since the start of the attacks on the Ark were purely to protect us all to this day. I think you know Gunter is right about finding a final anchoring place. Let's give all the info we have on the Mafia to the Americans. You might even get some help on a place of permanence, especially with all that useless cash we have.'

'You're right Amy. But first of all I must apologise to Gunter for calling him a dumm-kopf. He did not deserve it.'

'Albert you didn't, call him that, did you? You go to him right now and say sorry. You know how sensitive he is.'

Amy took Esperanca from Albert. They got up and he went to find Gunter. The order was given from Albert to drop the sails and slow down to a standstill but not to anchor and allow the sub to be alongside them. He then gave the Americans a communication, thanking them for taking out the attackers and he said he would like to thank them personally as soon as they were alongside. The message was received and understood and they replied they would be with them as soon as they could, although sea conditions would mean keeping a short distance from the Ark, but not a major problem.

'Gunter can I have a word with you?'

'Yes, what is it Albert?' Gunter was abrupt and obviously still upset with him.

'My sincere apologies for the name I called you, you didn't deserve it because we didn't warn you of the repercussions of not keeping sat-silence. I'm deeply sorry.'

'It takes a real man to apologise like that Albert and I thank you for bringing us through the dangers we have encountered, but my ignorance was also a fault.' They shook hands and went about cleaning up the broken glass. All hands joined in. The shattered windows were covered temporarily with clear polythene. Then preparations were made for a welcome for their saviours from the USS Tina Turner.

The sub fully surfaced shortly after taking out the attackers and soon caught up with the Ark, very quickly moving parallel to them as they slowly lost momentum together. There was excitement from the Ark as to who would come aboard from the sub and a certain someone was having a heart-thumping experience hoping it was Buster. As soon as she heard that the Commander and company were to board Mi went to the swimming pool deck on her own to look out for them. She wanted to be private with her emotions if it was him arriving. Leaning on the rails that overlooked the foredeck with the now shattered biome just below, waiting in anticipation, she started imagining various scenarios. She wondered if it's *him* and how he would respond to her. She felt very deeply for this young American. What will Pete be like with him? Will he be jealous if I make a fuss of him? He has not said anything so far and he has seen I'm very fond of him, but I suppose that is Pete. He does not show much emotion, I suppose that is what makes him a professional fighting soldier.

The party boarded and were greeted by Albert and Amy. Everyone else was still busy making preparations and cleaning up. Four people came from the sub: The Commander, Buster and two others. Commander Grey introduced the two newcomers to Albert and Amy, shaking their hands and greeting them. It was a CIA official Wayne Kerr and a naval intelligence Officer, Captain Lenska Korsky. They were welcomed along with the Commander and Buster. Mi was having difficulty making out the faces. They all had peaked baseball type caps on. She was so frustrated she had to find out and could not help herself.

'Buster,' she shouted out. He immediately looked up to her and waved.

'Well that's a good welcome Buster I think someone is pleased to see you,' said Albert. Buster was slightly embarrassed.

'That must be Mi,' he said. 'She's a very good doctor, isn't that right Albert?' The remark flummoxed Albert.

'Mi, oh yes she is an excellent doctor and we are pleased to have her expertise onboard. When Buster was pulled out of Somalia I understand he was given a clean bill of health by her. Let's go on to the canteen and have a discussion and some refreshments,' said Albert. 'I think things should be cleaned up and

163

ready to use by now.' Amy changed the conversation from the Buster and Mi topic, thanking the Commander for being close by at their time of need. Then Albert walked ahead with the Commander. 'Commander, we are most grateful for your help back there. With you still being around us, it is obvious to me that you want something else.'

'Yes, that's correct. But let us all sit and talk about the situation, for benefit of both parties.' The CIA officer followed on with the group with his head down looking at where his feet were going. The young Captain had to keep looking back not believing the things she was seeing. A mobile farm! What's this got to do with the Russian Mafia? She asked herself.

The group sat down around a table with Albert facing the Commander, Pete facing Buster, the Captain facing Amy and the CIA man on his own. Melanie was there to serve drinks for them. She enjoyed this, because she found out what was going on and would pass the knowledge around to the rest. The drinks were served and the business began.

'Right Albert, I'll come straight to the point. We need more information because the small piece of info you gave us was 100% correct and has, or is being dealt with. So, on that basis our intelligence staff's assumption is that you have a lot more to give us. Now we will not always be available to be on your tail providing backup at the US Government's cost to take out an attack like you seemed to be struggling with,' deliberated the Commander.

'Point taken,' said Albert, 'So how can we help you this time?'

'Let me explain,' replied the Commander. 'Our Government has done some research on you Albert and your friend Pete here and the records show you were both very distinguished in the battlefield, never failing an operation for Her Majesty's Government of the time. Now that is something I would be proud to have on my record. What has happened now is that the work that was under the control of the CIA our friend on the end there is now back where it always should be with the naval intelligence our lovely young Captain Lenska Korsky. I'll pass you over to her to explain.'

'Thank you Commander.'

'Albert, my understanding is that you dislike any other form of title.' She addressed Albert as though she was talking to a private in the US Army. 'Yes young lady. We have no titles on the Ark. We all multitask as much as possible and I would appreciate calling each other by first names, as we are not in any military set-up. I finished with all that years ago, besides I didn't think we were here to discuss what to call each other, is that a problem?' There was a pause from Lenska while taking in the situation, but then she returned a volley.

'I am dwarfed by someone with such a gallant military history, but we are here today with a different set of problems to solve, so we must get it sorted out. We are here to help you and for you in return to help us. We know you are loners and as far as we can detect, self funded. From what I have seen in a short space of time you are very well organised in surviving a good lifestyle, but like us you have enemies so why not just give us all the information and its source. We know the problem they cause us, the same as any Mafia based organisation but I am mystified as to what a well organised and well funded ruthless mob would want with a floating farmyard?'

'The last comment was disrespectful to the Ark and its community and on that note you will have to decide who needs who. I suggest we have a short break for some food and refreshments and continue the discussion afterwards, with a different attitude,' Albert retaliated.

Albert had vibes about this young Captain and thought she had been thrown in at the deep end to prove herself, and presumably by her name was a Russian speaking officer. He knew they would want him to give up the computer equipment they had obtained from the Revelation. He would be relieved to be rid of it but would that solve the constant attacks? He was definitely not giving up his arsenal. That would be suicide. He conferred with Pete while at the bar.

'Well Pete what do you think? I don't want to make it too easy for her.'
'Yes, you're right. Let her stew for a while, she'll mellow.'
'I just cannot do with that arrogant, bossy, patronising attitude. It makes me cringe, especially from someone so young.'

Meanwhile the Commander had words with the Captain.

'Captain Lenska you will not get far with an approach like that. Albert is not an idiot. I suggest you start the conversation the other way around, ask him what can we do for them first?'

12. PLEASANT INTERLUDES

The food arrived. Patricia and co. had been very busy and trays of fish, meats and salads were set out for them, followed by glasses of homemade wines. Each of the guests were eager to taste all. Albert proposed a toast.
'Here is to a good workable relationship between us, Cheers.'
'Cheers,' was the reply. Then Albert fired a shot at Lenska.
'Not bad Lenska, for a floating farmyard Lenska?'
'Cheers Albert, my apologies, can we start again?'
'Certainly my dear, enjoy the food and wine. Tomorrow's another day. There's no rush.'

The occasion settled down to an enjoyable sociable evening with eventually the whole community arriving for their meals. Lenska was surprised at the number of children and how healthy everyone looked. Then Mi arrived and went over to Pete giving him a kiss on the cheek and then to Buster shaking his hand.
'Buster, it's lovely to see you again so soon, I hope we will see a lot more of you. You didn't have much leave did you? See you.' She went to the bar to get a drink and then joined Millie.
'You're very sweet on Buster aren't you?' said Millie.
'Yes, I think he is gorgeous.' She blushed and then continued. 'I should not say this, it would be considered totally unprofessional, but you are a very close friend and I know it won't go any further. You know that night when Albert and Pete brought him aboard? He was in a bad state and later I asked for him to be brought to me for a health check. Well Pete delivered him to me the next day and waited outside the surgery while I inspected him. I asked him to strip off and when he did I was drawn to his wonderful male physique. Lovely formed biceps, no paunch and then I asked him to lie on the couch so I could check his penis. He did and I turned to put on surgical gloves. By the time I turned back to him he had an erection, it wasn't that big but it was so thick, I would struggle to get it in my mouth!' Millie was totally fascinated.

167

'Then I did the professional thing and flicked it hard with my finger and watched it deflate, it was sad.' They both burst out into girly giggles.

'How much do you fancy him?' asked Millie.

'Enough.' Mi replied.

'How will that work and what about Pete?'

'I don't know how long Buster will be about yet, but if there is a chance and he is around for a while perhaps you could keep Pete happy? I know you like him and Pete enjoys you.' They both started sniggering naughtily confirming their agreement.

'I'm going over to talk to Buster. Pete's all yours Millie. Please keep him occupied.'

Millie was taken aback by Mi's boldness as she went straight to Buster. Millie was a little apprehensive and decided she would have another drink. She received her glass and turned away from the bar to be faced by Pete.

'Oh Pete I thought you were sat down talking business. I turned around and here you are, you do move quickly.'

'Millie what's going on? I could see you two having an in-depth chat with giggles and then she goes straight to her desire of the month.' Millie took a big gulp of wine, and then tried to explain.

'Mi has serious hots for Buster and she wants me to keep you occupied for a while.'

'I've no problem with that, have you?'

'Not at all, it suits me fine, but it all has to come to a head sooner or later, there is too much deceit going on. It's not fair on others, commitments need to be thought of and made.'

'What sort of commitments are we talking about?'

'Well first of all you and me. Would you be prepared to live with me and stay with me here on the Ark?'

'Yes and no is the honest answer. Yes I'll live with you on the Ark as a commitment and no I can't guarantee I will stay.'

'Thank you for your honesty, the thing is I don't want to leave the Ark, so if you left, I would stay so how do you feel about that?'

168

'I don't know but you are forgetting another part of your life, that's Ched and your children.'

'No I haven't forgotten. If you look over there, who is Ched in deep conversation with and accompanied by the children? I'm not positive but I'm sure those two are getting it together. I do feel sorry for Marigold. She's had a rough time and she's so young. I think they would make a good couple so that leaves me to be sorted. It's strange living in a small community, where you get used to looking out for one another. At first there were some differences between people but as things went on, through the attacks and other problems, we've all stuck together and Albert saw us through.'

'I know what you mean but I've always found I don't really belong anywhere, I stay for a while and get uncomfortable and feel the need to leave.'

'Have you any children?'

'Probably, but I've never stayed anywhere long enough to find out.'

'How would you like to stay and find out?'

'You mean you would have my child? Is it a good time of month now then?'

'Well you had already started when we were scuba diving and after you returned from your night out with Albert, but you haven't hit the target yet so you will need to keep trying and now is a good time and a good chance if we act quickly. It won't happen by talking to each other stood here.'

'I'll see you by the swimming pool in ten minutes.'

Mi and Buster were sitting down together chatting away, as were the others, Albert with the Commander, Lenska talking to Jane, Amy saddled with the CIA man who suffered from verbal diarrhoea once he found a victim. Albert had an in-depth conversation with the Commander, talking a lot of shop. The Commander had been briefed on what an ideal outcome would be, giving hints to him as the wine went down, this gave Albert something to think about. His sole aim was to get rid of the threat of the attacks once and for all. Meanwhile Jane realised that she'd stayed longer than intended she immediately explained she must go and look after her baby Alberto to relieve Antonio who would need to eat.

169

'Pete are you sure you want this commitment?' Millie asked as they found a secluded spot. They locked their lips and then entwined tongues as if they had been apart for years. He grabbed her shoulders and gently pushed her away to look at her.

'You are beautiful,' he murmured then he put his thumbs under her skimpy top resting on her shoulders. He lifted it over her head like a tablecloth pulled rapidly leaving the china on the table, and revealed those still pert breasts. Her nipples stared him in the eyes and he fell to them like a baby wanting to feed. Millie pulled him to her holding and caressing his head. Like a man on a mission he worked down over her tight stomach rolling her elastic waist skirt along with her knickers and sent them heading for the deck. She stood there before him completely naked. He got up and stepped back again to admire her. Millie went to him and kissed him in the way she knew he liked while she released his shirt and trousers to fall from his torso, leaving him in just his underpants. She looked down.

'Pete can you please remove your underpants slowly. I want to stand back and watch it unravel out, then I'll look after it.'

Millie waited to see his lengthy tube fall. As it arrived she fell to her knees and took it in her hands. As soon as she touched, it obeyed her wishes, stiffening rapidly, taking the shape of a long bent banana pointing upwards. Knelt in front of him holding her prize in both hands she pulled back the foreskin to reveal the bulbous end then immediately covered it with her mouth, but not for long she wanted that wonderful muscle inside her. Pete was not in control and he wanted her quickly. Lying down on his back Millie followed astride him and held his erection, guiding it into her. Steadily she moved up and down on him, driving him wild with excitement, she wanted him to last until she came to her climax. A sudden lifting from his buttocks followed by the sound of agonising pleasure, then she felt him pump his precious fluid into her.

'Oh Pete, that was wonderful I want to stay with you tonight where can we go?'

'I know your place.' Pete replied.

'Don't be silly Ched will be there.'

'No, the farm, I'm sure there will be some bails of straw or hay to sleep on.'

'That will be great. I'll go first and wait for you and bring something to drink, preferably a soft drink I want to pay full attention to you.' Moving off of him she stood up looking down at him but giving him a pose, legs slightly apart, hands on her narrow waist and then moved her hands upwards to caress her breasts. Pete rested his head in his hands behind.

'You are something else lady, you make me feel good, naturally. That's worried me.' Millie put her clothes back on.

'I'll see you in an hour. I'll make our bed and wait for you.' She bent down to kiss him.

'Please make it less than an hour because I want to snuggle up to you and be close.'

'I'll be with you as soon as I can. I hope I don't bump into anyone on the way. See you soon.' Millie left him and went to the bow farm to make preparations for her night out.

The canteen was still active with more drinks flowing and the CIA man getting plastered, to the amusement of the Captain Lenska, who was also enjoying the banter from the group which now consisted of Albert, the Commander, Ched, (Marigold was looking after the children) Buster very close to Mi, Gunter, Antonio, Magnus and Patricia. Pete popped in to get some soft drinks no one noticed being all deeply involved in conversations. He left as inconspicuously as he could and off to his date. The evening ended up a full session with Albert trying to work out where the guests could stay. He began to organise places for the night. Amy had left some time ago to take Esperanca from Melanie.

'Lenska, if its ok you can stay in our quarters on the sofa, it's very comfortable.'

'That's great Albert.'

'Mi, can Buster stay on the couch in the surgery?'

'No, he can stay with Pete and me, on our couch.'

171

'Thank you Mam, that's very kind of you.'
'By the way where is Pete?'
'He's probably gone for some fresh air,' Mi replied.
'Well Commander it looks like its surgery for you.'
'Do I look that bad?' The banter began to bring out the silliness as the alcohol took its toll. It was time for them all to make it to their various places to stay the night all but the CIA man, who was left slumped over a canteen table.

Ched noted the absence of Millie and Pete and thought he had better go and relieve Marigold from 'his' children. He let himself into her quarters to find them all fast asleep and was faced with the question of should he wake them up to take them back to their own beds or should he let them sleep?
He then went into Marigold's bedroom where she was also fast asleep under a thin white sheet showing her naked form.
'Shit.' he softly said to himself. 'She is beautiful.' He rapidly pulled his clothes off, lifted the sheet and climbed in beside her. Gently moving toward her trying not to disturb her, just wanting to be body-to-body and sleep with her. He managed to be in cuddling distance putting his arm around her and his hand onto her right breast. Marigold stirred.
'Hmm Ched,' she turned over to face him. 'Ched I love you, tell me you love me.'
'I love and want you always.'
'You will have me always you are the kindest man I've ever known.' They kissed and held each other tight finding fulfilment just by holding each other close, drifting off into a deep sleep.

'Goodnight Albert,' Mi said as she held Buster's hand. 'Let's go and find Pete to tell him you are staying with us. You don't mind staying with us tonight do you?' Mi asked, as soon as they were away from earshot of Albert.
'Not at all Mi, as long as Pete doesn't mind by the way, where is he and I haven't seen Millie either? Is there something going on I should know about?'
Mi put her fingers to her lips to emphasise quiet, then still holding his hand led him to her cabin. They went in and she locked the door behind them.

172

'Can I get you a nightcap Buster? There is some of Albert's Flash spirit or a soft drink, and fresh lemonade in the fridge?'
'Lemonade will be great. I think I have had enough alcohol for tonight.' Mi sorted out the drinks while Buster relaxed making himself comfortable on the sofa.
'You have a really nice place here. Do you think Pete will be long before he gets back?' By the time he had finished his sentence Mi had the two glasses of lemonade in her hands with her arms across her naked breasts. She stood in front of him uncrossed her arms to give him his glass and a full frontal view. He was stunned to see such a tiny fully grown woman with a perfect physique.
'Mi, I think I get the message, my only concern is Pete, what will he say or do if he came in?'
'He would probably join us, and ask you to do the work first.' They chinked their glasses and sipped the cool refreshing lemonade.
'So where is Pete now?'
'He is with Millie somewhere on the Ark. There is a good chance they are making love as we speak.'
'Oh and you don't mind?'
'We have an understanding and it works fine so let's take our drinks to the bedroom and I will check out that lovely tool you have, because I have an apology to make to it.'

She grabbed him by the arm. He lifted himself from the sofa and was led to the bedroom like a lamb to slaughter. Placing their drinks down Mi began to undress him, gradually removing his tropics, first his shirt, then he released his trousers and pulled them and his underpants to the floor leaving him standing as she was, naked. She went over to the bed, pulled back the sheet, climbed in and waited for him to follow. Being a little dumbstruck, he could not resist her so he climbed in and lay on his back. Mi immediately moved on top of him and began to nip at his neck and muscular chest, he became aroused very quickly Mi felt the swelling close to her.

173

'Buster I want you inside me.' He gently rolled her over to place her on her back and then straddled her putting his thick trunk towards her little bush. 'Are you sure about this?' he asked. 'Yes, I want you.' He pointed his excited penis to her moist anticipating lips and holding it with his hand rubbed it up and down and around her opening just to say hello. 'Oh that is nice very nice, please more.'

Buster continued in his foreplay and she was delighted, then she begged him to fill her. He waited a few seconds before obliging and gently entered her slowly, knowing how thick his penis was he did not want to hurt this small, beautiful lady. She gasped as he moved into her. 'Oh, Oh,' she cried. He lowered himself to her to kiss and then he moved in and out to their utter pleasure, just steady away, controlling himself impeccably. All he heard was 'Oh, Oh' delighted moans from Mi. 'Quicker, please quicker Buster.' He obeyed. Mi went into a climax she had never experienced before, shaking and juddering clinging to him then petered out to exhaustion. When she had finished and her body went limp he continued moving into her, he held her buttocks in his hands while he thrust his still rampant cock in and out until he let fly his sperm at full throttle to another groan of pleasure from Mi's welcoming body. She was satisfied with her quest, rolled over and went to sleep; Buster snuggled up behind her dwarfing her petite body, both content.

'That didn't take you long Pete, what was happening back there?' 'Not much, Mi and Buster were close and all were quite jolly, still drinking away.' 'Where was Ched?' 'He was still there chatting.' She put her arms around his neck and kissed him. 'This is very erotic Pete. I want to make love alfresco again. Let's go to the orchard and peel off together. It's a warm evening. What do you think?' 'Lead the way my dear. Have you any other fancies?' 'No just you.'

174

Hand in hand they went the short distance to the fruit trees, that always had some fruit to pick but now there were more fruit in the orchard of the human kind, the fruit of life. They stood as they did earlier and felt good about it, in front of each other undressing and letting their clothes fall to the ground, standing back to look at each other's beauty. Then the resistance broke down to move to each other and touch, caress and entwine like a dance in nature, their hands all over each other. Pete loved the shape of her breasts. He moved his fingers constantly over them gently. Millie wanted to hold his penis in one hand, run her other hand up and down his spine while kissing him passionately. Pete could not take anymore his cock was bursting in Millie's hand.

'Millie please let me in, you can you feel how hard it is?'

'Let me turn around, I'll hold the tree. Millie bent to brace herself. Pete was so desperate to be inside her he slipped in immediately.

'Pete steady, please, just slowly at first and then as quickly as you like.'

'Millie, Oh Millie,' Pete stopped to hold her breasts and tried to pace himself but he could not hold back any longer. Millie straightened up as Pete held her tight, still inside her. She felt all of him throbbing then it stopped, no movement, they stood totally still for several minutes after. She turned to him as his strength faded to a wilt. She was content with their love making, realising you don't have to reach the heights of ecstasy every time to have fulfilment with your man. The bond between them was strong. Pete had found someone he truly connected with at last, although again it was to be another man's wife, whose passion for sex had brought her to him. His passion for women had found her. He felt complete at last after the years of searching. The pressure he found himself under for being so well endowed had come to its end, love had taken him over.

'I never ever thought I would feel like this Millie, I didn't think it was for me.' Moving her cheek from his chest to look up to him, he looked to her and their eyes met.

'What are you saying Pete?'

'Umm, I've never said this before in all my adult life,' She smiled at him warmly in anticipation of his words.

'I think I'm old enough to say this now and you know I'm a lot older than you.'

'Say what, Pete?'

'Do you mind the age gap?'

'There is no physical age gap, say what Pete?'

'I love you.'

'I love you too.' They kissed and moved hand in hand to their night's quarters along with the animals of the Ark. Snuggled down together they pulled straw over themselves and soon went into a deep sleep, both content with the outcome of the day, not bothered they were not under clean white sheets on a body forming foam mattress.

The sun popped its head over the horizon. The cockerel had already alerted the farm's extra guests, and they dressed, pulling away any straw that was stuck to them, checking for anything that would give them away, any telltale sign of where they had been.

'I have a spare boiler suit here Pete and wellingtons so I can milk the cows and tend to the animals as normal.'

'Ok, do you want any food brought down?'

'No, I'll manage until later and go to the canteen at about my usual time when I put the cows in the field after milking.'

'Ok my love, I'll see you later.'

13. HONESTY AND COMPROMISES.

'Millie can I have a one-to-one word with you in private please, when you are not too tired through your work?'

'Yes Marigold, is there something wrong with Vicky or Rose?'

'No, no, nothing like that, please leave it until you have time because it may take a while to explain things.'

'I'm intrigued as to what you want to talk to me about so we had better make it soon otherwise it will drive me mad thinking about it. So how about coming down to the Bow farm tomorrow morning and we'll have a wander in the fields and you can tell me what it's all about?'

'Yes Millie, that's a good idea. I'll ask Greta to mind Rose while I come down to see you, thank you Millie.'

The next day, the meek and mild Marigold left Greta with her and Millie's children set on a mission to try to deal with a situation that had been going on far too long for her. She wanted to have a heart-to-heart with Millie. Millie was expecting her and had been thinking about why, but deep down had an idea.

'Morning Millie,'

'Hi Marigold, just one moment and we'll go for a walk. Antonio can you watch that runt? He's not getting a fair share of his mother's milk.'

'Sure Millie,'

'I'm just going for a walk with Marigold, won't be long.'

They set off and strolled to the orchard, Millie still slightly puzzled, then out into the open fields before saying a word.

'Ok Marigold, let's hear it.'

'It's a bit difficult, but I'll put it from a woman's point to gain some sympathy if you like. I'm very lonely and I can't see if anyone will turn up for me. I spend a lot of time with your children and Ched and I have become very fond of them all. It's a very small community and I don't want to upset anyone. I know you and Ched have not been that close of late, and I don't know or want

177

to know why. I've been through bad situations myself and know the pain but I don't want that, I want harmony.'

'So spit it out girl. What are you saying?'

'Well,' she gulped, 'would you mind if I shared a bed with Ched now and then?' Millie was not that shocked in her mind at the request, but went very quiet without replying immediately. She was only thinking of the things she had done in the past and recently. How selfish she would be if she said no.

'I'm sorry Millie, I shouldn't have asked, it's just that I'm so desperate to have someone to love me,' and she burst into tears.

'Marigold,' Millie comforted, 'I understand the three of us will have to talk to see how it could work.'

'You mean you might agree?'

'Yes Marigold. What have we to lose? We can only gain.'

'Gain, I can understand part of that for me but what is your gain?'

'Love and deep happiness, I've had a different point of view on life for a long time now and it's strengthened even more since my illness, and I've become to love living on the Ark. This is the home that we all love so what's wrong in helping each other in our needs to be happy here. She put her arm around Marigold.

'Don't worry, we'll work it out.'

'Thank you. I was so worried that you might have been violent to me. I couldn't take that.'

'No, don't be silly. I wouldn't dream of it. Leave that to Pete and Albert against those who attack us.' They walked arm in arm back to Millie's work then Marigold felt an inner joy and excitement well up inside her, and left to go back to her duties with Greta at the upper decks in the school and crèche.

'Ched I had a strange request today from Marigold.'

'What's strange about that? I thought all women were strange.'

'I'm being serious Ched and I think you know what it's about and if I agree you might benefit by it.'

'What do you mean?'

'How close have you two been?'

178

'We've become very close. She's a lovely girl and I'm quite fond of her. She fancies me and I fancy her. We talk about it a lot, because neither of us are getting anything just lately since you had your illness and spend so much time with your new friends. She's worried that if she doesn't get someone soon it might heal up!'
'It can't be that bad, Ched.'

'We've spent a lot of time together looking after the children and become almost like a couple and as you would imagine, being the healthy male that I am, I wouldn't say no to her if asked, but it all depends on you and if you are getting it from somewhere else. Because I know you, you've always liked sex and considering we haven't been together for months I would wager that there's someone else that's keeping you happy. I don't want to fall out with you because I still love you, but you must admit things have only been tolerable since Rose's birth. To add to the situation one night when I finished my shift I crept into bed as quiet as I could because you said not to disturb you or the kids. I lay awake for a while you were out for the count but dreaming aloud and saying just one name, *Pete,* so where does he fit in? At a guess between your legs,'
'Well Ched you have been storing things up and I expect that there's more to you and Marigold than you're saying.'
'Millie, why not let's just tell each other the truth and sort our problems out? We could ask each other questions and only answer by saying yes or no, without any nastiness or repercussions at this stage or at any other, just to let us see where we stand between each other. I like living on the Ark and I know you do so we can't be warring in such a small community. And the most important thing we have to consider is our children.'
'That sounds reasonable, let's give it ago. Who goes first?'
'We should toss a coin but we haven't any.'
'We have a pack of cards somewhere, have you seen them lately Ched?
'No, but I know where they will be, where they were left from the last time we played strip poker and you lost for a change. I remember that well.'

Ched found the cards, placed the pack on the coffee table and asked Millie to shuffle them. As she did so he said to throw two cards out and whoever picks the highest card asks the first question. Each picked up their card, Millie had the nine of hearts and Ched had the Queen of spades allowing him to ask the first straight question.

'Oh dear, 'he said, 'Millie I want you to know that there will definitely not be any animosity between us no matter what, I promise you.'

'Thank you Ched, I appreciate that and you will always be close to me.'

'Right question one.'

'Millie, am I the father of Rose?'

'No.'

'Ched, have you made love to Marigold?'

'Yes.'

'Millie, has Pete made love to you?'

'Yes.'

'Ched, have you been seeing to Marigold for some time?'

'Yes.'

'Millie, is Antonio the father of Rose?'

'Yes.'

'Ched, does anyone else know about you and Marigold?'

'Yes.'

'Millie, does Mi, know about you and Pete?'

'Yes.' This startled Ched and he had to pause to think about what was going on and couldn't think of another question to ask.

'Ched, do you love Marigold?'

'Yes.'

'I have no more questions, have you any?'

'No Ched, I think that sums the pair of us up, don't you think?'

'Yes it certainly does and you know it's a huge burden off my shoulders and I hope it is for you when we are totally honest about things. It won't make a blind bit of difference in how I feel about Rose or Pete, as long as we live our life in harmony, the one we chose on the Ark.'

Millie rushed to him putting her arms around him hugging him, with tears in hers eyes and then sobbing.

'Oh Ched where did all those words come from and what will happen to us now?'

'We talk more and let each other know what's happening and I think the first people to tell that we have a new situation, are Albert and Amy. So when you feel you are up to it let's arrange a meeting with whoever's involved and get it in the open.'

'Ched I'm not ready for that yet. I don't want anyone else to know. You mentioned Albert and Amy, are they the only ones that know about you and Marigold? If so I need a bit more time.'

'Yes, but where does that leave Marigold and me? We promised Albert and Amy we would not continue. It was very embarrassing Amy caught us out in full thrust.'

'You are joking?'

'No we forgot to lock the door and there we were doing it doggy when Amy called and tried the door and it opened as we were at it.' Millie started to laugh seeing the funny side of it and tried to imagine how Amy would have reacted to the shock and surprise of Ched at his vinegar stroke when she put her head through the door.

'What did she say?'

'Ched, Marigold! That was it, but we had to go and explain to them what had been going on and then promised to stop the affair. But it's been very difficult and now being so close to each other with looking after the children and with you spending more time away, things have developed. What more can I say?'

'I know Ched and I understand. So at the moment, let's arrange things so that you see Marigold and I see Pete and cover for each other making sure the children are loved and cared for. Do you agree?'

'Yes, but I want you to speak to Marigold to assure her that you are alright about us. She's a very sensitive girl and has had a rough time in her past. As you are probably aware I want to make her happy as well as still being your friend.'

'Ched you do like her don't you?'

'I'm sorry Millie but yes I do, but you are still my wife and I still love you and wouldn't do anything to hurt you. You understand that don't you? The way I see it, living on the Ark has its problems and benefits, the latter outweigh the problems, risks etc. We are comfortable and enjoying a very good life and it is a joy to wake up every morning, not like it was back in Hull in the UK, dreary and miserable and no guarantee of sunshine there. But on the Ark you are quite happy if it rains, 50% of the time. You can be certain it will be warm rain and good weather to follow. What I'm trying to say is my theory, that's because we've made our day-to-day lives so good and content on the one side, we, you and I have found some excitement elsewhere, resulting in us drifting apart and getting involved in other relationships. Well that's my theory anyway.'

'Sorry to throw your theory out of the window but I've been as randy as hell ever since we boarded the Ark and I feel guilty of putting us in this situation. We had a sound marriage until I made a big mistake and I'm very sorry Ched.' Millie was hugging him again as the tears appeared once more.

'Don't be upset. Just think of what our honesty with each other has done. We couldn't carry on the deceit. It would have ended in disaster. Besides we don't hate each other so why brew hatred?' 'Oh Ched, deep down you are a very wise man with a heart of gold. I didn't really realise that before this. I knew it was there but not the intensity that you have shown here and now, thank you. But please, as I said earlier, let's keep it quiet for now and I'll talk to Marigold for you, and for me, for that matter. I should have been kinder to her in the past, I didn't realise how lonely she might have been, even when Monty was about.'

'That's fine by me Millie. I'd better get to my watch shift. I'll catch you later, bye,'

'Bye Ched.'

Millie sat down and put her hands on her head and burst into tears. 'What have I done?' she cried. 'It's my fault.' She continued until there were no tears left to cry then took a deep breath, got up and went to the farm to lose herself in her work. Then she started to think of Pete and Mi. Would Pete stay

182

with her if she let Ched go? And would Pete leave Mi? And what if Mi wanted to have Pete back and if I end up on my own would Marigold share my husband with me? Oh, I'm so confused. It must be sorted out, I love Pete, does he really love me? I still love Ched, who can I talk to? Well it can only be Amy and Albert of course, but I'll leave it for the moment and see what the Americans are up to and how long Buster is around.

'Hi Millie, yet another lovely day here in the Indian Ocean.'
'Pete!' She jumped up from her confused state and wrapped her whole body around him so tightly.
'Steady on, I only popped down to tell you something.'
'Oh Pete, I love you and just want you, just you and me here on the Ark.'
'Millie I came down to tell you something and you can relax because I want to be with you too. I've had a good talk with Mi, because things are not working out between us. She and Buster are serious, so it's what happens between you and Ched. I'm sorry but there has to be a loser.'
'No, Ched's not a loser and never will be. He has Marigold and our children and I will always be his friend and share the responsibility of them.'
'Will he take responsibility for ours as well?'
'Pete, that's a good hint at commitment. But yes he probably would. Does that mean we have to have divorces? How will that work? It will be a tall order for Albert, and then do we marry?'
'Bloody hell! Steady on girl. We'll be lined up to be buried in the orchard at this rate. Let's take one step at a time and make sure each of us are clear of the implications, because from what you tell me about Ched and Marigold, there will be a big swap around and the children won't understand what the hell is going on. So lets sort things out from their perspective and then deal with the rest of the community.'
'Pete, do you love me?'
'Yes, you know that. I told you in the orchard and I won't change my mind. At last I've found someone to be happy with. I feel at ease and very good with you, like I never felt before.'
'Pete, I want to be with you. Can you make it happen soon?'

183

'Yes I will. So don't worry too much, it will work out fine.'

Clutching him she felt better. The mixed up feeling was slowly disappearing. He was her knight in shining armour, she kissed him and then Pete pulled away slightly.

'We still don't know what the Yanks are really up to but I know Buster is on our side now for two reasons, which are pretty obvious. There's a meeting organised on the sub tomorrow to sort out what each party want and see if we can help each other without losing our security, gaining some if possible. We will just have to see. And the other thing is we will have to pull into Cape Town and have some repairs done after the jet attack. The problem is I don't know how the Ark would pay for them.'

'Now don't you worry I'm sure Albert will find a way,' said Millie.

'Pete I've had a talk with Ched and a totally honest one and before that Marigold wanted to talk to me so we met and her only request was to see if I would allow her to share a bed with Ched now and then, because she was so desperate to be loved. I said I would talk to Ched. She knew that our feelings for each other had changed. But the talk with Ched turned out to be quite bizarre with us asking and giving honest answers to questions, yes or no! I have to tell you that Rose is Antonio's child, only he, now you and Ched know. Does that change anything between us?'

'What, with my background? You must be joking.'

'Oh Pete I love you. I can face the music now, the sooner the better. Let's sort it. I'm sure it will be agreed all round. Just think, we don't have to go through the courts and to be ripped off by lawyers. The children are here on the Ark with full access at any time to each parent. That's no different than what's been happening before. We have no assets to quarrel over. The hardest thing will be facing the community and explaining things in a way that does not cause any bad feeling between us but being so close to them and knowing how kind natured they are, I think they will understand especially if we are all happy with the new arrangement.'

'There's one thing that has not fully been resolved and that is Mi and Buster. They say they want to be together but where will that be? That's the weak link in the chain. She can't live with him on the sub and won't like it here on her own. As you know she likes her needs to be met and I don't think that will work anymore, do you?'

'No I did it and enjoyed it because I wanted you and you found me through that, but I don't want to go back there, it's only you now, I promise. Will you promise it's only me?'

'You drive a hard bargain, but yes.'

'You are a cheeky sod, come here!' Millie kissed him passionately.

14. THE DEALS

The meeting on the submarine USS Tina Turner had commenced. In attendance were Commander Grey, Buster, Lenska and Wayne Kerr for the USA and Albert, Pete and Jane for the Ark. Jane volunteered to take the minutes for Albert. The Commander thanked them for their cooperation and their past hospitality.

'I will now hand you over to Lenska to do the dealing and extracting the information and anything else that might help us destroy the enemy. I will oversee and be assistance wherever required.'

'Thank you Commander. Now we must move on quickly and I believe if we work together we can destroy this thorn in our side. I have been authorised by our Chief of Staff to help the Ark in any way we can in return for the complete information you have on our common enemy, so I will commence by asking you what can we give you in return for us to receive that information?'

'I would like to thank all on the USS Tina Turner officially for the backup you gave us by knocking out the two jet attackers the other day, and our community would like to say that entertaining you all on the Ark was a pleasure,' Albert said. Buster smiled which Pete thought was apt. Albert continued, 'There are a number of things that we on the Ark have talked about and would like, and there are things that due to the attack are going to be necessary. The first thing we need is to have some repairs done to the damage caused by the missile and machine gun fire. We have no method of paying for this, nor a way of organising it.' Jane thought to herself, we have enough cash to cover that and plenty more, but kept quiet.

'The main thing that we would like is our own static place of residence, a small but fertile island, with fresh water somewhere in the Pacific, north of the Tropic of Capricorn. That was where we were heading before the attack.'

'Your first request,' Lenska replied, 'will not be a problem. You will need to head for The Cape of Good Hope and then will be able to stop at our base at Cape Town for repairs. This will be organised all at US expense. As to the other request, I will need to find out which islands in the area you are thinking

186

of, to see if they are available and suitable, because many beautiful tropical islands have already been bought by celebrities and the mega rich. Most are very close together, so you could end up with noisy neighbours, I don't think that would suit you or them, knowing your action filled history.'

'That's not a negative for us,' Pete commented. 'We could quieten down the area and make it respectable.'

'I like your sense of humour,' said the Commander, 'but these people are huge taxpayers to the US and upsetting them would not go down very well, if you know what I mean.'

'Yes, I can imagine, it wouldn't help the poll ratings for the government of the day.'

'Correct Albert,' said Lenska, 'so your requests are not out of the window. They can be achieved. Now let's see what you would give us in return. We know that you are able to track the movements of the Russian Mafia so you must have that technology on the Ark and that means you have access to the rogue satellites as our surveillance tells us. Are we agreed that is the case?'

'Yes replied Albert.'

'How you came about them must have been sheer bravery. We have been trying for a very long time. I say "we," but it was his department on the end there, Wayne Kerr's, is that correct Wayne?'

'Yes Captain,' the stone faced man replied.

'What we would propose,' she continued, 'is that we install temporary staff on the Ark to use the equipment you have as a surveillance strategy until it can be transferred to a vessel from the US. This may take up to four or five months by the time we can commission a suitable ship, organise and man it for the task etc. For your protection during that period this submarine will be at close quarters, but if other more serious situations arise and the sub is required elsewhere, then you will be on your own.' Albert, Jane and Pete looked at one another and Jane leaned over to ask Albert a question.

'Who and how many people from them would we have to cater for, extra accommodation and so on?'

187

'How many and who would that be? Albert asked. How would it work? There would be extra accommodation and costs in energy production etc., we cannot expect our people to wait on and cater for many numbers of the US Forces.'
'No, No Albert the numbers required at this stage are small. We are talking initially just two: that would be Buster and I. We would be visited by a supervisor every two weeks for three to four days and that is it.'
'Oh, that's reasonable but we need to confer with the rest of the community so can we adjourn for a few hours and would you like to meet again at 1500 hours in our canteen?'
'Yes Albert, Pete, Jane. It would be a pleasure.' They all shook hands and the three of them left to go the short distance to the Ark.

Albert congregated all the community in the canteen as soon as they returned to discuss the proposals. Albert explained that the only real downside would be that they could still be a target for four months while the Ark's equipment was used to extract information from the communications that were being transmitted via the Russian's rogue satellites. He gave his view on the situation.
'From the survey Gunter and Greta did in finding out if the majority of you would like to be anchored in one place with a suitable climate, most of you agreed. The only difference in this proposal if it went ahead would be that we would possibly own a piece of the world to take care of and be our permanent home, but we would have to put up with having two guests staying with us and a visitor occasionally for a few days every couple of weeks for that short initial period.'
'Who would the two guests be?' Mi asked.
'Buster and Lenska please don't ask who the other visitor will be. I don't think they know themselves.'
Pete looked at Mi's reactions to that and could see she was delighted which made him think he was doing the right thing by choosing Millie. Millie also watched Mi's face and then glanced over at Pete without a smile just a look knowing of calm and relief. The community talked between themselves for a

188

few minutes discussing the pros and cons of *The Deal*. Slowly they quietened down to a hush and then Jane was appointed to speak.

'It seems we have a full vote of confidence in 'The Deal' in its outline form at present and would like it to go ahead. It appears that we can trust the people we are working with at the moment. The rest of us are concerned that they may decide to change their personnel and bring in some obnoxious twat, oh sorry, I meant person. Can we ensure that the two mentioned are to be the only temporary residents on the Ark Albert?'

'That's not an unreasonable request. We will put that to them at the meeting this afternoon. Are there any other questions that concern any of you?'

'Yes there is Albert,' Patricia spoke up. 'What will happen to all that money we have that Miles left?'

Albert immediately thought shit! Pete and Mi have not been told and Patricia unwittingly has just given me some explaining to do.

'What money is that Albert?' Pete asked.

'It's a stash of dirty money and should not be touched. That was the agreement that was made, when it was discovered.'

'Why didn't you tell us about all that when Mi and I joined the Ark?'

'Why should you be told about it? It does not mean a bean to us. It's a burden just having it onboard can you see money changing hands on the Ark? I'm surprised Patricia has even mentioned it. I'll tell you what we could do with it, if and when we find our place of permanence. We could say to the Yanks we want to pay for this island with the cash. We don't know of its origin and we want to dispose of it, or if they could give it to a good charity as long as the US president sends us a signed written receipt as to where it has gone, they can have it.'

'How much money are we talking about?' asked Pete.

'Why does it matter how much it is? We have never counted it and do not wish to and why should its value matter to you? When you joined the Ark, money was of no importance. That is one of the main reasons why we are a solid community, a cashless society.' Millie wondered why Pete was so concerned about the money, it is, as Albert said, of no importance and his continued interest made her wary and asked herself what is this man about? I

189

will need to talk to him about this she decided as her mind became more and more disturbed. Pete got the message and realised it was not a good thing to be asking about the cash and kept quiet. Magnus was furious with Patricia for letting the cat out of the bag and was brewing a temper that he had never experienced before.

The meeting came to an abrupt end with a tremendous amount of disruption to their minds because of Patricia's outburst. All of a sudden she had made herself an unpopular person. Albert thanked the community for attending the meeting and said he would disclose the outcome of the talks with the Americans here later, as soon as it had all been concluded.

The guests arrived and very soon were made to feel at home. This time there were just three of them: the Commander, Buster and Lenska. It was taken that the CIA Chief had no role in the affair anymore. They were greeted in the normal respectful manor by Albert, Pete and Jane who escorted them to the canteen. It was the same format, just less a CIA man. The meeting commenced.

'Welcome back to the Ark. We have had a meeting and come up with a vote of confidence and we can do a deal subject to some minor requests.'

'Thank you again for your hospitality,' the Commander said, 'it is a pleasure being here on the Ark again. I must congratulate you Albert on creating such a wonderful place to be. I've heard the expression of living in an ideal world and you have almost made it. If it wasn't for the outside interference I think your community would be content living in that world, now over to you Lenska.'

'As requested, I have confirmation from our Chief of Staff that there are a number of islands that are available and suitable for your use and one could be allocated for the Ark's community if we can do a deal.'

'Thank you. That sounds very promising Lenska, but does that mean we would own the real estate outright?'

'Oh no Albert, the US government owns all its national property since the world's financial crash some years ago, so it will be a ninety nine year lease,

we cannot offer more than that and let's face it, the way China and Iran are going your island may just be a particle in the atmosphere.'
'Point taken and understood Lenska, we will face that if and when it comes. The one thing we would like to confirm at this stage is that we only have yourself and Buster as the guests for the transition period, because we like and trust you both,' Lenska and Buster looked at each other and to the rest, and smiled, thanking them simultaneously for the compliment.
'I don't see that as a problem do you Buster and Lenska?'
'No Sir,' they replied to the Commander.
'Does that mean we have an agreement and it will be put into action?' asked Albert.
'On the face of it I think we can do The Deal. The only thing that remains is when can we get started? Do we wait until you have found your island of preference, which we will need help from you by marking charts for us or can we get working on the enemy on the way?'
'Let us get our repairs done and extend the accommodation for you and Buster, and the other occasional visitor, then on transit to the destination we will show you the equipment we have acquired and then take it from there.'
'That is reasonable, so it shall be,' said Lenska with the Commander nodding in agreement.

Hands were shaken and the Commander passed a pre-prepared document of the outline proposals to Lenska to put forward to Albert, not to be a binding contract just a formality to say an agreement has been made.
'Albert I arranged this to be sent to us in anticipation to be signed in good faith.' She showed him paperwork from the US government, signed by the Chief of Staff, albeit electronically, but in principle a commitment. Albert then said it was time to move on to Cape Town and he would appreciate being escorted there for the repairs. We would prefer to anchor outside the port for security and manoeuvrability. They didn't want the hassle of tugs moving them into a berth, besides the repairs and alterations should not warrant that.
'Oh, Lenska there are a few security things that we will require while the repairs take place.'

191

'Go on Albert, tell me!' She expected difficult additions.

'They are not so much added extras more like prudent security measures. The repairs I understand will be organised by your contracted teams of skilled workers.'

'That's correct Albert.'

'Well, I would prefer local black South African skilled personnel onboard for that task as one requisite. The next would be that you and Buster stay on the Ark, on combat duty while we are under repairs. There was something else but I haven't written it down, now what was it?'

'Methane gas Albert?' Jane prompted.

'Oh yes, you couldn't spare us a few hundred thousand litres of methane gas could you? These extra journeys make us use more than we would like.'

'Are you sure that's everything Albert?'

'I can't think of anything else at the moment, but there probably will be more.'

'If it's only minor things like that, that's ok. Now Albert, there is one other thing that we would like to do.'

'I thought you had all you wanted.'

'Yes we have, more or less, this is just to help us setting up a decoy ship. We have satellite photos of the Ark but not in enough detail. We want a deeper view of the layout and workings of your systems without interference whilst getting this information. It will be done by video and photographic recordings.'

'That's not a problem as long as none of the community are on the images.'

'Of course Albert, that goes without question.'

'Then I take it our business at present is complete.'

'Yes Albert, we will be with you on the way to Cape Town so whenever you are ready to sail?'

'Thank you Commander and Lenska, we shall sail at first light.'

The Ark steadily gained speed the next day under sail power. It was some hours before they could tell that they were moving.

There was a figure constantly looking out for the submarine to make sure it wasn't far out of her sight, Mi was really in love! Millie was annoyed about Pete's questions on the money and wanted to tackle him on the subject. This kept gnawing away at her and, as usual when she had a problem, she would be down on the Bow farm to concentrate, putting her thoughts on the really important things; her livestock and crops. Pete had other ideas and wanted more information about the cash. Knowing where Millie would be, he wandered off down to the farm to pursue his quest for more details.

'Good morning Millie,' he moved towards her to kiss her, but she pushed him away. He expected more of a welcome.

'Be careful Antonio could be about,' and moved further from him.

'You seem a little off Millie. Have I done something to upset you?'

'Yes quite frankly.'

'Like what?'

'Your concern about the money at the meeting,'

'Well it was a surprise to hear that you were all sitting on a huge sum of cash and didn't want it. No wonder Patricia mentioned it. If you don't want it then I'll have it and you won't see my arse for dust!'

'That just about sums you up Pete. It's obvious that your brain is the size of the end of your dick and is only good for fucking. Now fuck off and leave me alone. You've upset me to say the least.'

Millie turned away and continued her work. Pete was shocked at her outburst and returned to the bridge at a slow pace trying to understand why anyone would not want a huge sum of money, then he started to think of Millie and how he preferred being with her to Mi.

'Shit I've blown it again!' he said aloud to himself. 'Women, I never understood them.'

Albert was at the helm when Pete joined him.

'You didn't stay long at the farm Pete? I thought you liked to work out down there. You were fast to get there and slow to come back. I see it all up here, is your labour not required?'

193

'Yes there's not much to do down there, so I thought I would come and annoy you instead.'

'You sound a bit negative, are you dreaming of untold riches?'

'What do you mean?'

'It was bloody obvious from the meeting that as soon as the money was mentioned you were agitated and wanted to know about it. The whole community had been through the shock of finding out about the cash and eventually we came around to a conclusion. That was if we threw it in the sea the Russians would still come after us, so it wasn't doing any harm where it was. Besides it's a 99.9% chance that it was ill-gotten anyway and it does not belong to us. So if we can disperse of it through the latest development then it's a problem solved.'

'Surely it's like winning the lottery? Just think what you can do with all that cash and now heading for Cape Town you could buy a big chunk of real estate there.'

'Pete, I'm not getting through to you. We don't want any mainland shit. We want to be separate, our own little piece of the world and no interference from the outside. We don't want money or anything else associated with it. The Ark had the benefit of that in having the Ark's building conversion so that we could make it on our own. But it will take the help of the US to balance the Russian problem and hopefully we'll pass it on to them. If you cannot live here in these conditions then you will have to think again. You have got until Cape Town to make your mind up, so forget the money. It is a no-go subject you will not be taking one single euro or US dollar from the cache with you if you decide to leave.'

'No, no, don't get excited Albert, I'm just trying to come to terms with the community's ethos on living the way you do and I must admit it has its benefits. The problem I have is what do I do in a perfect environment? I don't want to end up like some retired ex-pat in Spain with nothing to do but eat and drink himself to death in paradise.'

'How about having some children? You and Mi must have thought about it. That would keep you busy. You're a lot younger than me and I've realised that you can't be an active Marine all your life.'

194

'That's where I have a big problem.'

'Oh! I thought you were 'master stud?'

'No, not in that sense, well I may just as well tell you before you find out elsewhere. Hmm, you see I have been getting on very well with Millie, well up until an hour ago and then I upset her.'

'I thought something was going on between you two, Mi and Buster as well. So what's the score on it all now?'

'Mi and Buster suit each other and I don't mind if he took her on. She's a lovely person and I'm very fond of her, but I am more comfortable with Millie. She and Ched have drifted apart now Marigold is on the scene, so at the moment if I knuckle down to Millie's wishes I will be with her, Ched will be with Marigold and it looks like Mi will be with Buster.'

'You certainly have been busy since you arrived onboard! It's like some old TV soap opera. Now has the trouble between you and Millie got to do with the money because we are not used to having someone we all love here upset?'

'It's as I said, I can't understand not wanting to spend that cash. Millie won't leave the Ark under any circumstances so if I want her I will have to stay and learn how to live in paradise, that's why I took so long to walk back because I was deep in thought about myself and the situation.'

'Come on Pete, it's not that bad. How old are you now? You must be fifty surely, and to have the opportunity to have the choice of two young fit ladies to be with, how old is Mi? Thirty, how old is Millie? Probably in her early thirties, when did you want for anything since being on the Ark? Pete you don't know when you are very well off.'

'Albert, you sound like my old man, telling me how bad things were when he was a kid, perhaps I should have listened to him as I should listen to you now.'

'It's like this so far, the only problem we've encountered to be in real danger has been the Russian mob. We have a male female imbalance and that may increase if Lenska stays for a lengthy period, because there won't be anyone available to get inside her knickers, you know exactly what I mean?'

195

'Yes, could be trouble Albert, we'll be a man down, but then she possibly won't be staying with us for very long. Also Buster has a limited time here as far as we know, so who knows what will happen?'

'You sound a bit like me when Melanie was concerned about her future. I would always reply. *You never know what's over the horizon.'*

'Very true Albert, so I'd better go back to Millie and tell her I don't need the money, just her.'

'Before you go please make sure that nothing negative evolves from the partner changes you have suggested. The main priority is the children. They are so young and can be easily hurt. I know that there are no signs of problems so far because they are well looked after. I have a task on my hands now to explain to Amy and the others the possible forthcoming changes, but that will be when you have all made a commitment between each other by a confrontation ending in full mutual agreement. It will have to be a formal arrangement between all parties, so make sure you are aware of this if you all decide to make it happen.'

'Thank you Albert. Talking to you has made me feel better about being here. I've just got to find a way of making my life, in what is basically retirement, an occupied and fulfilled one.'

Pete left to go to Millie and felt a lot better realising that Albert had brought a message home to him. The main thing was his age, nearly fifty. He had rarely thought of the years creeping up because he had always been active and busy all the time. He knew he was still able to attract younger attractive females and make them happy! But how long would that last? Hmm Albert's right, I had better be thankful for what I've got. Walking at quite a pace he was at the Bow farm in very little time and speeded up when he saw Millie.

'Millie I'm so sorry. I'm not interested in the money I just want you and to stay with you. Will you have me?'

'Yes as long as there are no more goings on with any others. Is that clear?'

'Yes I promise.' They hugged and kissed, held each other tightly then separated and took each others hand to walk together to the orchard and stopped at a spot next to Miles' grave and sat to talk of what would lie ahead of them. The pair began to ask each other how they would sort out their lives and how it would affect the others involved and made plans minimising damage to them.

Albert and Amy lay awake after feeding Esperanca in the early hours of the next night after his discussion with Pete. Albert was frustrated with not being able to get back to sleep,
'Did you know that Pete and Millie were having an affair and are going to be together in the very near future?'
'Yes, Millie told me.'
'Oh, when was that?'
'Tonight in the canteen, she was the happiest I've seen her in a long time and without the aid of a drink. Didn't you notice?'
'No I was with Magnus and Melanie who was concerned about Zimbo, who they say is not pulling his weight and in fact becoming overweight. He doesn't like getting up in the morning and has developed an attitude problem. I must admit I don't see much of him but now I have another problem to solve.'
'I'm sure you'll sort it out darling. Can I do something to help you sleep?'
Turning to his side she lowered her hand onto his limp cock, and moved it gently back and to. It soon reacted by swelling as the blood rushed in.
'That's a rapid response.' No more was said as they connected passionately as always, then fell into a deep sleep after their lovemaking, feeling complete and happy.

15. DIVORCE THE PROPER WAY

The commander was true to his word having his sub within shouting distance of the Ark all the way to Cape Town. Table Mountain appeared at dawn with the sun rising behind them as they sailed towards the South African port. A pilot boat was there to meet them and indicated to follow to the place where they were to anchor, an area just less than a mile from the harbour, a position given to them by the Port authority. The submarine went into their own base where prearranged berth accommodation was allocated for them in the military compound. From there the commander organised the repairs and instructed Albert ready to receive Buster, Lenska and the workers in two days time.

Buster and Lenska arrived almost twenty-four hours earlier than expected with their necessary security equipment. Then their temporary accommodation was sorted out. It was at that point that Albert said to those that were in changing partner mode that he would like a meeting with them, including Buster now that he was involved. They all agreed and most in many ways were relieved that the situation was going to be opened up and hopefully closed. Mi had welcomed Buster straight away by jumping up at him and clinging to him by arms and legs to his embarrassment in front of Lenska. 'Buster we are having a meeting with Albert, Pete, Ched, Marigold, Millie, you and me to sort out our quarters, plus a few other things,' Mi immediately and excitedly informed him. 'So bring your things to the canteen. Oh Lenska could you go to Amy's quarters she is expecting you? The meeting will need to finish before we know where you will be staying.'
'Sure, I know where it is, no problem, I'll catch up with you later Buster!'

The three couples and Albert congregated in the canteen. No other person was permitted at that point to be a party to the discussions. Albert had put a lot of thought into this with the invaluable help of Amy, who wanted to be present but had problems with Esperanca and also needed to sort out accommodation for Lenska. Albert had laid out the tables to have each prospective couple that wanted to live and love together opposite each other with him at the head of the table so he could see all their faces and reactions.

They all sat and Albert began his deliberation. He was slightly nervous and talked in his official voice.
'This is a very difficult situation for you all and for me. I am to sort out in a formal manner the separation and joining of you adult people in our community. It does not surprise me that in this small but solid community those changes in relationships happen. I personally do not condone it but I do not want to stop fulfilment and happiness. There is one thing I want you all to remember and to pass on to your children as a priority, and I have asked Jane in the past to create a true family tree and record of who, putting it plainly, came from who. Because we are a small, growing social group, I believe from proven science that is a must. We do not want any close interbreeding between us. It could be disastrous. So I will make a rule that will be unchangeable, under any circumstances the mating of direct first cousins is strictly prohibited. The family tree record will be available to all at the mating age of fifteen years this also will be known as Ark's law. It gives the children the true knowledge of who their biological mother and father are, and, if they are lucky, grandmother and grandfather, plus a very important thing: half-brothers and sisters.

Now at the moment my understanding is that you Ched and Marigold want to be and live together, is that correct?'
'Yes,' they replied, speaking together looking at each other.
'Millie, have you any problem with that situation?'
'No Albert.'
'Millie you and Pete have formed a strong relationship, is that correct?'
'Yes Albert.'
'Mi and Buster, have you formed a solid relationship which would be sustainable through the interruption of the US forces who employ Buster and, if ordered could be drafted away at a moment's notice?'
'Yes Albert,' they both replied.

199

'Can I now have assurances from you all that, that is the case and there is no animosity whatsoever between you, because the consequences could be huge to our wellbeing on the Ark?' They all agreed looking at each other and nodding in agreement.

'That's good and I'm pleased you all can do that and now, I have to ask Mi and Buster to leave the meeting and sort out their accommodation temporally although only until we have repairs and alterations completed whilst here in Cape Town.'

Albert addressed the remaining four.

'This is the hardest bit both for me and for your children. My view is that there will be no priority over any custody of them Ched, Millie and Marigold because it is irrelevant. All four of you will be, as the rest of us are, responsible for all children that are on this Ark, their care, their emotional needs, their education, their physical development, mental stability and health etc. How you do that is by the means that we all have worked for and are in place. Now you can object to my view if you like, but you will have to have a sound reason for an alternative method or answer.'

'Albert, I want to say something that needs to go on the family tree record. Ched knows now and I'm certain Marigold knows. I have told Pete that Rose is the result of Antonio and me, my biggest concern is that Jane would be doing the records and I don't want to upset their solid relationship.'

'That was a shock to Amy and I.' Millie looked down. 'We had suspicions as all did. Pete, first of all does that make any difference to your love for Millie?'

'No.' Millie looked up and smiled at him comforted by his direct answer.

'The only thing I can do is to ask you all at this stage to be totally silent to any of the community on the true parentage of the beautiful girl Rose. I will ask Amy to take on the task that Jane had started of the family tree record that is now out of date, until such times that the true situation can be revealed without the possible threat of upset within the community. That may be some years and it will not be relevant to do so until our offspring are at the age of puberty.' Again the four were in agreement and nodded their heads.

200

'Now I want to conclude this meeting by telling you where you will be quartered. As I see it Ched, you and Marigold retain the place you shared with Millie, mainly because you have the space to accommodate all the children, which I understand you have more or less been doing.' They looked at each other and smiled. Millie I think you would be best in Pete's home. Mi and Buster will share Marigold's place once her personal things have been moved. Now are there any other items to be discussed?' They all shook their heads and could not wait to get out of the canteen and move to the places where they were organised to be. The rest of the day was spent sorting out the accommodation, with all the change around of cohabiting partners.

The evening meal bell came and all of the Ark's community attended including the American guests. Albert took this opportunity to address everyone. He stood up before anyone had collected meals and knocked on the table.
'Can I have your attention please for just a few minutes before you have your meals?' He looked around to make sure all were seated and parents/carers had the children under control.
'I would like to take this opportunity to tell you all, now that we are one hundred percent together and in one place. Over the past year relationships have changed between various members of our community. To put straight any rumours that may have been flying about, I will now give you all the latest information of who will be with whom; the most important subject is our dear offspring.
Ched will now be living with Marigold with the children Vicky, Lucy and Rose. Millie will now be living with Pete and will have direct access to her own children at all times. Mi will now live with Buster. I'm not so positive about this because Buster is employed by the US government, but we all know that he wants to become one of us along with Mi, who we are so lucky to have here as our in-house doctor. We can only hope that things will work out and that he can stay permanently. The final part of this is our other guest who will be with us for the next four months or so, Lenska a Captain in the US Navy is here to extract the information from the equipment we have

201

installed in the communications room and hopefully remove the threat of any further attacks from the Russian Mafia who keep attacking us. Please make her very welcome. That is all, please enjoy your evening.'

Albert was so relieved to get that out in the open and out of the way. Without sitting down he went straight to the bar and poured himself a glass of water with ice. Amy looked and thought that's strange. Albert sat back down next to her.
'Are you alright, it's not like you to be drinking plain water at this time of night?'
'I'm expecting to be bombarded with questions from some people and if I have a pint of bitter in front of me I will have a sip after every question and I will be wanting another, before long it will be too many, bearing in mind we will have workers arriving at some time of the morning and I want to be present for that and fully compos mentis.'

Just then Marigold came over to ask Albert a question. Amy smiled at Albert.
'Albert this thing about being responsible for all the children on the Ark, I couldn't possibly look after all the children at one time all on my own. I would not be able to cope.'
'Marigold that is not quite the meaning of the responsibility, what it means is that we all have the duty of making sure at all times that our children are cared for and if you see a problem, a child that needs help in any way, such as if the child has wandered off and lost on this vast area, because that is what it looks like to them, it is your duty to tend to that child's needs whether it is your child or any others on the Ark. I could go on about situations but the basic thing to think of is, the protection of all, knowing where each of them is at any one time.'
'Oh, I understand now. Sorry I must sound thick to you.'
'No, not at all Marigold, I'm not the best on this planet at speeches.'
'Thank you Amy and Albert for what you have done for me, Lucy and Ched.'
Marigold went back to her table only to be quizzed by Ched.
'What was that all about? It's not like you to approach Albert.'

'I just had to thank them for what they've done for us Ched.'
'Yes, my love and I will too.'

0600 hours the next morning a tug boat laden with men and some materials hooted for attention as they were by the side of the Ark waiting to board, the night watch manned by Gunter had seen it approach and called Buster and Lenska to be ready to accept the arrivals for security checks. It was too early to call Albert to be involved, so Gunter thought, and left the situation to the chosen, Buster and Lenska. Their first problem was how to gain access. The person that usually controlled that was Magnus and he was still in bed. Buster and Lenska went to the bridge to consult Gunter.
'Gunter we have people waiting to board to do the repairs. How can we give them access?'
'Only with Magnus, he will shut down the electrified fence and operate the ladder.'
'Gunter, please could you call Magnus?'
'Certainly Buster, but how is it that we were not told of a 0600 hours start this morning, have you had confirmation of that?' Buster looked at Lenska, and she shrugged her shoulders,
'Albert knew workers would be here this morning,' she said.
'I think we should check with Albert. Gunter, call Albert and Pete this is urgent,' Buster requested.

Gunter acted immediately and in ten minutes the pair appeared already armed. Albert thanked Gunter for letting him know the workers were here.
'Right what's the situation?'
'Sir,' Buster explained, 'we have no knowledge of this delivery of workers so early to board the Ark for repairs, we need to take precautions until I contact the Commander for confirmation, but in the meantime I guess we should check out the status of the personnel in the boat waiting to board.'
'Which side are they on and where are they?'
'They are Port side and about foredeck position so they have an idea of where to access,' said Gunter.

'Right Pete, let's take a look,'
'Albert, Lenska and me will be with you,' Buster said, not wanting to be left out.
'You can come if you want but don't get in the way.'

Albert and Pete were long gone, checking their automatics on the way before the two security people had decided what to do.
'Lenska we are supposed to be doing what they are doing, so why are we still here?'
'I don't know. Which is the port side?'
'It's where they've gone.'
'Buster that's bloody obvious is it left or right?'
'I don't know it depends which way you are facing, towards the front of the ship or the back. I don't know.'
'Buster this is stupid, let's just go and find them.'
'That won't be hard if there's a problem you will hear them. They don't fuck about!'
'What do you mean they don't fuck about? I thought that's what you did?'
'Lenska I'm being serious here, when these two guys move they do damage. I owe my life to them. If they had not been so professional I would have been splattered all over Somalia.'

Pete asked Albert when they had arrived at the point of access for the visitors if Magnus was up yet, if not to get him out of bed to shut down the fence.
'Magnus are you out of bed yet?' Albert waited for a few seconds for a reply.
'Magnus I repeat, are you out of bed yet?'
'Yes Albert, I hear you, but I haven't had my breakfast, it's a bit too early.'
'Magnus fuck your breakfast and shut down the fence we have visitors. We don't know if they are friend or foe, so be ready for action.'
'Yes Albert.'

It took ten minutes for Magnus to get to operate the shut down and then he radioed to confirm it was off. Albert and Pete opened the gate to see who was

204

waiting to board. They lowered the steps to the boat looked down and could see two coloured males in tee shirts, unarmed and as soon as they saw the gate open with Albert and Pete's head appearing, the two men jumped to the foot of the metal steps to board and started to climb, then four more males appeared from within the tug boat but they were white and had thick coats on, a big giveaway to Albert and Pete.

'Hold it there?' said Albert. He and Pete raised their weapons pointing them to the tug.

'You lot down there,' Albert shouted. 'Take off your coats you won't need them today it's going to be a hot day!' The four looked at each other and one just nodded to the others, the coats were off and automatic's were firing at Albert and Pete but hitting and killing the two poor local lads on the access steps. They fell into the sea through the aggressors' gunfire, and one by one they jumped to the access steps only to be shot on their attempt to board the Ark. The last one stayed on the tug and shouted abuse at the pilot because he wasn't moving fast enough. The arrival of Buster and Lenska came as the shooting ceased.

'What's happened?' asked Lenska.

'We didn't like the look of them,' said Albert. He closed the gate and radioed to Magnus to switch the fence back on.

'Right Buster, contact the Commander or whoever is on duty and get that tug apprehended and the persons onboard in US custody without the South African authority involved.'

'Yes Albert Sir, straight away.' Buster dealt with the communication via the radio on the bridge.

'I have confirmation that it will be done Albert.'

Meanwhile Pete was being hit by questions from Lenska.

'How many were there?'

'How many did you kill?'

'Were any of them just injured?'

'Hey, hey, hey, just a fucking minute lady. We've just done your job, how many did you kill or injure? Why were they here? Who is the leak? Why are

205

we having this conversation?' Lenska stood and looked at him, realising she would not be getting many answers from him at present.

'I'm sorry Pete I've never been this close to action before, I guess I haven't got the balls yet. We have let you down.'

'Don't bother getting any balls you are just fine as you are!' Lenska smiled seeing the funny side of his remark.

'What are you two smiling at?' said Albert, 'You behave yourself Pete you are in enough trouble with women as it is.'

The tug was taken by US Navy Seals and the men captured before getting back to the mainland, they were taken directly to US Base and put under guard for initial interrogation.

The sleeping community on the Ark gradually emerged from their beds to resume a normal day unaware of the incident that had already taken place. Others at the Bow Farm: Millie, Antonio and Zimbo were also oblivious of the action. In the canteen the arrivals one by one and two by two collected their breakfasts. Magnus was the first to ask questions while tucking into his usual breakfast prepared by the love of his life, Patricia.

'What was that all about so early this morning Albert?'

'Nothing to worry about Magnus just the normal stuff,'

'Oh, that's ok then.' Albert shook his head in dismay. The canteen soon filled up with most of the community plus Buster and Lenska who both made a beeline to Albert to give him confirmation of the taking of the assailants. The two spoke together.

'Albert, the Navy Seals have captured the two that got away.'

'Do I have to hear that in stereo?'

'Sorry Albert,' they both said, realising they were still speaking at the same time.

'You explain Buster, and I'll go to the bridge to tell Pete.'

'Sorry again Albert, the Commander has confirmed that they have the two men from the tug and they are in security at the US Base.'

'The Navy Seals didn't kill them, but actually caught them alive.' Repeated Albert.

'Yes Albert, so I've been told.'

'Well that's an achievement for them. They will be able to go to the top of the class and give out pencils or should I say laptops now.'

'Yes, you must be forty years behind with the use of pencils in the classroom.'

'Maybe, but I didn't need any laptop to sort those poor sods out a couple of hours ago.' Magnus overheard.

'What poor sods was that Albert?'

'Just a failed attempt to board us by the usual undesirables, which ended in death for some of them,' Magnus was shocked, not realising that while he was at ease slowly waking up to Albert's heated request there was action happening.

'Sorry Albert, I thought this would be a safe haven from the Russians, besides the US were with us and supposed to protect us.' Buster looked at Albert and was just about to say sorry.

'Don't say sorry. That's all I've heard since I got up this morning and it's not even 0900 hours yet.'

Millie told Antonio that she was going to the canteen for her breakfast early, would he mind if he went for his on her return?

'I'll come with you, I'm very hungry *fatso'* here can look after things for a while.'

'I'm not fat I'm a young man still growing,' Zimbo retaliated.

'You are fat Zimbo, just look at you.'

'Stop it you two, let's go for breakfast.'

'You are right,' Millie said as they walked to the canteen, 'he is getting fat. Can you have a word with Jane to work out a diet for him, I know we've had our differences in the past but she is intelligent and diplomatic in such situations and gets things enforced.'

'Thank you Millie I will give her that compliment.' Millie smiled looking forward to seeing Pete and to have her breakfast.'

'I must say Antonio; your English has improved remarkably.'

'Thank you Millie.'

207

Pete had finished his meal and was still sitting with Lenska, just chatting about what had happened when Millie arrived. Seeing him talking to her put her hackles up. Albert could feel the vibes from her as he watched her walk into the canteen and immediately intervened, jumped up and grabbed her by the arm.

'Millie, Pete is just explaining some of the details of the failed assault early this morning, that's all.'

'Assault, what assault? I didn't hear anything. We must have been in the cowshed milking.' He took her to Pete and Lenska's table, still holding her by the arm. As soon as Pete saw her he got up and greeted her, immediately he kissed her on the lips which quelled any jealousy straight away.

'Pete, please could you explain to Millie what happened? While I go and get her some breakfast, what would you like Millie?'

'Thank you Albert that's very kind of you. Please can I have bacon and two eggs, toast, butter and some of that fantastic marmalade Amy made.'

Pete explained. Then Lenska gave her version of the event from the US side of things to Millie. Then Millie realised that she and Antonio were up and long gone by the time the action took place on their way to the farm and would not have heard any shooting over the side of the ship. Zimbo didn't arrive until much later, as usual, well after the incident. Millie was still hands on the situation with the animal side of farming. Albert delivered her food. 'Thank you Albert.' She soon tucked in while listening to Lenska.

At 1100 hours Buster received a message from Commander Grey via the ships radio.

'Albert the Commander is coming to see you at 1200 hours, can I confirm that is OK?'

'Yes Buster, that's fine.' Later the Commander was welcomed, not alone but with another high ranking officer, who was introduced as Commanding Officer Felix Chapman of the Communications Division, seconded to the Intelligence Corp.

'Pleased to meet you Albert,'

208

'And you Felix.'

'Felix is here to get some idea of the equipment you have acquired. It's just an assessment so that he can pick the right engineer to operate the system when it's recreated on the decoy ship. Would it be alright to let him have a look at the set up?'

'Yes Commander, Pete will show him the communications room.' Pete greeted Felix by shaking hands.

'Welcome aboard the Ark. Let's go ahead. I'm sure Albert and the Commander would like a chat.'

'Sure Pete.'

'Commander, how come we got into this situation this morning, which left five dead, two of them were probably just paid to look like local workmen to get access for the others to follow and do the business?'

'I don't know Albert; I can't possibly imagine that there is a leak somewhere. I can only think that they knew you would be headed to your normal winter retreat and took the opportunity when you pulled into Cape Town for repairs and, as soon as our contract people started looking for personnel to carry out the repairs, the word got to the wrong people. The thing is it was a last minute attempt when you anchored here, then an attack was ordered. The other point is that it shows you have had most of your attacks not that far from land and in the southern hemisphere where they seem to have a grip on persons willing to take a risk for a few dollars.'

'Well, Commander nothing changes much does it? It has been like that ever since the white man went into Africa, whether it was missionaries, traders, mercenaries, warlords, Taliban and thousands of other types including ourselves. We all caused poverty and death to the indigenous people. Some of the worst were the so-called privileged ones, heads of tribes etc. They were given an Oxford type education, only to return to be a despot or dictator whatever you can call them just to give the people extended misery.'

'Bloody hell Albert you have got a chip on your shoulder. No doubt you must have been involved in some of that shit. Do I read you right?'

209

'Yes Commander, regrettably and that's one of the reasons for creating the Ark and it seems that yet again I have been used.'

'Look on the positive side Albert, if you hadn't created the Ark and been so resilient in your protection of her, you wouldn't be where you are today with the US government at your aid. There are talks going about that you have uncovered a big can of worms. There are statesmen and politicians on both sides of the Atlantic disappearing and committing suicide. The stretch of the Mafia's stranglehold is bigger than was ever thought, so there is at least one government that is indebted to you for creating the Ark, but we know there are other naive governments that are out for your demise. That sounds worse than it might be. I need time to talk to you and explain what has been happening and hopefully, will take place in the next six months. This is just between you and me Albert, is that OK?'

'Yes of course.'

'As you know, we are recreating the Ark to be almost identical from the physical image but extremely well equipped within her bowels so as to deliver shit where required, that is why you will have this type of visitor but only for the next month.'

'I understand and they will be accommodated I will see to that. What have you got on the two captured men from the tug that the Navy Seals managed to avoid killing?'

'Nothing as yet, we are waiting for our specialist interrogation squad to arrive. It is different now. Since the Guantanamo Bay disaster bringing the intervention of "do-gooders" on the scene, any prisoner must be interrogated in a humane manner. The US military are not permitted to directly question anyone who is suspected of being a terrorist and taken prisoner and since then, no useful information has been extracted from any prisoner taken.'

'I see, so I won't hold my breath then?'

'No I wouldn't, and on the Navy Seal's issue, there again you have made an impact Albert, after that debacle when you gave the Navy Seals a loss of pride and a top class submarine heading to be unbalanced. There was a huge concern about the big headed bullish way things were being done, so it was addressed. The team that took the men prisoners were still Navy Seals but were trained in capture, they still sunk the tug though.' They both laughed at that. Albert enjoyed the Commander's sense of humour.

'I think that deserves a drink Commander. It's gone 1200 hours so that's alright. Are you up for it?'

'Yes why not?'

'Commander I don't know your first name. I'm not one for titles as you are well aware.'

'It's Frank, Frank Trevor Grey. I can understand why you don't like titles, but then you have that choice when you are out of the service.'

'True.'

At the canteen they both went to the bar, Albert moved to behind the bar as no one was there.

'What can I get you Frank?'

'I had some raspberry wine I think the last time, it was very good. I'd like one of those, do you have any?'

'Yes there's plenty, it's one of my favourites. It's not too strong but a good quaffing wine when chilled and does not give you a bad head the next day if you have exceeded more than you should have.'

'I don't think the replication of the Ark will go to this detail, it will be imported food and refreshments.'

'Cheers Frank here's to survival.'

'Cheers Albert.'

'So Frank have you found our promised land?'

'No not yet, we haven't found what you are looking for. The main problem is that the present ideal locations are on the top of fractures, plates that when they move, could erupt, causing earthquakes and could be devastating to you at some time. Just be patient, I'm sure the experts will come up with something.'

'How do you propose the changeover from this Ark to the replacement without the Russian Mafia knowing?'

211

'We've thought this through and there are certain places in the southern hemisphere that are unable to take any satellite coverage. It will be at one of those areas that we hope the swap over will take place, then the decoy will start transmitting periodically when it has returned to satellite coverage area, allowing you to travel to your promised land.'

'What about the rogue satellites, do you know if they cover those areas?'

'They mainly cover the Northern hemisphere but we believe they have one that covers the Southern hemisphere down to as far as a just a few hundred miles south of here, because there's nothing going on for them south of that yet.'

'It sounds neat but will it work?'

'We have to make it work. This threat to the US, Europe and many other countries is growing by the day. There are also rumours that the undefeated Taliban is being supported by the Russian and Italian Mafia's organisations, so the problem now is Third World War status.'

'So, am I reading this correct? The money that the Mafia make from extortion is going to feed terrorist organisations?'

'Exactly Albert,'

Albert realised that his original assumption of the purpose of Mile's stash of cash was intended was not far wrong, but where would that place be? Miles knew that the idea was just to season hop up and down the Atlantic, so where did he plan to get off with the cash and how would he do it? This was bugging Albert to the extent that the conversation between them stopped.

'Are you still with me Albert you seemed *miles* away?'

'Sorry Frank, yes I was 'Miles' away. You sparked something off in my mind that has been troubling me for a while. It's like another piece in a jigsaw puzzle has just been put in its correct place, my apologies. How about another glass of wine, would you like it refilled?'

'Yes please, it's very quaffable, as you said.'

'The lunchtime food will be on soon. I hope you are hungry Frank.'

'I've always looked forward to meals on the Ark, they are something else. The lady Patricia is a fantastic cook.'

212

'Thank you, I'll relay the compliment.'

The pair had just finished their lunch when Pete and Felix came in to eat.
They were greeted and Albert asked what Felix thought?
'Well I hoped it may have been simple to just download everything and reload
onto our system, but there is a huge possibility that it will self destruct in that
situation, so you did the right thing by removing and reconstructing the
computers as they were when you found them.'
'You can thank Magnus for that. He is always meticulous when it comes to
engineering.' Albert received a call from Gunter to say there was a US ship
next to them with methane and fresh water tanks on board.
'Ok, I'm on my way. Call Ched to give me a hand to fill our tanks as soon as
possible please.

16. PAST OLD GROUND

Finally, after ten days all the repairs and alterations were complete and the Ark was ready for its little operation for the US, then hopefully to its final destination. The tanks were full, up to date medical supplies and other equipment required for the guests were now onboard and the Ark was ready to sail to its winter home and for its ruse, then hopefully to its ideal resting place. Oddly enough, the area the Commander advised them to go for the winter was just west of Tristan Da Cunha, their normal winter retreat but the opposite side of the islands. They would wait there then change ID with a decoy ship. Pete commented that while he was on patrol as coastguard, it was that area that had the most illegal factory fishing operations by the Chinese and others, because with no satellite cover there was presumably low risk of being detected.

There were many thoughts onboard from the community whether the trip to their promised land a South Pacific Island would be a successful one in the near future or would it elude them due to outside world political circumstances? They all had faith in Albert and the Ark's defence team, including themselves knowing the distance they had come in time, travel and to overcome the tyranny of external threats and attacks. They believed they still had the confidence and qualifications to survive. The only attack they had while at anchor at Cape Town was dealt with rapidly by the ageing pair. Albert and Pete still had the ability to think on their feet, ready for the unexpected, and dealt with the situation as an everyday job as their duty to protect the Ark.

The Ark had its fuel of methane gas boosted to full capacity and also received a number of extra storage cylinders for the continuous supply from the Ark's own source. It was hoped by April when the decoy ship should be ready to do the swap, then, they could sail on to Cape Horn, through Drake's Passage in the Scotia Sea to where they wanted to be. Millie and Albert were concerned about the lower temperatures on route and the damage they could cause to the various Mediterranean species of fruit they were growing, but hopefully the transit in that area would not be for long. When they enter the South Pacific from the east, they intended to travel north-west and then to the west to the Polynesian Group of islands, passing Easter Island, and then onto the Pitcairn Islands. Some of these islands have a romantic history and some not so!

The switch around of partners went surprisingly smoothly and was well organised and now accepted by the rest as almost normal. Ched was with Marigold who mainly looked after Vicky, Rose and Lucy, taking on a more responsible role now she had a proper loving relationship. A permanent smile developed that could not be seen without a smile back. Millie had settled with Pete, content with their relationships. She worked with Ched and Marigold to make sure the children were loved and cared for by all of them. Vicky still spent most of her spare time with her mother, tending her garden and taking a full interest in farming. This was natural and she developed very much like her mother, caring for the land and animals, although unfortunately Millie secretly thought she had the physical features of her father Ched. Mi and Buster had a honeymoon for a week and not much was seen of them, until he volunteered for night watch. Rumour had it and by the way he walked, he was very sore down below and Mi slept a lot afterwards.

The anchor was raised and soon the turbines with their new supply of fuel were thrusting to power them away, turning the huge propellers and leaving a massive foamy wake behind. The magnificent sight of Table Mountain was soon in the distance. Albert insisted that the use of sails would still be a preference when conditions were suitable. The USS Tina Turner left shortly after and kept a short distance away from the Ark, always in its sight and near enough to respond if any sign of attack, and were very much appreciated for knocking out the aircraft attack that caused immense damage. But were disappointed with the debacle, when an early morning attempt to board the ship by intruders, with Buster and Lenska running about like headless chickens. They had been taken aside by Commander Grey and told to get their act together because the success of the operation was critical to the nation's

215

future security. Buster and Lenska had a word with Albert that because it was unreasonable for just the two of them, to keep a twenty four hour, seven day security watch, could he organise some help to break down their shifts? Albert's reply was.

'You two continue your rotas between you how you like because we will not rely on you to protect the Ark from attack.' Albert replied. 'It will be too much of a stressful task for you anyway, so do shifts that you are comfortable with and we will still maintain our own system of defence 24/7.'

'Oh, are you sure?' asked Lenska.

'I'm positive. Just inform me of your watch times and if you change them, give me good notice so that I can inform the others on watch that you are about; if you don't you could be mistaken for the enemy and then what do you think would happen?'

'Fully understood Albert and we we'll go with that. Thank you Albert.'

ALBERT'S LOG December 2019

Well almost back to normal, just need to get the next six months over with and hopefully we will be left alone to settle by our island somewhere. The search will be interesting. I hope Gunter has taken into account that the depth of sea around some of the Pacific islands will not take our draft; I had better remind him of that. From the communications I had from Frank recently they have narrowed the search down for us to a couple of atolls/archipelagos. Some of the islands have high ground and fresh water, it couldn't be better for us. Gunter and Greta seem to be the most excited. Gunter has done well with his navigation skills over the past and deserves a break from that task, as we all do ours. When we finally stop, Pete is going to find it difficult to keep actively occupied. We will think of something. I know Pete has thought about it but hasn't come up with a solution yet. I wonder if Gunter has considered his own situation, I'll mention it as boredom can be a very dangerous thing. Most of us have always been very active and I'm sure we need consultation about the

216

possible problems that could happen to most of us. Mind you, there are some that will take to boredom naturally, that's another problem. We must come up with the answer to make it all work out, after all, we have still got to maintain our food supply and keep ourselves healthy. I will need to prioritise these questions well before we arrive at our final destination.

According to what Commander Frank said, the interrogation of the men captured on the tug, will not come to anything so it would not make any difference to the situation now anyway. In hindsight Pete and I should have given those men on the tug with the big coats concealing their weapons time to get half way up the ladder, then hit them. It would only have been the boat's pilot that needed to be questioned which would probably have suited the investigation squad.

Commander Grey seems to be a good solid chap, very amenable and pleasant to work with. He has kept his word on everything so far and no reason for it to change. But what if the world's present stability changes? And it would not take much to cause a dangerous crisis at the moment or in the near future, and I can predict this. There are some countries bent on having world power not thinking of the consequences and it is not hard for any normal thinking person to point a finger. So, on that assumption I will take the view that we are still on our own and at all times, we must remain independent and able to defend ourselves.

The partner change threw me somewhat, especially Pete and Millie, but there you go! You cannot control peoples' emotions when they have a desire for another. At least now they've sorted themselves out and can adjust to a normal situation as far as the eye can see. I really don't want to do that sort out again. I just hope they stay settled and I hope all the couples make a pregnancy. I feel a little sorry for Ched at the moment, he and Marigold have three children to mainly care for, which they do very well, but I'm

217

positive that it won't be long before there is another child on its way. That will make four, I had better start thinking of bigger cabins with more bedrooms.

At first when Gunter mentioned a place of permanence there were thoughts of letting the Ark ground and making it join a part of an island, perhaps a coral reef. I've had second thoughts on this for three reasons, one is the damage we may cause to any coral reef, second: once grounded it will be impossible to move. Third the problem of keeping active men occupied, which could be done by maintaining the Ark and keeping it fully operational. Also I don't like the idea of not being able to up and move if there is a major problem.

Weather conditions were now suitable for raising the sails. All of the crew were used to pitching the sails to the best angle for the most effect from the southerly wind pushing them in a westerly direction to take the Ark some two thousand nautical miles to its winter stay. Their speed was ten knots by the end of their first day back at sea. Radar and the lookout were manned around the clock. It was estimated the trip would take about seven days at that speed. Either Albert or Pete, one of them would always be around, neither was going to let their guard down. Each did a twelve hour shift with Albert doing from 2200 hours until 1000 hours the next day and Pete 1000 hours until 2200 hours. Each had breaks during their shifts covered by Ched and Gunter. Albert thought it would be better that way now that Esperanca was more settled in her feeding and sleeping patterns. Lenska and Buster adopted the same rota as Albert and Pete with Lenska opting for the same shift as Albert which suited Buster who would have a normal day shift and nights with Mi, which kept her happy.

During Albert's night shift with Lenska present, she asked Albert a lot of questions on how the whole project of the Ark came about and how on earth it got involved with the Russian Mafia. She was always very polite and diplomatic in the way she questioned him. Albert could not see any harm in giving her the answers. After each shift she would immediately go to her cabin and write down all that Albert had told her. By the time they arrived at the east side of Tristan Da Cunha she had put together the complete story from the set up of the Ark in Wales, the funding of the project, the way it was designed with all the eco-systems installed, the farming and produce methods, the attacks, the rescues and the births, marriages and deaths. Primarily she collected this information for use in recreating the US replica ship to pose as Miles' Domain, but found the information so fascinating and thought that if she wrote a book about the Ark's extraordinary journey she was convinced she would make a lot of money from it!

'Buster, how are things going? I don't see much of Mi lately since we started doing these shifts; I hope things are working out well for you both.'
'Just fantastic Pete, I know it was a whirlwind romance for us, but she is one fine lady and Millie must be something else for you to give up Mi for her. It's strange how things work out in life, one minute I'm expecting curtains and the next I'm in your canteen eating bacon sandwiches and drinking spirits bringing me round from my ordeal. Then I fall in love with your wife, now I'm with her without any bitterness between parties. If this had happened back home you would have shot me by now, there is something very special about being on the Ark. What more can I say Pete?'
'You're right about the Ark being very special. It gives me food for thought about what Albert maintains, it is all worth fighting to keep it the way it is, it may be an old redundant oil tanker, but its contents are all good.'
'I couldn't agree more on that, it is all good. How are things with you and Millie?'
'They are just fine. She is a little workhorse it's a job to get her away from the farm.

Buster, I'm just looking at the charts and we will be approaching the islands of Tristan Da Cunha soon. That is where I re-met Albert and the first time the Ark ever wintered there. I was then a Captain for the coastguard based at

Tristan, my last post in the Euro-Navy before I retired. But before that Albert and I served together in the Royal Marines in the 1991 Gulf war. I would drop him and his squad off from boats on the Euphrates for a night's operation then pick them up with any prisoners they had and got them back to base.'

'What sort of prisoners were they taking?'

'The highest ranking officers they could find in the Iraqi army to bring them back for interrogation. It would be very rare for him not to bring anyone back.'

'Gee he must have been one hell of a soldier.'

'Yes and he still is. When I boarded the Ark for the first time as my coastguard duties required me to do, I just couldn't believe my eyes to see him greet me and when I saw what he had created, knowing I was due for retirement, I thought this was for me. But I needed a partner so I sorted that out then it was how to get onboard safely thinking I could just arrive by helicopter from Tristan when I knew they would be in the area again. So I hired a chopper from Tristan to fly out to the Ark, but Albert was there on the top deck brandishing an automatic, making sure the pilot could see it, as a warning not to land.'

'Why didn't you radio to get permission to land?'

'I knew Albert leaves the radio switched off because he doesn't want any communication with the outside world.'

'So how did you get onboard?'

'I asked the pilot if he had a parachute and luckily he did. I put it on, he took the craft to about 6000ft and I jumped. As I got closer I could see Albert as he raised the automatic and gave a burst to one side of me as a frightener. I shouted at him calling him a daft bastard and telling him who I was. So actually, your boarding the Ark was a lot easier than mine.'

'Could you have got a lift from the coastguard on their visit?'

'I checked that out but they were too busy, and were not due to visit for a few weeks, I didn't want to hang about Tristan for that length of time.'

'You are some team and I'm proud to be with you all. I had better go and do my rounds playing at being a guard. See you later Pete. It was good talking to you.'

220

Buster left Pete at the helm with an aura of proud contentment about him. His first checkpoint was the lookout post where he knew Zimbo was on duty. To his disgust he found him fast asleep, Buster was furious and immediately kicked him hard in the buttocks.

'Argh!' He woke rapidly, shouting. 'What was that for? I had only just dozed off this second.'

'That's strange I've been stood here five minutes and you were giving it some big Zeds. You are supposed to be on lookout which is very important work for the Ark's security. I will have to report you to Albert and Pete; you are not to be trusted at your post.'

'So what, what will they do to me, send me home? They won't waste fuel and time on that, they're stuck with me.'

Buster smiled at him thinking this guy is a 100% wanker and needed to be sorted. He looked around him to see if anyone was about, all clear, he grabbed him by the throat and with one arm lifted him completely off the deck.

'I think I'll save them a job and just pitch you over the side. No one will know a thing and you won't be missed.' Zimbo was struggling to breathe and his eyes were bulging from their sockets as he grunted and groaned. Buster continued with his deliberation.

'You are a disgrace to everyone onboard this ship, to the very people that saved you taking you into the bosom of their home, fed you and totally accepted you as part of them. From now on you will pull more than your weight, because I will not be telling Albert or Pete. You can if you like and I doubt very much if you will. I will be watching you and that big fat belly of yours.' Buster raised him even higher. All Zimbo could do was to look at the size of the biceps that were the power holding him in the air.

'So I do not see a problem in putting you over the side, do you?' Zimbo tried to acknowledge and looked down at his arm. Buster let him drop to the deck where Zimbo laid for a short while coughing and spluttering before he returned to his lookout duties without a sound. Buster folded his arms flexing his muscles and watched over him for the next ten minutes. Zimbo looked

221

around a few times to see if he was still there only to return his head quickly to look through the binoculars.

After finishing his rounds from stern to bow, Buster returned to the bridge. Pete was still there at the helm watching the radar.

'Anything exciting going on out there Buster?'

'No, nothing exciting, only disturbing, apart from that it is all looking good.'

'What's disturbing Buster?'

'It's that lad Zimbo on lookout. He has a huge fat belly on him, not like anyone else on the Ark. How come? He's dozy as well.'

'Yes Albert knows as we all do and it will be tackled soon.'

'Pete can you show me how to control the ship from here? Once I'm confident I would be able to give you a break now and then.' Pete obliged and gave him a session at the helm on each shift. Gunter would make a regular visit on all shifts checking their course and set new when required.

During the days of transit to Tristan, Millie gathered the harvest and had all the help she could muster. The harvest was later then usual, by nearly three weeks and some crops were almost overripe, mainly because of all that was going on during the attacks, the diversion and delay while repairs were going on in Cape Town and the emotional changes that had come to a head but now well sorted out. Millie was back on form and more content than ever. By the time they were at anchor she realised she had missed a period. She kept quiet about it until she was certain. When the harvest was complete Millie took life a little slower and one morning she decided to stay with Pete in bed for a well earned sleep in. When she did get up she wasn't feeling too good.

'What's up Millie?'

'It's morning sickness Pete, I'm pregnant!' Pete was dumbstruck, speechless; he went to her and held her close.

'Thank you Millie.' Were his first words then a pause for some minutes, 'you have made me a very proud man,' she looked up to him and into his eyes to shed a trickle of tears.

'Why are you crying my dear?'

'Pete I'm frightened you might leave me now.'

'No way my love, I will be there beside you to bring that child of ours up and show it how to survive.'

'Oh Pete, thank you,' clutching him as tightly as she could, reassured with his words.

The news was soon out and congratulations from all, was quickly received, even from Ched. His immediate thought was, he has beaten me to it. I know it won't be long though, the way my Marigold has been since we became a permanent couple. Oh she is so wonderful.

A communication came from the sub to Albert. It was the Commander, or Frank as Albert now called him, to arrange a meeting because something had cropped up and needed urgent discussion. The Commander's preference would be a meeting on the Ark because the hospitality was far superior to anything Tina Turner could provide. The meeting was arranged for 1200 hours the next day with the Commander requesting it to be in private with only Albert, Pete, Lenska and Buster to attend. Frank was to arrive alone.

'This sounds serious Pete.' Albert commented.

'Well we are alright out here for a while with or without the sub. Perhaps they want Buster and Lenska to go elsewhere. Lenska leaving isn't a problem but for Buster to leave now could really upset Mi!'

'We will just have to see what comes up at the meeting Pete, it's no good speculating.'

'You're right we'll see what tomorrow brings. Oh by the way, changing the subject, has any thought been given to what to do about the overweight and lazy Zimbo yet?'

'Jane has tried to get him to eat better and do more exercise, but she said that he claims he's being picked on because he's black, pulling the discrimination card, which is absurd.'

'So what's next?'

'Amy is going to have a word with Melanie to see if she could help in bringing him into line with the rest of us. We will have to wait for the outcome of that.'

'Sorry Albert I feel that will be negative as well. You and I know what the answer is, don't we?'

'Yes I'm afraid you're right but we have to let them try it their way first, at least we won't be criticised when we sort him our way!'

'That will be fun Albert! And a nice little job for Buster if he's around.'

17. NAÏVE WESTERN GOVERNMENT'S

Albert greeted the Commander the next day and escorted him to the canteen where Pete, Lenska and Buster were waiting. Albert had already arranged for Gunter and Ched to make sure no one entered the room. They guarded the access doors to the canteen from the outside. The meeting began as soon as they all sat down together acknowledging each other while they did so. There were only glasses of chilled water on the table.

'This won't take long.' the Commander said. 'I have to inform you that my sub must leave immediately for the Black Sea for the defence of Turkey, which has been threatened by Iran with a nuclear attack on Istanbul, if it does not remove the US and its allies from the borders of Iran and Iraq. NATO's Security Council are meeting as we speak, and because it was a threat to the democratic free world, the US had moved quickly. Another conflict looks like it may get out of hand. Pakistan is now overrun by the Taliban using the Afghans trained and armed by the west, I should not say it in my position, but all this at the expense of hard working taxpayers and decisions made by naïve western governments. Some might say that the Taliban and Al Qaeda along with Mafia organisations had this arranged all along, arming and training the insurgents indirectly funded by Iran. All this is to the western world's detriment, then it would only be a matter of time and I fear, that time has arrived.'

'Well,' said Albert who was still bitter on the subject. 'The "do good western world" has finally got to see the shit hitting the fan. Yet again the poor foot soldier will pay the ultimate price and the taxpayer will pay the bill, leaving the politicians sitting pretty as usual.'

'What about our two guests here on the Ark, are they required to join you?'

'No Pete, that part of the strategy must continue because we know the Russian and other Mafia organisations are well in with the Taliban and what are left of Al Qaeda, along with splinter terrorist groups. I know you won't like this but we need your equipment connected to tell us what is going on before you hit the no satellite coverage which is about two days sail away. The target source

225

of information is in the UK. Intelligence tells us that the Russian Mafia and Al Qaeda have a site they use for joint operations. We need names and where they are operating from etc. If I could have that before the sub has to leave Albert, it would be much appreciated.'

Lenska and Buster acknowledged the Commander's wishes.
'Yes Frank, I'm sure Pete will supply that information before you leave today,' Albert assured.
'By the way, you will be having a visitor sometime during your stay at your winter retreat, to take any information you have collected between now and when you hit the no satellite area. He or she will come from a US Navy submarine that will track you at the co-ordinates 37° 10′ south and 12° 42′ west. The sub will find you anyhow it will just make it quicker if you stay there.'
'How will we know if the person is genuine or not, doesn't it leave us a sitting target?' Albert asked.
'The person will arrive with a Naval Officer from the surfaced submarine which should make it obvious to you where they are from. We know from the report that Felix made when he surveyed your computers, that any top secret data information would self destruct if it was downloaded, but we also know that any day to day operational details can be downloaded and even printed out. So we want that data on these good old fashioned memory sticks, once on there the information will be scrambled, and at worst, if we do not receive the info and it falls into the wrong hands, it will be some time before anyone could decipher it. After you have left the no satellite coverage area you will move on to your place of permanence. By then the decoy ship should have removed the computers and communication system and reinstalled them on the US ship. Then you will not be bothered by us.'
'Two things that I'm concerned about,' said Albert.
'Firstly, I would want the person that visits us to collect that information known to us before you leave even though he or she had arrived on a US Navy sub. Secondly, because we will be staying at this holding position only until the end of March, if the decoy has not arrived by then it will have to find

us because after that we will be heading for new pastures. If we stayed any longer the weather would not be suitable for our plants and some of our livestock to sustain the extreme temperature and weather conditions when we pass Cape Horn on our way to our as yet unknown destination.'

'Albert I can only do my best to have your request for the identity of the collector, and if the decoy has not arrived for the changeover it will delay things somewhat but could chance blowing the ruse apart.'

'Frank I cannot risk all the things we have worked for here on the Ark. We know when we have to move and normally we go directly north, but we will need to go south west before going north, so we must not leave it any longer than the end of March.'

'I'll see what I can find out before we leave today Albert and will inform you of it if there's anything at all.'

'Thank you Frank, will you join us for a spot of lunch?'

'I would love to but I must get back to the sub to make a communication which will take an hour, so if you could make it for 1400 hours, that will be great.'

'Yes of course we all look forward to seeing you then, thank you Frank.'

The Commander shook hands with those present at the meeting and quickly went back to the sub to see if he could get the identity of the collector and details of how far off the decoy was in being ready for the changeover.

'Pete can I have a word with you on the bridge in a few minutes?' Albert met Pete straight away.

'What is it Albert?'

'The information that Frank wants, can you sort it as soon as possible and then get Magnus to disconnect the system and lock the communications room so no one can access it. I do not want anyone to be able to make any communications, no matter what Frank has asked for.'

'Good thinking, can you keep Lenska and Buster away from there while I do it?'

'Yes I'll think of something. I'll get them to trim the sails.'

227

Frank knew he wouldn't get an answer straight away so he went back to the Ark for lunch leaving instructions to the communications officer that if he received a positive reply to send it to him on the Ark immediately. On his return to the Ark he requested a private chat with Albert, who obliged by taking him for a short a walk around the foredeck in front of the re-glazed biome dome.

'Albert, being an ex-military man, I guess you might have known something like this would happen, having to be sent at a moment's notice to any situation wherever in this mixed up world. I can only give my personal apologies to you.'

'Thank you for that Frank it is much appreciated, sincerely. My concern is the identity of the collector. I'm sure you will understand the reason I say this, that if I do not have the ID confirmed by yourself before you leave us then no one, whoever they say they are, will be permitted to board the Ark. Any organisation with enough cash can buy a sub these days and pose as someone else and, as for the other matter we will find a place for the community to put the Ark on our own if we have to. That Frank is all I can say other than let's go and have some lunch.'

'Yes Albert, I would do exactly the same if I were you. So let's eat. I know I shall miss these times on the Ark with all your splendid hospitality.'

'Thank you.'

The Commander's last meal on the Ark was very much enjoyed but over far too soon. It was time to leave and no undertaking had been received by the Commander to give to Albert, so it was as Albert said a closed shop. The position they were soon to be in moving into, not known to have satellite coverage and no communication with the outside world for the next three to four months, quietly, that suited Albert very well. The information was given to the Commander by Pete without anyone else being involved. Goodbyes were said from all the residents of the Ark to the Commander, leaving him feeling he had let them down by not giving them a permanent place to go to. As for him not being able to give Albert the collector's ID information, that, he suspected suited Albert anyway, in less risk to the Ark. Once the Commander and his sub were on its long journey to the north, Albert gave Lenska and Buster an order, something he did not like to do but he pulled rank with this one and only order.

'Buster and Lenska as of now the computers will be shut down and the communication room will be locked. There will not be computer links or any other communication with the outside world under any circumstances. So you both had better find some way of occupying yourselves for the next few months or more, I'm sure you'll think of something.'

'But Albert we still have satellite coverage and will have for probably twenty four hours yet,' appealed Lenska.

'Yes exactly, I do not want our direction and position tracked any longer. I have one project I would like you both to implement, and you will have the resources supplied to do it and that is sport, keeping the community fit, besides your guard duties for the US military. I am sure you know the areas where fitness is required.'

'Yes Albert, I most certainly do,' Buster replied and smiled.

Albert pulled Pete aside once Buster and Lenska left them.

'Pete, has Magnus made the room extra secure?'

'Yes, it's not what the Yanks wanted but tough shit, they've left the scene.' Albert then contacted Gunter on the short wave.

'Gunter can I meet you on the bridge. I now have the position we need to maintain for the winter stay and for the Yanks.'

'Ok Albert I'll be there in a few minutes.' The two met while Ched was at the helm. Albert had changed the co-ordinates to his own choice prior to giving them to Gunter without saying anything to anyone, his view was it wouldn't make any difference to the established community, but for anyone else it will be more difficult to find them.

'Right Gunter these are the co-ordinates for us to maintain our anchor point, 36° 56′ south and 13° 33′ west please don't mark them on the chart and make sure they are locked away.'

229

'Yes certainly Albert.' They continued their journey and made anchorage two days later.

Because of the late move to their winter retreat, Christmas was upon them before even giving it much thought, toys were created for the children and a feast arranged to celebrate, but all in all they did not feel much different than any usual Sunday get together. The only difference was to see the children play with their new toys that mainly Magnus had constructed. How can you better the best and why try if your everyday life is as good as you want it? The New Year was seen in respectfully with reminiscing of the past year. This happened after a New Year's dinner and they all sat around one long table made from a number that had been put next to each other and just for a couple of hours there was no one on watch. Albert took the risk thinking they were so remote there and the last watch was scanned visually and radar was on continuously, but after two hours Albert followed by Lenska resumed the watch.

With the help of Antonio and Pete a fallow field just in front of the foredeck towards midships was allocated as a designated sports field. It was fenced off and the grass cut and rolled to form a small football pitch which was marked out for five-a-side, male and female. This was something that Antonio had missed. He loved his football and had been excited about it since the project was first mentioned. One of the things that Albert had omitted from his original 'Stocking the Ship' list was a football. There were every other kind of balls; tennis, cricket and ones for swimming pool use, but not for the likes of rugby or football. It was time for good old fashioned craftsmanship. Leather was a by-product of the slaughtered cows and pigs which had been saved, tanned and stored. They needed something that would be airtight for the inside and a pig's bladder was chosen. But who would make a football good enough to be able to be kicked and pounded thousands of time per session? Magnus, as usual was the person that assured everyone he could do it. He cut out leather circles and shaped the circumferences to point down leaving a shape like a bottle top shiny side up. Some thirty of these segments were

230

made and then stitched together at their perimeters to form a sphere. This was done inside out to allow for stitching to be inside the ball. A slit was left to allow the treated pig's bladder to be inserted inside and then filled with air from a compressor. He tied a knot as you would do a balloon to retain the air. That was tucked inside the leather case and stitched to seal the ball. The first attempt was just about usable but very unpredictable because of its imperfect less than round shape. But it got them started and a game was played at least once a day with Antonio being the star. This in its way provoked competition mainly between Antonio, Buster and the very paunchy Zimbo who was the butt of Antonio's jokes. Buster took this opportunity to tackle Zimbo on his lack of fitness for his age and because he liked playing the game he was annoyed with himself for not being able to be as quick and as good as Antonio or Buster. This made it easy for Buster to put him under pressure to get a healthy physique for a male of his age and stature, through a training and dietary programme without Zimbo objecting.

Magnus was now on his tenth ball and each time they improved in bounce, shape and endurance.
They never managed to get a complete five aside game it was mainly Antonio, Buster, Zimbo, Lenska, Pete, Jane, Gunter and Ched that enjoyed the game but it set precedence for a fitness programme that mostly the younger element kept up. The usual training session would start by jogging around the sports area and then followed by stretching exercises before the football was kicked about.

The end of March was approaching and everyone was delighted with the winter season. There were no interruptions from visitors or the like, a good period was spent, with plentiful crops and produce, good fishing and most of all contentment throughout the community. Millie was five months pregnant and as far as known, no others had any on the way. Ched and Marigold were trying their hardest but that sometimes seems to have an adverse effect. The time had come to move on. Their plan was to sail south-west across the Southern Atlantic, east to the foot of Chile, then around Cape Horn to change

231

direction to north-west into the Eastern Pacific. The distance to the Cape from their present position was about 2500 nautical miles, and at their average speed, some ten days away. Once around Cape Horn and changing direction to Easter Island (under the rule of Chile) which would be about the same distance, this would put them just south of The Tropic of Capricorn. They wanted to be somewhere north of that line. All were prepared and security had been stepped up with weapons set, checked and armed, with Lenska and Buster drilled in Albert's way in the full use of the weaponry. It was April 2nd 2020, exactly four years ago since leaving Milford Haven in the UK. As always at first light the Ark moved from its winter haven, a little push from the turbines and then it was sails. Albert was at the helm and Gunter close by working on the charts. They had been sailing for about five hours just up to their average speed. Albert spoke out to himself but overheard by Gunter. 'We are being too predictable.'

'What do you mean?' Gunter asked.

'I will explain when Pete gets here.' He immediately called for Pete to join him on the bridge, and he arrived within minutes.

'Yes Albert, is everything ok?'

'Close and lock the door and switch off your short wave, you too Gunter and listen. Something has just come to me and has made me think, the thought was as you heard Gunter. We are being too predictable.'

'If you mean by going to the same seasonal retreat this time, we are not,' said Gunter.

'Not exactly that but we are doing what we said we would do, planning out our route and making it known to all, including the Americans. Now at the moment everyone thinks we are going around Cape Horn and then north-west towards Easter Island and then on to the Pitcairn Islands. I know you, Gunter and Greta have your hearts set on this new place of permanence but our security is more important, don't you agree?'

'Yes of course it is.'

'Well as a security measure I want to change course gradually and go north straight up the centre of the Atlantic and see what response we get, if any. If you remember we had two attacks in short succession after the US sub had been with us and that business of the tug with armed attackers onboard. How did they know about the coloured workers?'

'I see what you mean and because it was not possible to get any satellite communication in the area we have been for the past months, preparations could have been made to have a go at us when we are in amongst the numerous islands of the Pacific,' Pete said.

'Yes and if you think about it, that is the sort of planning we would do if the shoe was on the other foot, so to speak,' said Albert.

Gunter was a little confused, and scratched his head.

'When you say shoe on the other foot did you mean if we were going to attack this ship?'

'Yes Gunter, so if we think what they might do, we should change what we are going to do and head for a different destination and at the moment it is unknown and will stay unknown until we get there. The only thing is that just the three of us know that we are changing course to go north and let me repeat, no one else on this ship is to know that. We will deal with altering the sails as if we are sailing normally, gradually changing our course over a long distance and then we will see who makes a fuss, if at all, when they realise the sun appearing from the starboard side of the ship.'

'What if it's one of our own that recognises the change in direction?' asked Gunter.

'We will say we have changed tack to gain more speed with the wind and if we need to use the turbines to help, so be it.'

'Sounds alright to me Albert,' said Pete.

'Greta will not be happy when she finds out.'

'We can cross that when we come to it. As for now, no one else will know of this plan can I have your assurance on that please?'

'Yes.' They all agreed. Gunter went back to the charts to see how wide he could make the change of course. Albert surveyed the charts with him. Gunter was about to mark out the first change and Albert stopped him.

'Gunter don't mark the charts, just make a note and lock it away, is that clear?'

'Sorry Albert I did not think. I should have known from the last time.'
'You must think twice on everything you do at the moment. You may think I'm being over cautious but believe me, I know what I'm doing. Pete left the room mulling it over and thinking, Albert's right and I had better keep a close eye on Buster and Lenska, because if there is a leak onboard that is where it will come from.

Gradually over the next two to three days the Ark was heading north making a third of a circle over two hundred nautical miles. The first reaction was from Ched, as Albert expected. Ched took his shift from Gunter and asked him why we were keeping a course mainly heading north and Gunter paused for a moment.
'Ched I need you to talk to Albert before you say anything to anyone else. I'll get him to come here now so please don't ask anymore questions.'
'Oh, there is something going on then that they didn't want me to know?'
'No, Ched it is not like that. I will call Albert now and I will not say any more. Please respect me for that.'
'OK,' he said, disgruntled. Gunter called Albert to the bridge. As he entered Ched was standing with his arms folded facing the bridge entrance. As soon as Albert saw him he knew what to expect. He turned and locked the door behind him and went to face him. Ched wanted to get his words in first.
'What's the big secret that I'm not privileged enough to know then?'
'Ched there was no reason to tell you anything yet. Does it matter to you where we spend the next season as long as it is somewhere out of harm's way and productive?'
'But that's not the point Albert. The fact is you chose to leave me out from decisions. I suppose Mr Action Pants is in on the act?'
'Ched grow up! This is a very delicate situation we are trying to tackle and actually it has been known in the past for you to say things to others where you should have kept your mouth shut. You are not the only one not to be told a thing. Apart from you, now it is Pete, Gunter and me, so that is how the situation is. Now I want your word that no hint of anything goes from this room. Is that 100% clear?'

'Yes Albert it must be serious.' Ched answered more respectfully.

'Since the sub and our guests have been with us we had two attack attempts in succession. Now I'll say this, it may be purely coincidence that the Russians are on the ball. But one thing is gnawing at me is the tugboat issue when the two coloured workers were sent up the ladder to their deaths. I purposely asked the Commander in the earshot of Buster and Lenska for that type of labourer, so it was well known to them and that would be passed on to their contracts supplier. What I'm trying to eliminate is the leak coming from the Ark. If someone kicks up a fuss when they realise we're not going where we said we were going, for what reason should they? So from this Ched you now have a burden of an extra responsibility.'

'What do you mean?'

'To keep your mouth shut at all cost, even to your nearest and dearest at the moment, and to be vigilant taking note of who is doing anything out of the ordinary.'

'Yes Albert, understood. But why can't things just be as they were supposed to be when we all started out?'

'That's all Amy and I wanted, Ched, and then look what's happened to you since this all began!'

18. DESTINATION "UKNOWN"

Four days had passed and there were no signs of anybody querying the direction they were travelling. All well and good Albert thought but he was still puzzled at the attempted attack in Cape Town, and then news of something he did not want to happen came via Jane.
'Albert, why is Lenska using a mobile phone from the stern of the top deck?'
'When was this?'
'Not ten minutes ago. I'm sure she is still there.'
'Jane thank you, keep everyone out of the way, is that clear?'
'Yes.' Albert thrust the short wave to his mouth.
'Pete, come in please?'
'Roger Albert.'
'Stern top deck, side arm required, Lenska is using a mobile phone.'
'Five minutes Albert.'
'I'll be with you, careful, she's armed.'

Pete being that bit quicker was there and out of sight, ready to approach her as soon as Albert arrived. A little out of breath but ready, they quietly and calmly walked over to her. She had her back to them, still with mobile in hand and not speaking English. Each moving to either side of her she turned, surprised to see Albert, and immediately threw the phone over the side and then reached for her automatic, but found that Pete's hand was in the way. She turned back to Albert and looked at the barrel of his automatic. Pete removed her weapon.
'Have you made a mistake Lenska or did you not want to talk to your boyfriend anymore?' She was silent knowing that she had something to hide and it would not have made any difference whether she had kept the phone or not. Pete prodded her with his weapon to move; she gave no resistance and went forward. Albert called Ched on the short wave.
'Yes Albert.'
'Ched, you remember Monty's isolation cell. Can you have it ready for a guest in ten minutes, and make it secure please?'

236

'Yes no problem at all.' Ched did not want to ask questions over the radio but could not wait to find out who the guest was and speculated. Yeah, I bet it's that Buster, too dam smart and too much of a goody goody.

Slowly the two pointed Lenska in the direction of her new home. No questions were asked, no explanations were made. Albert then called Jane and Amy on the short wave.
'Can you two meet me at Monty's old cell as soon as you can get there?'
'Yes Albert.' Jane had a notion what had happened, but Amy was clueless until they met on the way.
'Oh,' said Amy, 'I wondered why the sun wasn't coming up from the stern anymore.'
'You mean Albert hasn't mentioned anything to you at all? I thought it strange myself and just put it down to sailing, thinking it was because of going to new territory. I wouldn't have a clue which direction we were going.'
'That's Albert, Jane.'

By the time Amy and Jane arrived at the cell Lenska was locked in it with nothing in there that she could possibly do any damage to herself. Albert, Pete and Ched were waiting outside for their arrival.
'What's going on Albert?' He brought his two arms together with open hands pointing them in the direction of Lenska and said.
'You ask her.'
'What have you done?' Amy asked Lenska. She looked her straight in the eye and Lenska said nothing.
'Come,' said Albert, 'let's go to the bridge and have a chat.' They left Lenska in complete darkness, no food, water, blankets or a pillow. Shut off and no opposition to her cell conditions from Amy or Jane.

They entered the bridge to join Gunter who was at the helm. The six of them had to discuss the situation. Albert explained to Amy and Jane of his decision to go north instead of where everyone thought they were going and his

237

reasons. But now there was a dilemma and he started by asking them all a number of unanswerable questions.

'You all saw the response from Lenska, Jane saw her using a mobile phone and Pete and I caught her. She immediately threw it over the side. Why the attempted attack in Cape Town using coloured workers, which I had requested, to gain access? Where did that information come from? The amount of time she was on the mobile phone would be enough to give them our location and direction. Also it was obvious she had a good signal. All this points to her being the leak but we cannot be one hundred percent positive until we question her. Now we have a problem, in which direction to go? Do we carry on going north or do we stick to our original plan which would be to backtrack and go around the Horn and into the Pacific? The other alternative is to go back to the east around the Cape of Good Hope and into the Indian Ocean and then the Western Pacific where the climate will be better for the crops, plants and trees etc.'

'Firstly, and I think you would agree Albert,' Pete chipped in, 'we should continue north for a day or so and let them reorganise themselves to be mobilised to somewhere, where they think we are heading and then we could make the shortest turn around and fastest speed to be back in what must be a no satellite coverage, then to emerge from it to whichever direction we choose, keeping as far away from land of any significance as possible. But before that we must make sure she has not planted any tracking devices onboard.'

'OK, said Albert. 'Any questions before we get to work?'

'Yes Albert, how can we find a tracking device on the Ark, it could be anywhere?' asked Ched.

'I'll have a word with Magnus and see what he comes up with, but the first place to look is in her cabin.'

'Oh, I'll help with that.' said Ched. He was hoping to get glimpses of her undies lying about.

'No.' said Jane. 'We know what you will be looking for Ched don't we?' Jane was referring to an episode concerning a pair of red knickers (hers) a couple of years earlier.

238

'No need to be like that, I was only trying to help.'

'Let's go there first Amy and pull the place to pieces,' said a determined Jane.

'What sort of thing are we looking for? I'm not up on modern technology, I haven't a clue?'

'Anything you are not sure about. It doesn't matter what it is, could be an odd looking pen, toothbrush or electrical gadget, just smash it, and see the contents.'

'Oh, right.'

'What are you going to do with Lenska?' Amy asked Albert, before they left.

'Nothing for a couple of days, she will be left alone but checked every four hours without food or water in darkness.'

'Don't forget she is a woman.'

'Does it matter who fires a gun at you male or female Amy?' Pete said quickly. With that the pair left the bridge for Lenska's cabin.

'Gunter what is your view on which direction to travel?'

'I would say east, back the way we came past Cape Town and around the Cape of Good Hope and then across the Indian Ocean to the Timor Sea and enter the Pacific there.

Buster called in at the bridge to see if Albert or Pete were there. The door was open as the ladies left it, but he knocked before he entered. Gunter and the others were still studying the charts and they turned and greeted Buster.

'Has anyone seen Lenska? And how come we are heading north? Have you changed your minds where to go for the next season?' Albert and Pete looked at one another.

'Does it bother you where we go for the next few months Buster?' Albert asked.

'Hell no, just as long as I can stay on the Ark and not go back to other duties.'

'Well that is good to hear and yes, we have changed our minds on which direction to go and yes we have seen Lenska.'

'Oh where might I find her?'

'Come with us Buster and we'll show you.'

239

Albert and Pete led Buster to Lenska. They looked through the door window to see her lying on the bunk undisturbed by the noise of her visitors.

'Why is she in there?' asked a puzzled Buster.

'We caught her using a mobile phone on the stern top deck and she'd been talking for some time. When we approached her she immediately threw the phone over the side and went for her side arm. We knew we had a possible leak of information and now have the problem of getting information out of her.'

'Oh this is serious Albert. If it's true that she has been passing information to the Mafia then it could also be other information she has knowledge of, being in her position and that is greater damage than what could be done to the Ark! Let me have a word with her and see if she will give any indication of what she has been up to.' Albert agreed and unlocked the door, Buster entered first, followed by the others.

'Hi Lenska, what's this all about? What have you been up to? Lenska wake up its Buster.' He grabbed her shoulder and nudged her. Nothing, Pete went over, picked up her wrist to feel a pulse but there was nothing. She was dead!

'She knew she was in some deep shit to have to resort to that. Just open her mouth and see if there are any remains of a capsule, she is still warm, it might not have fully dissolved yet,' said Albert. Buster opened her mouth. Her tongue was discoloured with a small part of a capsule left.

'Is that standard issue for the Intelligence Corp. Buster?'

'Yes it is, but this one was used to protect the enemy and we do not know how much damage she has done to American security.'

'They will probably never find that out and she has left us the problem of what to do with her. By all accounts she is still the property of the US Military Service, so we had better put her in a body bag and think about it,' said Albert.

'Albert I must notify the service so they can identify the areas she had been connected to and look for any problems it might have caused.'

'I'm not allowing any communication, if that's what you mean.'

'Which way will you be heading?'

'We haven't fully decided yet, it is destination unknown at the moment Buster. We had better get Lenska sorted out and then tell the others what has happened. After that we will think again.'

Albert called all the community together to meet in the canteen. Amy and Jane left their search to attend. Albert asked if they had any luck yet.
'No but we'll continue,' replied Jane. He checked around to make sure all were there.
'You might have noticed that we changed direction to go north a couple of days ago. This was for a security reason and it worked, but not with a result I would have wanted. Lenska who had been living amongst us and we trusted, had other plans it seems, and by all accounts they could have been to our detriment. It was noted that she was using a mobile phone on the stern top deck. She was approached, still using the phone in the Russian language. Realising she had been caught she immediately threw the phone overboard and tried to pull her side arm at me. She was apprehended and taken to a secure place that most of you are aware of and locked up. But we have just discovered she has taken her own life using a deadly poison capsule that she must have had secreted on her person.' There was utter shock and cries of dismay from all that did not know of the earlier events of the day. Albert continued.
'The only reason, I can think,' Albert continued, 'that would have caused her to waste her young life was that she knew she had been caught and was in deep trouble and probably had more to fear from the Russian Mafia than the US Military. That is all I can say about the situation at the moment and I will keep you all informed of any further development's.' They left the room with mainly the women totally devastated that such a lovely young girl could be driven to do such a thing.

'Albert could I have a word with you and Pete in private please?' requested Buster.
'Yes of course we will see you out on the foredeck, I need some fresh air.'
'What is it Buster?'

241

'Would you mind if I made a suggestion it may help you all, it probably won't help me but I'll tackle that when I come to it?'

'Go on,' Albert was eager to hear.

'Why not head for the US Navy base in Cape Town and offload the computers and communication equipment. It would also be right to leave Lenska there. I will be debriefed and explain all and you may get topped up with methane gas for delivering the goods which I'm sure they would not see as unreasonable.'

'But what about you Buster? You may have to stay there, and that leaves Mi here, unless she stays with you?'

'No she will not be allowed to stay with me, but with some help from you, something else might work.'

Albert looked at Pete as they listened. Both were puzzled as to what was coming next.

'Well you know Commander Grey has great respect for you and the Ark and his last orders were for me to stay on the Ark on security duties and intelligence gathering work. Well that is unlikely to be changed because it will be recorded and accessible to the Base Commander there, so if you could confirm that to him if it becomes necessary when we are in Cape Town. If all goes the way it should then we should be able to get on our way, *Destination Unknown.*'

'You have been chewing things over and it does not sound like a bad idea. What do you think Pete?'

'Sounds quite positive, he is right that the Base Commander would assume that he would continue his Commander's orders while the conflicts continue and it would be in the interest of the US government to put him back to his duties without delay.'

'That's it then Buster we will take the chance and go back to Cape Town.'

They went straight to the bridge and explained what they wanted to Gunter. He agreed without question because it was more less what he had suggested earlier. The new course was set to east with sail and turbines to give them maximum speed. After all the different changes there had been an air of relief

242

at last as they now had a positive direction to go. The security had been stepped up intensely the nearer they got to Cape Town. They made their final change of course to approach the area to anchor in more or less the same place as before. The sails had been lowered five miles out and then the turbines cut to move in on it's momentum until the engines were put in reverse to stop the huge floating structure, and finally the bow anchor was lowered. Albert asked Magnus to switch on the electric fence and then to join the defence team on the bridge for a briefing.

'Now that we are all here I must stress to you to be on top alert, is that understood and clear? Zimbo have you any problems with that? There will be no sleeping on duty. You will be checked upon by secondary guards and lookout. We only want to stay the minimal amount of time here just to do as necessary and then put out to open sea as quickly as possible. Hopefully we will get refilled with methane gas and fresh water as we are still working indirectly for the US. That will be done as before, without anyone having to board us. Buster will go to the Base alone in the inflatable and in uniform. He will then organise Lenska to be collected. We will have her ready to pass over to their waiting vessel. Magnus how far have you got with the dismantling of the computers?'

'They are ready to be moved on deck. We just need a container to put them in, along with the dish and antenna.'

'Buster, could you arrange for the Base to bring a crane barge of some description, to lift a shipping container onboard for us to fill with the equipment? Albert asked.

'I'm sure they will, considering they have wanted the cargo for some time now?' 'Yes I will.'

'OK, that's all for now, are you ready for your little trip Buster?'

'I can't wait to get it over with and get back here.'

'Have you said goodbye to Mi?'

'No, there is no goodbye because I will be back.'

He was quickly lowered over the side and on his way to the Base. Everyone kept their fingers crossed for him, hoping all would go to plan. The hours

243

went by and nothing was heard. Darkness came, shift times were met, the night team heard nothing. Then day broke, with the sun pushing up over the east.

The community were in and out of the canteen for breakfasts and drinks, more so than normally, mainly to ask if anything had happened. It had become tense. Albert stood on the bridge constantly looking through his binoculars at the Base to see if there was any activity. It was 1200 hours and a crane mounted on the midships of a small coaster was heading towards the Ark, but no sign of Buster.

The vessel became clearer and Albert could see they had mounted a mobile crane with a telescopic jib, obviously as a make shift measure, and chained it to the deck of this small cargo ship. Albert radioed Antonio to stand on a good viewing point at the Ark's bow and wave to the ship with something highly visible, to send them to the port side. Albert then went to meet it. The equipment was there ready to load. The ship's Captain acknowledged Antonio's frantic wave and came along the port side to the foredeck where Albert, Pete and co. were waiting. The crew from the ship were all in naval uniforms and looked genuine so Albert opened the access gate to make communication. The Captain appeared from the bridge and shouted for Captain Albert. Albert moved to the gate to be seen showing his automatic at the ready.

'Yes I'm Albert, where is Buster?'

'He is on his way Sir he wanted some stores and things to bring with him.'

'Can you open the container and tie the doors back before lifting it on board Captain?'

'Yes of course.' Two ratings quickly opened the doors as requested.

'Ok, you can lift it up.'

The crane lifted the container into the air showing it to be empty which was a relief to them all. Albert and Pete still kept a close watch on everything while Ched, Gunter and Zimbo put Lenska in first and then all the equipment, finally closing the doors Albert signalled to lift the container. In minutes the job was complete and the crane's engine cut.

244

'Captain Albert Sir,' the Captain shouted. Albert appeared and acknowledged. 'There will be a delivery of gas and water at 1600 hours. Good luck.'

The vessel slowly moved away along the port side to the stern and then made a wide berth to pass on the starboard side to go back to the Base. It was 1430 hours and a little black spot was coming into view, this excited everyone. They hoped it would be Buster. It very soon became clearer because of the speed it was doing, bobbing over the waves towards the Ark. Albert kept his binoculars pinned on the object then a short wave radio message came from Mi who had been at the bow with some binoculars looking all day.
'It's Buster, its Buster!' she shouted jubilantly. Then she ran as fast as she could to meet and welcome him back onboard. Everyone was cheering for him. The hoist was ready and waiting for him to connect to the shackle and he was quickly lifted back onboard with a fully laden cargo. Mi ran at him jumping up wrapping as much as she could of her tiny body around him. Everyone was delighted to have him back.
'Well Buster so far so good, but we are not out of the woods yet. We have to wait until 1600 hours for the gas and water and the time it takes for that to load, then we will get as far away from here as fast as we can. Have you any news of what's happened out there with all the conflicts going on?'
'There are still many conflicts continuing, mainly in Iran and Pakistan. The US president has said that US will annihilate any country that presses a button to launch a nuclear attack on any other nation. This threat abated the situation but the ground wars and civilian bombings continue and the borders around the western countries are so tight it is almost impossible to move freely anywhere. The only large movement of people is the repatriation of immigrants from many western countries.'
'It was inevitable that would happen. Our challenge looks minor compared to the millions of other poor souls on this planet.'
'Yes it is a pity the Ark cannot fly and take us off this planet because it is just destroying itself.'
'By the look of what you've brought with you Buster you must have robbed the Quartermaster.'

245

'I told him I was on a secret mission and would need supplies for a few years as I won't be able to get certain items like coffee and tea etc.'
'Come on let's get to the bridge and wait for the gas and water.' On the way Buster explained that they did not need you to confirm the Commander's orders, the Base Commander wired Commander Grey and he gave Albert a copy of his reply.

Captain Buster Manta will continue with the orders of intelligence gathering for the US Military Intelligence Corps as he has done so courageously in the past, and for this gallantry he is now Captain. Please assist him and return him to his post as soon as possible.

Please inform Albert of the Ark that I will seek and thank him personally one day for the help he and his crew have done in assisting the maintenance of the security of our nation The United States of America.
May God Be with You All.

Commander Frank Grey.

Albert was taken aback in fact stunned at the words, although not being a religious person he respected the Commander's own views.
'Congratulations Captain Buster Manta on your promotion. I will look forward to seeing the Commander Frank again.'

A tanker laden with gas and water had been spotted. The Ark had moved around on the bow anchor so that the bow was facing open water. As soon as the ship was alongside, the nozzles from the hoses were connected. Gas and water were pumped through them into receiving tanks. All the crew were still on full alert watching everything that moved in the water and in the air, weaponry at the ready. As soon as the nozzles were released the anchor chain was winched up moving over its guide and into its hold. The turbines were already running and all clear was given to sail. It was pitch black when they

246

headed out to sea. An hour of sailing and the community were relaxed and soon adapted their routines and rotas. It was 2200 hours and time for Ched to relieve Zimbo on lookout. Ched was not looking forward to his night shift and would rather be tucked up in bed with Marigold. He arrived at the post but there was no Zimbo.

'Where is the lazy bastard?' he said aloud and immediately radioed Albert.
'Albert I thought Zimbo was here on lookout. It was his shift. Do you know where he is?'
'No he should be there. I'll check with Melanie and the canteen and let you know.'

He went to the canteen as it was on the way to Melanie and Zimbo's cabin.
'Patricia have you seen Zimbo or Melanie lately?'
'Melanie will be in her cabin and I would expect Zimbo in here at any time. He should have finished his watch duty by now.'
'OK, thank you.' He left the canteen swiftly and went to Melanie's cabin and knocked on the door, she opened it and was in tears and her tearful emotion burst further at the sight of Albert as she moved to him to clasp her arms around him.
'Oh Albert, why has he done this to me, I don't deserve this?' She was holding a piece of notepaper in her hand she showed it to Albert, it read:

Mel

I have to go. Look after Chuva as I know you will
This is not my type of freedom
Albert will understand and they will take good care of you
both

I'm going to hitch a ride on the tanker to the mainland and take my chances
I've been lucky so far
Bye, Zimbo

'Let's go inside, and talk about this Melanie.' Albert closed the door and sat down with his arm around her. She put her head on his shoulder with tears still trickling down her cheeks and onto Albert's shirt.

'Melanie there are some people who are not cut out for disciplined daily routine and responsibility, Zimbo was one of those. He was happier doing the things he wanted to do, like fishing. The only time he was a team player was when he played football. He lost weight and became fit just to do that. So deep down, he was not happy and did not want to face the rest of his life not doing what he wanted to do and in some ways you can admire him for that. He is an opportunist and that was the reason he got onboard the Ark. No doubt some of that spirit will be in Chuva as you will see. So take a deep breath and face the facts. You know he has gone for his freedom. You have a wonderful child to love and take care of. You have family and a community that loves you both and another horizon to look at.'

'Oh Albert,' putting her arms around him again. 'What would we do without you?'

'You stay here with Chuva, and I will explain to your mother and father first, and then the rest. You know we cannot go back for him? Apart from the possibility of never finding him, the risk would be too great Melanie.'

'I know Albert, and thank you.'

He left to seek out Magnus, calling him on the short wave but there was no response so he went to the canteen. He saw a short wave on one of the tables

248

and thought he was probably in the kitchen with Patricia; true enough they were having a discussion.

'Hi I'm glad I caught you two on your own because I need to have a chat with you both.' Patricia spoke before Albert could start.

'Why is everyone looking for Zimbo and where is he?'

'That's why I'm here if you would let me explain.'

'Sorry Albert, just anxious that's all.'

'The truth of the matter is that he's jumped ship, putting it bluntly. He left a note for Melanie and I would appreciate if you would go to her now and she will explain to you in her own words. She will need comforting until she gets over the situation. I will explain to the rest of the community as soon as I can get them together.'

'Thank you Albert for letting us know first.' said Magnus, who was not really surprised at Zimbo leaving at an opportune moment and they immediately left to go to Melanie.

Albert went to the bridge first but called Ched to inform him on the way.

'Hello Ched come in please.'

'I hear you Albert. Have you found the lazy bastard?'

'Now, now Ched, I've known you to be in that category yourself at one time. No we haven't found him but we know where he will possibly be.'

'Oh, where's that then?'

'He's jumped ship and headed for the mainland on the tanker.'

'Oh, *you do surprise me.*'

'Enjoy your evening,' said Albert and continued to the bridge. Pete was waiting for Albert to take over his shift at the helm.

'Sorry Pete I'm a little late. I've been trying to find Zimbo. Ended up he's jumped ship in Cape Town on the tanker.'

'He probably had his reasons for not wanting this way of life. Melanie might miss him for a while but I don't think many of the others will, he was slacker than slack and you couldn't rely on him in an outfit like this.' Pete replied.

'Yes Pete I know that, but its Melanie that's hurt the most and yes, she will get over it. So we will have to keep a lookout for another young shipwrecked sailor.'

'See you tomorrow Albert, Gunter will be here shortly to brief you on the change of course. He's due in a couple of hours.'

'Thank you Pete.' Gunter made his visit to tell Albert of the course to take and Albert explained about Zimbo and asked him to let others know when he saw them as there wouldn't be many people about at that time of night, the rest of them would be updated in the morning.

19. THOSE ISLANDS IN THE SUN

Albert made the change to the course towards the east and thought that they should put some sails up, but it was 0100 hours and most of the crew would be fast asleep by now so thought better of it. We will see what the morning brings they all need a good night's sleep. It had been a hectic couple of days. He continued at the helm and frequently looked at the radar with an occasional call to Ched.

'How are you up there Ched?'

'It's a bit nippy tonight. It soon changes once the sun disappears over the horizon. It's like autumn.'

'It is autumn down this end of the world.'

'Oh yes, I forgot about that.' To them it seemed a very long night and they were glad to see the sunrise over the east. They chatted together before they took a break.

'At least we know we've been heading in the right direction when the sun is over the bow Ched.'

'Yes and what a lovely sight it is too.'

Buster relieved Albert, Jane gave Ched his break. Antonio had left Alberto with Greta and was off up to the farm for milking. Their first day of many on their way to "Those Islands in the Sun" and they had not a clue where they would end up, undeterred they sailed on. The two went to the canteen to take a break before returning to complete their shifts. They sat together and could have a good cup of ground coffee and not feel rationed as they did before they had the gift from the Commander of the submarine.

'This is welcome Ched. We will have to look into growing coffee and tea I don't know if it was covered when the seeds were originally purchased. It's something I know very little about I'll ask Millie when I see her.'

The two went back to their posts and completed their shifts. Ched went straight off to his cabin and to bed. Buster, Gunter and Pete arrived back at the bridge for their shift. Gunter checked the course.

251

'Everything all right, nothing to report?' asked Pete.

'No, just a night that never seemed to end, no sightings of any vessel at all, not even one of the thousands of round the world single handed sailing type. Before I finish my shift I think we should get some sails up. We are relying on our gas supplies too much. Can you give me a hand Gunter? I'll call Magnus as well.'

'Yes everything is spot on with our course. There is nothing between here and the Timor Sea to contend with and that's over six thousand nautical miles, so some weeks off yet.'

'All the more reason to use the sails, come on Gunter let's go.' Off they went and at a steady pace and put all the sails up, pitching them to the best angle for maximum wind take. The further they moved into the Indian Ocean the safer they felt.

Amy and Jane still continued their search for a tracking device that Lenska may have left behind. They visited every place they could think of that she might have been. They asked for Buster's help as to what type of device it could be. He thought she probably just relied on her mobile phone because no one, not even he, knew she had a phone. It is not something you are issued with when on active service, nevertheless they continued searching.

Millie was still down on the farm but taking it a lot easier now, being over five months pregnant. Antonio was always there and Millie could count on him to take any undue work pressure from her. Melanie took hold of herself to concentrate on the welfare of Chuva and her daily life. Zimbo was never mentioned to her by anyone. Everyone now was looking forward to getting up in the morning to see the sunrise over the Ark's bow. Since circling about in the Southern Atlantic the residents took more notice of where the sun was coming up in the mornings, something many of them had not done all the time they had been at sea. With each day being a repeat of the previous one, with no sightings, nothing to report, it was as if they were the only ones on the planet. The progress they made was very good, sometimes making a speed of fifteen knots which if maintained it would be three weeks to the Timor Sea,

252

and then another week until they would be in the Pacific near to The Solomon Islands. From there, the search for somewhere would begin.

'Marigold you've missed a period you know that don't you?'
'Yes I have, but I'm not one hundred percent yet. I don't feel any different. It's too early to be sure and I didn't want to build up your hopes if it was a false alarm.'
'Don't worry you will do more harm than good if you are worried about it. If it happens fantastic, if not then we'll keep trying. We've got at least four weeks until we find our island in the sun, our Utopia. So we can relax and take it like a once in a life time cruise. There is everything we need here. I bet you haven't wanted for anything, other than me of course, have you? And all that money we have doesn't mean a thing to us. It probably isn't worth half of its original value due to the high inflation we've been told about. So there you go, just do your daily thing and relax my love.'
'Ched, what's inflation?'

Sailing became a routine and very little sail adjustment was required. They were now well into the Australian Basin and would have their first sight of land for three weeks. This would be the islands of Ashmore and Cartier on their port side. They knew then they were approaching the Timor Sea with Darwin in the north of Australia to starboard side, where a lot of hot air came from the mainland of Australia, off the Gibson Desert mainly. This changed the pattern of sailing entirely and it became totally unpredictable and too much for the small crew numbers to tackle the changes to the sails. It was not manageable, the only thing they could do under the circumstances was to drop the sails and use the turbines for propulsion. Also once into the Timor Sea it would be a massive challenge for Gunter because the navigation would start off with a few minor changes to their course but throughout he would need to be well on top of his skills to negotiate the area between the northern tip of Australia and Papua New Guinea before they could enter the Pacific Ocean.

'Gunter how are we going to be for draft going through some of these areas, they seem very shallow for this size of vessel?'

'We will be alright providing we go slow and make five knots maximum, and start the change of our course well ahead of the position we are making for, so we are turning at that point and moving in the new direction, you see it's simple Albert.'

'You're going to be doing some long shifts when we get to that area there Gunter, I don't want our Ark's bottom scratched or any damage to the coral we travel over.'

'I cannot do it entirely on my own Albert. We all will have to be here at that time when we pass through the narrow shallow channels, but it will not take long.'

'I can assure you of that Gunter. How far do you think we are off that stretch of the journey?'

'Four to five days at a reduced speed of ten knots, and reduced again as we approach the passage.'

They passed the Ashmore and Cartier Islands that were well in view to their port side, then into the Timor Sea. It would be two days until they reached the Gulf of Carpentaria. A deep gulf that can only be described to the not so geographical mind, as that bit between the Scottie dog's ears and the top of its head! This area is large enough to put the whole of Ireland in. The difficult navigation would begin once across this gulf and then the sighting of Deliverance Island to their starboard side. Because Gunter would be under so much pressure to get the course exactly correct, Albert had had words with the rest of the crew that manned the shifts to be available to help at all times. It would only be for twenty four hours maximum, no one flinched at the request because they knew they were in new territory and everything was at stake. The next island to look out for was Buru which they would see on their port side. Then three islands overlapping each other from where they would view them were Dauan, Kaumag and Saibai. It would seem like one long island to their port side, then Maza on its own. Once past this it would be relatively open water as they head in the direction towards the main town of Port

Moresby on the south west coast of Papua New Guinea. After using that as a point of direction the course would change to south-east and then east into the Coral Sea leading into the Pacific Ocean to find their home.

The time had come for them to enter the narrow and shallow channels that separate Australia and Papua New Guinea. With Pete at the helm and Gunter marking and plotting their exact position at regular intervals as they sailed through, noting their position and the islands they passed, naming them and knowing the next one to be spotted. The passage did not take long and they were relieved to be out in open water again.

'That went very well Gunter, congratulations! It should be plain sailing now to find a nice little island base. Not long now and we will be in amongst The Solomon Islands, a group of over nine hundred islands, some inhabited and some not. That seems like a good place to start looking.'
Gunter was extremely relieved that that part of the journey was over and they were nearer the place he and Greta wanted to be. As soon as he had navigated the Ark through the channel he left the bridge to tell her.
'Greta, we are through and out into the northern part of the Coral Sea. After that we will be in The Solomon Islands. I'm so excited. We will have to have a little celebration when we find our island in the sun.'
'Oh Gunter I'm so proud of you, let us just hope that we are left alone then.'

The next few days took them from the change of course at Port Moresby down the southwest coast of Papua New Guinea and then east towards the island of Utupua in the Temotu Province of The Solomon's. They sailed between Lord Howe Island and Utupua which is distinctly recognised by its volcano shape. All the islands they had passed seemed extremely fertile with lush growth of greenery and trees. Gunter altered course to the north-east to take a look at a small group of the Duff Islands, consisting of several of various sizes, the largest being Taumako. Then there was Bass, Obelisk and Treasurers Island.

255

It was 1046 hours, Buster was on lookout. He had only been at his post for forty five minutes and was very alert. His binoculars scanned the horizon. There were clouds to the north and he could see something happening on the horizon which he thought didn't look right and immediately called Albert. 'Albert there's something happening on the horizon. It looks like a big wave heading towards us.'

'A tsunami, it's a big tidal wave, get down here quick. We need to drop all the sails and get the animals in the sheds and all personnel back here.' Albert then radioed Millie and Antonio. Millie was in the canteen and Antonio at the Bow farm. He immediately got the animals in their sheds and then went to help, getting the sails down on his way back to the bridge area. Albert instructed Magnus to switch all drainage pumps on and to divert them to pump all water back to the sea so as not to contaminate their watering system. All available men got the sails down in record time. Everyone moved quickly to the shelter of the bridge and canteen. The turbines had already been working now the ship was to face this huge wave. They pointed the bow of the ship straight at it and just waited for impact. All eyes were concentrated at this huge wall of sea.

'How high do you think Pete?'

'I would say ten metres at least, could be fifteen at a guess.'

'It will do us some damage if it breaches the sides of the ship, especially the Biome that will go.'

The Ark was now square onto the wave and everyone braced themselves firmly to whatever they could and then it hit the bow with such force it made the ship shudder and then the bow lifted, putting her angle at what seemed almost 30°. Albert was at the helm and quite some time prior to the impact, he had put the turbines to full power making sure the ship was in control of its direction. As the ship was at the angle the top of the wave engulfed the area behind the orchard flooding the fields, but as the power of the engines kicked in, the ship was lifted over the wave and became stable as though it had moved up a step and now was just dipping up and down with the flood moving back and forth over the fields, and the water gradually disappearing through the drainage system that was pumping the flood at maximum force back into the sea.

A big sigh of relief and cheers of joy erupted as the Ark became steady again. 'Well done Albert,' came from all around.

'And well done all of you for acting so quickly. Thank you Buster, it was your alertness that gave us the time to prepare, its teamwork. One thing that we must do now, that is to look out for any survivors that may be in the wake of this tsunami. So Mi, can you organise the medical side of things and ask for whatever help you need? Magnus, Ched, Pete and Buster have the inflatable and fishing boat ready to launch? Antonio could you check the animals I hope there aren't any casualties there, if so we will just have to do as necessary with them?'

'Wait Antonio I'll come with you,' Millie shouted.

'Please be careful,' Pete called after them. 'There's still a lot of water moving about out there. Take good care of her Antonio?'

'We had better change our course back to where we were heading to the Duff Islands because the wave would have hit there. Let's see if we can be of any help to anyone. What do you know about these islands Gunter?'

'The largest island is Taumako it is 5.7 km long and has steep sides going to a height of four hundred metres. The whole population of this group ten years ago was about four hundred people and on the decline. There are no roads, communication or electricity on Taumako. So there is no contact with the outside world and it would not surprise me if there was no satellite coverage in the area.'

'Thank you for that, we had better keep our eyes peeled and be ready to launch the boats.'

They kept up their speed using the engines to get them to there as quickly as possible. Knowing that it would be night-time when nearing the area, Magnus rigged up a searchlight fitted on a pole to the mini tractor. Antonio drove this around and around the perimeter of the fields with Ched directing the light across the sea in the pitch black night. Now they could pick out the outline of

257

the islands. The engine power was cut allowing the ship's momentum to take them in close. As they moved to within half a mile of the south western side of the main island they dropped anchor. Nothing could be seen at all, no lights, no life. Lookouts were posted and the others went to their cabins to rest because the next day teams would be out searching. Jane volunteered for lookout duty through part of the night to allow Antonio to rest and be with Alberto. Albert also would do a night stint to allow the others to get some sleep and be fit and alert the next day.

Jane managed to get the last few hours of darkness snuggled up to Antonio before he had to be up to look after the farm and assess the damage to the fields and try to get the creatures back to a settled routine. When Jane finally let him go at 0630 hours, he kissed her and Alberto.
'See you later.' Alberto was wide awake now and wanted to be fed. Jane picked him up and brought him to her bed and snuggled up with him. She soon dozed off and Alberto did too thinking, that it's not a bad alternative and fell asleep with his mother.

Albert was glad to be relieved by Pete and it was not long before all adults were arriving, scanning the area to see if there was any life about. They saw the devastation the wave had left behind, a clear cut line about fifteen metres above the shore level, wrecking all in its path, but above that just seemed normal.
'I need to get some sleep Pete, just a couple of hours and I'll be back. Can you and Ched take the inflatable around this island to assess the situation, its calm enough it should be about twenty kilometres in distance. I know I don't need to say this but just in case you might have forgotten, take a side arm.' Pete smiled at him. Albert shook his head and wished he hadn't mentioned it knowing Pete probably would do anyway. Just then Ched arrived.
'What's the score then, any sign of life at all? Oh by the way, talking about life, Marigold's pregnant.'
'Congratulations!' they both said together.
'You finally made it then?' Pete added.

258

'Stop it you two. Right I'm off. You had better tell Ched what he will be doing. See you later.'

'Come on Ched I'll fill you in on the way. We are going for a little trip.'

'Oh, I see you're prepared with that thing. Are we expecting trouble?'

'Ched you should know better. We should always expect trouble, and if you think you need one I should get it now. We will be out for about three to four hours, so let Marigold know.'

'Yes I will, I'll pick up a side arm, you never know do you?'

Ched went straight to the armoury. Being a key holder he entered and chose a .38 calibre Taurus, checked it, loaded a clip and put one in his pocket. Then he strapped the gun to his side, locked the door behind him and went to the foredeck to meet Pete and Magnus. On his way he thought that was easy, he didn't seemed bothered about the gun as he had done in the past and wondered why his attitude was so different! It can't be because of Millie, she has always been against guns but now she is with Pete and he carries one nearly all the time. I don't think it would worry Marigold and if it meant it betters my chance to get to back to her, then that must be why. The pair got in the inflatable and Magnus lowered them over the side. The water was calm as they released the shackle and they were soon away, steering close to the shoreline going up the coast in a north-westerly direction. Ched piloted while Pete scanned the shore with binoculars. The only communication they had with the Ark was the short wave radio and their distance would reach a few kilometres at the most.

'I hope you had a good breakfast Ched, because we could be out for several hours at this rate?'

'Yes I did thanks. That's one thing about Patricia she is the best in that kitchen.'

'That she is. You would struggle to find better.'

Steadily they moved around the island and then they were going south-east down the other side. Pete had been moving his binoculars along the shore and up towards the higher ground, knowing that if anyone had their wits about

259

them they would move to high ground. Their intensive search continued and just as you see in the films, they were about to give up hope when there they saw some smoke coming from the trees about one hundred metres up in a small clearing.

'We've got something Ched, smoke just up there. Can you see?'

'Yes I can. Any sign of activity?'

'No the trees are in the way from this angle. Can you find a place to beach and we'll take a look?'

'It's a bit rocky here but there's a clearer bit over there. I'll cut the engine. We will need to push ourselves in by those rocks.' They jumped out and pulled the boat ashore. Pete said to isolate the engine, as he took away the paddles. They started to climb the sheer slopes of the island. Moving in a zigzag upwards, to the area where the smoke they had seen.

'This is strange Pete. This is the first time I've been on land in over four years.'

'I thought the Ark was land that just moved about.'

'I suppose so but not in the true sense of terra firma.' They reached the area where they were greeted by a young man.

'Thank you for coming,' he said in Pidgin English. 'You must help us, my brother and his wife are hurt and they have a baby.'

'Where are they?' asked Pete.

'Just over there. Come I will show you.'

'Ched you stay here. I'll go and take a look.'

'OK.' Pete followed the man to a makeshift shelter and it was as he said. Pete took a look at the young girl holding the baby. Her leg was broken and the lower calf bone was sticking out the side. The young man had broken his right arm and there were several lacerations about his limbs.

'How did you get them up here?'

'I pulled them up so much each at a time.' He showed Pete physically by movements and then pointing at the baby and to his back.

Pete signalled to Ched to come and he sprinted over in just half a minute.

'Oh dear this is going to be awkward and painful.'

'I think the best thing to do Ched is for you to take this young man and the baby back to the Ark, tell Mi what we have here, two broken limbs with one very bad. Bring her back here with her medical kit. Tell Albert we will need the fishing boat and one stretcher, Buster, Antonio, Gunter and yourself to help us down with the injured.'

'Right young man can you take the baby?' Ched was pointing about, gesticulating with his arms hoping that he would understand. The young girl understood, but did not want to let her baby go. The man retaliated in their language. She then cried and released the baby to him.

'Come on.' Ched waved his arm forward and they trekked down the slope to the inflatable. Ched retrieved the paddles from their hiding place. He put them in the inflatable and pulled it to the water, then indicated to the man to get in and then pushed it further and jumped in with them. He reconnected the isolator and powered the craft around the remainder of the coast. As soon as he could see the Ark he radioed Albert.

'Albert, come in please do you read me?'

'I hear you Ched.'

'We've found causalities. There are two with broken limbs, Pete is with them. We need Mi and some medical supplies for the female. She's got a broken leg and it is quite bad. She will require pain relief and a stretcher. Plus could you send Buster, Antonio, Gunter or yourself in the fishing boat. I have here with me an able survivor and a baby, please prepare for us to board.'

'Understood Ched, we will be waiting.'

Albert snapped into action and called Mi and all the other adults to the bridge to explain their tasks. Mi ran for her doctor's bag and arrived at the foredeck as quickly as she could where Magnus was ready. He lifted the fishing boat from its hold. Ched arrived at the starboard side where Magnus was waiting to lift them entirely from the water, Ched attached the shackle and in a few minutes they were placed on the deck. Mi took the baby to check it over and then passed it to Amy who was close by.

'The baby boy is fine Amy although he will need feeding I'm sure.' Amy smiled at the delight of holding the young child.

261

'Amy could you take this young man with you, I don't know what relationship he is to the child, please make sure they stay together and are well fed.'

'Of course I will Albert,' she answered as she carried on regardless talking to the little one.

Albert was getting frustrated at Amy's slowness to act on his request.

'Go with her and be fed.'

'Yes Sir, thank you.' He followed Amy.

'Gunter can you take charge? I'll go out with them and assess the situation on the island.'

Ched, Mi and Albert got in the fishing boat. Magnus had already put the stretcher inside the boat. They were lifted over the side and down to the water. Ched started the engine, which fired immediately. Albert released the shackle. Ched then pointed the boat to the southern part of the island. Buster and Antonio were in the inflatable and ready to be put over the side and it wasn't long before they caught up with the fishing boat.

Amy took the baby and the young man to the canteen. He had obviously never seen anything like the Ark before and just gaped at everything in amazement. A congregation of the rest of the women and children soon gathered around, all wanting to see the new arrivals, especially the small baby. Jane stepped in with a quiet word in Amy's ear.

'Amy shouldn't we be sorting out feeding our guests and finding out about them and their plight?

Young man welcome to the Ark. What is your name?' He thought about the question then answered. 'Lomlom Mam.' She pointed at herself.

'Me Jane, this is Amy, Marigold, Patricia, Melanie and Greta. Come.' She pointed to the food counter where Patricia went to Jane's aid and helped Lomlom choose something to eat and drink. All the time he kept looking back at the baby unsure of the attention his nephew was getting. He picked out a plate of food and orange juice and went back to the table and sat next to Amy and baby. Jane followed and sat opposite him.

'Lomlom what is the baby's name?' she asked. He picked at the food with his hands, and answered with his mouth full.

'Nukapu Mam,' and continued to chew. Melanie had a bottle of milk for the baby. She passed it to Amy who put the teat to the child's lips and it was onto it without any encouragement, which made Lomlom smile as did the rest of onlookers.

Ched relocated the place where he had previously beached the inflatable with Pete. He pointed it out to Buster. He and Antonio entered the same spot as they did, jumped out and pulled the boat ashore. It was a little more difficult with the fishing boat being a lot bigger and more draft to contend with, but Ched's skill soon brought the boat through to allow the bow to rest on the beach. Remembering what Pete said, he asked Antonio to isolate the engine and remove the oars as did Ched with the fishing boat.

'Good thinking Ched, you never know who is around do you?' Albert said as he helped Mi out of the boat with her medical equipment. Antonio took the stretcher and then they followed Ched up the slope to the clearing where Pete and the two injured lay. Mi ran to Pete as soon as she saw him. He took her bag and led them to the shelter. When she saw the young girl and her leg the first thing she did was to anaesthetise her so that she could reset the leg. Mi wasted no time at all and got to work as soon as she tested that the anaesthetic was working. With her surgical gloves already on she attempted to put the bone back inside her leg to rejoin the two jagged edges together. She grunted and groaned trying to push. Pete could see her struggle and bent down to watch what she was trying to do. He took over using his strength to neatly marry the leg together.

"Keep it there Pete while I stitch the skin then we will put the splints on and bind them tightly before putting her on the stretcher." Later while the men carefully rolled the young girl over onto the stretcher, Mi attended to the man. His right arm was broken but not as seriously as the girl. She reset it quickly. He moaned while she did so but then he was OK, just relieved his wife was cared for. Again Mi put a splint on the arm and bound it tightly, then into a sling to keep it steady until they were back at the ship's surgery. Next she treated some of his lacerations, firstly with antiseptic and then bandaged or covered them with plasters. The girl was strapped to the stretcher and carried by Pete, Buster, Antonio and Albert. Ched helped the young man and led the way carefully down the slope with Mi behind.

They were all glad to be back to the boats after the tricky descent with the stretcher. They laid the girl into the well of the fishing boat and helped the young man onboard, then pushed the bow off the beach and one by one clambered into the boat, Mi, Albert, Ched and Pete. Buster and Antonio soon followed in the inflatable which raced ahead as the fishing boat had to take it steady to minimise any jolts from wave impact. The inflatable and crew were already onboard the Ark by the time the fishing boat was in sight. The word hit the canteen that the others were being hoisted onboard. Lomlom stood up to ask Amy for Nukapu. Reluctantly Amy handed back the child then Lomlom followed everyone to the foredeck. The fishing boat was just over the side and was lowered to the deck. It was all cheers for their safe return as the girl was carefully lifted out of the boat on the stretcher. She was awake but could not move for the restraints. She was looking around and Lomlom appeared with her child. He handed the baby back to her and pulled her arm from the strap to hold him, smiling at him, she was happy. They were carried to the sick bay and transferred to hospital-type beds. Food and drink were brought with Lomlom choosing their meal. Mi, Amy and Jane then took over cleaning them up and tending to their injuries. Lomlom was shown to Lenska's old quarters as temporary accommodation. Now the whole of the Ark's community was ready for a good night's sleep. No lookout was posted just the electric fence switched on. Albert doubted that anyone would look for them in the aftermath of a tsunami.

They had a sound night, even the injured guests benefited from some peace. They were all awake early to see a bright sunny day. Most were up and about, with Albert on the bridge and Pete soon joined him.
'What is Mi's view on the patients?'

'I don't know Albert I don't live with her any more. No doubt she will be along to give you a report on their progress.'

'Sorry Pete, I must be going senile.'

'So what's on the agenda for today Albert?'

'I'm not quite sure yet. There are other islands in this group I don't want to go searching aimlessly. It would be better to get some local knowledge from our guest Lomlom. We will invite him here after breakfast, talking of which I'm ready for mine now.'

'I'll join you.'

The canteen had never been so busy at breakfast time before because of the different shift rotas that were being operated in the past. Everyone had slept right through the night, and there was a queue for the bacon and eggs. Patricia managed to get all fed and contented until the next meal. Lomlom made his way to the food counter putting two plates on a tray and copied what everyone else took, the plates were filled and drinks were taken. He then looked around for Melanie and went to her to ask her for baby milk. She got up straight away.

'Yes I'll get some, just a moment please.' Off she went to the kitchen returning with a bottle of lukewarm milk and a smile. Lomlom thanked her and went to the sick bay to feed his family. Fifteen minutes later he returned with a tray and empty plates. Albert pointed this out to Pete.

'That's a good sign, their appetites look ok.' Lomlom then chose his own food and sat next to Pete, tucking in with his fingers, not saying a word. The pair did not interrupt him. He seemed to enjoy every mouthful and within a couple of minutes and the food had vanished. He sat back licking his fingers and drinking his orange juice. He looked around at everyone chatting and eating with an expression on his face as to what he might be thinking. *(It's not bad here)* Albert asked him if he would like to join them on the bridge, the vantage point, to see all the front of the ship from there and the farm. He nodded his head and got up ready to go. Albert and Pete followed suit and went to the bridge. Lomlom was amazed at the size of what was in front of him and all that he could see, the animals and trees in the distance. He was taken aback just moving from one side of the bridge to the other.

'Lomlom could we ask you some questions?'

'Yes.'

'Are you from this island?'

'No, I am from Lomlom a different island.' Pete was looking at the charts and there was an island by that name.

'Yes Albert it's over here.'

'It is in the same Province, the Temotu Province,' said Lomlom.

'How well do you know the islands around here?'

'Very well, I have been fishing here since a boy with my father.'

'Is there anyone else on Taumako, the one you were on, the one there?'

'No it's too hard to grow crops or keep animals there. You would have to climb to the top to find anywhere flat.'

'What about the other islands around it?'

'Yes there are some on other islands and they have radio to the outside world and would have been warned, giving them time to move to higher ground.'

'What do you think Pete is it worth looking at them?'

'Yes but not by moving the Ark around, we would be better to take this guy and the fishing boat, perhaps a couple of us and some supplies and go out for two or three days. The Ark is well suited here, it's close enough to the island not to be detected and we are weeks away from anywhere by boat, also there is plenty of fresh water on the island. The sun is shining, there are fish in the sea, what could be better?'

'Yes you are right but who can we get to spend three days away from their loved ones?'

'That's a difficult one. I don't think Millie would be too happy for it to be me and Ched at the moment is in a similar situation. That leaves Buster and Antonio. He likes a bit of adventure but then the farm is his at the moment, because Millie can't manage it for a while.'

'Then it looks like Buster and me, Pete.'

Mi and Jane came in and Albert immediately asked after the patients.

266

'They are looking good, they slept well and the baby just eats sleeps and the other. They have had a good breakfast that Lomlom brought for them and now they are sitting up.'

'That's fantastic, aye Pete?'

'Their names are Lomlom and Malo,' Jane told them, 'they are brothers eighteen years and twenty respectively. Malo's wife is Anuta and her child is Nukapu, Anuta is just sixteen and Nukapu, he is six months. They are all named after the islands they were born on.' Jane felt pleased with herself in providing this information.

'Lomlom how come you were on Taumako at the time of the tsunami?'

'We were using it to fish from and as a place to hide.'

'Hide! Hide from who or what?'

'Our parents, they banned Malo and Anuta from marriage so they ran away and I helped them. It is a problem going back many generations.'

'Is this going to cause trouble? Will they come looking for you?'

'No, once we have fled and make our own way in life and do not go back, we are free, but many that do this do not make it and are forced to go back to their families because they have the best islands to live on. Then they are separated and cannot see each other.'

'So what about you taking us out in the fishing boat around these islands to see if anyone needs help?'

'That is OK around Taumako but not the others where our names are connected, look I will show you on your map.' He went over and pointed to the islands where they could not go, which were quite a distance from this little group of islands.

'So your fishing boat must have been smashed in the tidal wave?'

'Yes my brother had just managed to get ashore and Anuta was waiting for him, I had the baby and was up high. She wanted to meet him and they were running to higher ground when they were hit. I had to put the baby down to go and look for them. They were clinging on to trees when I found them and I dragged them to safety. I lit a fire to dry them out, keep warm and attract attention.'

'You did well Lomlom. It was lucky we were just passing at the time.'

267

'Then you will be leaving soon? it will be difficult for Anuta to manage but we thank you for saving us.'

'No,' Mi jumped in, 'Lomlom we will not be leaving for some time. Anuta cannot be moved nor will she be able to walk for many weeks yet.' Pete and Albert looked at each other then Albert spoke.

'Mi, my dear, we have no intention of leaving just yet, if at all. Originally we were just passing by but circumstances have altered the situation somewhat.'

'Sorry Albert I know what you two are like, we could have sailed through the night and be on a different planet the next day, and no one would have known we had moved with you two in charge.'

'We're not that good yet Mi, but an interesting thought.' They all laughed.

'Mi, have you any idea where Buster is?' She went to the bridge window, looked out and scanned the fields.

'Yes, he is over there training, doing his daily workout routine.' Pete could not help himself.

'Hasn't he done that already?' Then he wished he had not said it. Mi was furious with him.

'At least he doesn't fall asleep half way through!' She stormed out of the room.

'Pete I think you owe her an apology,' Jane advised.

'Yes I know, I'll do it now. See you shortly with a bit of luck.'

'That was out of order Albert.'

'I know and it won't do much good for relationships on the Ark.'

'Is there a problem Mr Albert?'

'No, no Lomlom don't you worry about it. You have your own problems so let's see if we can help you with those. At the moment I'm sure the rest of us will agree that you can stay here on the Ark for as long as you wish, now lets organise that search trip.'

'What trip is that Albert?' Jane asked.

'We are going to look at the other islands to see if anyone requires help, that's Lomlom, Buster and I. We will be taking the fishing boat and will be away for about two days.'

'Does Amy or Buster know about this?'

'No not yet.'

The fishing boat was filled with supplies and some medical basics and put ready to go first light the next day. They all said their goodbyes to their loved ones and Lomlom looked around to see if Melanie was about, but she wasn't. Albert and Buster put their packs in the boat complete with side arms. They got in and were lowered over the side and soon on their way to the first island. It's name sounded like some historic novel: Treasurers Island which lay to the west of Taumako, then Obelisk and the number of islands to the north-east of it, then returning down the eastern side of Taumako to the Bass Islands south of Taumako. Lomlom seemed at home in the fishing boat, albeit a far cry from his proa wooden sailing canoe called Te Puke and known to westerners as Tepukei.

The three got on well together on their journey. Albert piloted the boat, Buster and Lomlom kept their eyes looking through the binoculars, scanning the shore line of the islands. Most of the inhabited islands had their dwellings up high, out of harm's way. There was no evidence of any housing beneath the level of where the wave had cut along the shore line. They could see radio masts and satellite dishes dotted around in high places on these islands. The only activity they saw was the building of new fishing boats to replace the smashed ones. Albert looked at the forestry that surrounded the main islands and noted there was no shortage of raw materials. There was no sign of a town as such just a few huts here and there. Lomlom would catch some fish and each night they pulled into a secluded spot and made camp cooking the fish over their fire, pulling the meat off the bone by their hands as Lomlom had at the table in the canteen. Their last day was to scout the Bass islands. These were very small and unlikely for anyone to be there but they thought they had better check just in case a fisherman had been stuck there. There was nothing to report. It was obvious to Albert that there was hardly any population in this group of islands and thought to himself that is just the way he liked it. They returned back to the Ark to the glee of everyone. The boat and occupants were lifted entirely from the water as normal. Amy clutched Albert, Mi grabbed hold of Buster and Melanie stood there smiling at Lomlom. All were asking questions and it was too much of a bombardment so Albert raised his arms. 'If we all go to the canteen now I will explain what we have seen and answer questions in an orderly manner.' This brought the peace and tranquillity that he had experienced for the last few days to an abrupt end, all gathered in the canteen eagerly waiting. Albert explained that there were very few people on the main islands. Those that they saw were coping with the situation and rebuilding. On the rescue side of things he was pleased to say that their services were not required. Gunter was eager to ask the first question. 'Albert is the area suitable for us to stay?'

'Yes but do not ask me for how long, remember we are in an area renown for frequent earthquakes, causing tsunamis, volcanic eruptions which fill the atmosphere with acrid smoke for weeks and you know what effect that would have on us.' Ched asked the next question.

'Albert from that I take it you would want the option to leave if we have to?'

'Most definitely Ched, it would be foolish not to.'

'Where we are anchored now is that our best position for the time we are here?' Millie asked.

'After the survey that Pete and Ched did when looking for survivors and our trip of the past few days, yes, it is the best position to anchor. We are the closest to the sheerest sides of the island and once the greenery returns to the fields on the Ark we should blend in nicely. The island has an abundance of fresh water and I'm sure Magnus will create a pipeline to feed us onboard. It will certainly be good water for the beer making.'

'It needs something,' shouted Ched.

With them all laughing the questions petered out and Albert called for their attention.

'Before I finish and have a drink of my lovely beer, I want you all to officially welcome our guests and I've stuck my neck out in saying that they can stay on the Ark as long as they like. So please welcome Lomlom who is here as you see, his brother Malo who is with his wife and son, Anuta and Nukapu. They are recovering from their injuries under Mi's care with her assistants. Now I think we are well overdue for a little celebration on our successful journey here, guided by our navigator Gunter, so please thank him for giving us our direction to here.' A round of applause was made for Gunter as Greta joined him. He put his long arm and huge hand around her. She looked up at him, so proud of her man. The evening continued with a meal and after dinner drinks and socialising. All the couples and children were together. Malo and his wife Anuta with their son Nukapu were still in the sick bay and very happy. Amy was there with Albert and Esperanca, Gunter with Greta, Stella and Venus, Ched with Marigold, Lucy, Vicky, Rose and one on the way, Jane with Antonio and Alberto, Millie with Pete and another expected soon, Mi with Buster trying very hard, Magnus with Patricia, finally Melanie sat next to Lomlom holding Chuva on his knee, all smiling.

20. ALBERT'S FINAL PRIVATE LOG – May 2020

Nature never ceases to amaze me how it can adjust itself in many mysterious ways. At first on the Ark's maiden voyage although an even number of male/female adults, there was a total imbalance of male/female children with females being the domineering number by 100%. Then the odds changed to 5 – 1 with the birth of Alberto, then to 5 – 2 with the birth of Chuva, then 6 – 2 when Esperanca arrived and now totally out of the blue came Nukapu putting the score at 6 – 3.

History has noted this adjustment many times before, the classic situation was The Great War, the First World War just over one hundred years ago, I don't know why they ever called it 'Great' because there was nothing Great about it in the normal meaning of the word. More like 'Monstrous' when all the young healthy men were needlessly, in most cases, sent to their slaughter, young men from all corners of this earth. This left an imbalance back in their home countries where the young females were left behind. Although the young females in most situations would settle for the older male to mate, that in itself is nature and today in most western free countries the match is pretty even. Not so in some other countries where the barbaric slaughter of female babies born to poor families still happens.

The two pregnancies we have of Millie and Marigold are developing very well, and we are all waiting for Buster and Mi to prove themselves in that area. But the way Melanie and Lomlom are getting on they may beat them to it!

The flood damage to the fields caused by the tsunami has soon repaired itself and the first sign of green was the grass poking those shoots through the ground to the delight of Millie and Antonio. How the rabbits survived I do not know. It must have been a shock to them, all that water running about, but then their burrows are mainly near the orchard which was protected when the wave breached the sides of the Ark.

Pete has found a very fast flowing waterfall on the island that has a pool below. Magnus has said he can convert one of the spare generating units with some fabrication using Ched's skills and between them they can make a Hydro Electric power supply which can feed the Ark to help boost its needs. But we will have to move the Ark nearer to the area and shoreline where the waterfall is.

Ched has taken well to fishing here and has a full time companion in Lomlom, who teaches Ched the native way of fishing and the different types of fish to catch. Lomlom has requested help to construct a traditional wooden sailing canoe, the Te Puke, another project to keep them busy.

I've taken to sailing in the black yacht which is moored most of the time to the bow anchor chain and I have mastered the art of sailing her single handed with some technical modifications courtesy of Magnus. I have tried to get Amy to join me on several occasions but to no avail, she said she could not see the point of just sailing around in circles. For me it gives me time to reflect on my past and clears my mind giving me peace with my achievements in life.

We have not a clue what is happening with the outside world. No doubt there will be war of some form or other in the usual places and over the same old problems, innocent people being slaughtered and maimed. Those men and women ordered to go to the front line for the honour of their country.

The Ark blends in well with the islands trees growing from the fertile soil that rises to the summit. There is a plateau but extremely difficult to get to, I will save that for when I want to see that little bit further.

21. EPILOGUE

Albert's determination to succeed with this project won through, but he did not do it alone, it was a main core of people all pulling in the same direction. The journey for this community changed them all in some way. The most important thing was to protect their families and their home and this is an ancient problem of how to protect your home and that will never change no matter what country you live in or what type of government is in control.

The Ark did make use of the outside world when it saw fit and when help was there to be had, but as Albert saw it, if you are going to be used by others then you must use them. The swapping around of mates was a way of diluting family strains so that breeding in a small community is not kept within family groups risking the danger of interbreeding and the addition of the occasional outsider is a bonus.

The Ark is now resting after a four year long trip covering thousands of nautical miles. The majority of time spent now was in total peace and harmony. The aggressive interruptions did not physically last long although mentally lasted longer and in some more than others. The elders of the community's main task now is to transfer their knowledge to the young by teaching them the skills required to survive, to be tolerant, along with as much information about the world around them and how they can be good to their environment.

The Ark will live on for many years to come.
Who will be their guide and defender when the inevitable happens?
Who will replace Magnus as the next engineering genius?
Who will be the farming expert?
Who will teach the future generations all the skills to be able to care in all aspects for one another?
They will do all these things to survive but, as Albert often said,
"You never know what's over the horizon".

274